D1365634

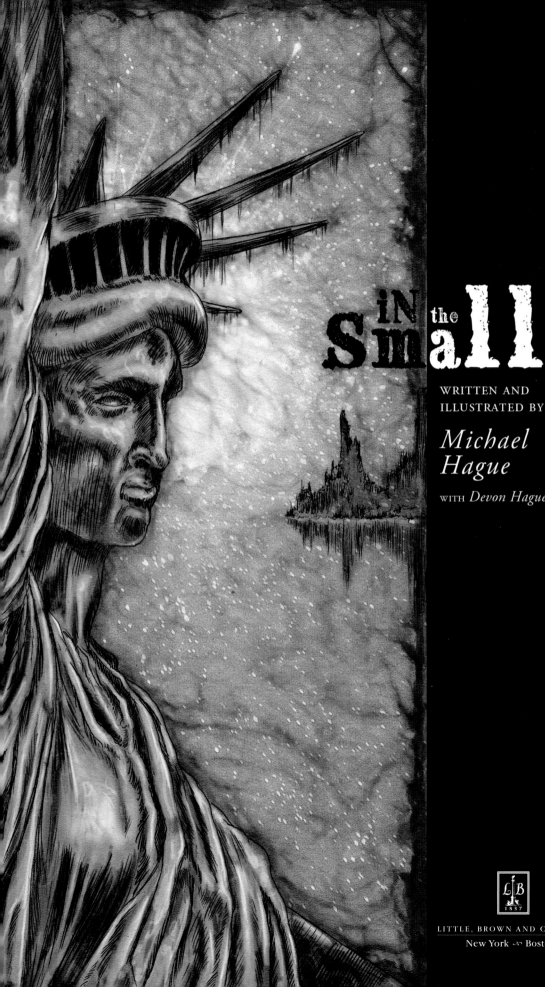

iN the Small

WRITTEN AND
ILLUSTRATED BY

*Michael
Hague*

WITH *Devon Hague*

LITTLE, BROWN AND COMPANY
New York ⚬ Boston

iN the Small

FOR DEVON,
WITHOUT WHOM THIS BOOK
WOULD NOT BE POSSIBLE.
– M.H.

Little, Brown and Company

Hachette Book Group USA
237 Park Avenue, New York, NY 10017
Visit our Web site at www.lb-teens.com

First Edition: May 2008

ISBN-13: 978-0-316-01323-9
ISBN-10: 0-316-01323-4

10 9 8 7 6 5 4 3 2 1

TWP

Printed in Singapore

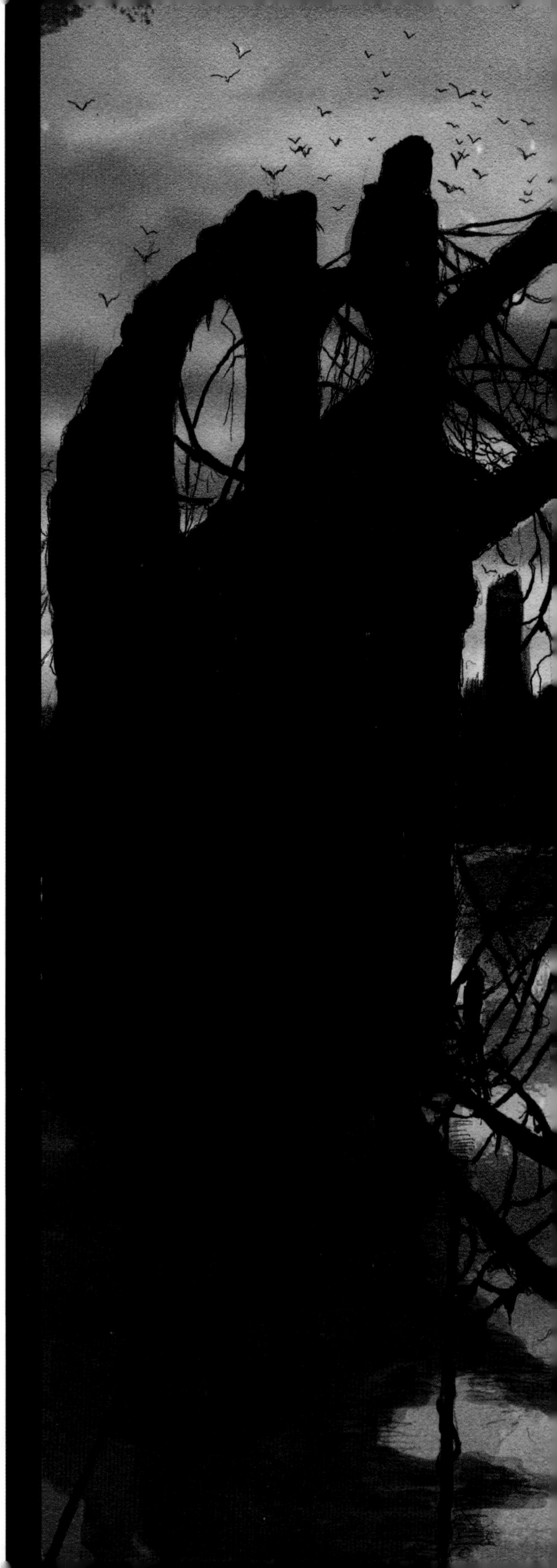

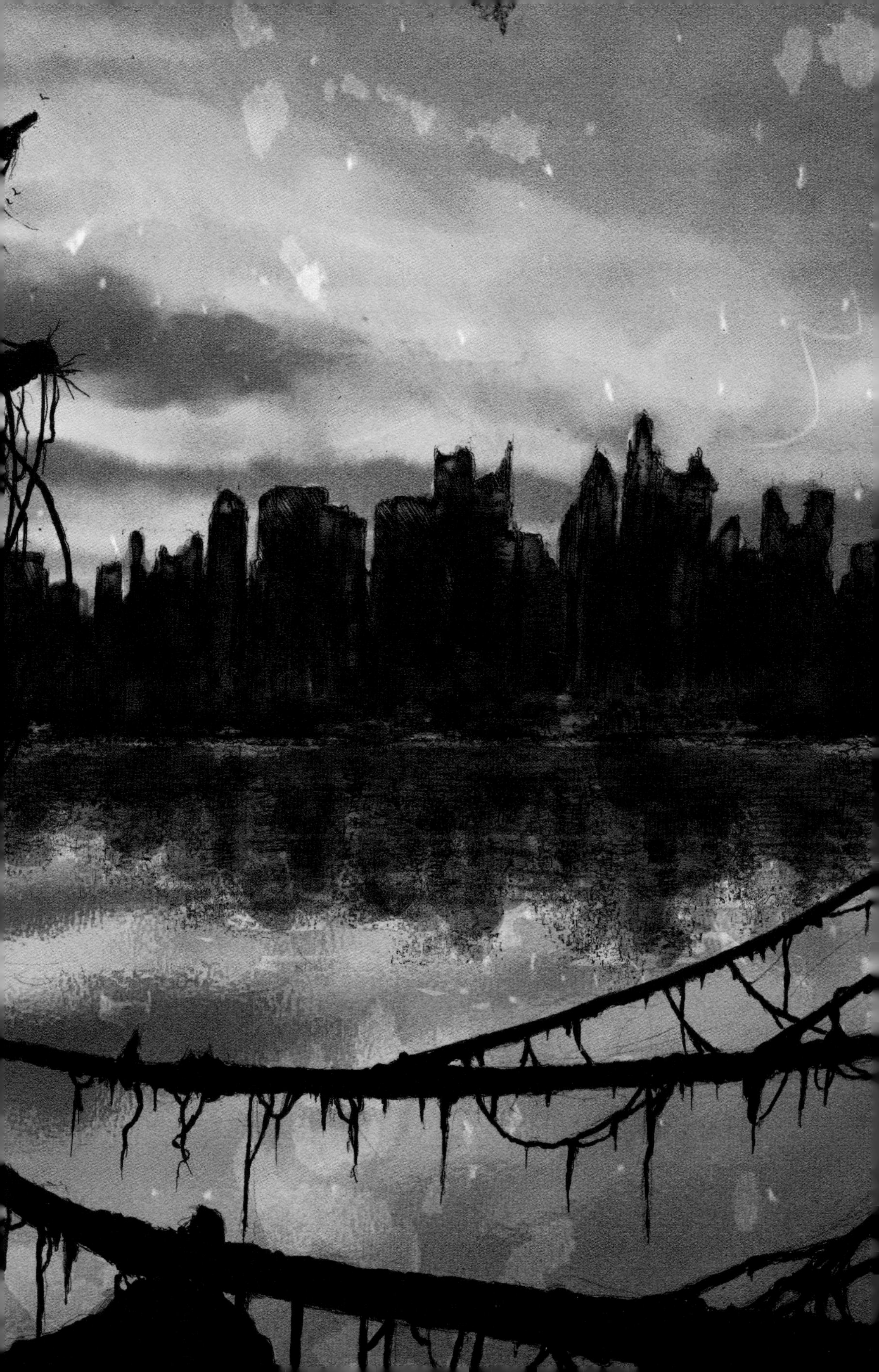

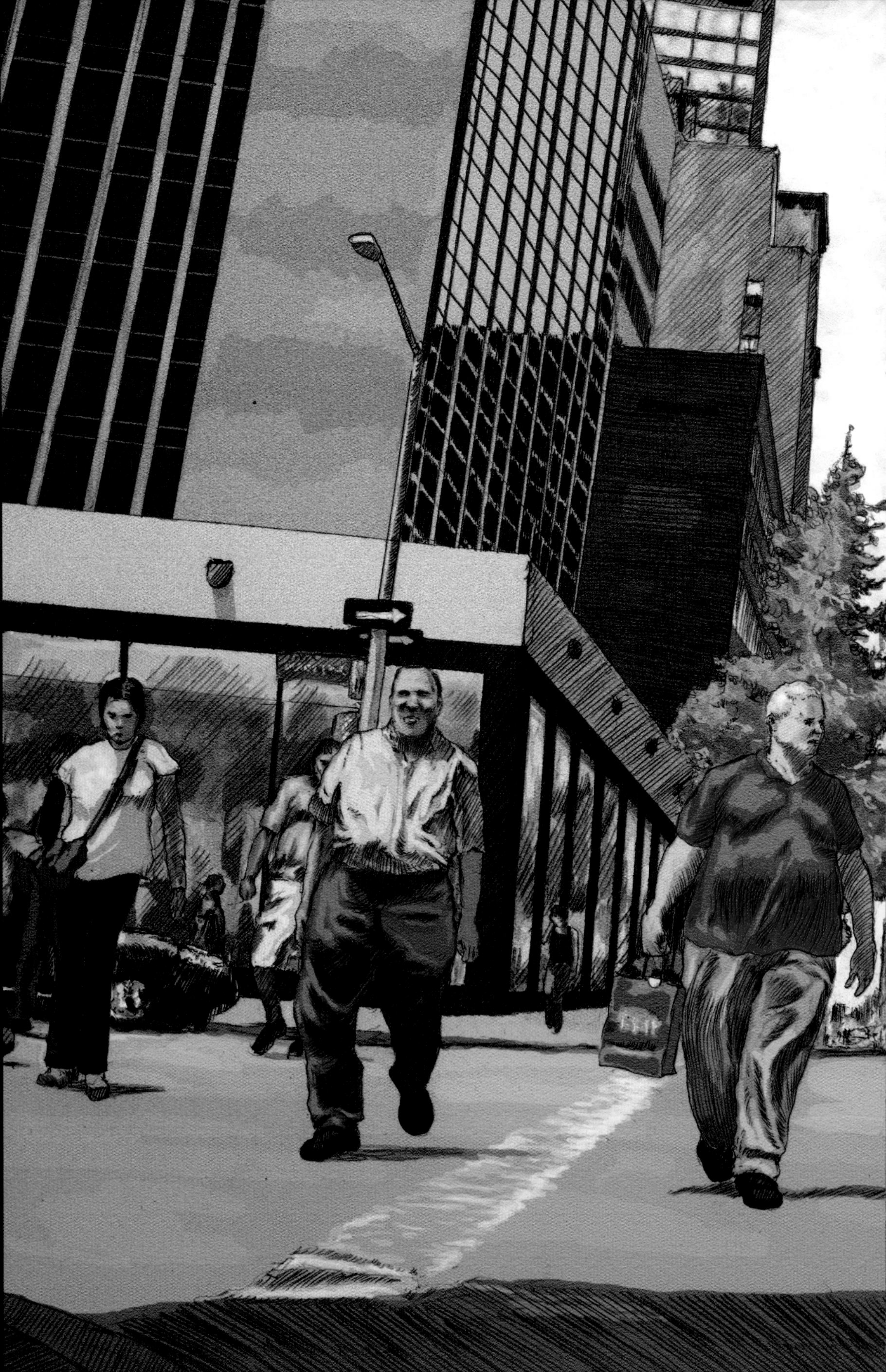

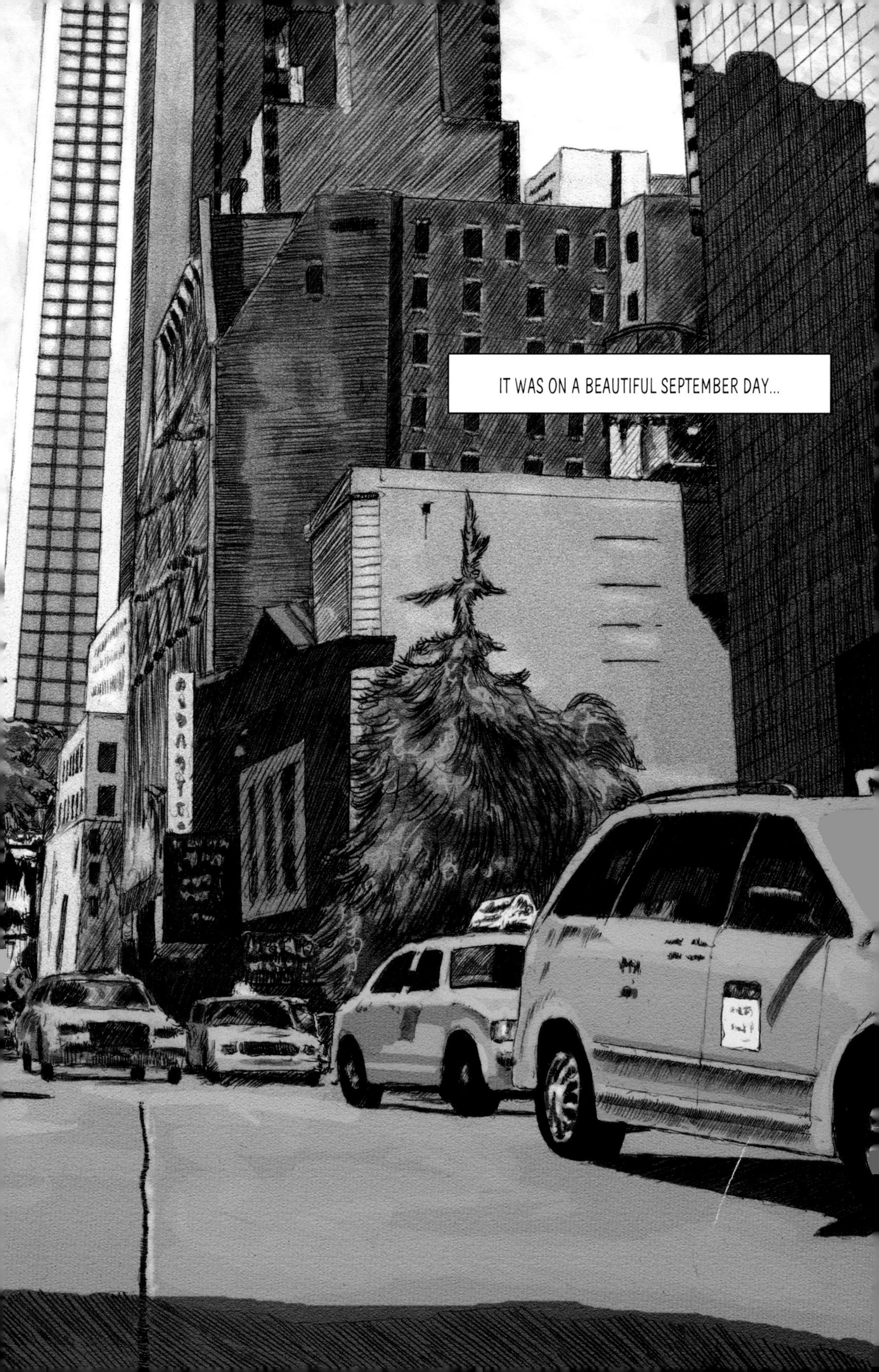
IT WAS ON A BEAUTIFUL SEPTEMBER DAY...

THE MYSTERIOUS BLUE LIGHT
BATHED EVERYTHING.

IT PENETRATED THE DEPTHS
OF THE OCEAN...

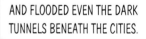

AND FLOODED EVEN THE DARK
TUNNELS BENEATH THE CITIES.

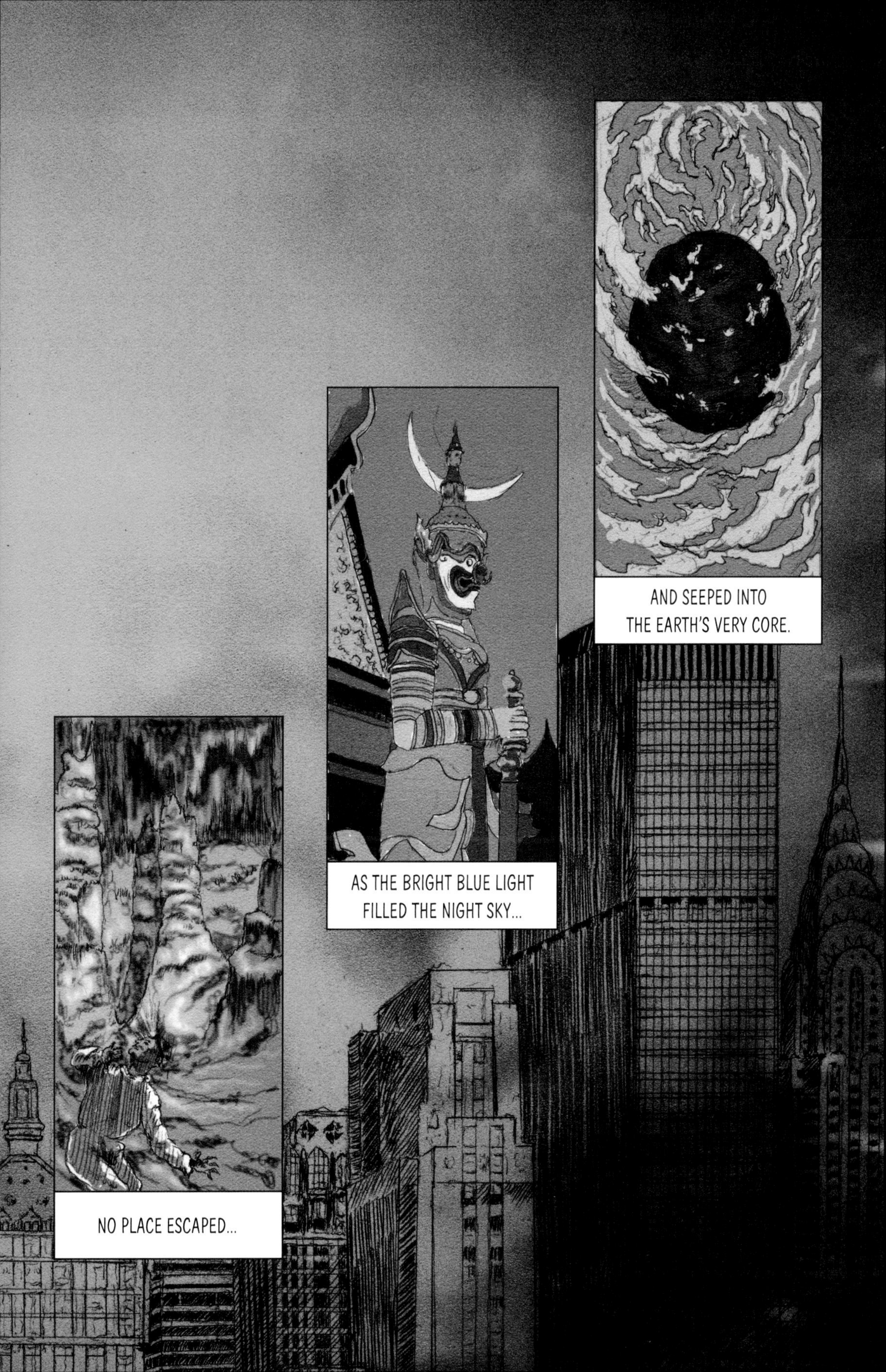
NO PLACE ESCAPED...
AS THE BRIGHT BLUE LIGHT FILLED THE NIGHT SKY...
AND SEEPED INTO THE EARTH'S VERY CORE.

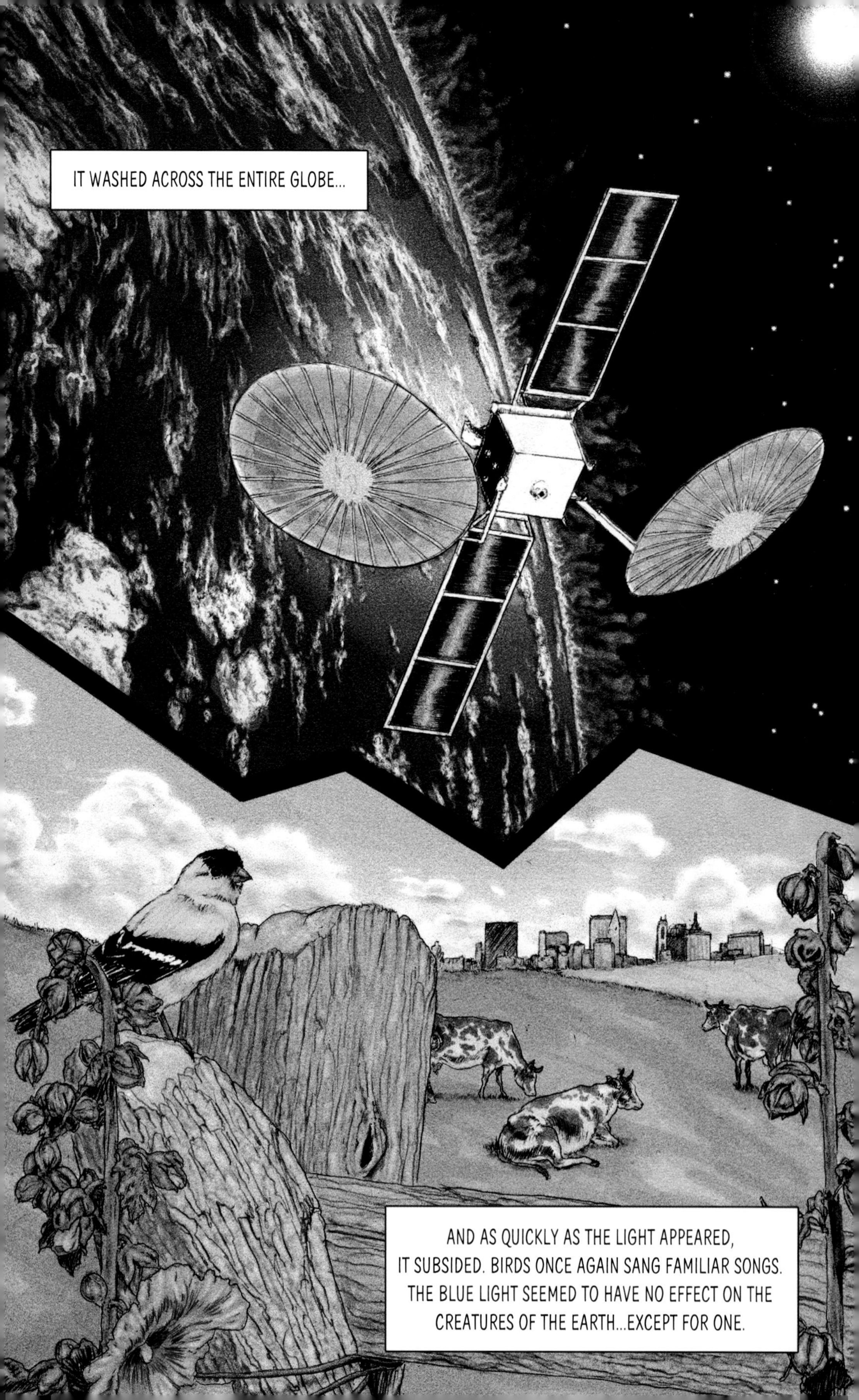
IT WASHED ACROSS THE ENTIRE GLOBE...
AND AS QUICKLY AS THE LIGHT APPEARED, IT SUBSIDED. BIRDS ONCE AGAIN SANG FAMILIAR SONGS. THE BLUE LIGHT SEEMED TO HAVE NO EFFECT ON THE CREATURES OF THE EARTH...EXCEPT FOR ONE.

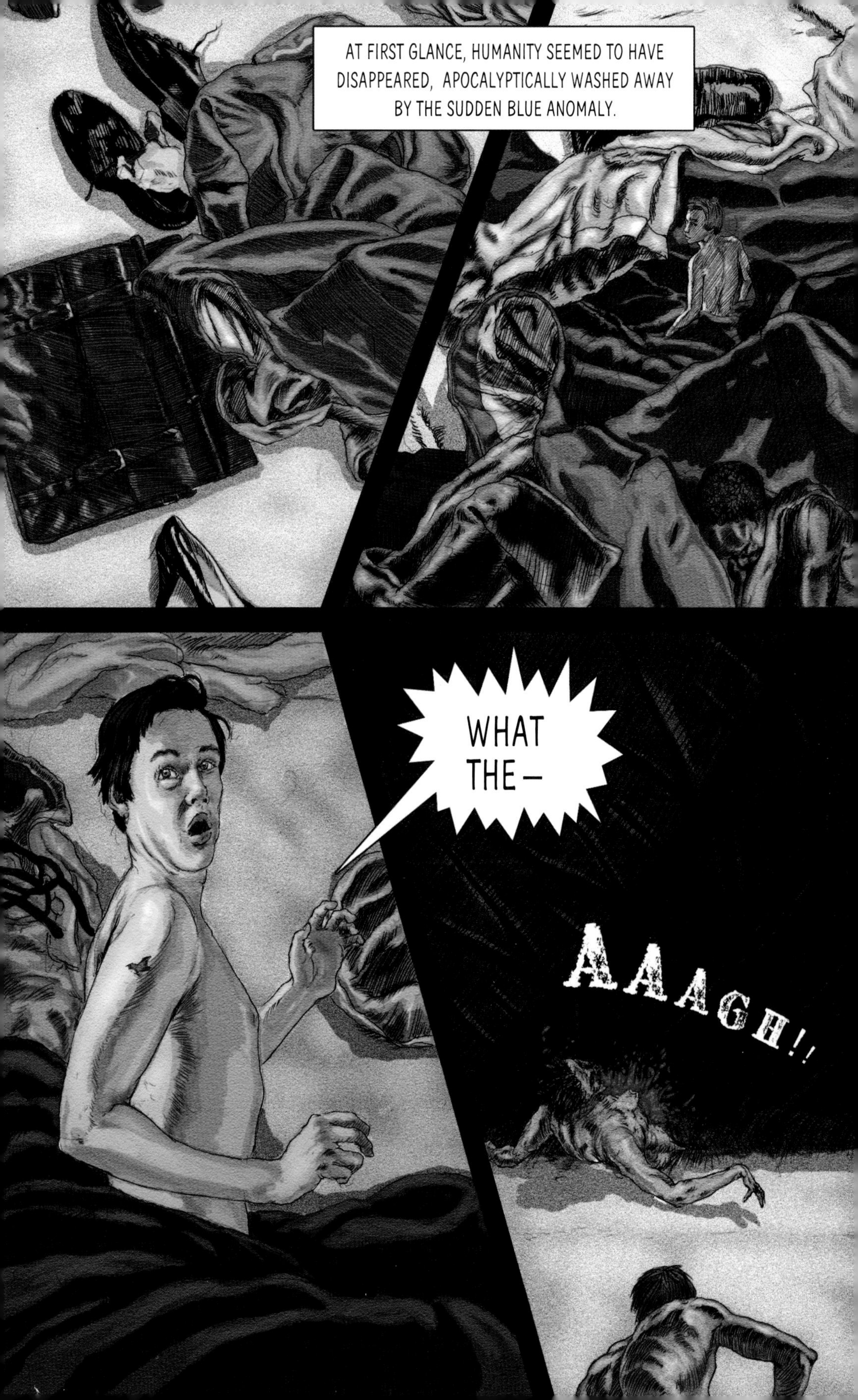
AT FIRST GLANCE, HUMANITY SEEMED TO HAVE DISAPPEARED, APOCALYPTICALLY WASHED AWAY BY THE SUDDEN BLUE ANOMALY.
WHAT THE—
AAAGH!!

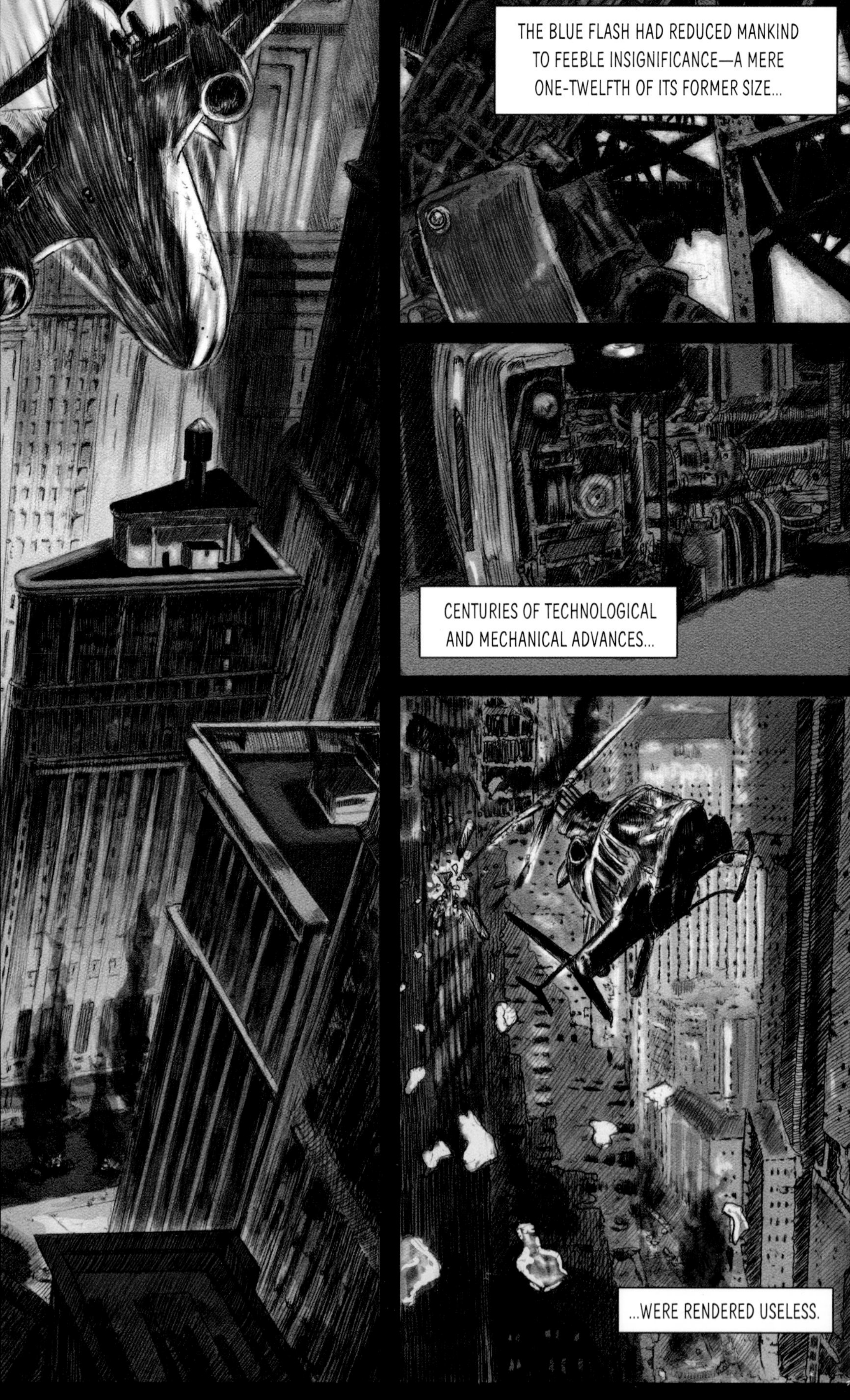
THE BLUE FLASH HAD REDUCED MANKIND TO FEEBLE INSIGNIFICANCE—A MERE ONE-TWELFTH OF ITS FORMER SIZE...
CENTURIES OF TECHNOLOGICAL AND MECHANICAL ADVANCES...
...WERE RENDERED USELESS.

THERE WAS NO ONE TO EXTINGUISH THE FIRES.

NO ONE TO TEND TO THE INJURED.

NO ONE TO RESTORE ORDER.

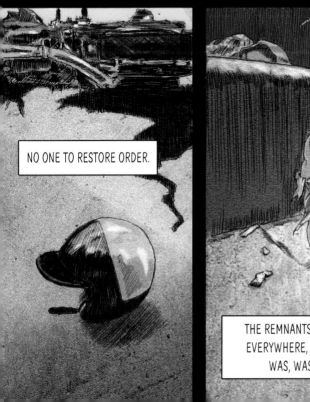

THE REMNANTS OF CIVILIZATION WERE EVERYWHERE, BUT CIVILIZATION AS IT WAS, WAS GONE...FOREVER.

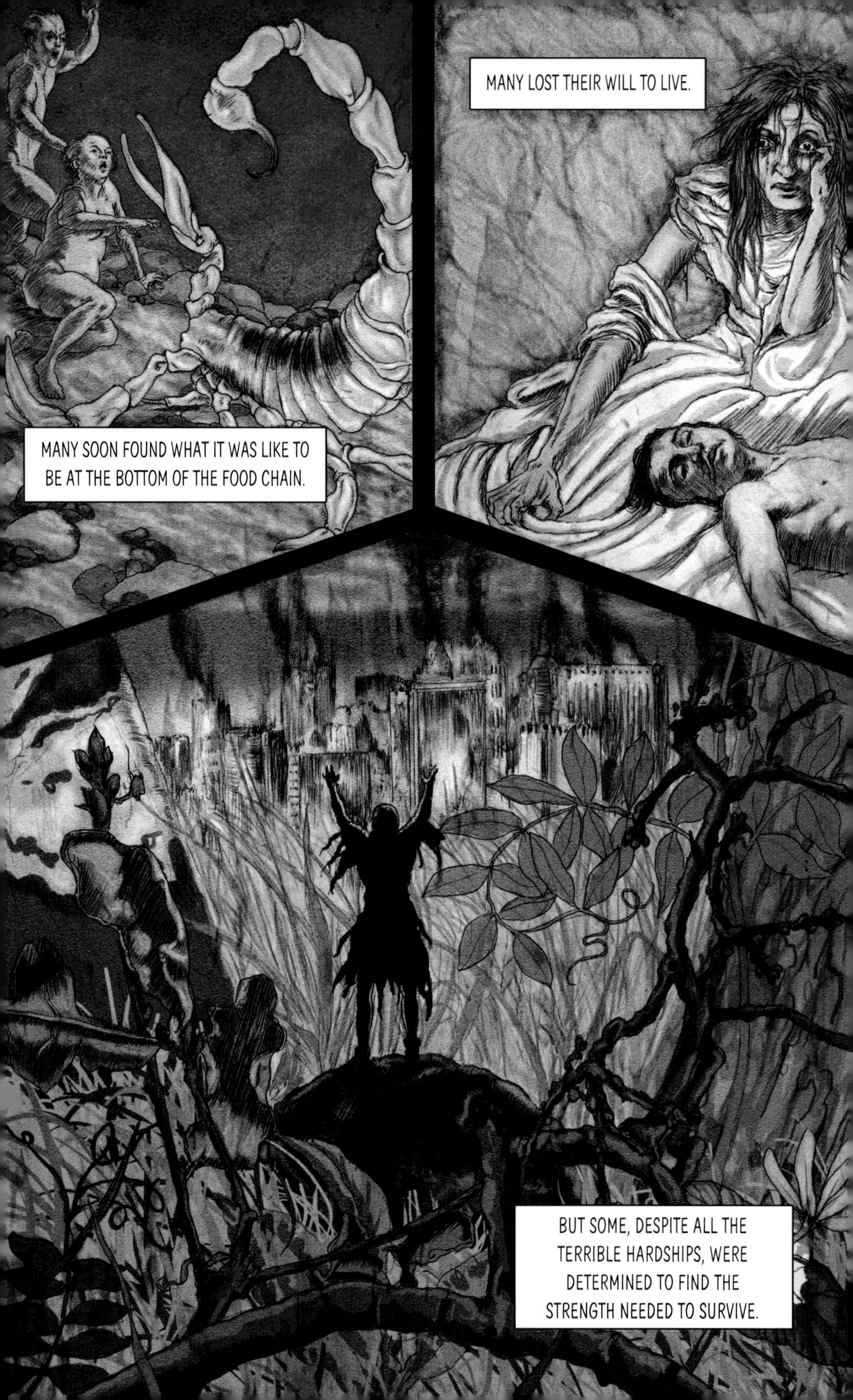
MANY SOON FOUND WHAT IT WAS LIKE TO BE AT THE BOTTOM OF THE FOOD CHAIN.
MANY LOST THEIR WILL TO LIVE.
BUT SOME, DESPITE ALL THE TERRIBLE HARDSHIPS, WERE DETERMINED TO FIND THE STRENGTH NEEDED TO SURVIVE.

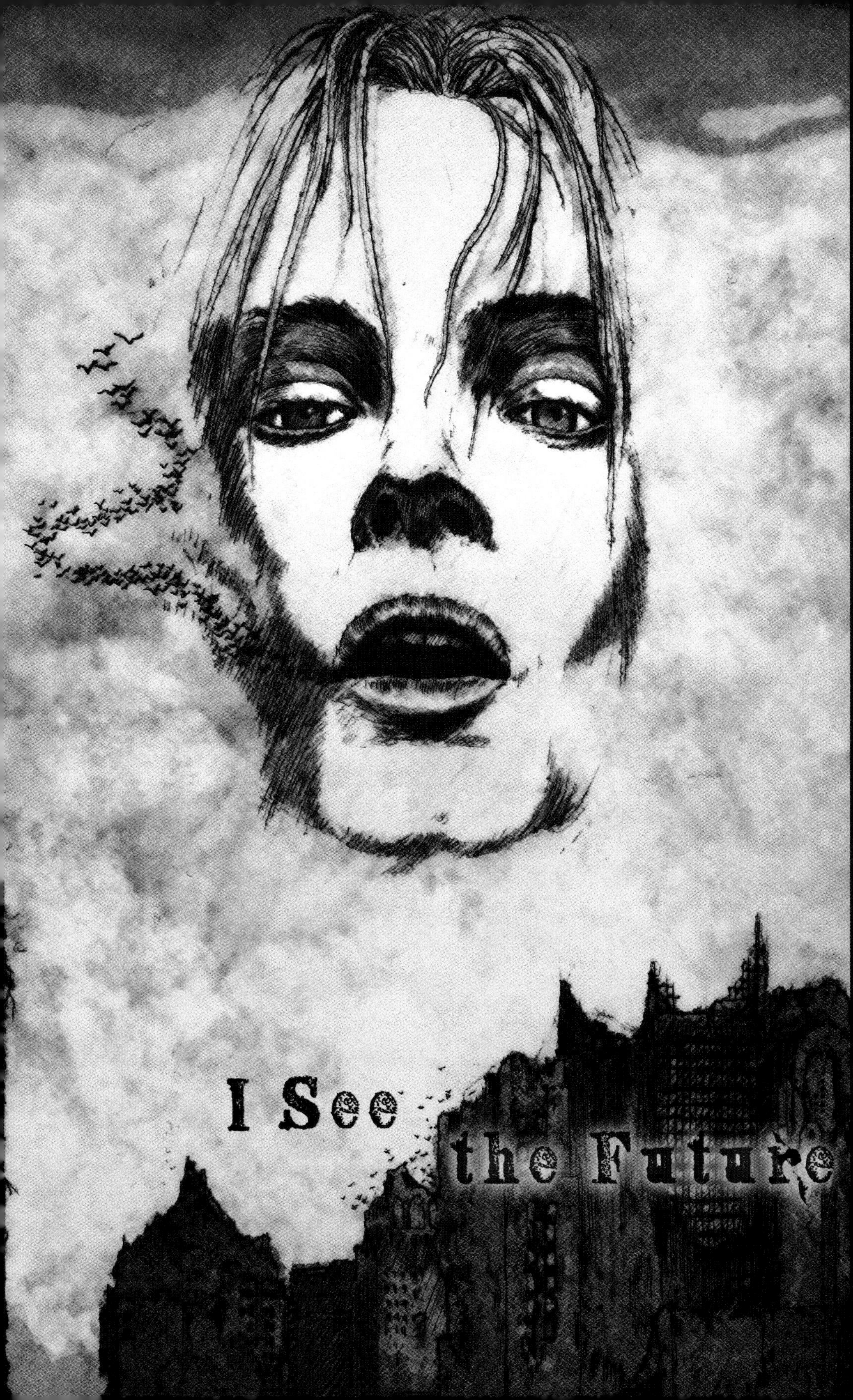
I See the Future

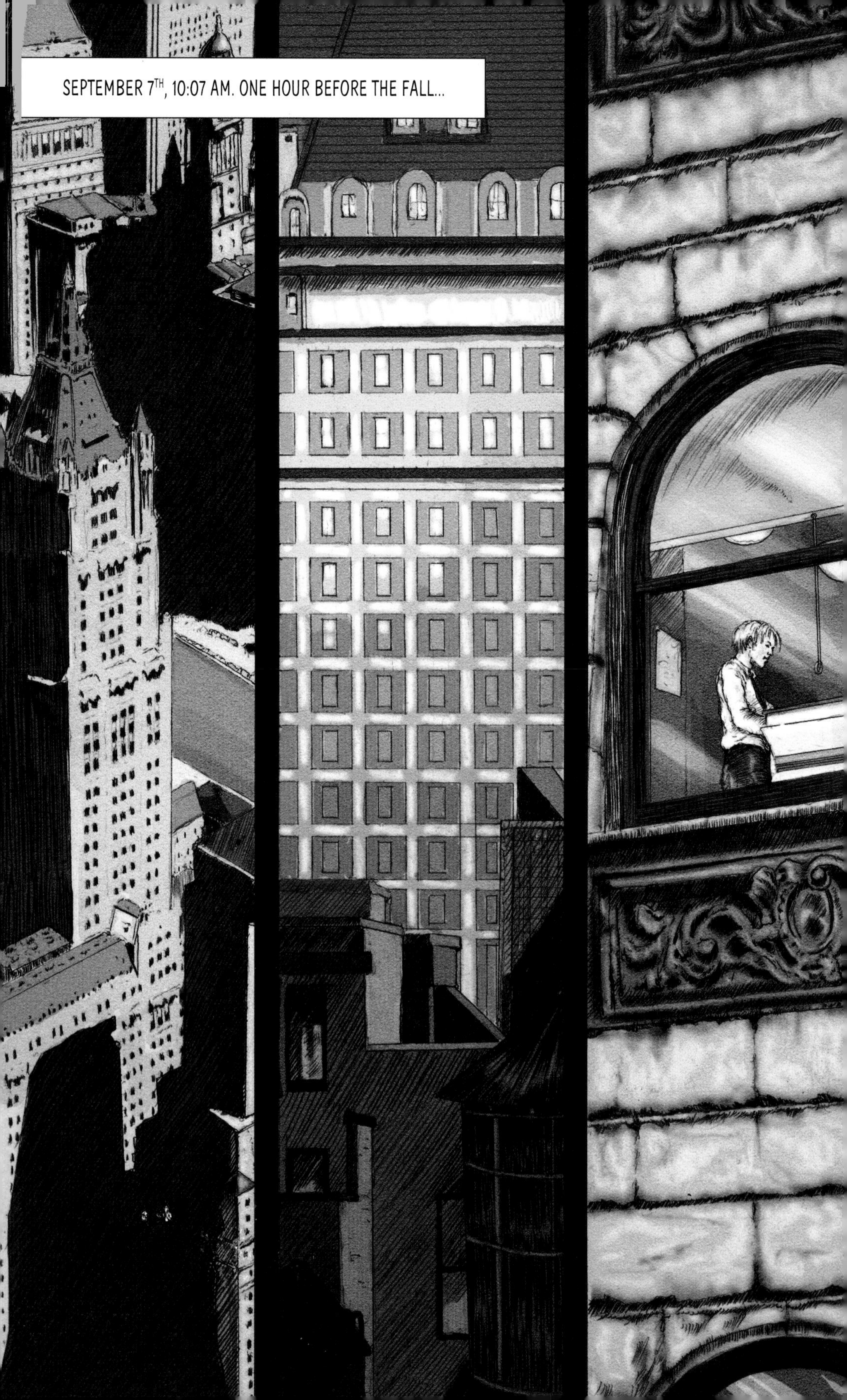
SEPTEMBER 7TH, 10:07 AM. ONE HOUR BEFORE THE FALL...

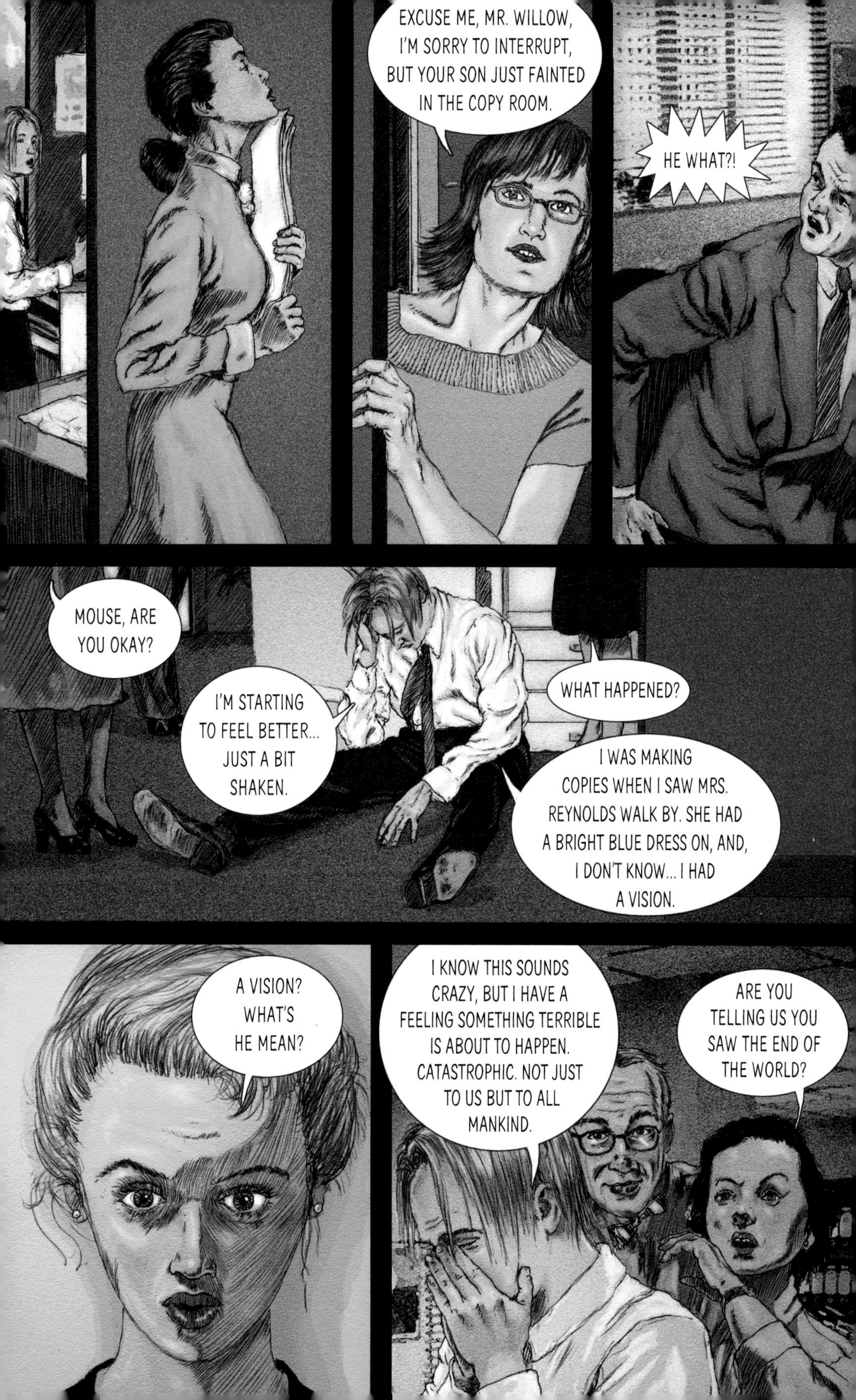
EXCUSE ME, MR. WILLOW, I'M SORRY TO INTERRUPT, BUT YOUR SON JUST FAINTED IN THE COPY ROOM.
HE WHAT?!
MOUSE, ARE YOU OKAY?
I'M STARTING TO FEEL BETTER... JUST A BIT SHAKEN.
WHAT HAPPENED?
I WAS MAKING COPIES WHEN I SAW MRS. REYNOLDS WALK BY. SHE HAD A BRIGHT BLUE DRESS ON, AND, I DON'T KNOW... I HAD A VISION.
A VISION? WHAT'S HE MEAN?
I KNOW THIS SOUNDS CRAZY, BUT I HAVE A FEELING SOMETHING TERRIBLE IS ABOUT TO HAPPEN. CATASTROPHIC. NOT JUST TO US BUT TO ALL MANKIND.
ARE YOU TELLING US YOU SAW THE END OF THE WORLD?

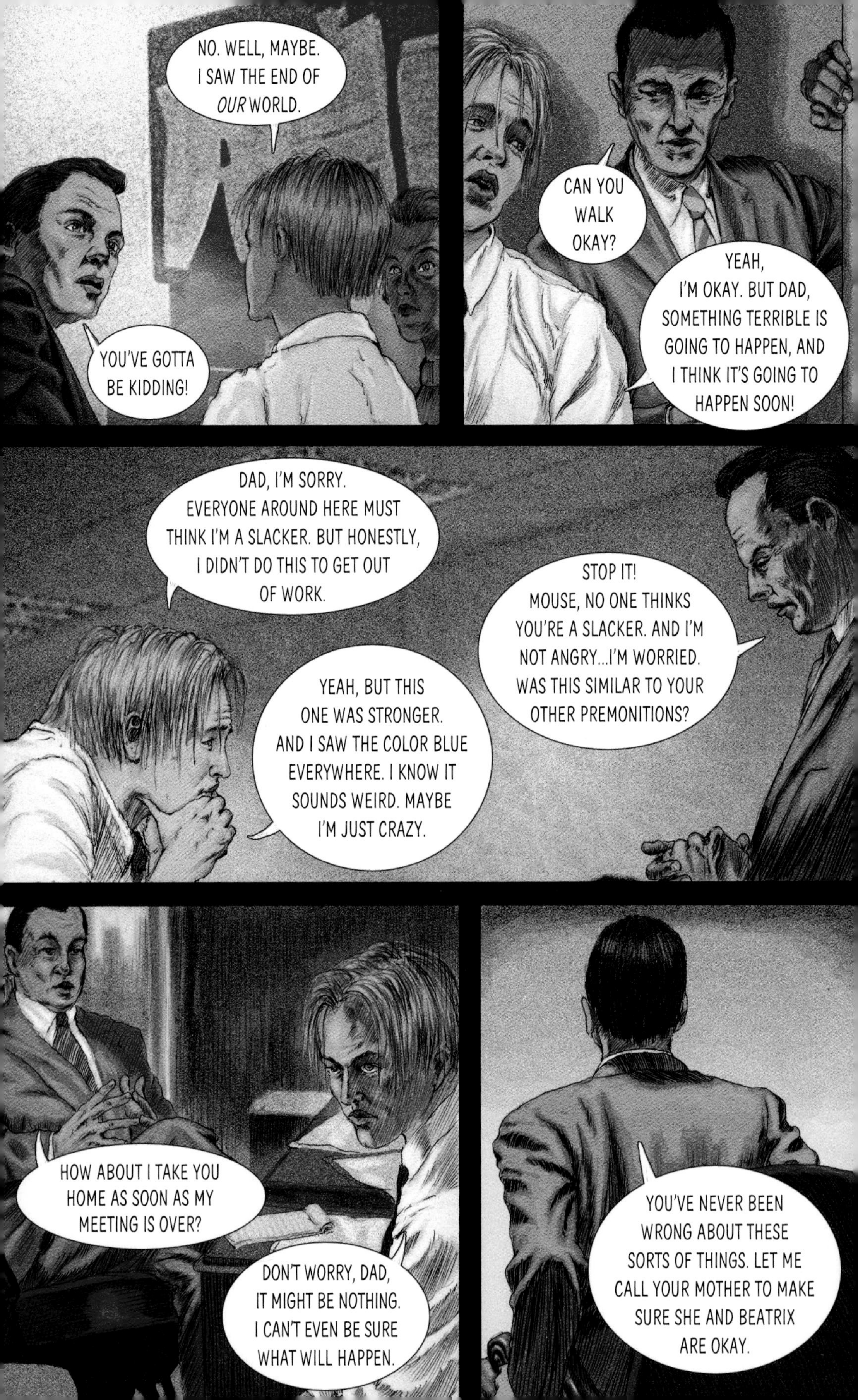
NO. WELL, MAYBE. I SAW THE END OF *OUR* WORLD.
YOU'VE GOTTA BE KIDDING!
CAN YOU WALK OKAY?
YEAH, I'M OKAY. BUT DAD, SOMETHING TERRIBLE IS GOING TO HAPPEN, AND I THINK IT'S GOING TO HAPPEN SOON!
DAD, I'M SORRY. EVERYONE AROUND HERE MUST THINK I'M A SLACKER. BUT HONESTLY, I DIDN'T DO THIS TO GET OUT OF WORK.
STOP IT! MOUSE, NO ONE THINKS YOU'RE A SLACKER. AND I'M NOT ANGRY...I'M WORRIED. WAS THIS SIMILAR TO YOUR OTHER PREMONITIONS?
YEAH, BUT THIS ONE WAS STRONGER. AND I SAW THE COLOR BLUE EVERYWHERE. I KNOW IT SOUNDS WEIRD. MAYBE I'M JUST CRAZY.
HOW ABOUT I TAKE YOU HOME AS SOON AS MY MEETING IS OVER?
DON'T WORRY, DAD, IT MIGHT BE NOTHING. I CAN'T EVEN BE SURE WHAT WILL HAPPEN.
YOU'VE NEVER BEEN WRONG ABOUT THESE SORTS OF THINGS. LET ME CALL YOUR MOTHER TO MAKE SURE SHE AND BEATRIX ARE OKAY.

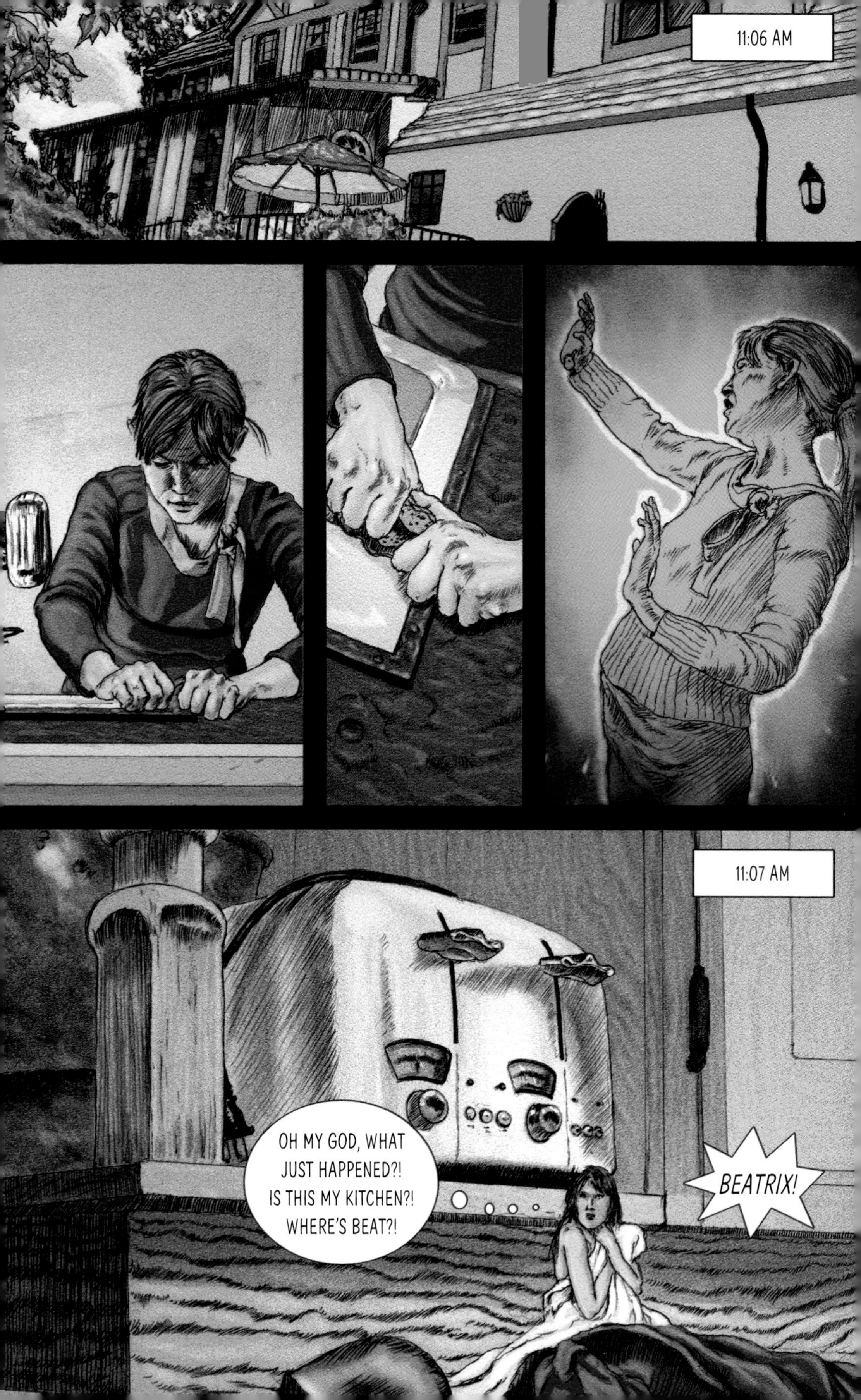
11:06 AM
11:07 AM
OH MY GOD, WHAT JUST HAPPENED?! IS THIS MY KITCHEN?! WHERE'S BEAT?!
BEATRIX!

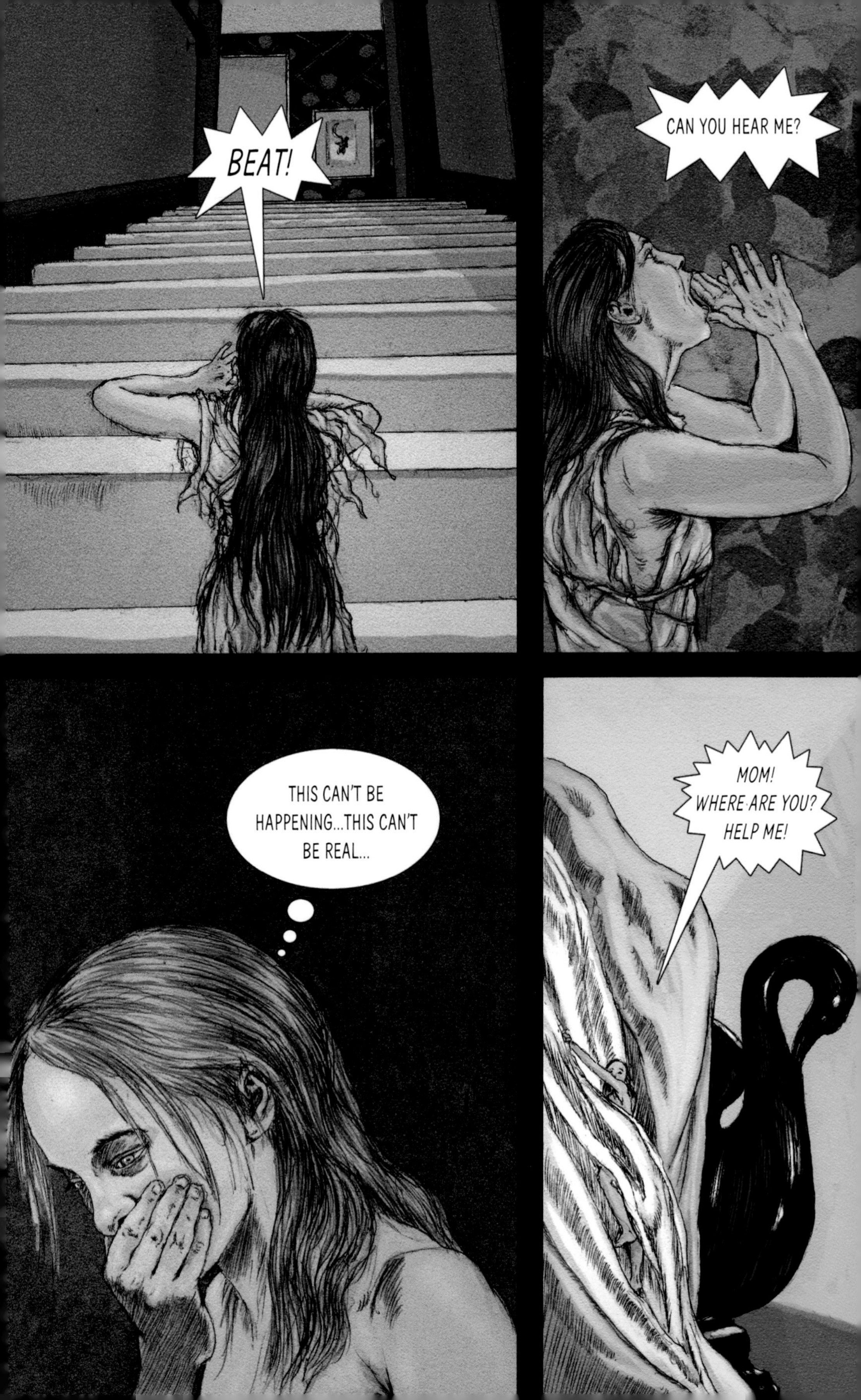
BEAT!
CAN YOU HEAR ME?
THIS CAN'T BE HAPPENING...THIS CAN'T BE REAL...
MOM! WHERE ARE YOU? HELP ME!

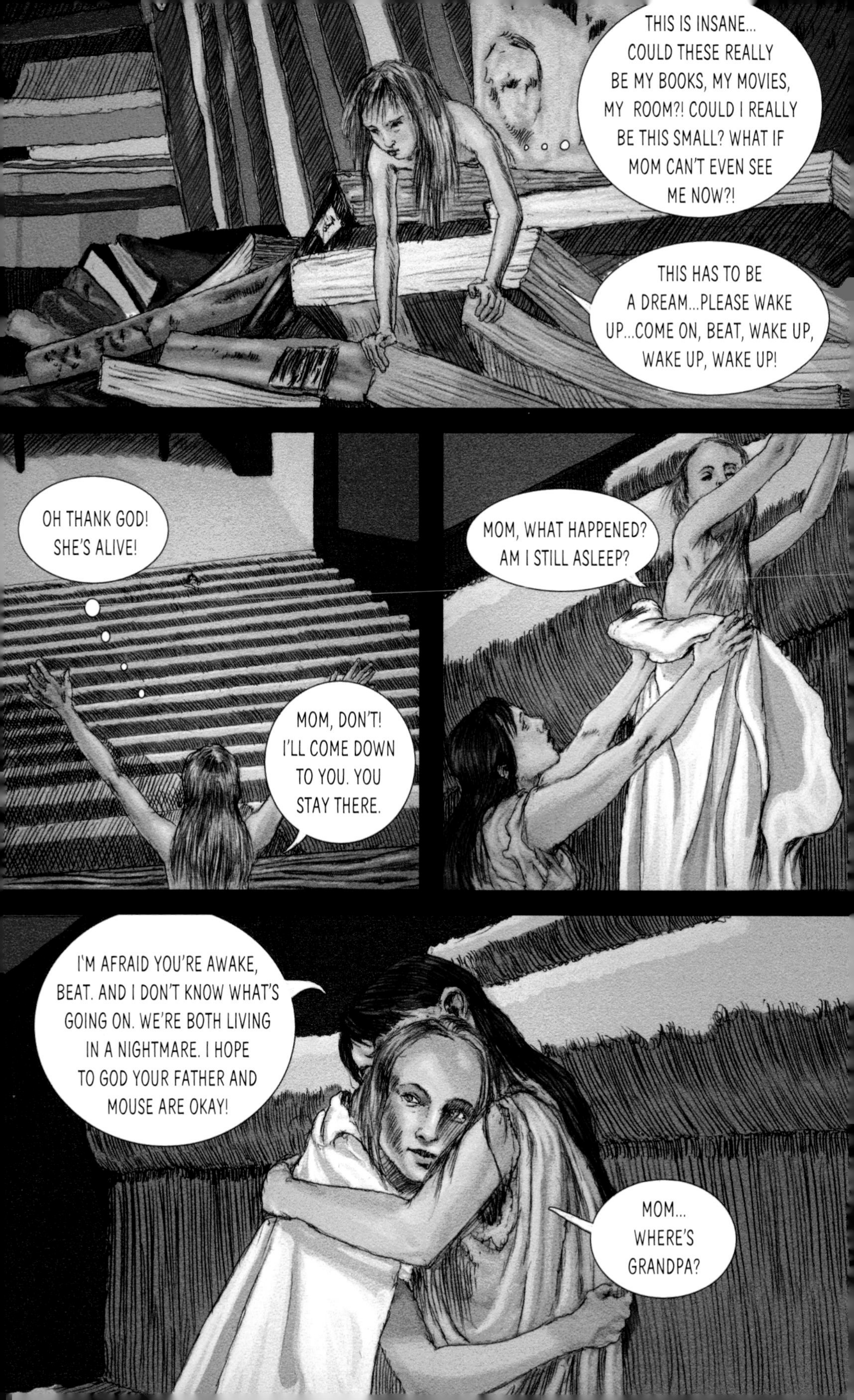
THIS IS INSANE... COULD THESE REALLY BE MY BOOKS, MY MOVIES, MY ROOM?! COULD I REALLY BE THIS SMALL? WHAT IF MOM CAN'T EVEN SEE ME NOW?!
THIS HAS TO BE A DREAM...PLEASE WAKE UP...COME ON, BEAT, WAKE UP, WAKE UP, WAKE UP!
OH THANK GOD! SHE'S ALIVE!
MOM, DON'T! I'LL COME DOWN TO YOU. YOU STAY THERE.
MOM, WHAT HAPPENED? AM I STILL ASLEEP?
I'M AFRAID YOU'RE AWAKE, BEAT. AND I DON'T KNOW WHAT'S GOING ON. WE'RE BOTH LIVING IN A NIGHTMARE. I HOPE TO GOD YOUR FATHER AND MOUSE ARE OKAY!
MOM... WHERE'S GRANDPA?

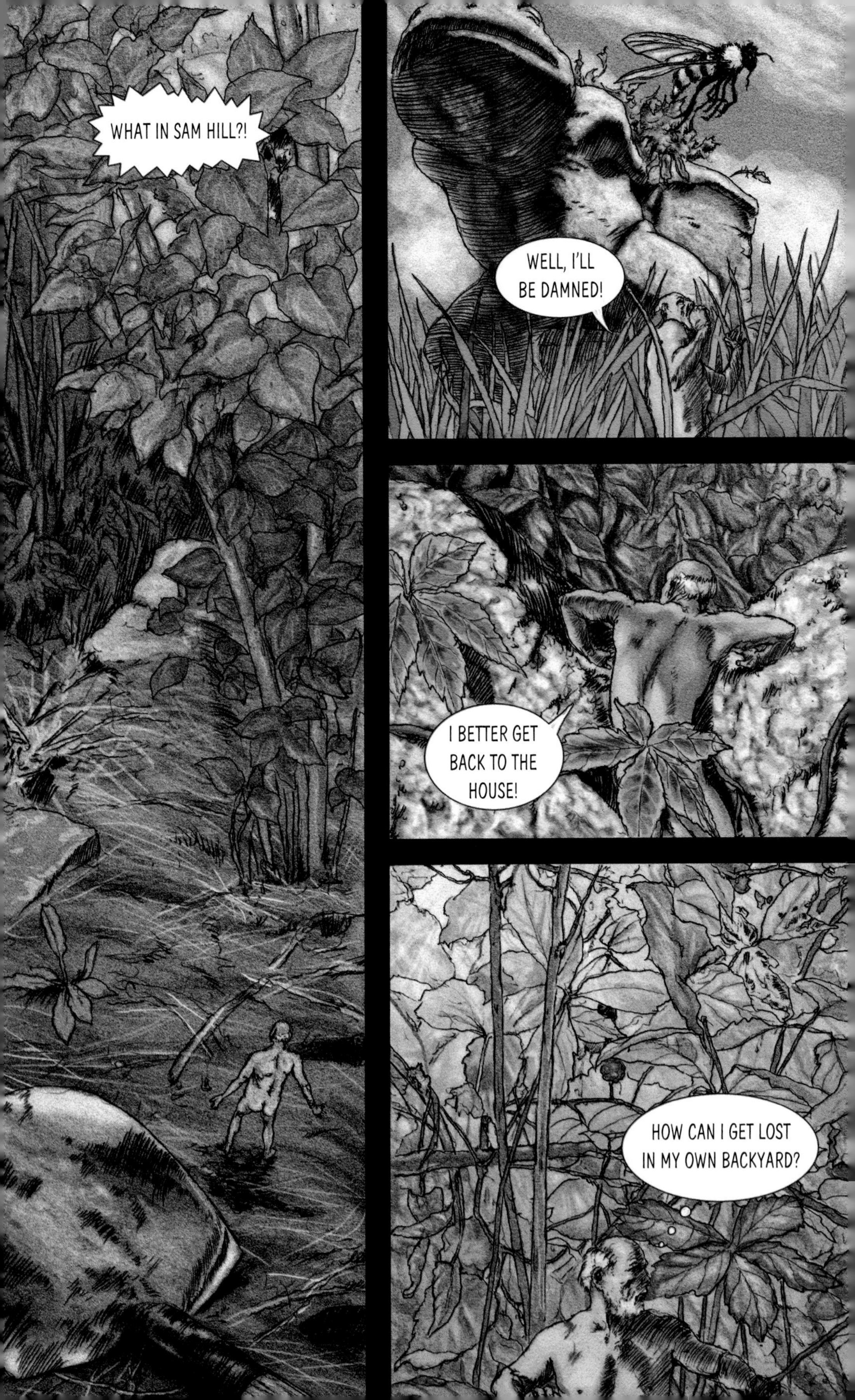
WHAT IN SAM HILL?!
WELL, I'LL BE DAMNED!
I BETTER GET BACK TO THE HOUSE!
HOW CAN I GET LOST IN MY OWN BACKYARD?

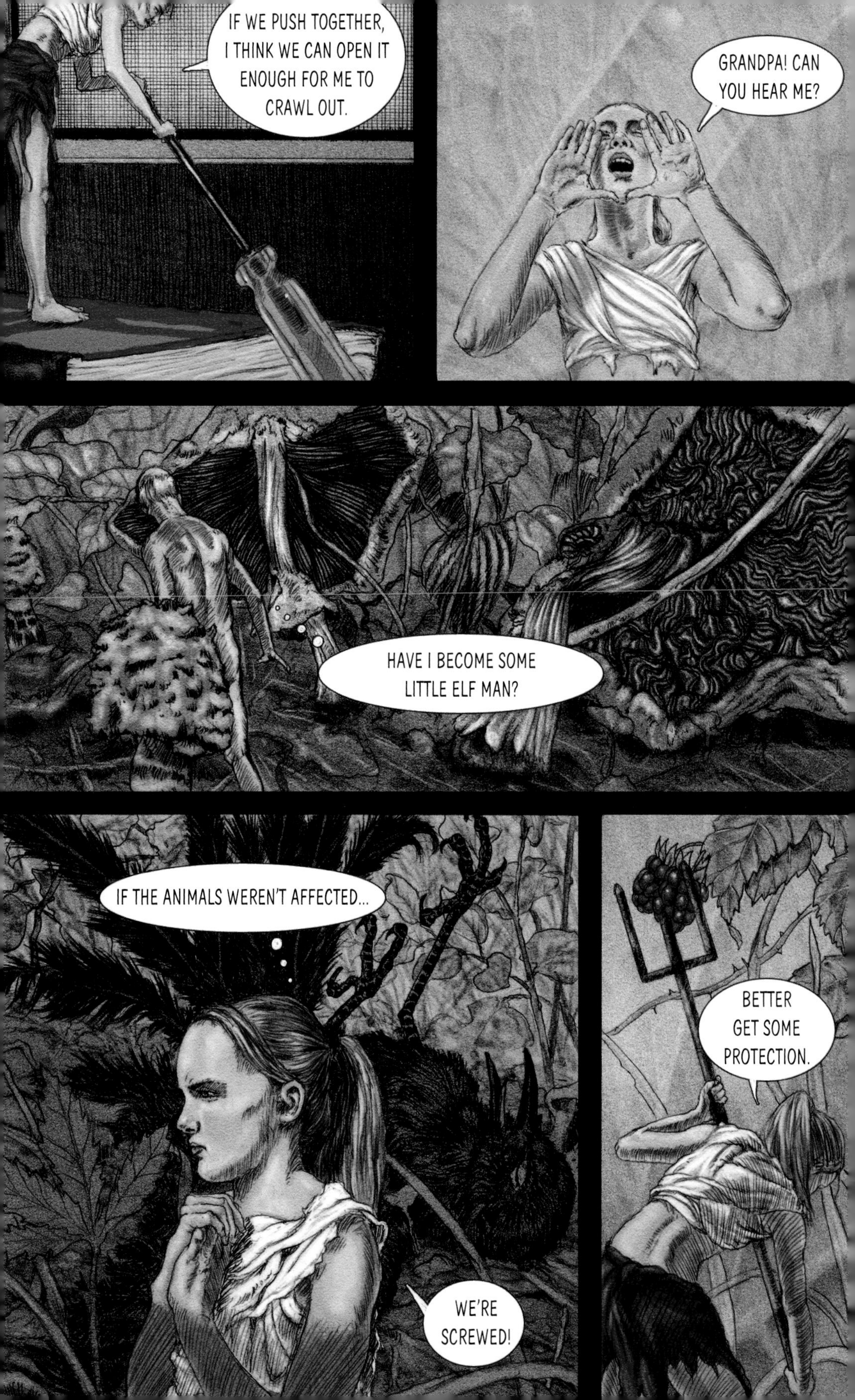
IF WE PUSH TOGETHER, I THINK WE CAN OPEN IT ENOUGH FOR ME TO CRAWL OUT.
GRANDPA! CAN YOU HEAR ME?
HAVE I BECOME SOME LITTLE ELF MAN?
IF THE ANIMALS WEREN'T AFFECTED...
WE'RE SCREWED!
BETTER GET SOME PROTECTION.

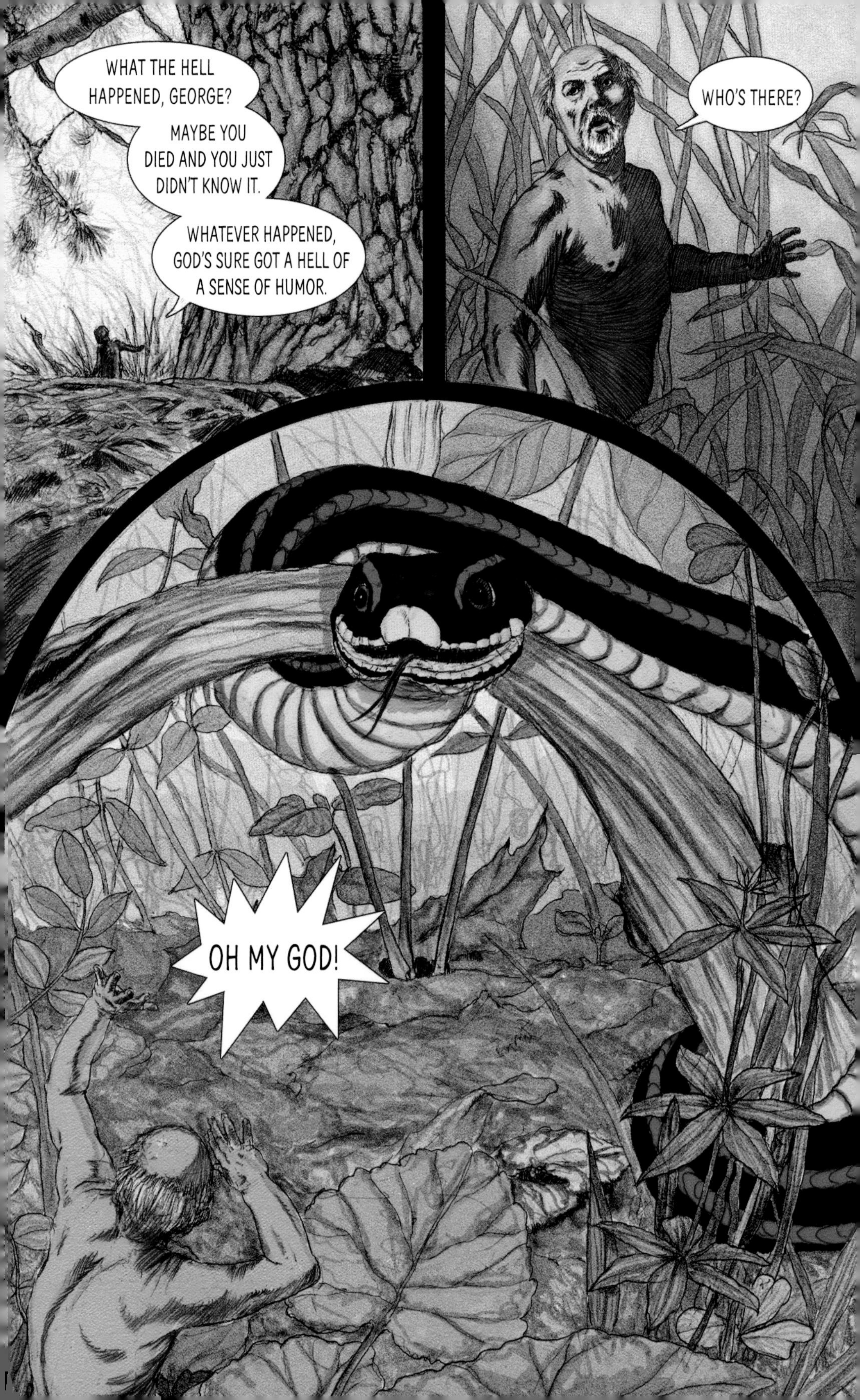
WHAT THE HELL HAPPENED, GEORGE?
MAYBE YOU DIED AND YOU JUST DIDN'T KNOW IT.
WHATEVER HAPPENED, GOD'S SURE GOT A HELL OF A SENSE OF HUMOR.
WHO'S THERE?
OH MY GOD!

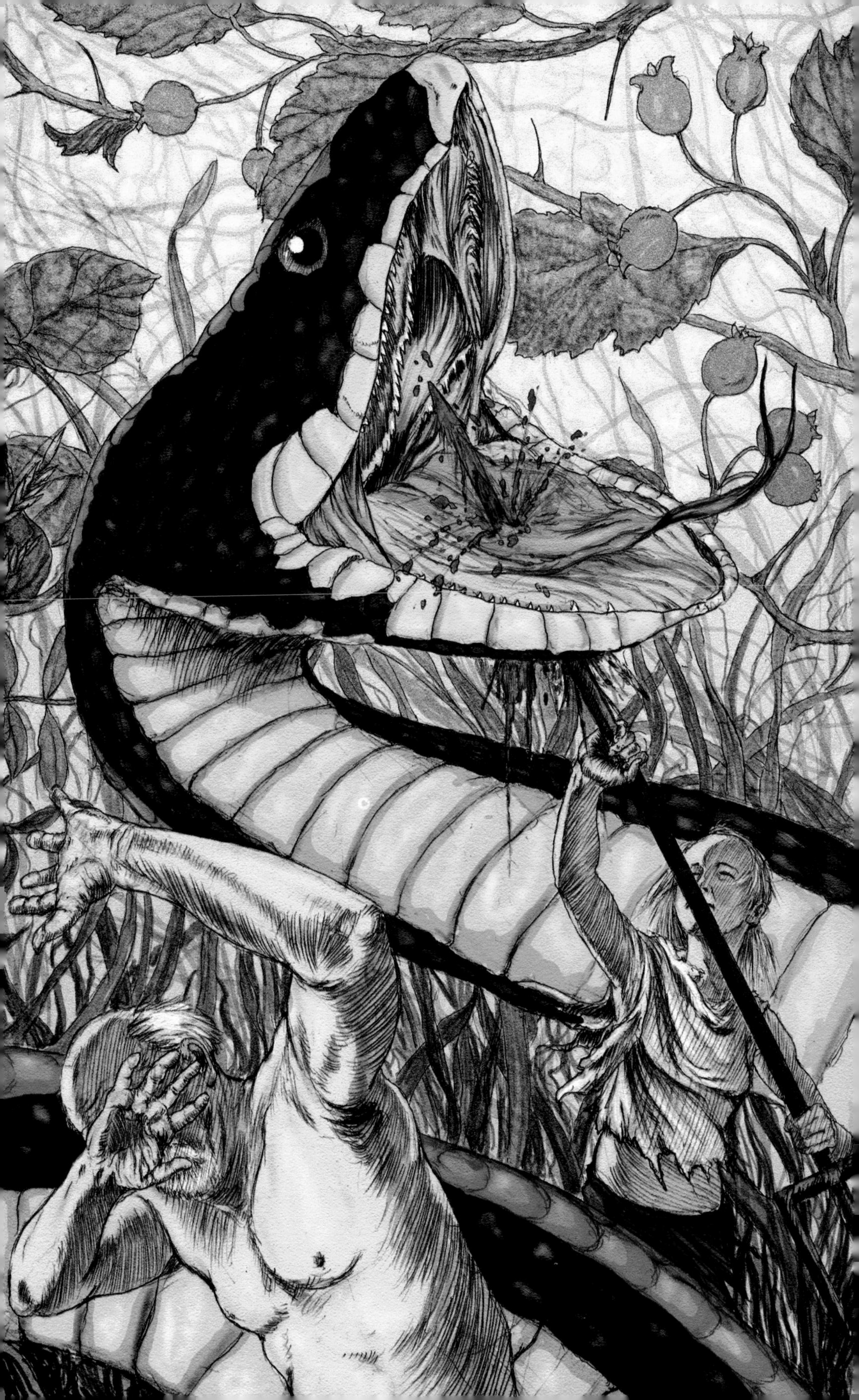

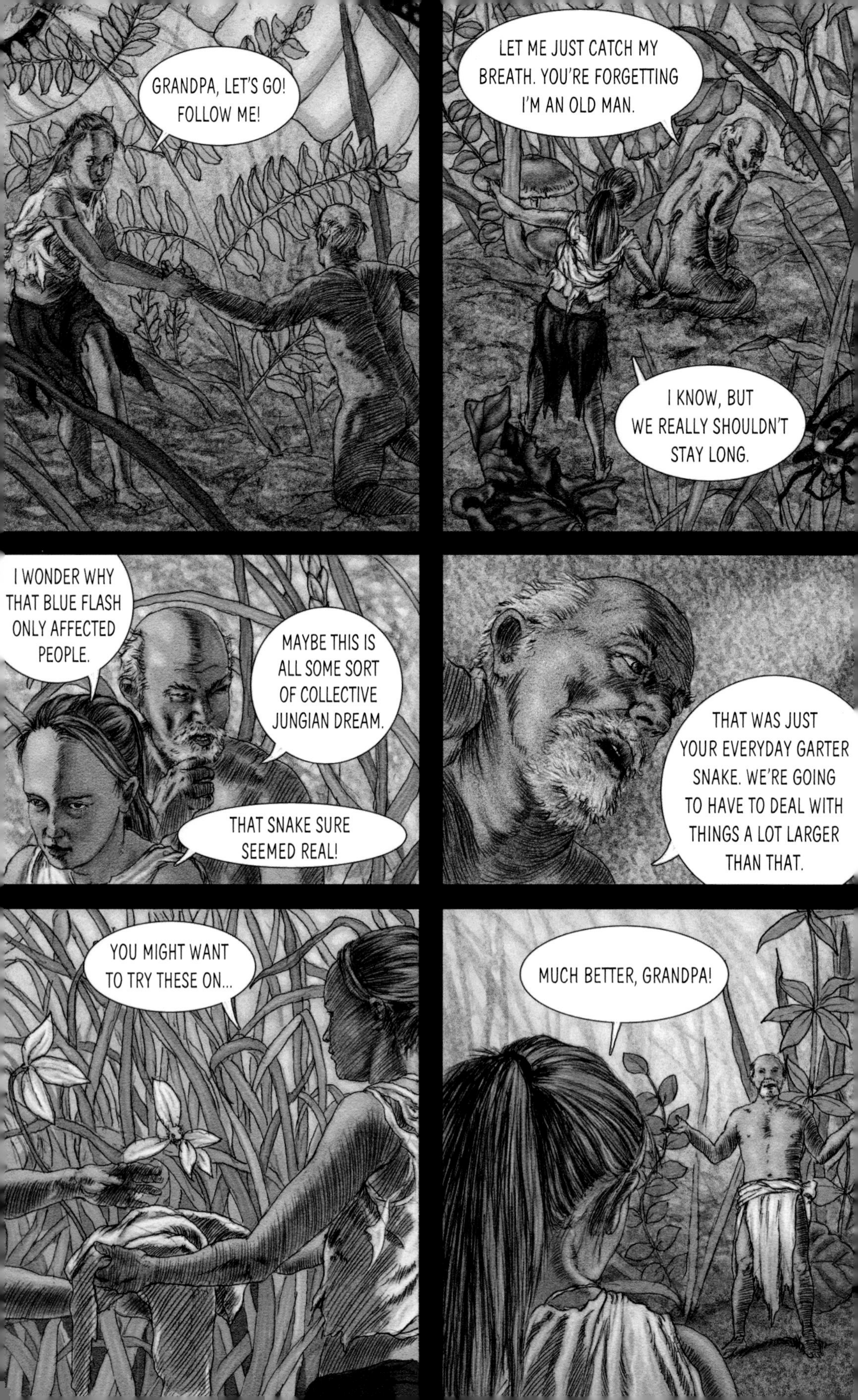
GRANDPA, LET'S GO! FOLLOW ME!
LET ME JUST CATCH MY BREATH. YOU'RE FORGETTING I'M AN OLD MAN.
I KNOW, BUT WE REALLY SHOULDN'T STAY LONG.
I WONDER WHY THAT BLUE FLASH ONLY AFFECTED PEOPLE.
MAYBE THIS IS ALL SOME SORT OF COLLECTIVE JUNGIAN DREAM.
THAT SNAKE SURE SEEMED REAL!
THAT WAS JUST YOUR EVERYDAY GARTER SNAKE. WE'RE GOING TO HAVE TO DEAL WITH THINGS A LOT LARGER THAN THAT.
YOU MIGHT WANT TO TRY THESE ON...
MUCH BETTER, GRANDPA!

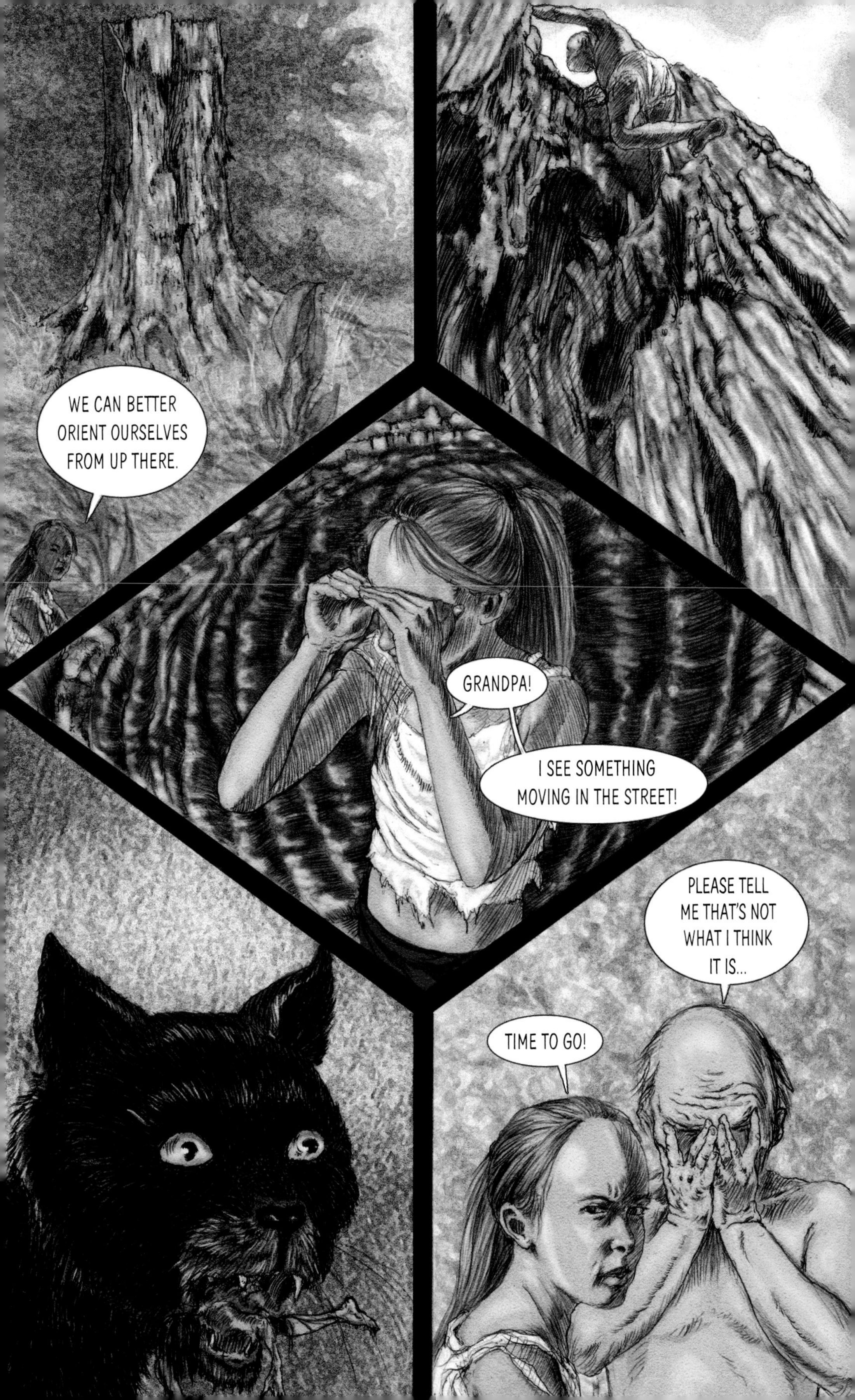
WE CAN BETTER ORIENT OURSELVES FROM UP THERE.
GRANDPA!
I SEE SOMETHING MOVING IN THE STREET!
PLEASE TELL ME THAT'S NOT WHAT I THINK IT IS...
TIME TO GO!

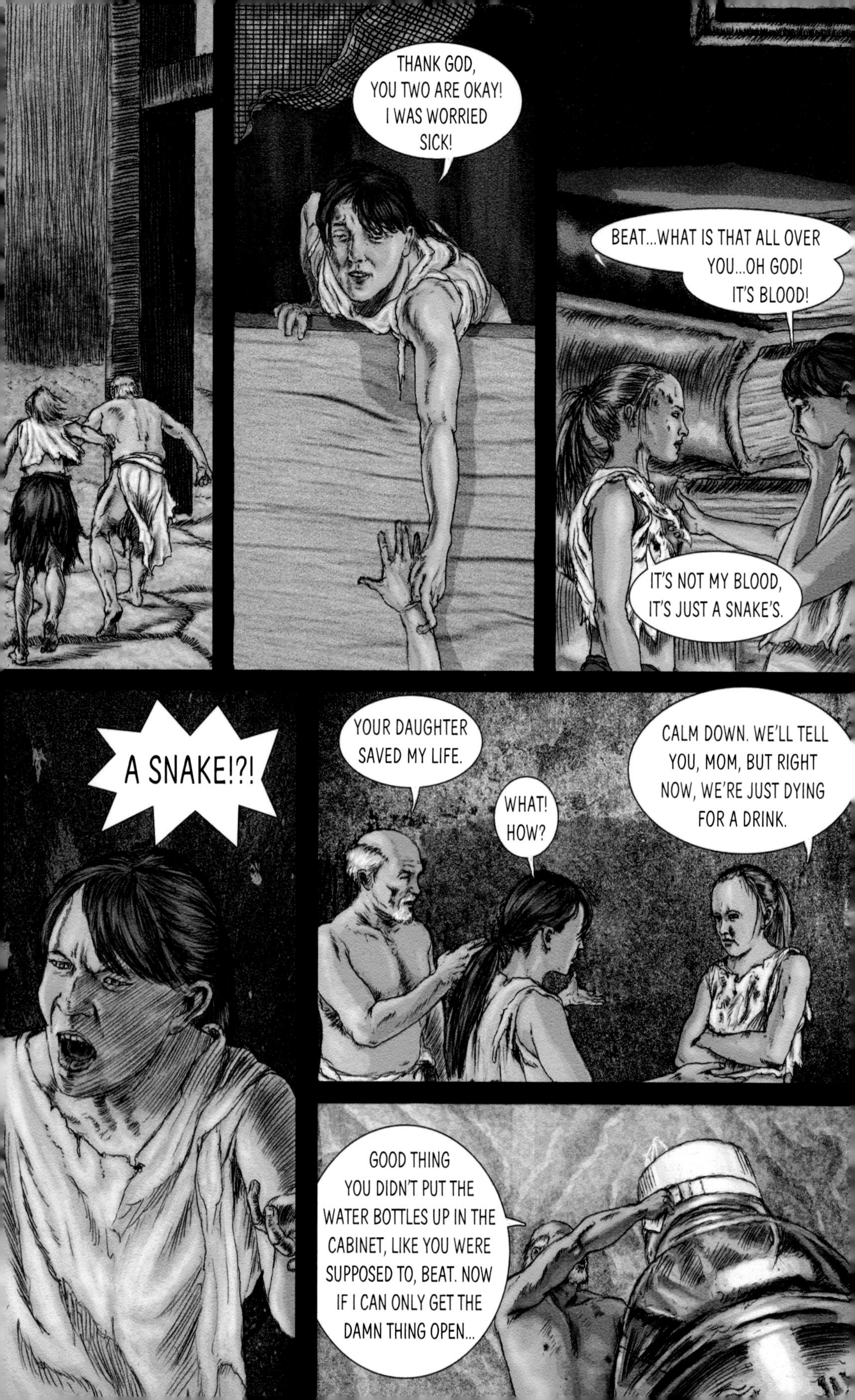
THANK GOD, YOU TWO ARE OKAY! I WAS WORRIED SICK!
BEAT...WHAT IS THAT ALL OVER YOU...OH GOD! IT'S BLOOD!
IT'S NOT MY BLOOD, IT'S JUST A SNAKE'S.
A SNAKE!?!
YOUR DAUGHTER SAVED MY LIFE.
WHAT! HOW?
CALM DOWN. WE'LL TELL YOU, MOM, BUT RIGHT NOW, WE'RE JUST DYING FOR A DRINK.
GOOD THING YOU DIDN'T PUT THE WATER BOTTLES UP IN THE CABINET, LIKE YOU WERE SUPPOSED TO, BEAT. NOW IF I CAN ONLY GET THE DAMN THING OPEN...

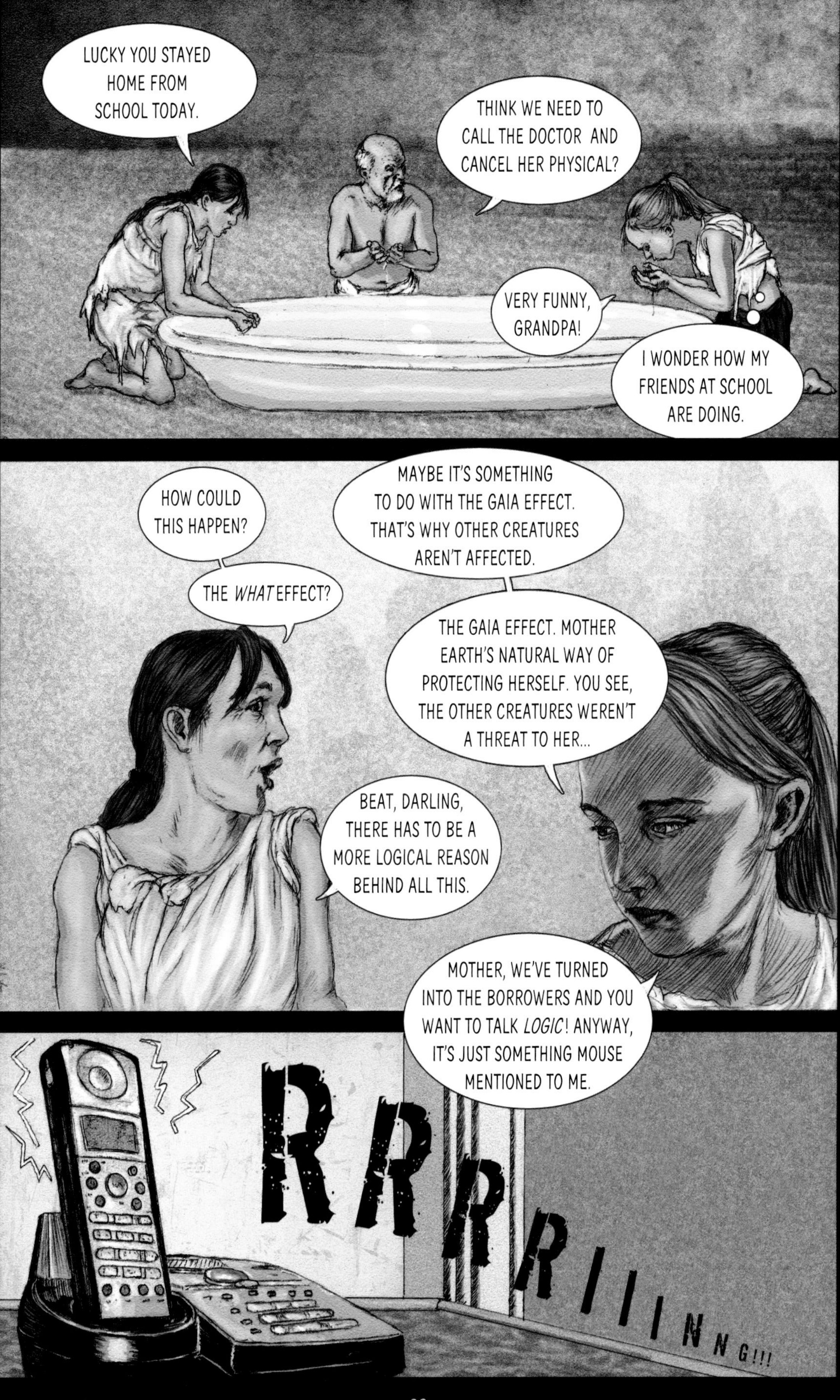
LUCKY YOU STAYED HOME FROM SCHOOL TODAY.
THINK WE NEED TO CALL THE DOCTOR AND CANCEL HER PHYSICAL?
VERY FUNNY, GRANDPA!
I WONDER HOW MY FRIENDS AT SCHOOL ARE DOING.
HOW COULD THIS HAPPEN?
MAYBE IT'S SOMETHING TO DO WITH THE GAIA EFFECT. THAT'S WHY OTHER CREATURES AREN'T AFFECTED.
THE *WHAT* EFFECT?
THE GAIA EFFECT. MOTHER EARTH'S NATURAL WAY OF PROTECTING HERSELF. YOU SEE, THE OTHER CREATURES WEREN'T A THREAT TO HER...
BEAT, DARLING, THERE HAS TO BE A MORE LOGICAL REASON BEHIND ALL THIS.
MOTHER, WE'VE TURNED INTO THE BORROWERS AND YOU WANT TO TALK *LOGIC*! ANYWAY, IT'S JUST SOMETHING MOUSE MENTIONED TO ME.
RRRRIIIINNG!!!

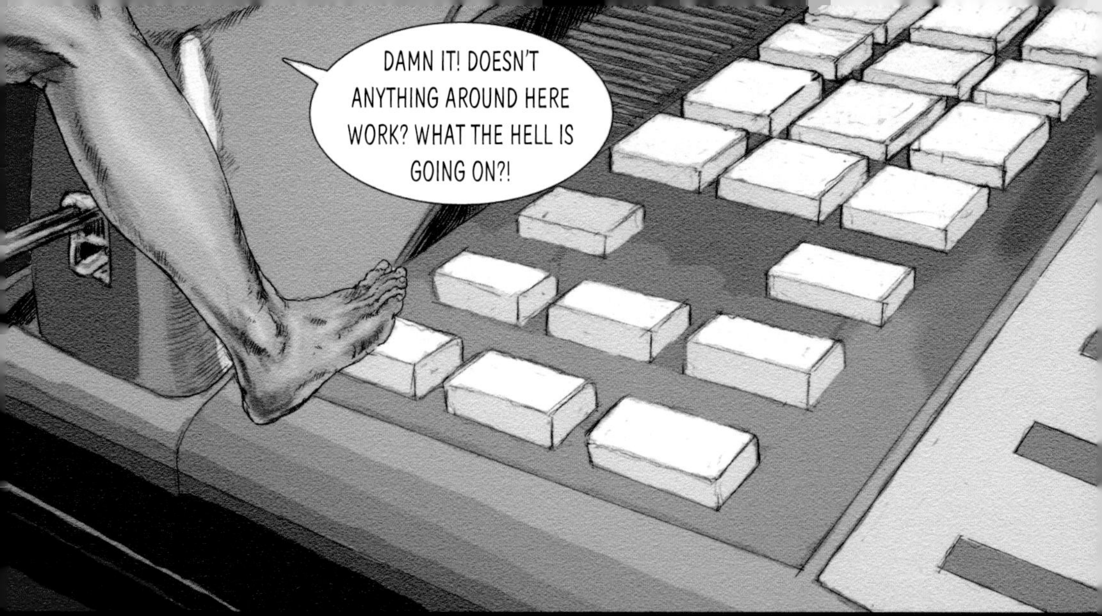
DAMN IT! DOESN'T ANYTHING AROUND HERE WORK? WHAT THE HELL IS GOING ON?!

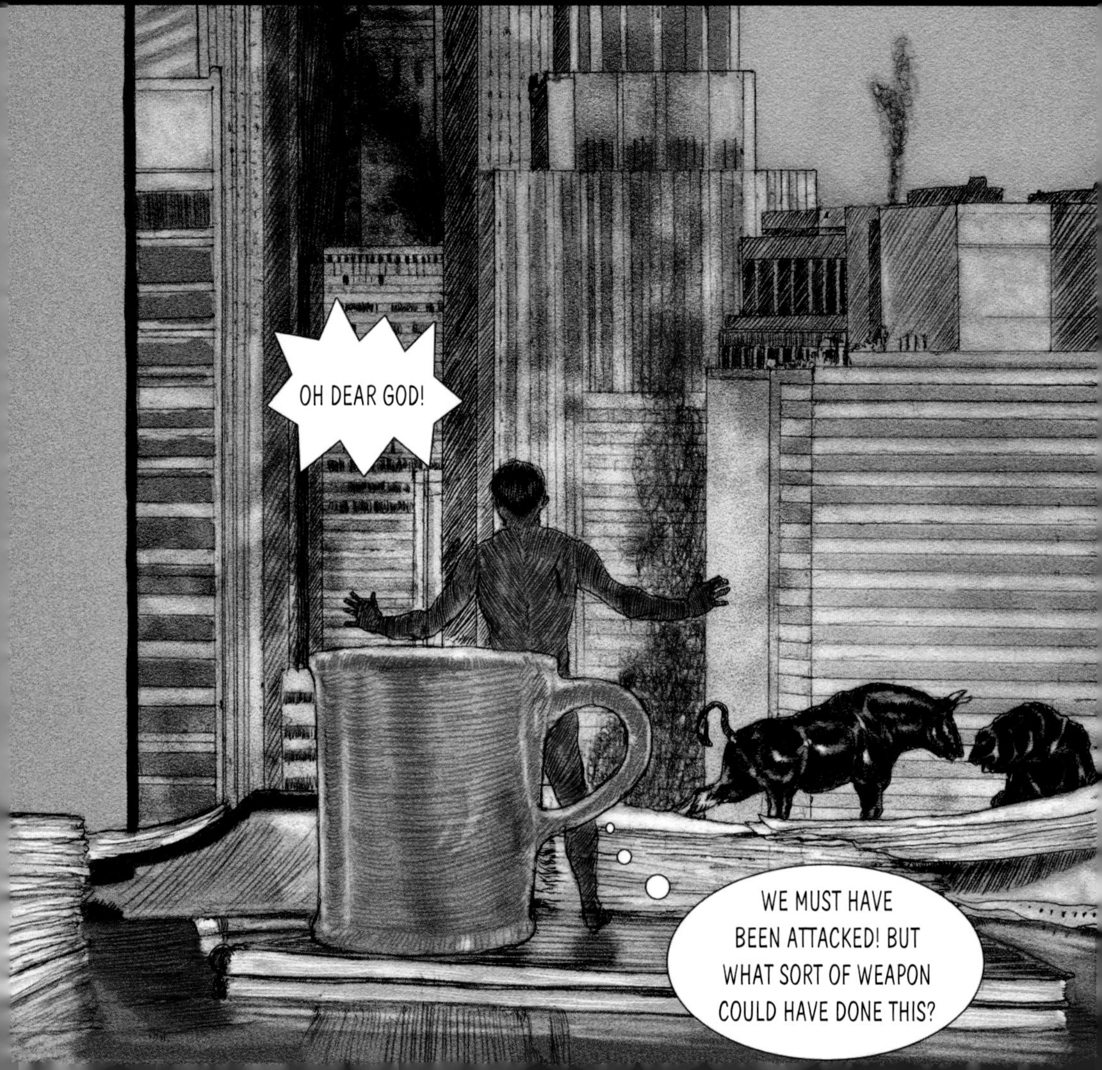
OH DEAR GOD!
WE MUST HAVE BEEN ATTACKED! BUT WHAT SORT OF WEAPON COULD HAVE DONE THIS?

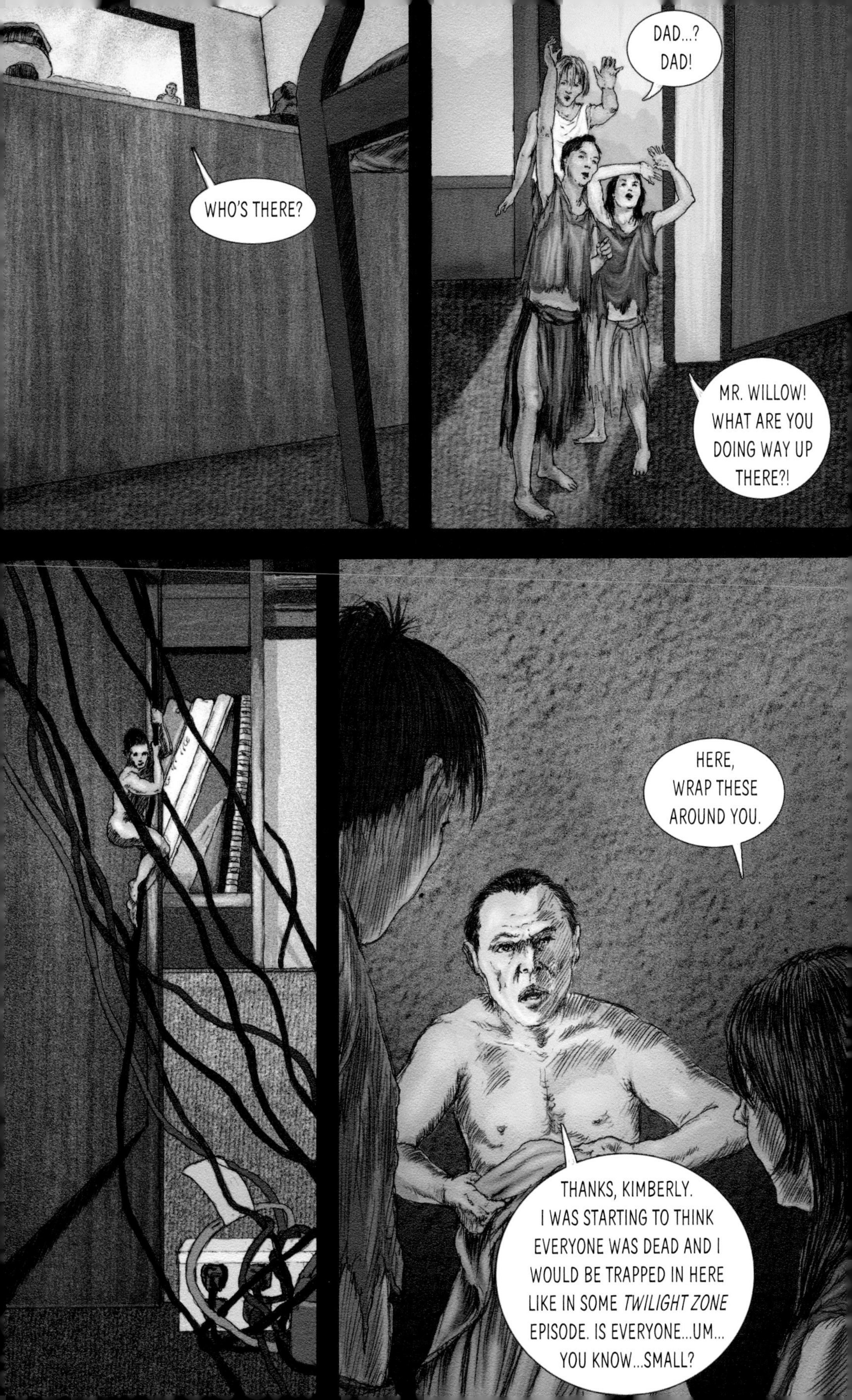
WHO'S THERE?
DAD...? DAD!
MR. WILLOW! WHAT ARE YOU DOING WAY UP THERE?!
HERE, WRAP THESE AROUND YOU.
THANKS, KIMBERLY. I WAS STARTING TO THINK EVERYONE WAS DEAD AND I WOULD BE TRAPPED IN HERE LIKE IN SOME *TWILIGHT ZONE* EPISODE. IS EVERYONE...UM... YOU KNOW...SMALL?

EVERYONE HERE IS IN THE SMALL. I THINK THIS IS A GLOBAL PHENOMENON— ALL OF MANKIND HAS FALLEN. REMEMBER MY VISION, DAD?

IF WE'RE GOING TO SURVIVE, WE HAVE TO START LOOKING AT THINGS DIFFERENTLY. WE'VE ALREADY STARTED COLLECTING FOOD AND WATER.

WHO COULD HAVE DONE THIS?

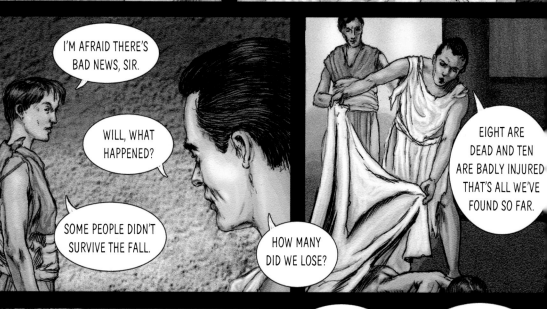

I'M AFRAID THERE'S BAD NEWS, SIR.

WILL, WHAT HAPPENED?

SOME PEOPLE DIDN'T SURVIVE THE FALL.

HOW MANY DID WE LOSE?

EIGHT ARE DEAD AND TEN ARE BADLY INJURED THAT'S ALL WE'VE FOUND SO FAR.

WE HAVE TO LEAVE THIS BUILDING NOW. I KNOW IT'S HARD, DAD, BUT THE INJURED NEED TO BE LEFT BEHIND.

HOW CAN YOU SAY THAT? I CAN'T LEAVE PEOPLE I'VE WORKED WITH FOR FIFTEEN YEARS!

THERE'S NO DOCTORS, NO HOSPITALS, NO AMBULANCE ON ITS WAY. THESE ARE OUR CHOICES — STAY AND DIE...

...OR LEAVE AND AT LEAST HAVE A CHANCE TO SURVIVE.

QUIET, EVERYONE. THERE'S NO NEED TO PANIC. IT MUST BE OBVIOUS BY NOW THAT WE HAVE BEEN THROUGH A MASSIVE TERRORIST ATTACK. THE MOST PRUDENT PLAN IS FOR US TO STAY WHERE WE ARE.

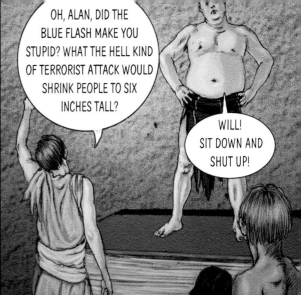

OH, ALAN, DID THE BLUE FLASH MAKE YOU STUPID? WHAT THE HELL KIND OF TERRORIST ATTACK WOULD SHRINK PEOPLE TO SIX INCHES TALL?

WILL! SIT DOWN AND SHUT UP!

I WANT TO HEAR WHAT BOB'S SON HAS TO SAY. HE SAW THIS COMING!

WE'RE NOT ABOUT TO LISTEN TO SOME INTERN. I'M THE HEAD OF THIS COMPANY AND WHAT I SAY GOES...

DON'T YOU GET IT, ALAN?

I GET IT, ALRIGHT— YOU'RE FIRED!

ARE YOU INSANE? THERE'S NOTHING TO GET FIRED FROM. COMPANIES AND JOBS JUST BECAME EXTINCT! MOUSE HERE WAS THE ONE WHO ORGANIZED US. HE FIGURED OUT THE DOORS. HE WAS THE ONE WHO GOT THE GROUP TO FIND FOOD AND DRINK. AND WHERE WERE YOU? HUDDLED IN THE CORNER LIKE A LITTLE...

FINE, FINE... LET'S HEAR WHAT THE KID HAS TO SAY.

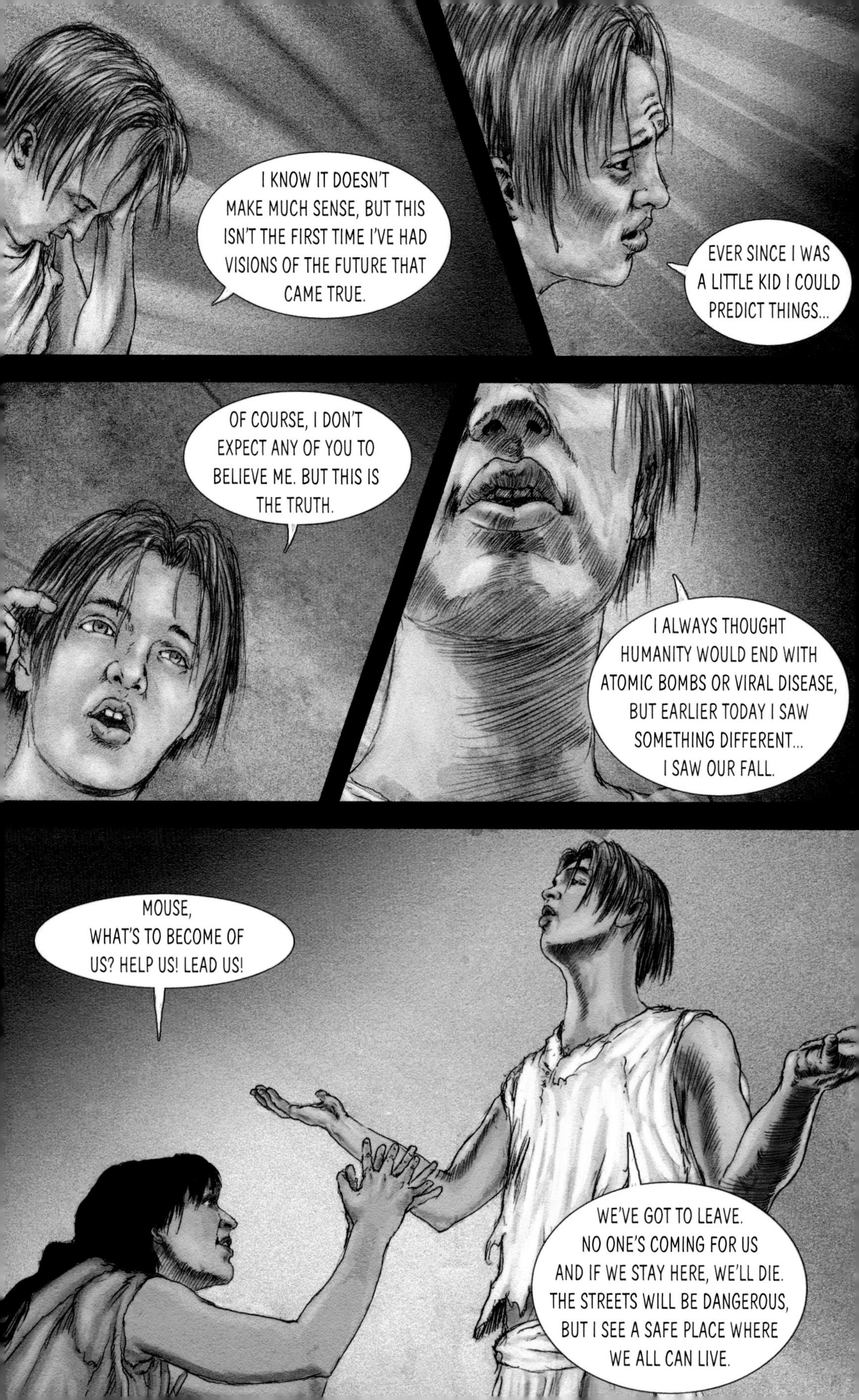
I KNOW IT DOESN'T MAKE MUCH SENSE, BUT THIS ISN'T THE FIRST TIME I'VE HAD VISIONS OF THE FUTURE THAT CAME TRUE.
EVER SINCE I WAS A LITTLE KID I COULD PREDICT THINGS...
OF COURSE, I DON'T EXPECT ANY OF YOU TO BELIEVE ME. BUT THIS IS THE TRUTH.
I ALWAYS THOUGHT HUMANITY WOULD END WITH ATOMIC BOMBS OR VIRAL DISEASE, BUT EARLIER TODAY I SAW SOMETHING DIFFERENT... I SAW OUR FALL.
MOUSE, WHAT'S TO BECOME OF US? HELP US! LEAD US!
WE'VE GOT TO LEAVE. NO ONE'S COMING FOR US AND IF WE STAY HERE, WE'LL DIE. THE STREETS WILL BE DANGEROUS, BUT I SEE A SAFE PLACE WHERE WE ALL CAN LIVE.

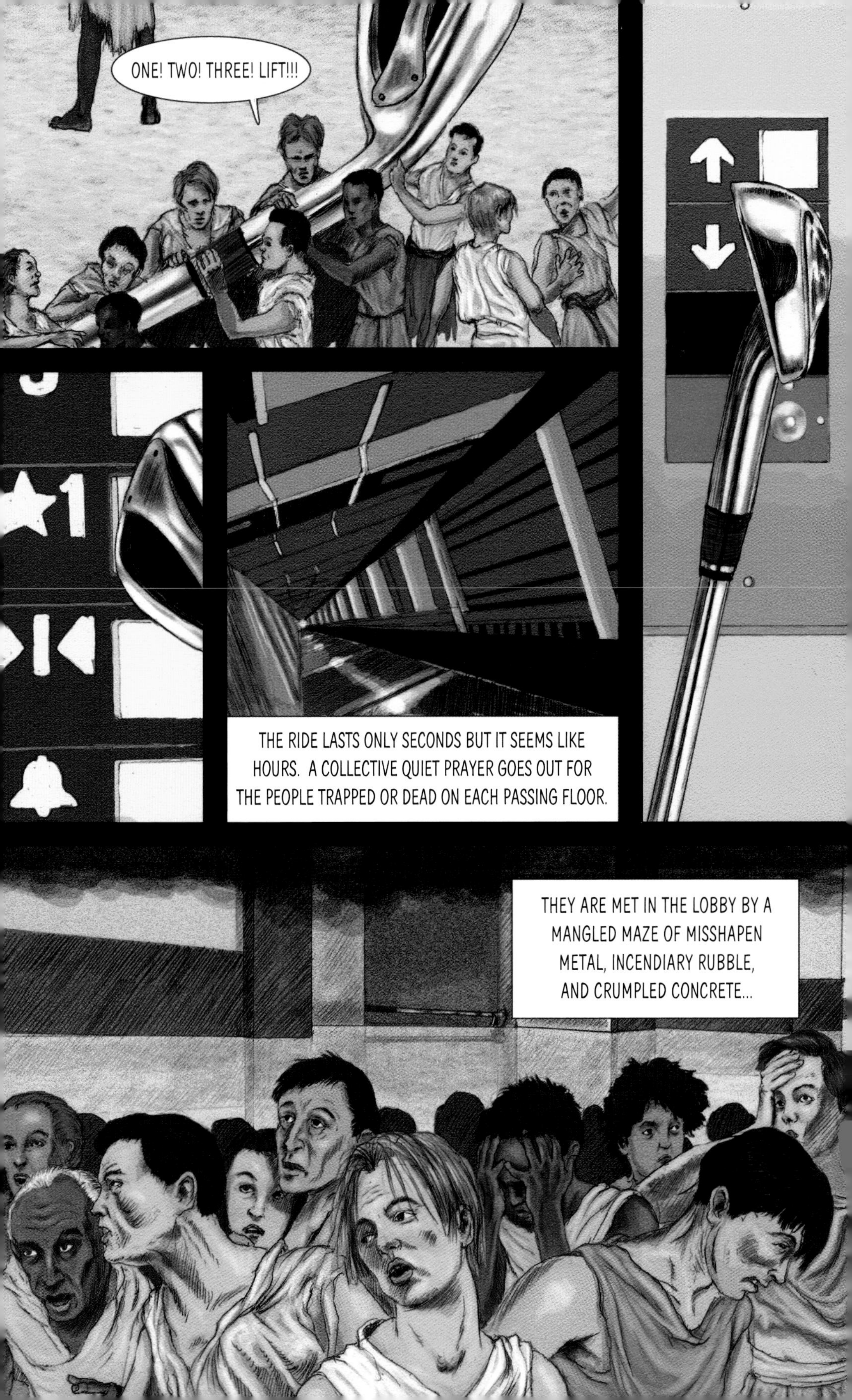
ONE! TWO! THREE! LIFT!!!
THE RIDE LASTS ONLY SECONDS BUT IT SEEMS LIKE HOURS. A COLLECTIVE QUIET PRAYER GOES OUT FOR THE PEOPLE TRAPPED OR DEAD ON EACH PASSING FLOOR.
THEY ARE MET IN THE LOBBY BY A MANGLED MAZE OF MISSHAPEN METAL, INCENDIARY RUBBLE, AND CRUMPLED CONCRETE...

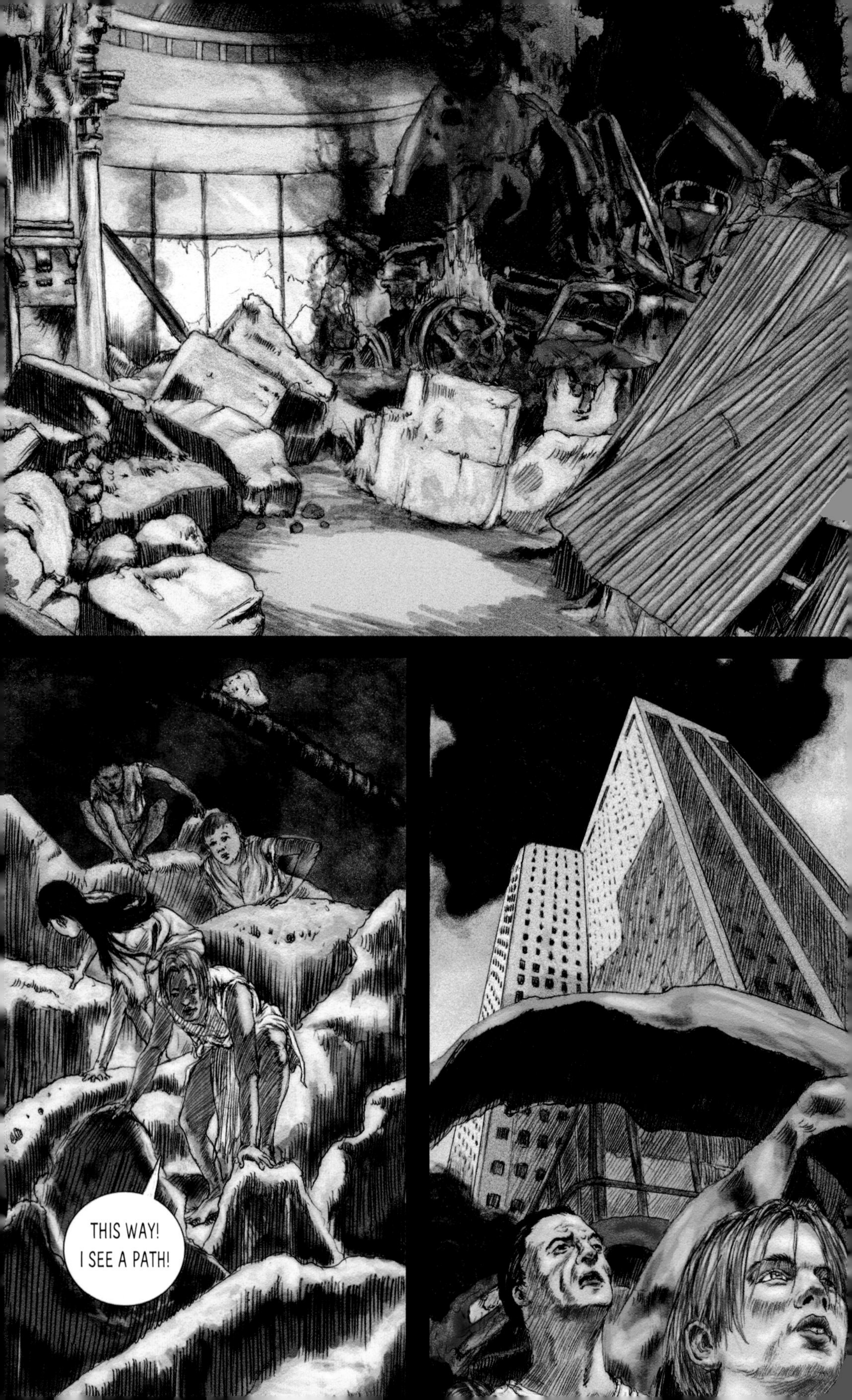
THIS WAY!
I SEE A PATH!

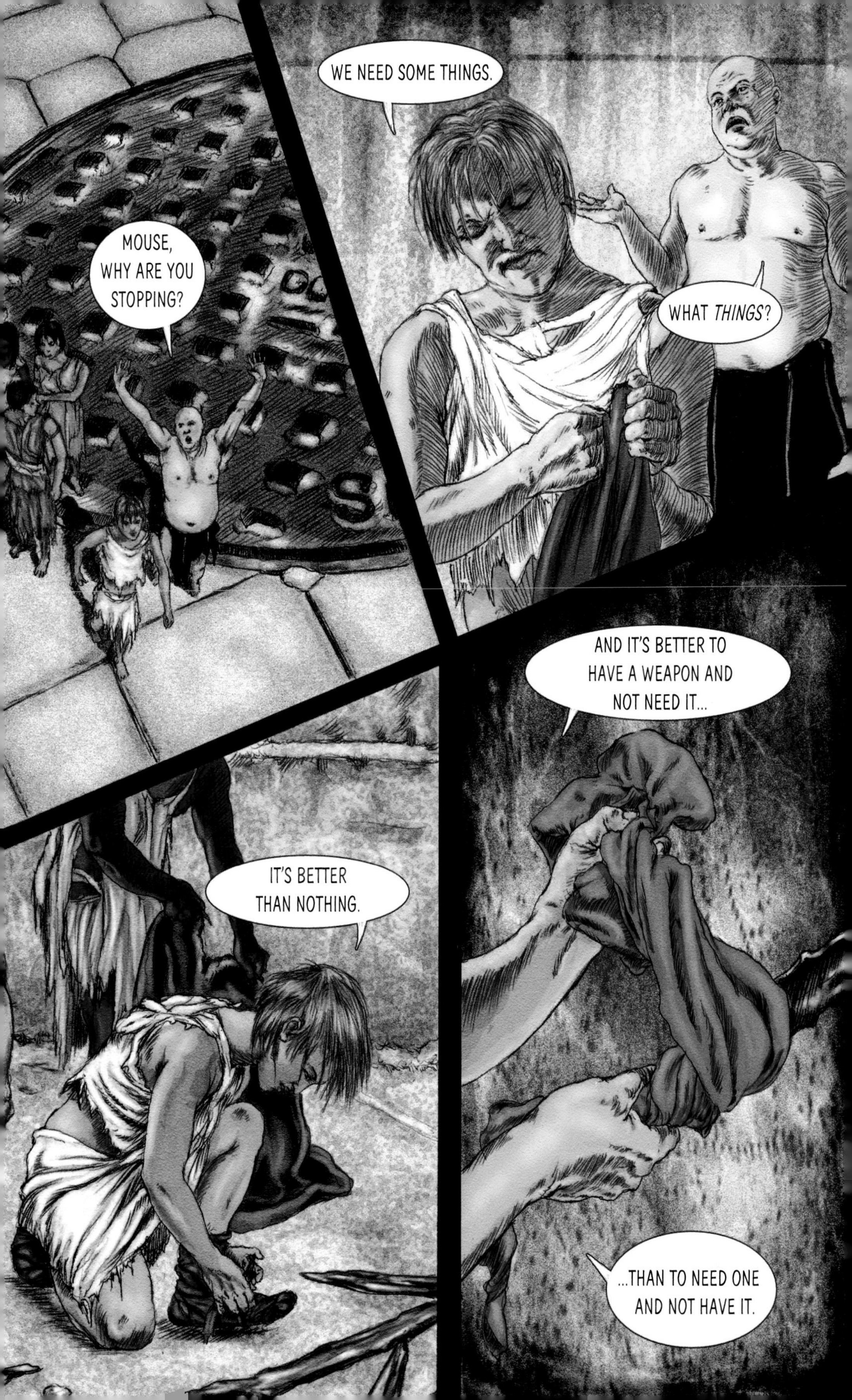
MOUSE, WHY ARE YOU STOPPING?
WE NEED SOME THINGS.
WHAT *THINGS*?
IT'S BETTER THAN NOTHING.
AND IT'S BETTER TO HAVE A WEAPON AND NOT NEED IT...
...THAN TO NEED ONE AND NOT HAVE IT.

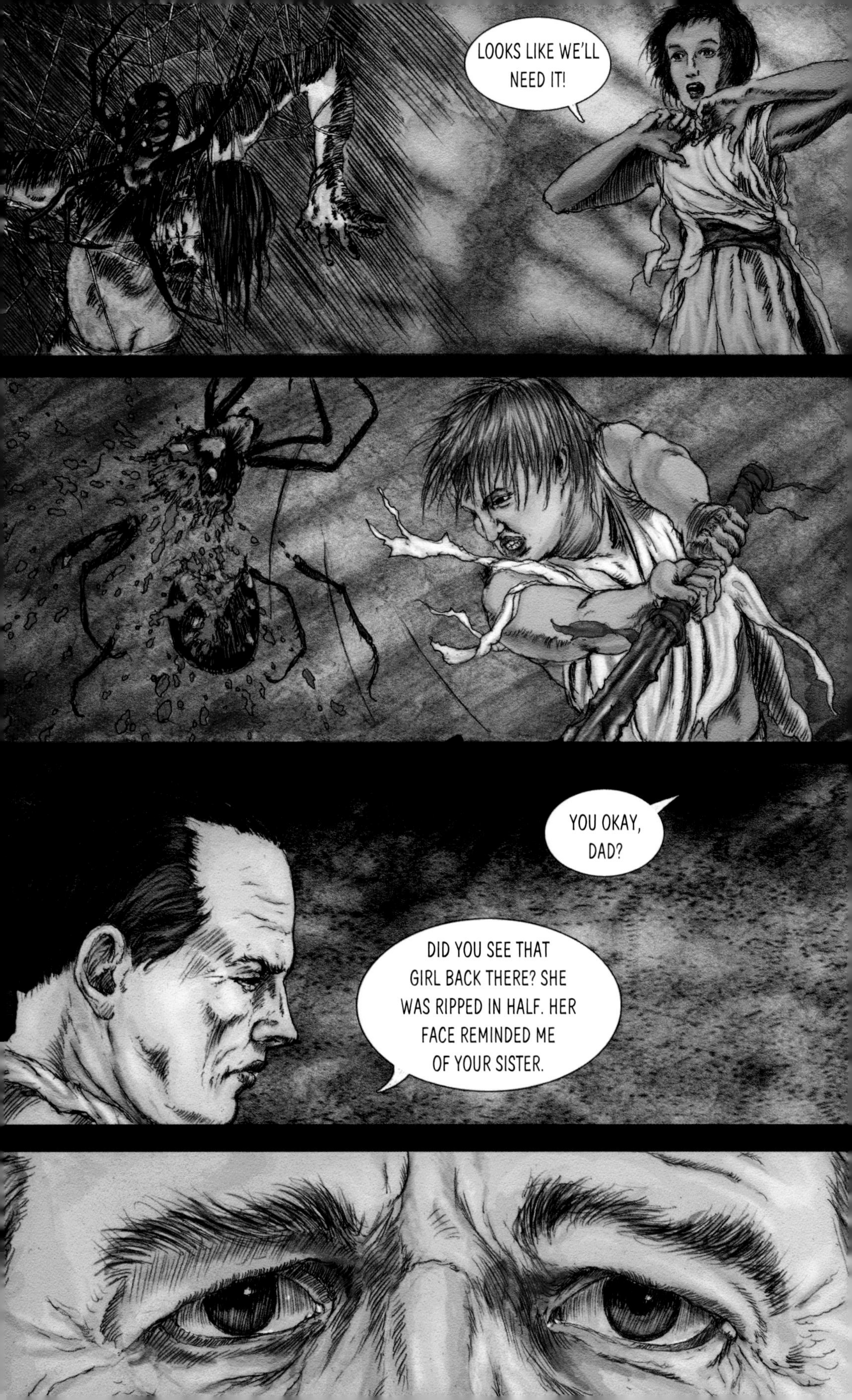
LOOKS LIKE WE'LL NEED IT!
YOU OKAY, DAD?
DID YOU SEE THAT GIRL BACK THERE? SHE WAS RIPPED IN HALF. HER FACE REMINDED ME OF YOUR SISTER.

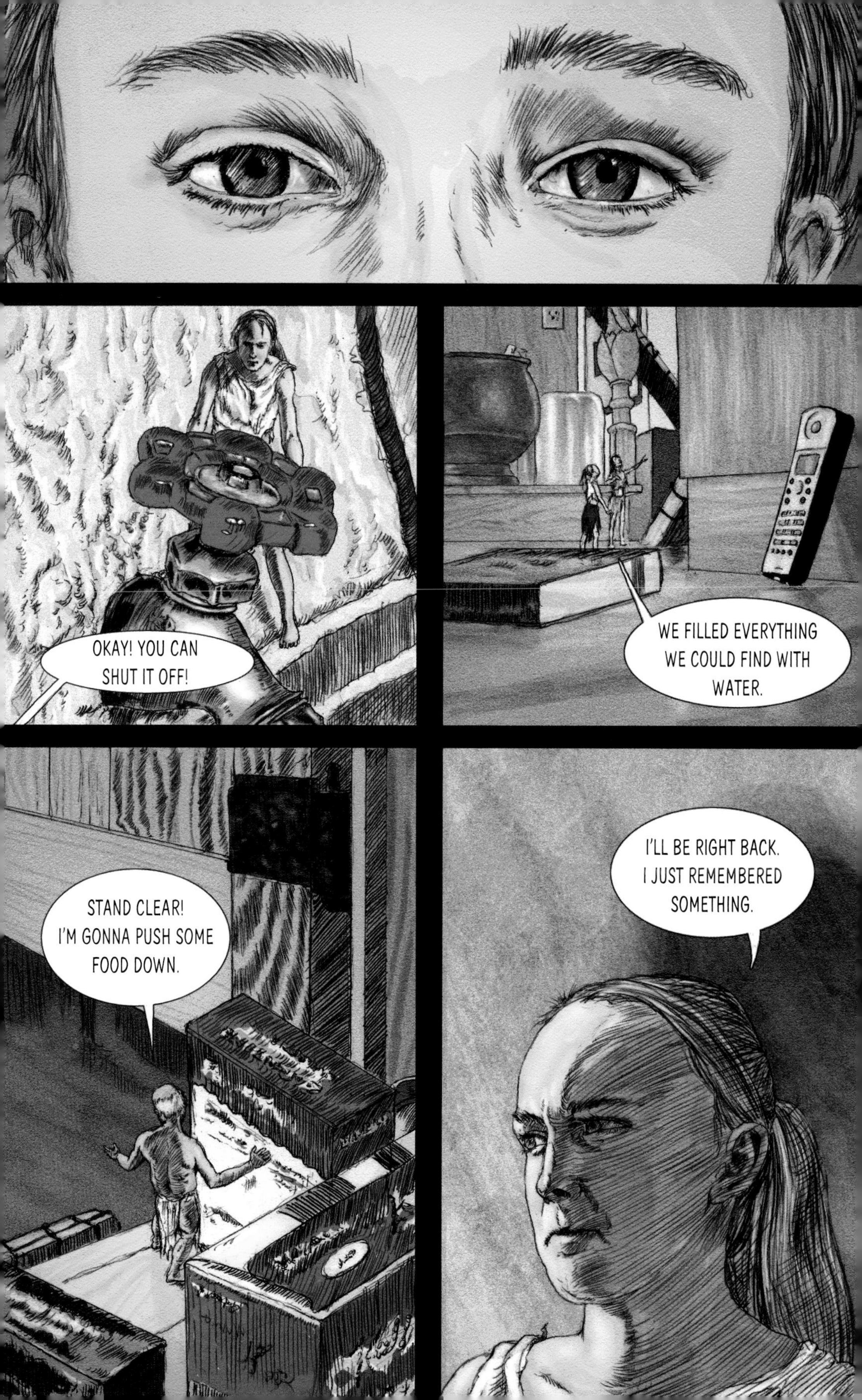
OKAY! YOU CAN SHUT IT OFF!
WE FILLED EVERYTHING WE COULD FIND WITH WATER.
STAND CLEAR! I'M GONNA PUSH SOME FOOD DOWN.
I'LL BE RIGHT BACK. I JUST REMEMBERED SOMETHING.

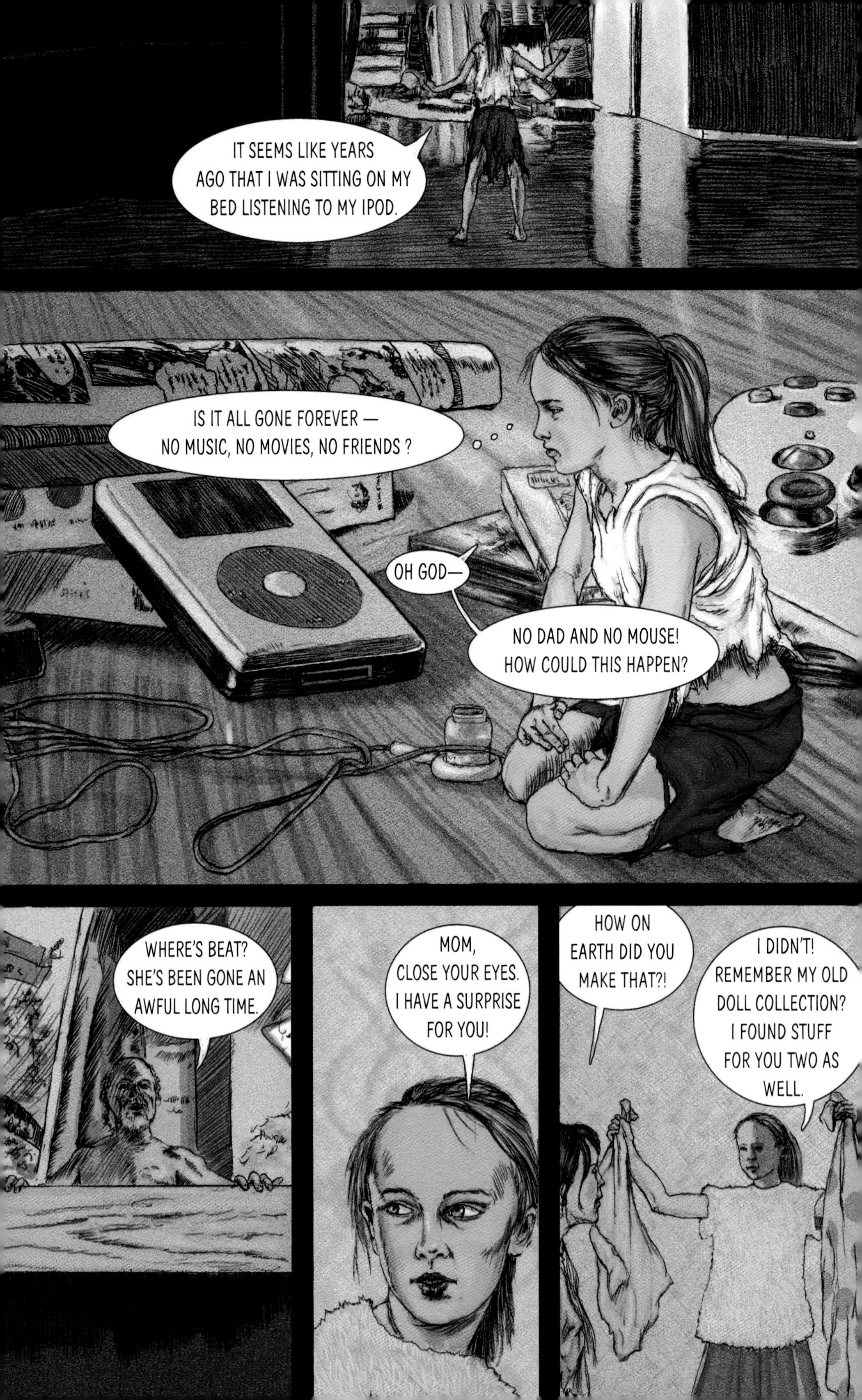
IT SEEMS LIKE YEARS AGO THAT I WAS SITTING ON MY BED LISTENING TO MY IPOD.
IS IT ALL GONE FOREVER — NO MUSIC, NO MOVIES, NO FRIENDS ?
OH GOD—
NO DAD AND NO MOUSE! HOW COULD THIS HAPPEN?
WHERE'S BEAT? SHE'S BEEN GONE AN AWFUL LONG TIME.
MOM, CLOSE YOUR EYES. I HAVE A SURPRISE FOR YOU!
HOW ON EARTH DID YOU MAKE THAT?!
I DIDN'T! REMEMBER MY OLD DOLL COLLECTION? I FOUND STUFF FOR YOU TWO AS WELL.

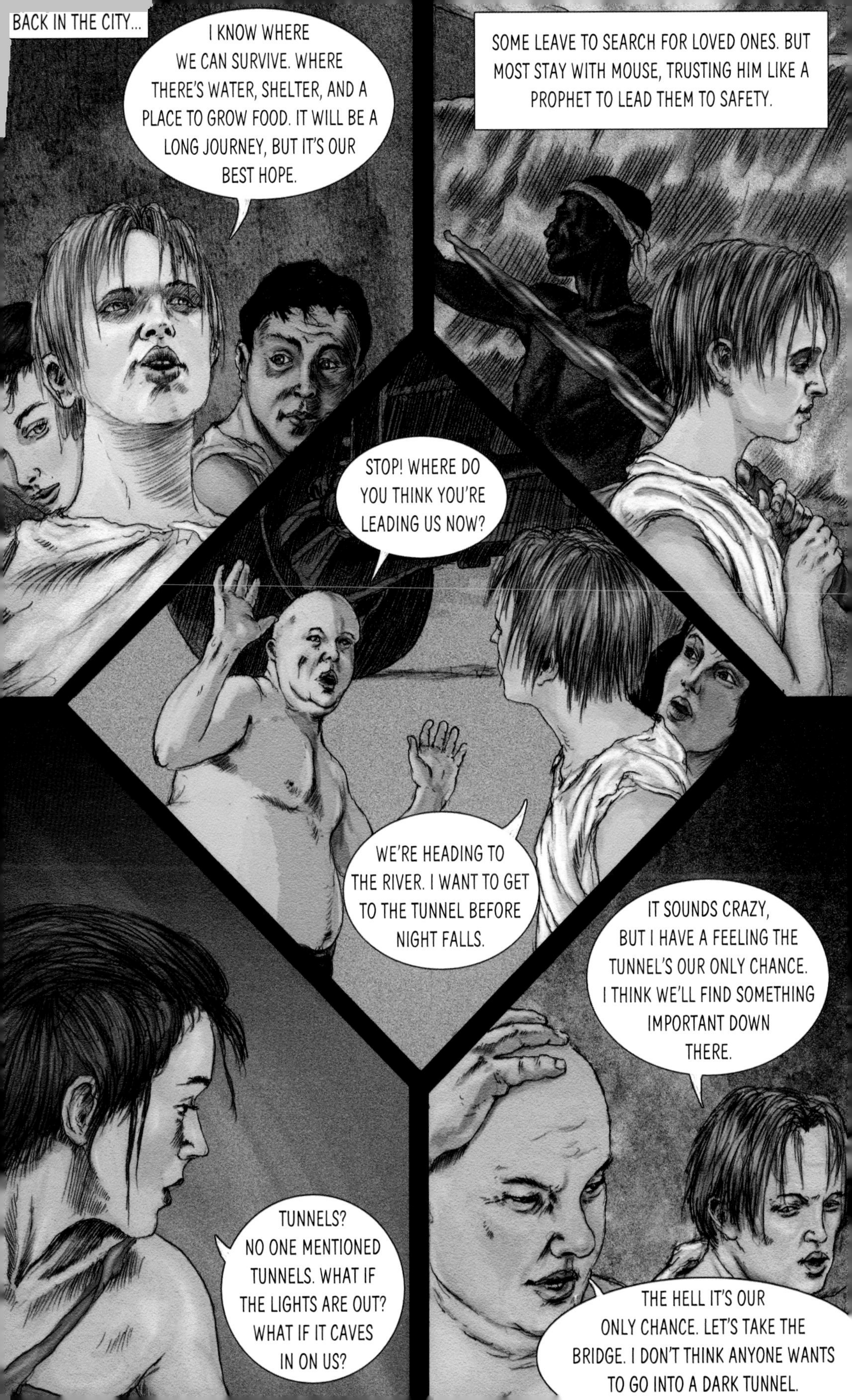
BACK IN THE CITY...
I KNOW WHERE WE CAN SURVIVE. WHERE THERE'S WATER, SHELTER, AND A PLACE TO GROW FOOD. IT WILL BE A LONG JOURNEY, BUT IT'S OUR BEST HOPE.
SOME LEAVE TO SEARCH FOR LOVED ONES. BUT MOST STAY WITH MOUSE, TRUSTING HIM LIKE A PROPHET TO LEAD THEM TO SAFETY.
STOP! WHERE DO YOU THINK YOU'RE LEADING US NOW?
WE'RE HEADING TO THE RIVER. I WANT TO GET TO THE TUNNEL BEFORE NIGHT FALLS.
TUNNELS? NO ONE MENTIONED TUNNELS. WHAT IF THE LIGHTS ARE OUT? WHAT IF IT CAVES IN ON US?
IT SOUNDS CRAZY, BUT I HAVE A FEELING THE TUNNEL'S OUR ONLY CHANCE. I THINK WE'LL FIND SOMETHING IMPORTANT DOWN THERE.
THE HELL IT'S OUR ONLY CHANCE. LET'S TAKE THE BRIDGE. I DON'T THINK ANYONE WANTS TO GO INTO A DARK TUNNEL.

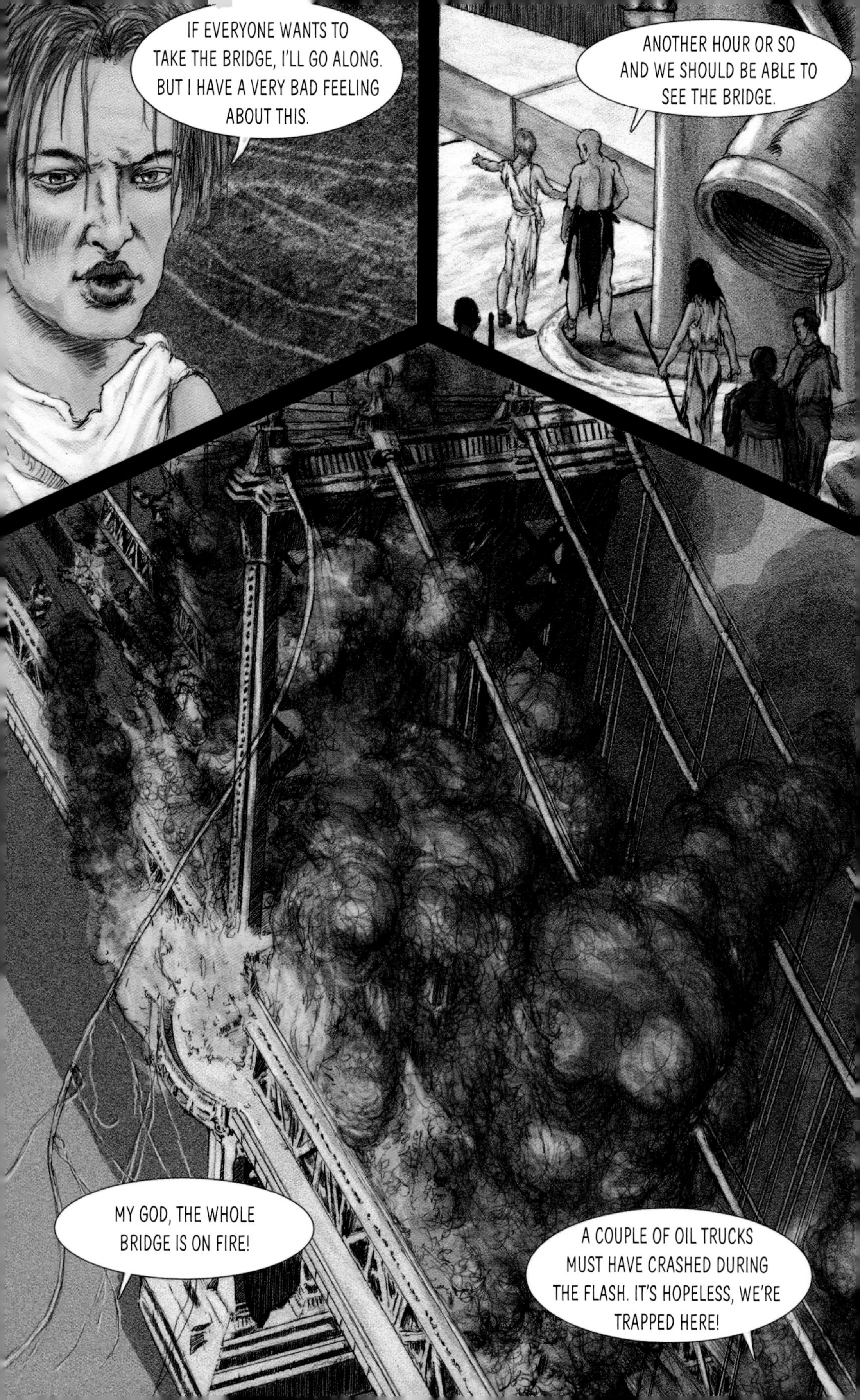
IF EVERYONE WANTS TO TAKE THE BRIDGE, I'LL GO ALONG. BUT I HAVE A VERY BAD FEELING ABOUT THIS.
ANOTHER HOUR OR SO AND WE SHOULD BE ABLE TO SEE THE BRIDGE.
MY GOD, THE WHOLE BRIDGE IS ON FIRE!
A COUPLE OF OIL TRUCKS MUST HAVE CRASHED DURING THE FLASH. IT'S HOPELESS, WE'RE TRAPPED HERE!

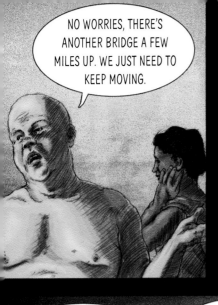

NO WORRIES, THERE'S ANOTHER BRIDGE A FEW MILES UP. WE JUST NEED TO KEEP MOVING.

NO WAY, ALAN. THE ONLY PERSON I'M LISTENING TO IS MOUSE!

WHAT DO WE DO NOW?

I'M SORRY. WE SHOULD HAVE LISTENED TO YOU, SON.

DON'T WORRY ABOUT IT. WE JUST NEED TO FIND SOME SORT OF SHELTER. IT'S BEST NOT TO TRAVEL TOO MUCH AT NIGHT.

GUYS, I KNOW A MOM-AND-POP RESTAURANT AROUND HERE. IF WE CAN FIND A WAY IN, THE PLACE SHOULD PROVIDE US WITH FOOD AND SHELTER FOR THE NIGHT...

IT'S NOT FAR NOW, JUST AROUND THIS CORNER...

ABOUT TIME, I'M STARVING!

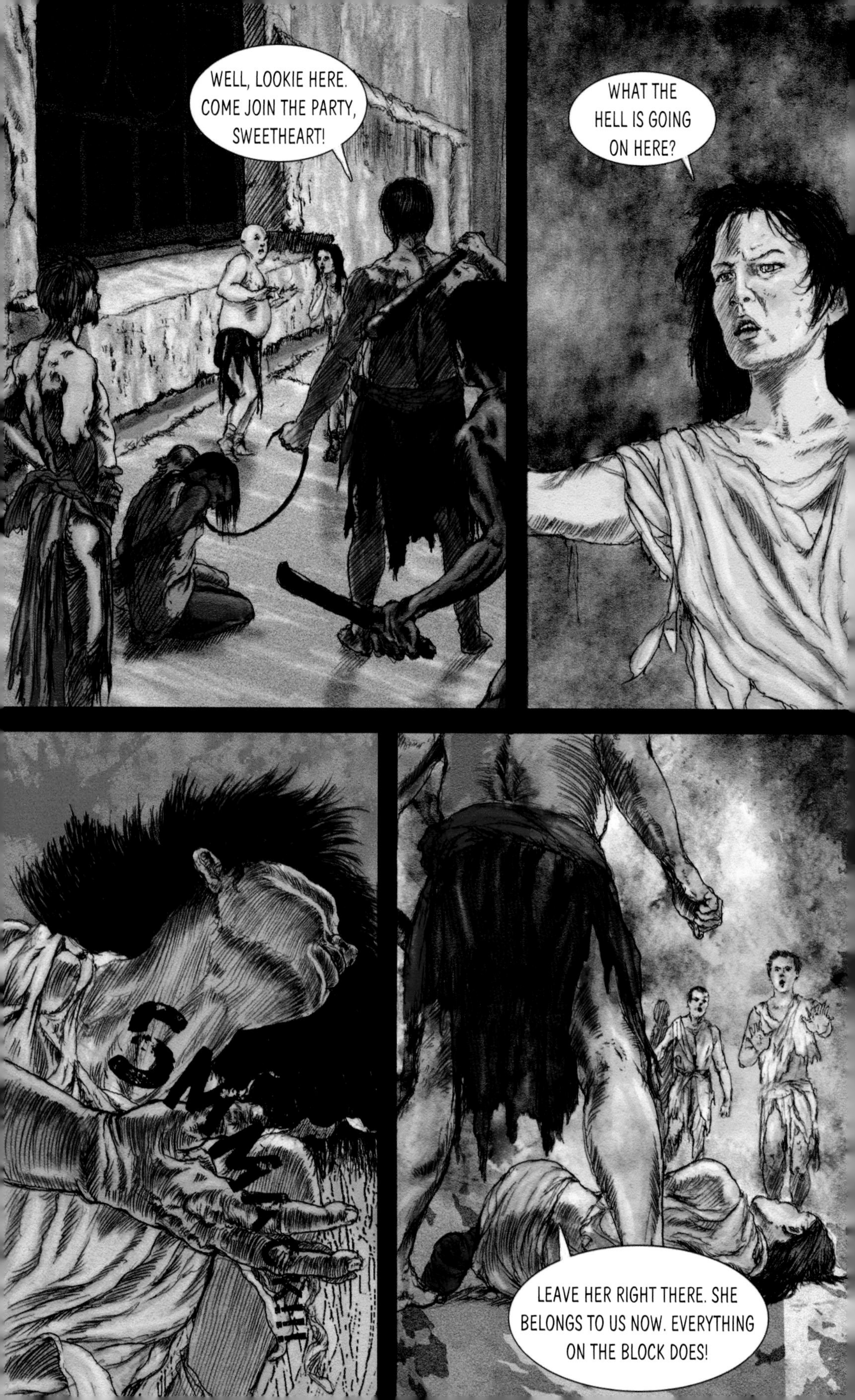
WELL, LOOKIE HERE. COME JOIN THE PARTY, SWEETHEART!
WHAT THE HELL IS GOING ON HERE?
LEAVE HER RIGHT THERE. SHE BELONGS TO US NOW. EVERYTHING ON THE BLOCK DOES!

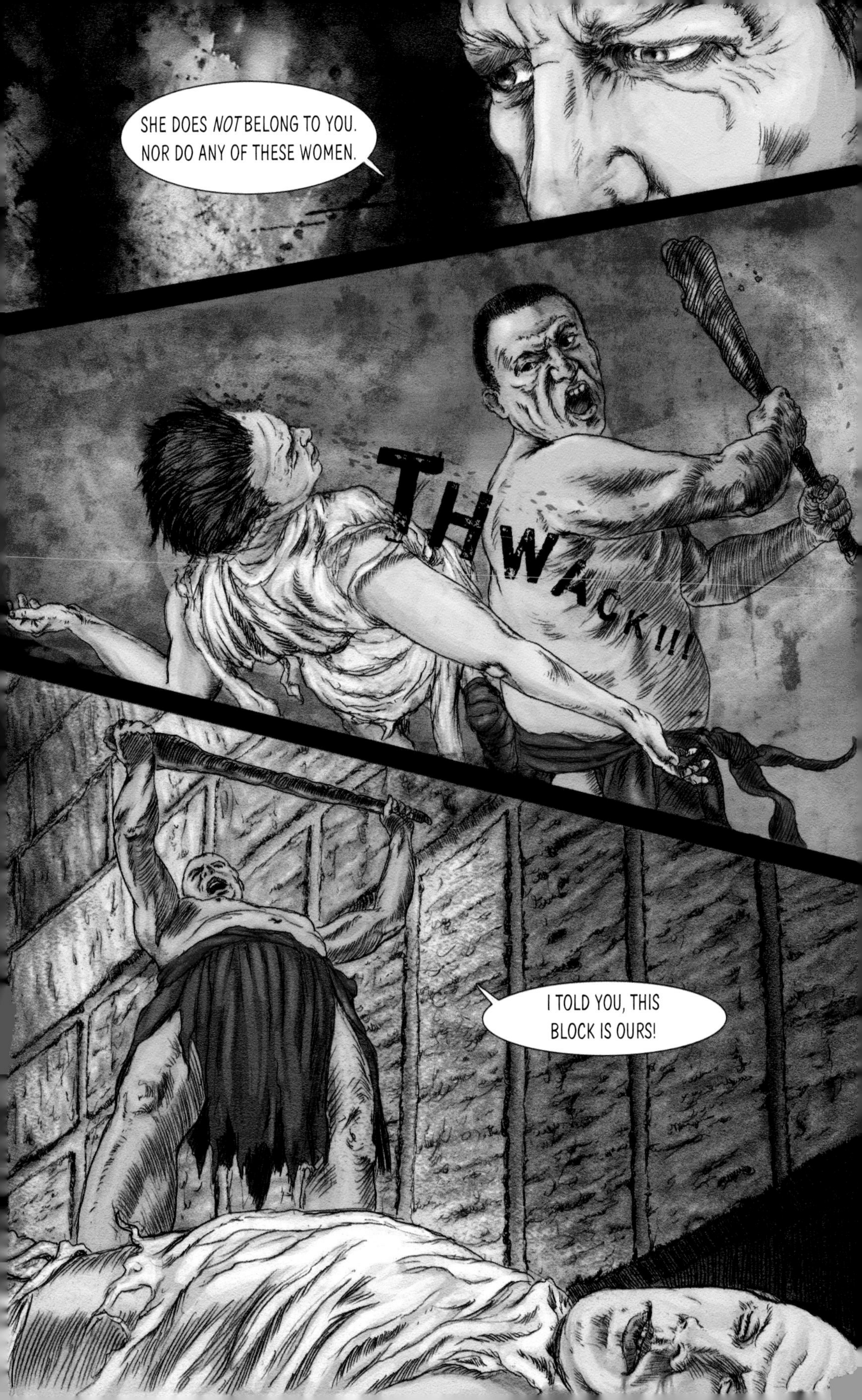
SHE DOES *NOT* BELONG TO YOU. NOR DO ANY OF THESE WOMEN.
THWACK!!!
I TOLD YOU, THIS BLOCK IS OURS!

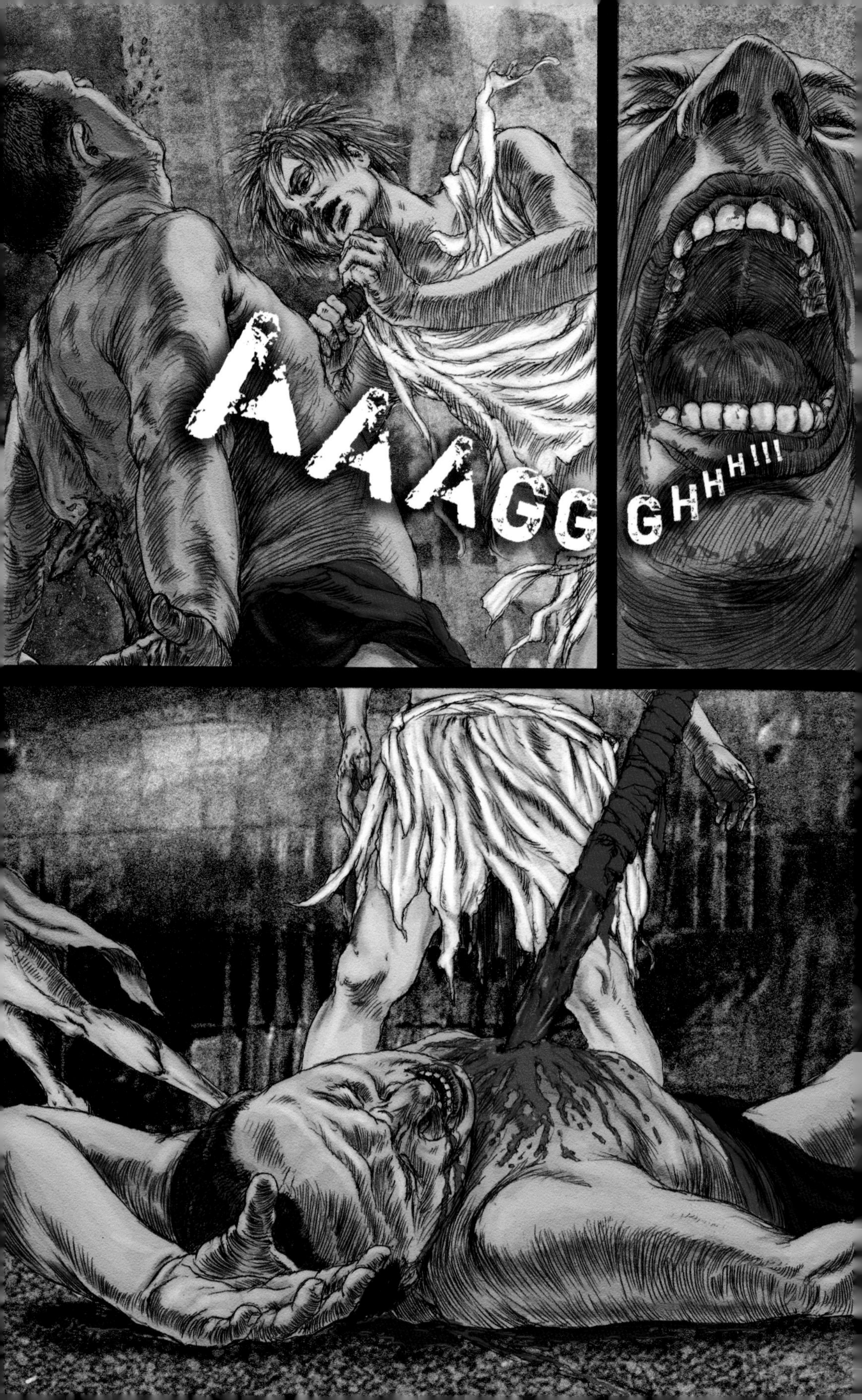
AAAAGGGHHH!!!

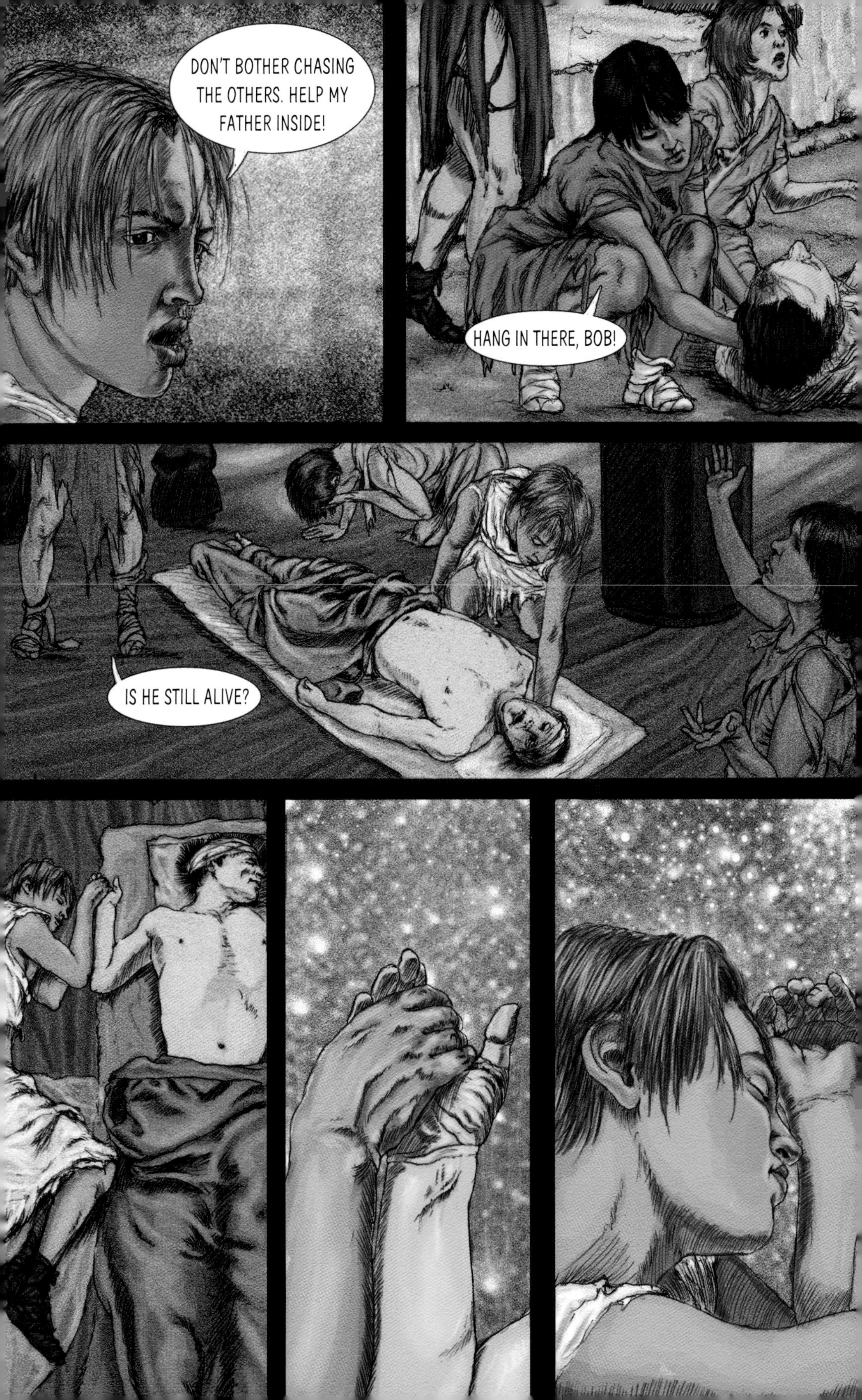
DON'T BOTHER CHASING THE OTHERS. HELP MY FATHER INSIDE!
HANG IN THERE, BOB!
IS HE STILL ALIVE?

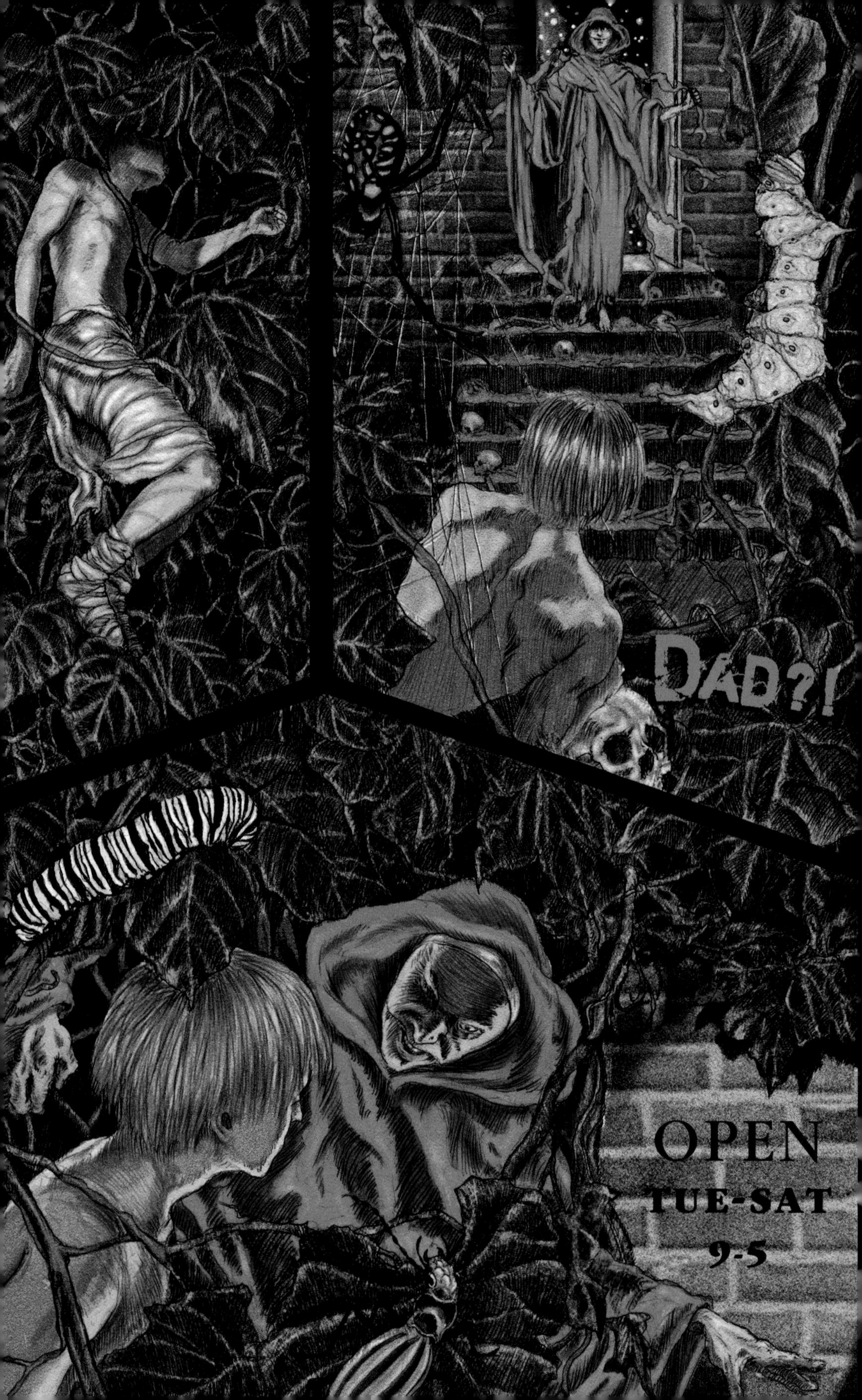
DAD?!
OPEN
TUE-SAT
9-5

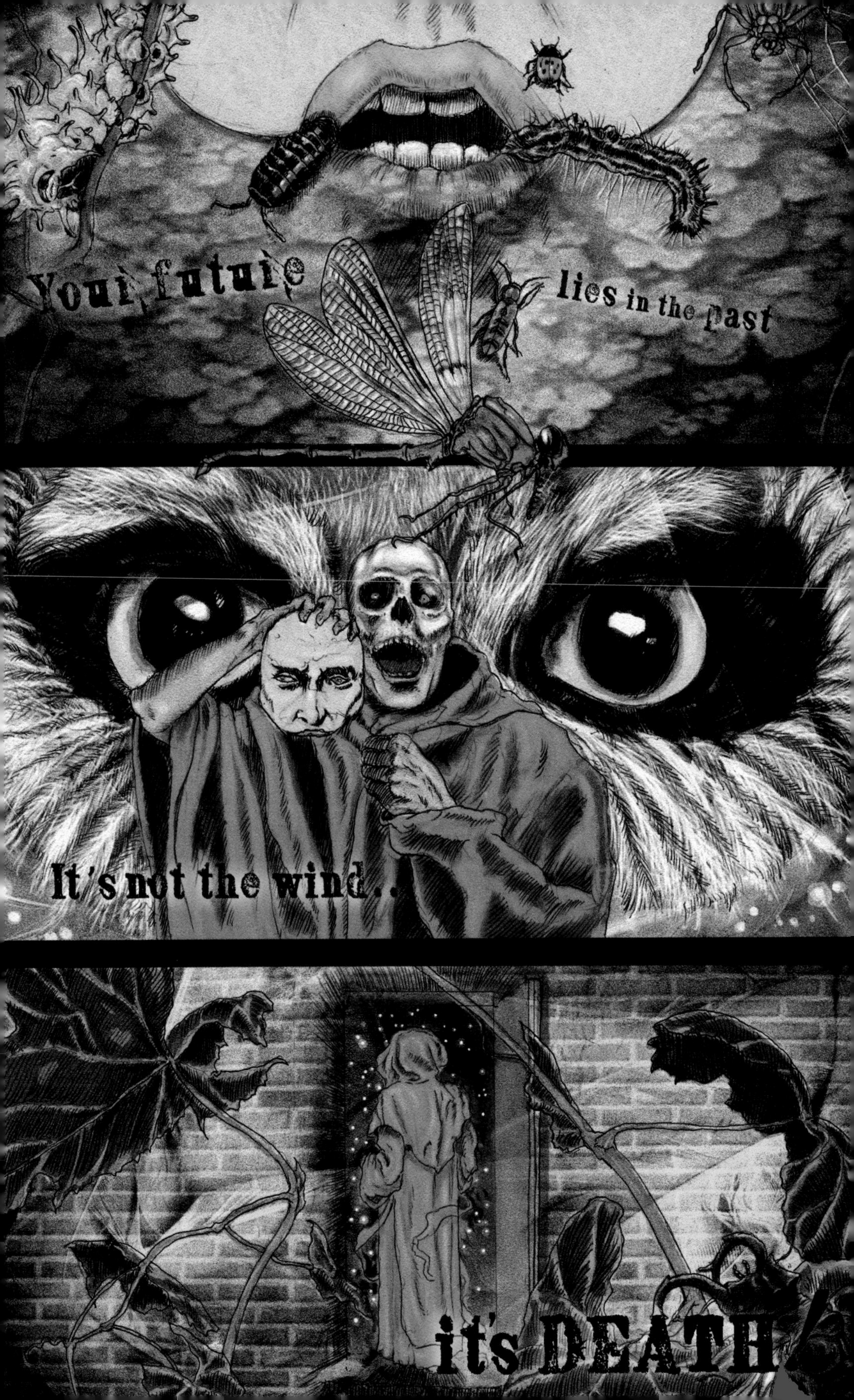
Your future
lies in the past
It's not the wind...
it's DEATH

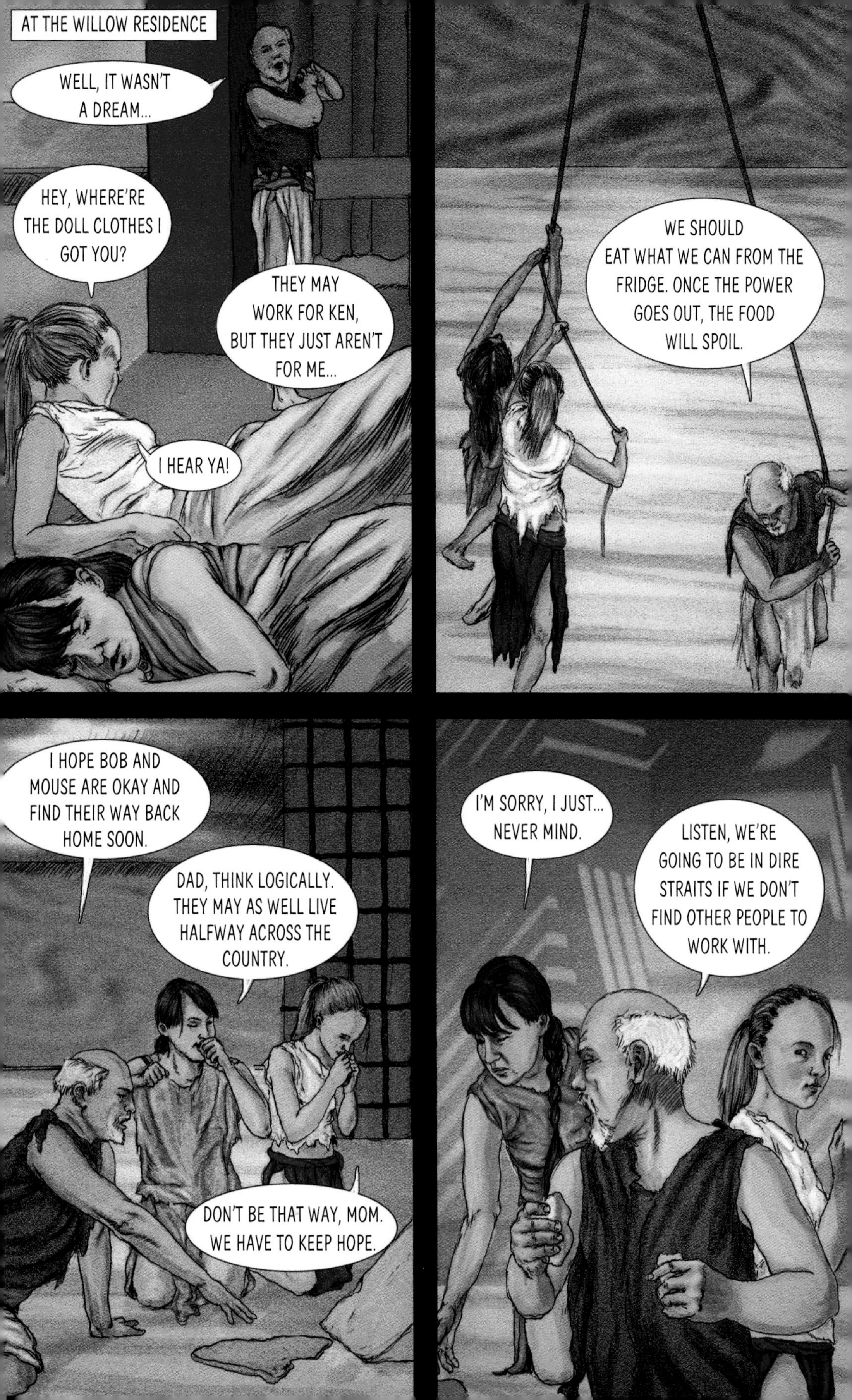
AT THE WILLOW RESIDENCE
WELL, IT WASN'T A DREAM...
HEY, WHERE'RE THE DOLL CLOTHES I GOT YOU?
THEY MAY WORK FOR KEN, BUT THEY JUST AREN'T FOR ME...
I HEAR YA!
WE SHOULD EAT WHAT WE CAN FROM THE FRIDGE. ONCE THE POWER GOES OUT, THE FOOD WILL SPOIL.
I HOPE BOB AND MOUSE ARE OKAY AND FIND THEIR WAY BACK HOME SOON.
DAD, THINK LOGICALLY. THEY MAY AS WELL LIVE HALFWAY ACROSS THE COUNTRY.
DON'T BE THAT WAY, MOM. WE HAVE TO KEEP HOPE.
I'M SORRY, I JUST... NEVER MIND.
LISTEN, WE'RE GOING TO BE IN DIRE STRAITS IF WE DON'T FIND OTHER PEOPLE TO WORK WITH.

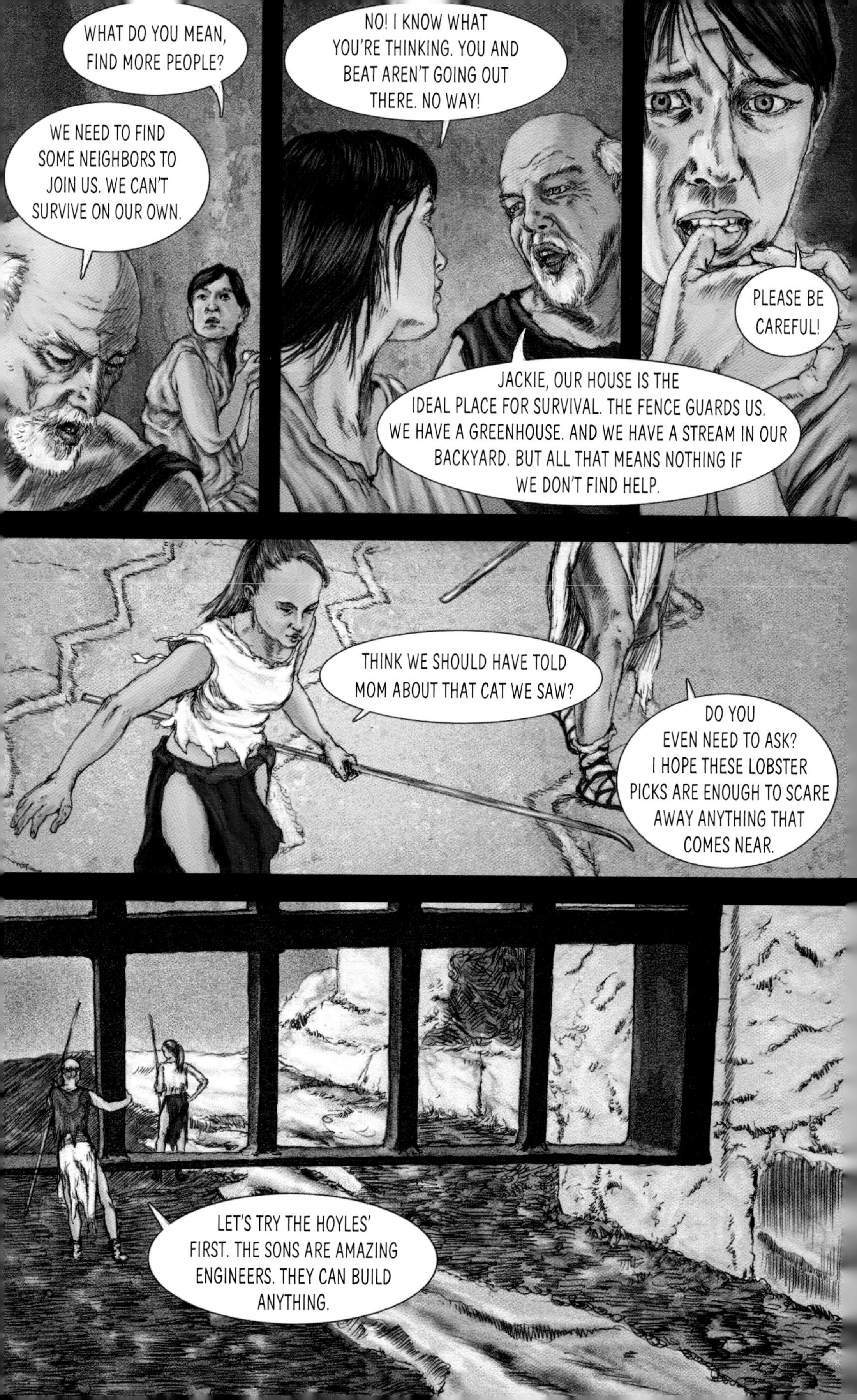
WHAT DO YOU MEAN, FIND MORE PEOPLE?
WE NEED TO FIND SOME NEIGHBORS TO JOIN US. WE CAN'T SURVIVE ON OUR OWN.
NO! I KNOW WHAT YOU'RE THINKING. YOU AND BEAT AREN'T GOING OUT THERE. NO WAY!
JACKIE, OUR HOUSE IS THE IDEAL PLACE FOR SURVIVAL. THE FENCE GUARDS US. WE HAVE A GREENHOUSE. AND WE HAVE A STREAM IN OUR BACKYARD. BUT ALL THAT MEANS NOTHING IF WE DON'T FIND HELP.
PLEASE BE CAREFUL!
THINK WE SHOULD HAVE TOLD MOM ABOUT THAT CAT WE SAW?
DO YOU EVEN NEED TO ASK? I HOPE THESE LOBSTER PICKS ARE ENOUGH TO SCARE AWAY ANYTHING THAT COMES NEAR.
LET'S TRY THE HOYLES' FIRST. THE SONS ARE AMAZING ENGINEERS. THEY CAN BUILD ANYTHING.

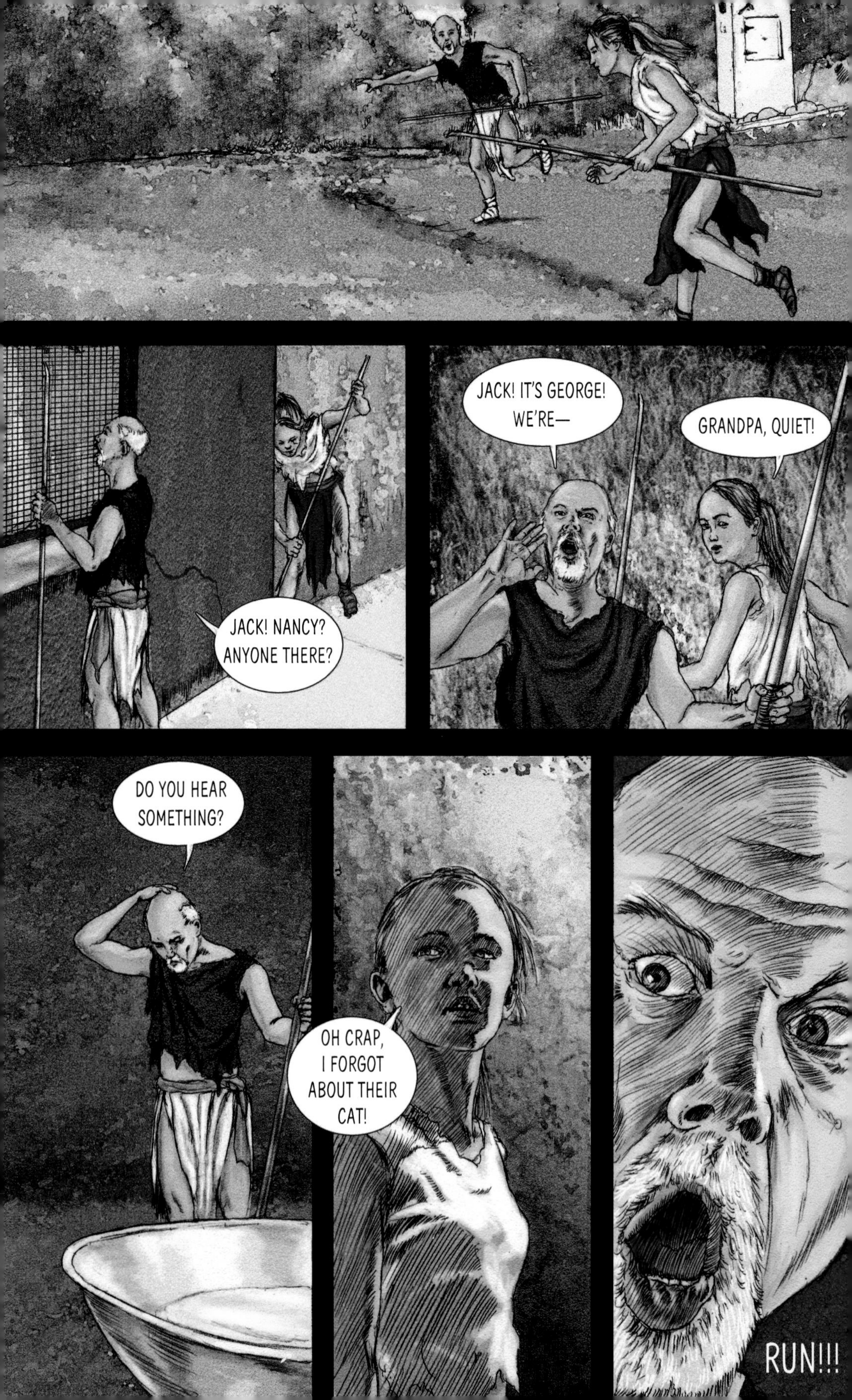
JACK! NANCY? ANYONE THERE?
JACK! IT'S GEORGE! WE'RE—
GRANDPA, QUIET!
DO YOU HEAR SOMETHING?
OH CRAP, I FORGOT ABOUT THEIR CAT!
RUN!!!

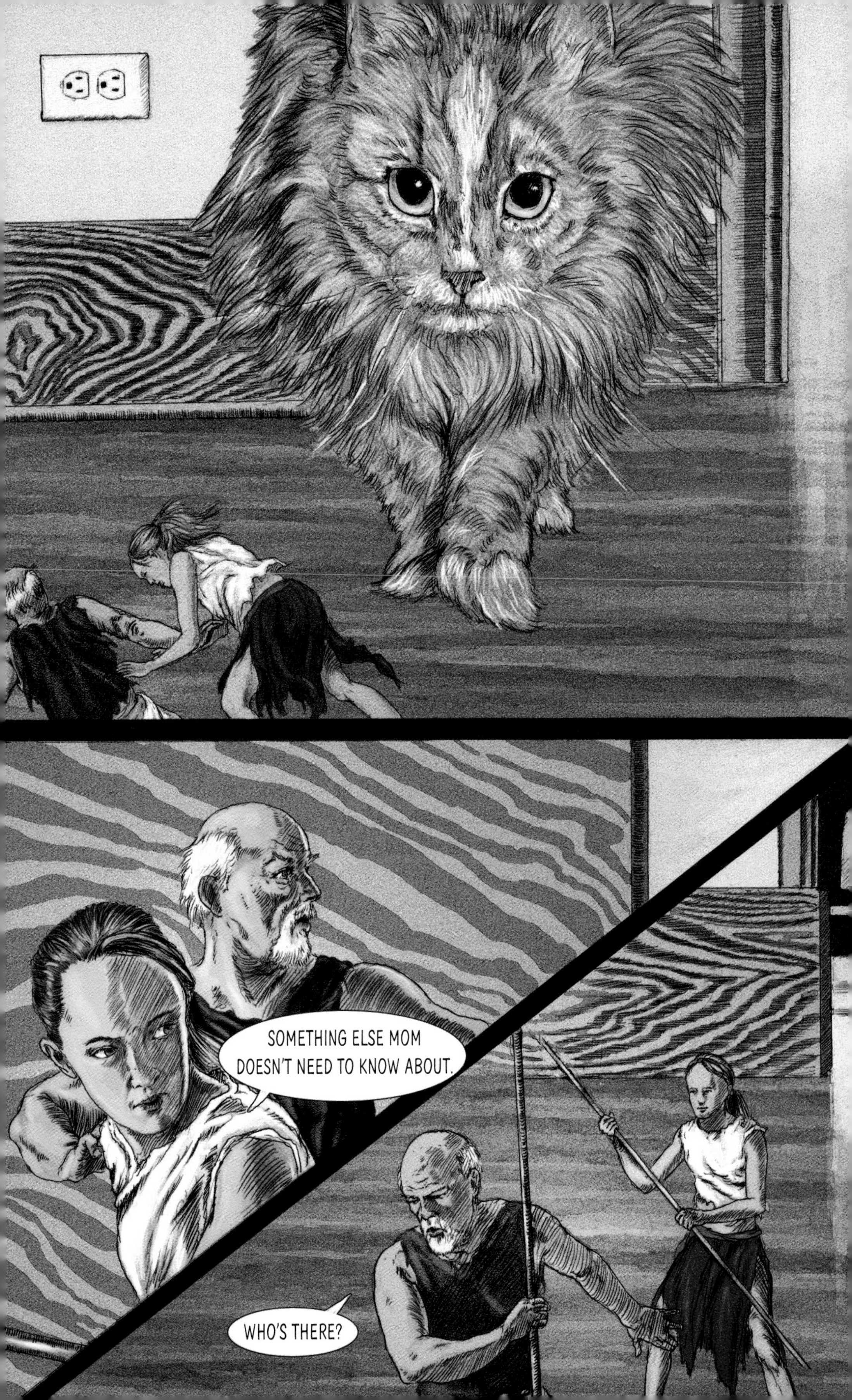
SOMETHING ELSE MOM DOESN'T NEED TO KNOW ABOUT.
WHO'S THERE?

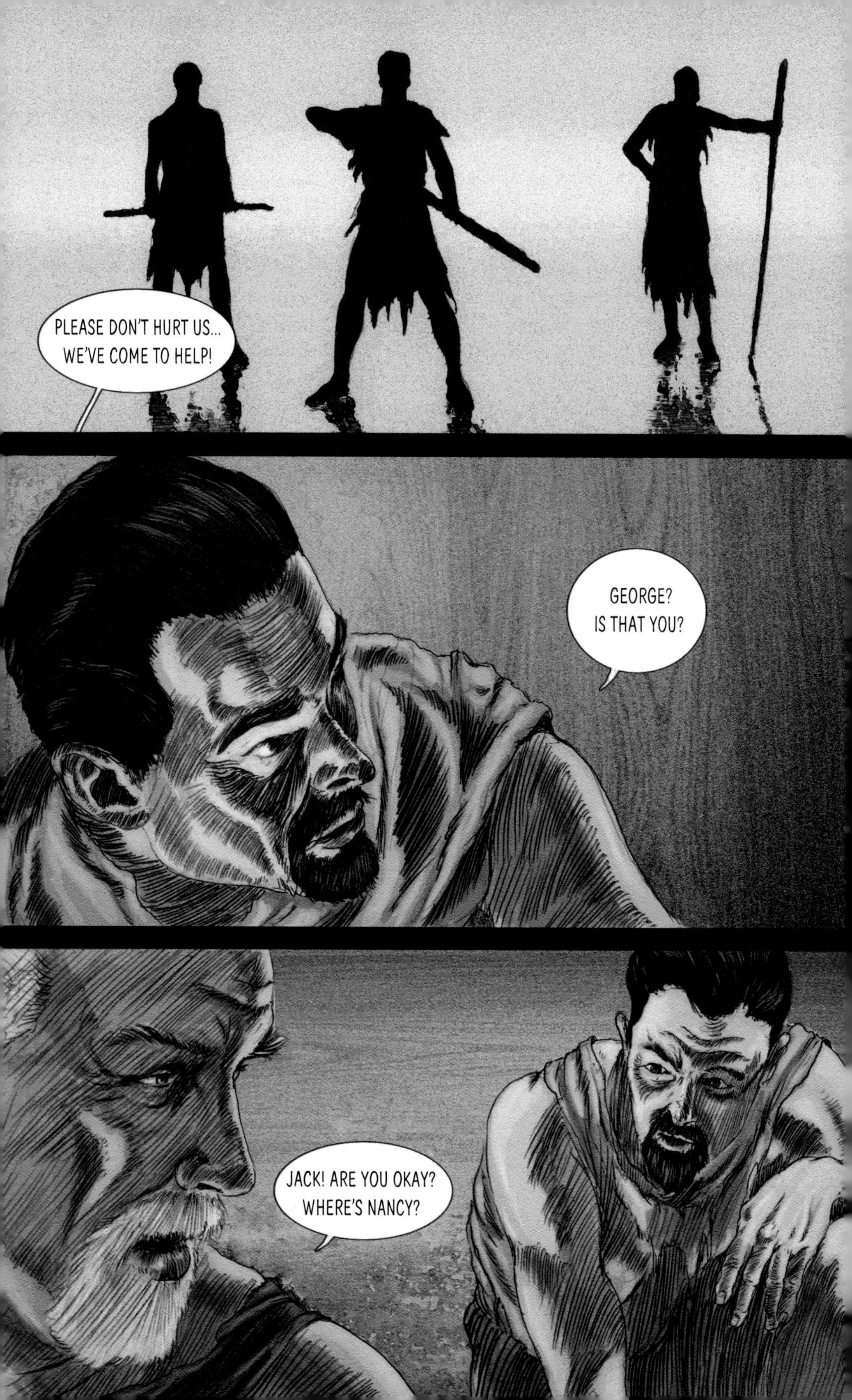
PLEASE DON'T HURT US... WE'VE COME TO HELP!
GEORGE? IS THAT YOU?
JACK! ARE YOU OKAY? WHERE'S NANCY?

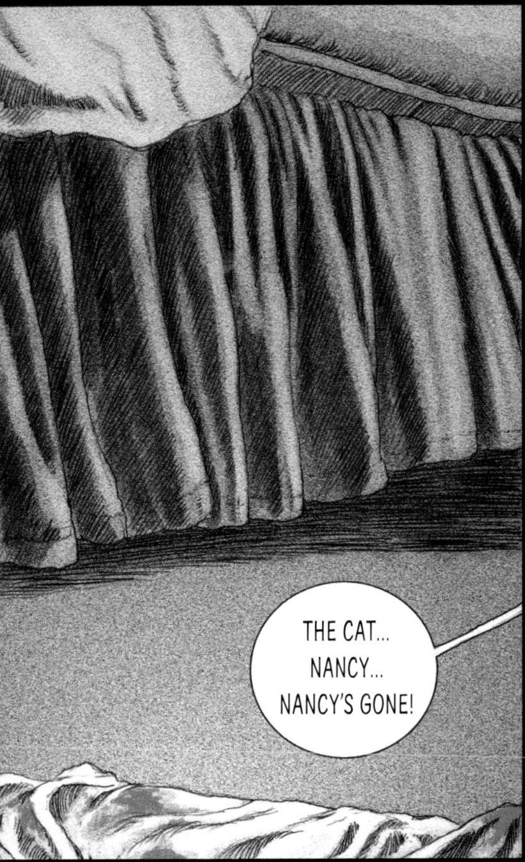
THE CAT...
NANCY...
NANCY'S GONE!

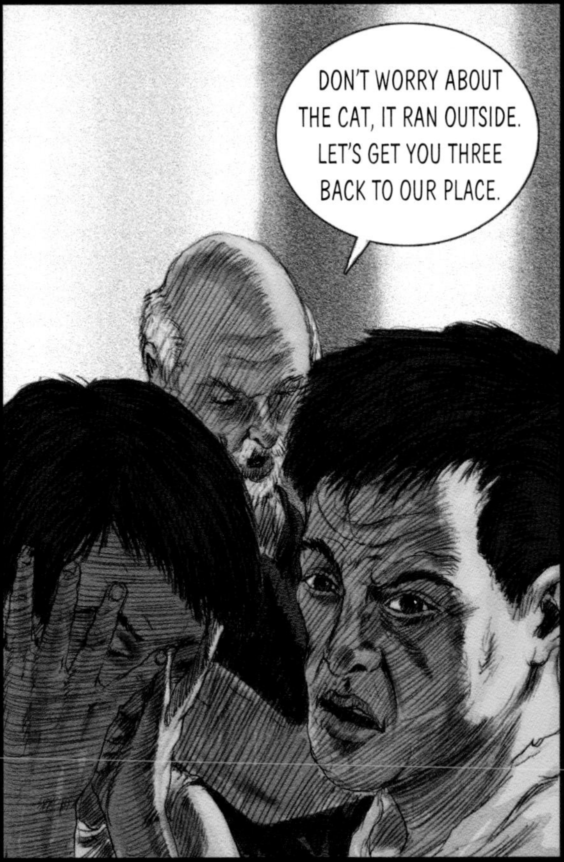
DON'T WORRY ABOUT THE CAT, IT RAN OUTSIDE. LET'S GET YOU THREE BACK TO OUR PLACE.

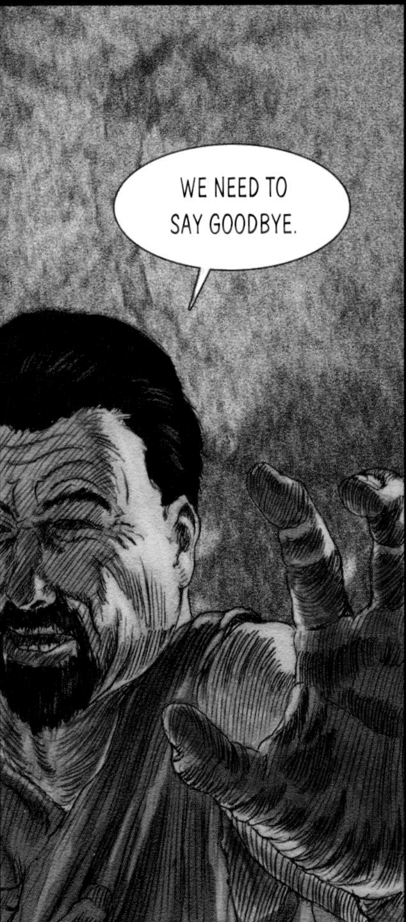
WE NEED TO SAY GOODBYE.

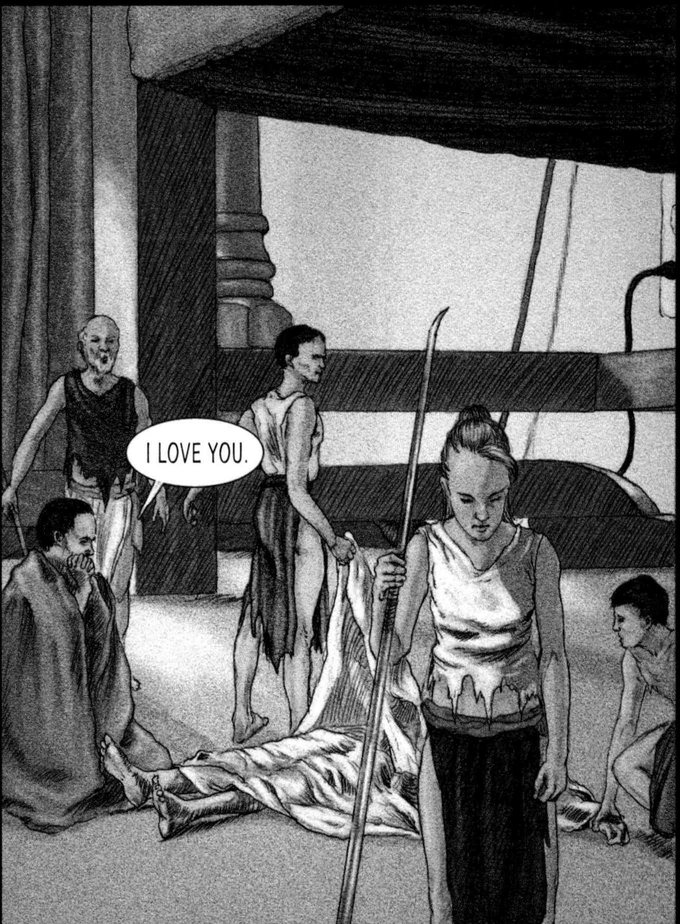
I LOVE YOU.

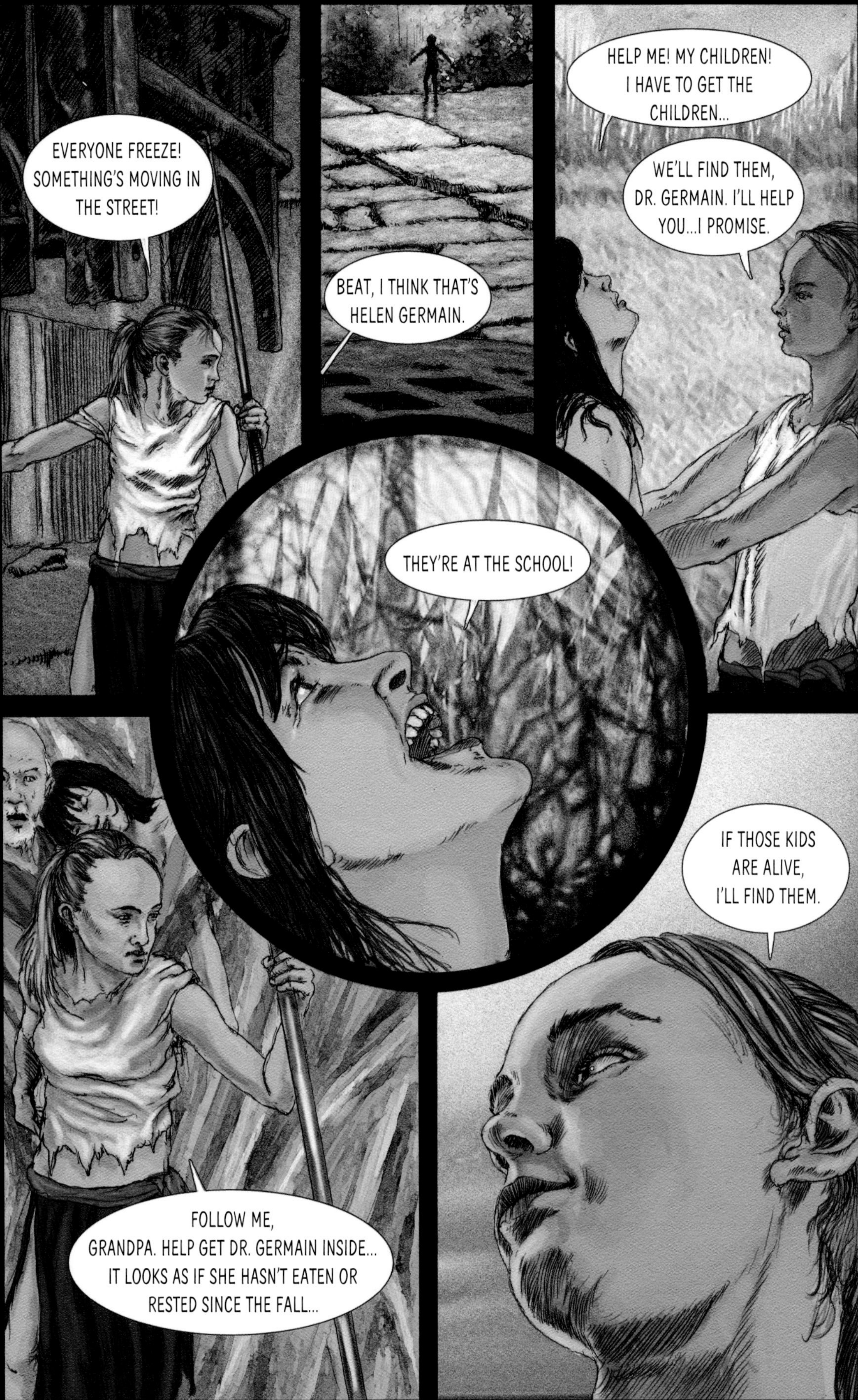

EVERYONE FREEZE! SOMETHING'S MOVING IN THE STREET!
BEAT, I THINK THAT'S HELEN GERMAIN.
HELP ME! MY CHILDREN! I HAVE TO GET THE CHILDREN...
WE'LL FIND THEM, DR. GERMAIN. I'LL HELP YOU...I PROMISE.
THEY'RE AT THE SCHOOL!
FOLLOW ME, GRANDPA. HELP GET DR. GERMAIN INSIDE... IT LOOKS AS IF SHE HASN'T EATEN OR RESTED SINCE THE FALL...
IF THOSE KIDS ARE ALIVE, I'LL FIND THEM.

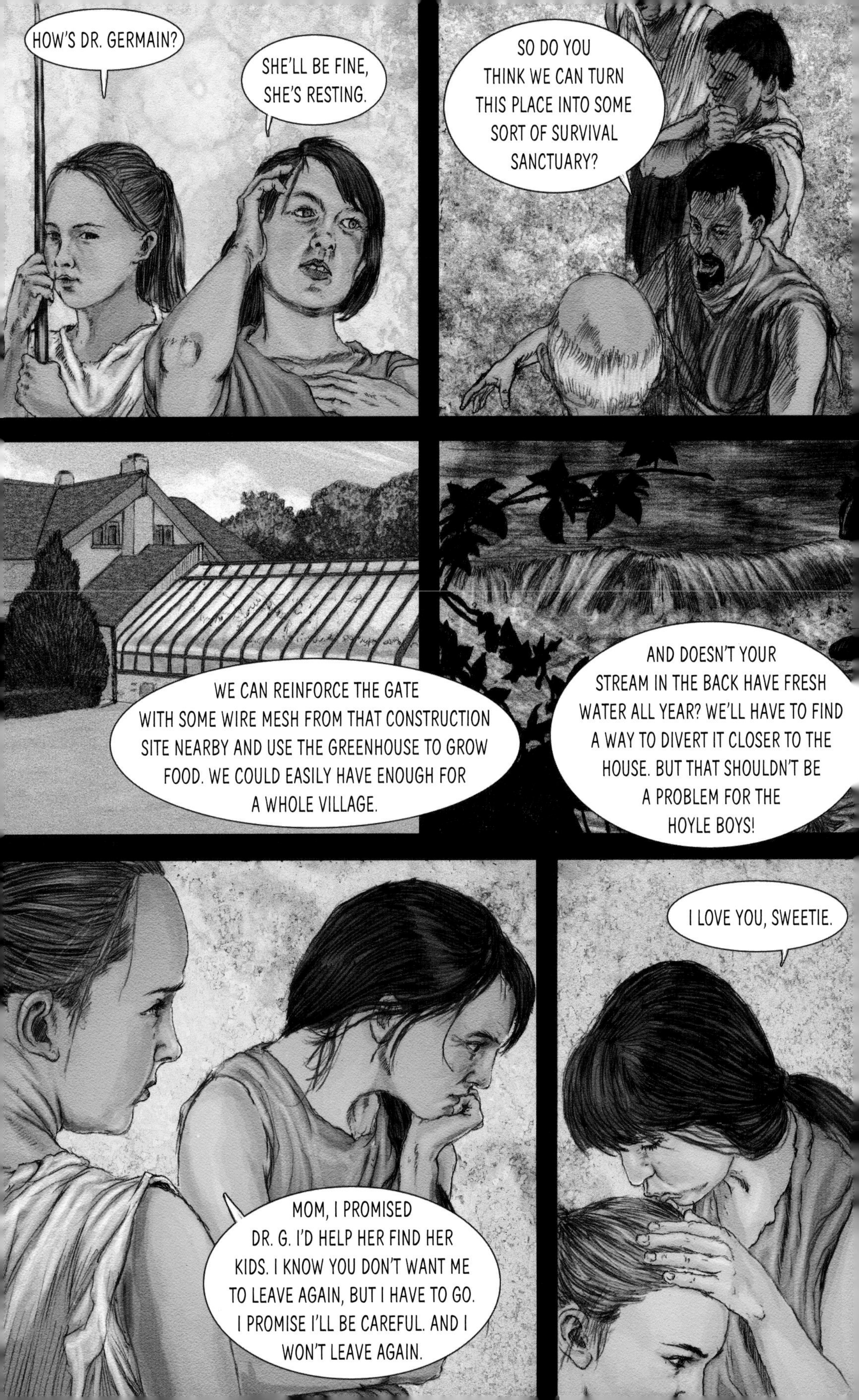
HOW'S DR. GERMAIN?
SHE'LL BE FINE, SHE'S RESTING.
SO DO YOU THINK WE CAN TURN THIS PLACE INTO SOME SORT OF SURVIVAL SANCTUARY?
WE CAN REINFORCE THE GATE WITH SOME WIRE MESH FROM THAT CONSTRUCTION SITE NEARBY AND USE THE GREENHOUSE TO GROW FOOD. WE COULD EASILY HAVE ENOUGH FOR A WHOLE VILLAGE.
AND DOESN'T YOUR STREAM IN THE BACK HAVE FRESH WATER ALL YEAR? WE'LL HAVE TO FIND A WAY TO DIVERT IT CLOSER TO THE HOUSE. BUT THAT SHOULDN'T BE A PROBLEM FOR THE HOYLE BOYS!
MOM, I PROMISED DR. G. I'D HELP HER FIND HER KIDS. I KNOW YOU DON'T WANT ME TO LEAVE AGAIN, BUT I HAVE TO GO. I PROMISE I'LL BE CAREFUL. AND I WON'T LEAVE AGAIN.
I LOVE YOU, SWEETIE.

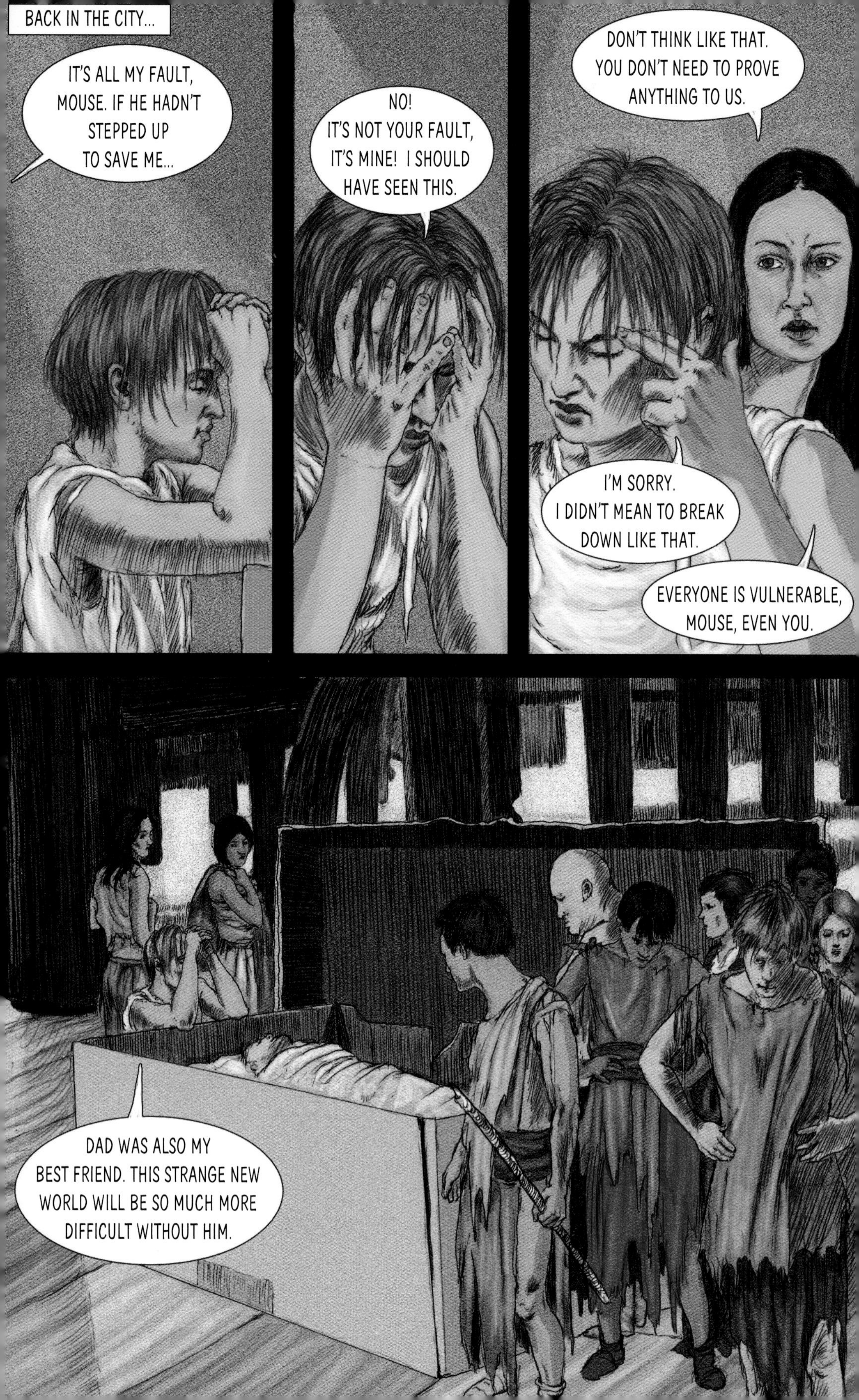
BACK IN THE CITY...
IT'S ALL MY FAULT, MOUSE. IF HE HADN'T STEPPED UP TO SAVE ME...
NO! IT'S NOT YOUR FAULT, IT'S MINE! I SHOULD HAVE SEEN THIS.
DON'T THINK LIKE THAT. YOU DON'T NEED TO PROVE ANYTHING TO US.
I'M SORRY. I DIDN'T MEAN TO BREAK DOWN LIKE THAT.
EVERYONE IS VULNERABLE, MOUSE, EVEN YOU.
DAD WAS ALSO MY BEST FRIEND. THIS STRANGE NEW WORLD WILL BE SO MUCH MORE DIFFICULT WITHOUT HIM.

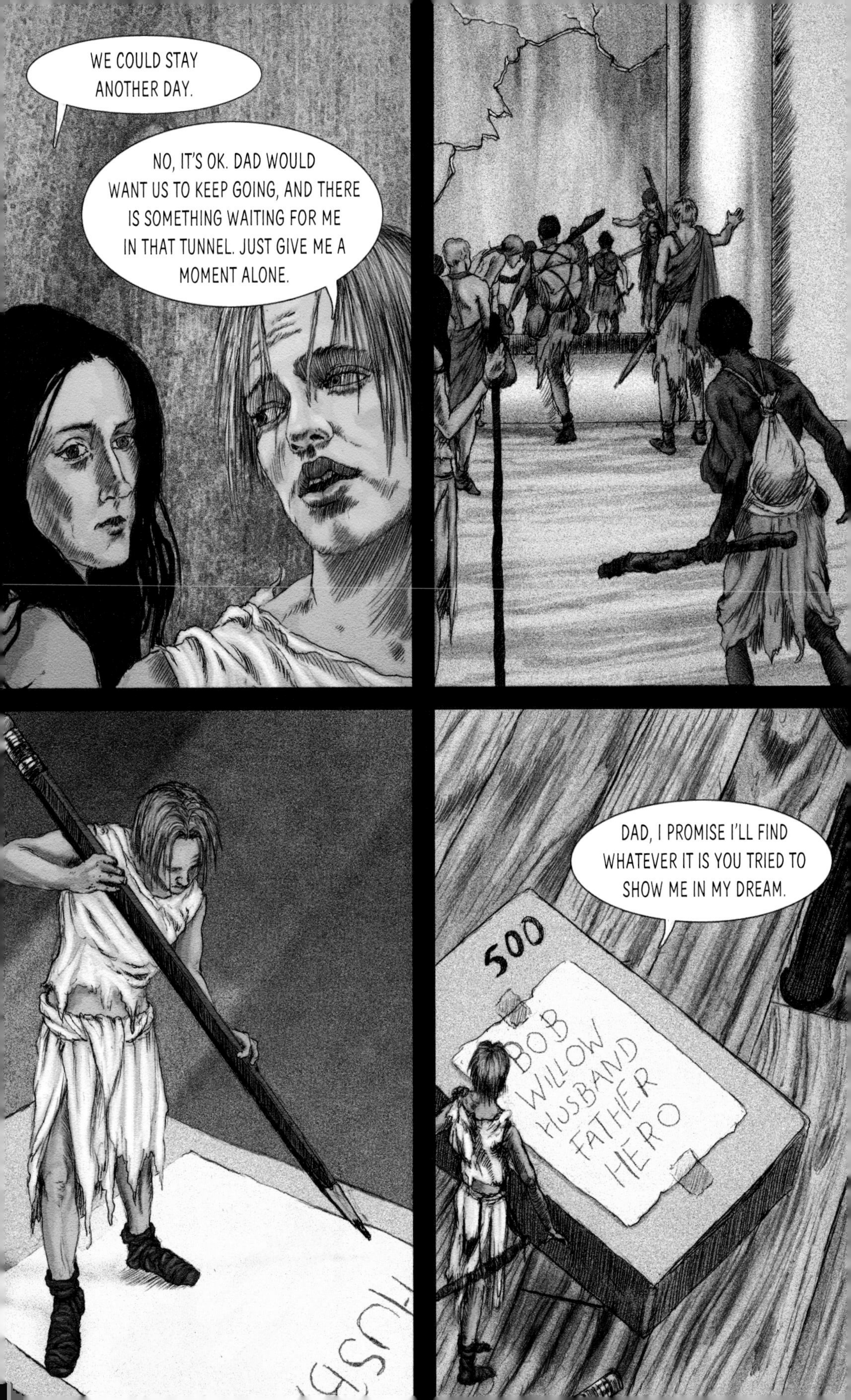
WE COULD STAY ANOTHER DAY.
NO, IT'S OK. DAD WOULD WANT US TO KEEP GOING, AND THERE IS SOMETHING WAITING FOR ME IN THAT TUNNEL. JUST GIVE ME A MOMENT ALONE.
DAD, I PROMISE I'LL FIND WHATEVER IT IS YOU TRIED TO SHOW ME IN MY DREAM.
500
BOB WILLOW HUSBAND FATHER HERO

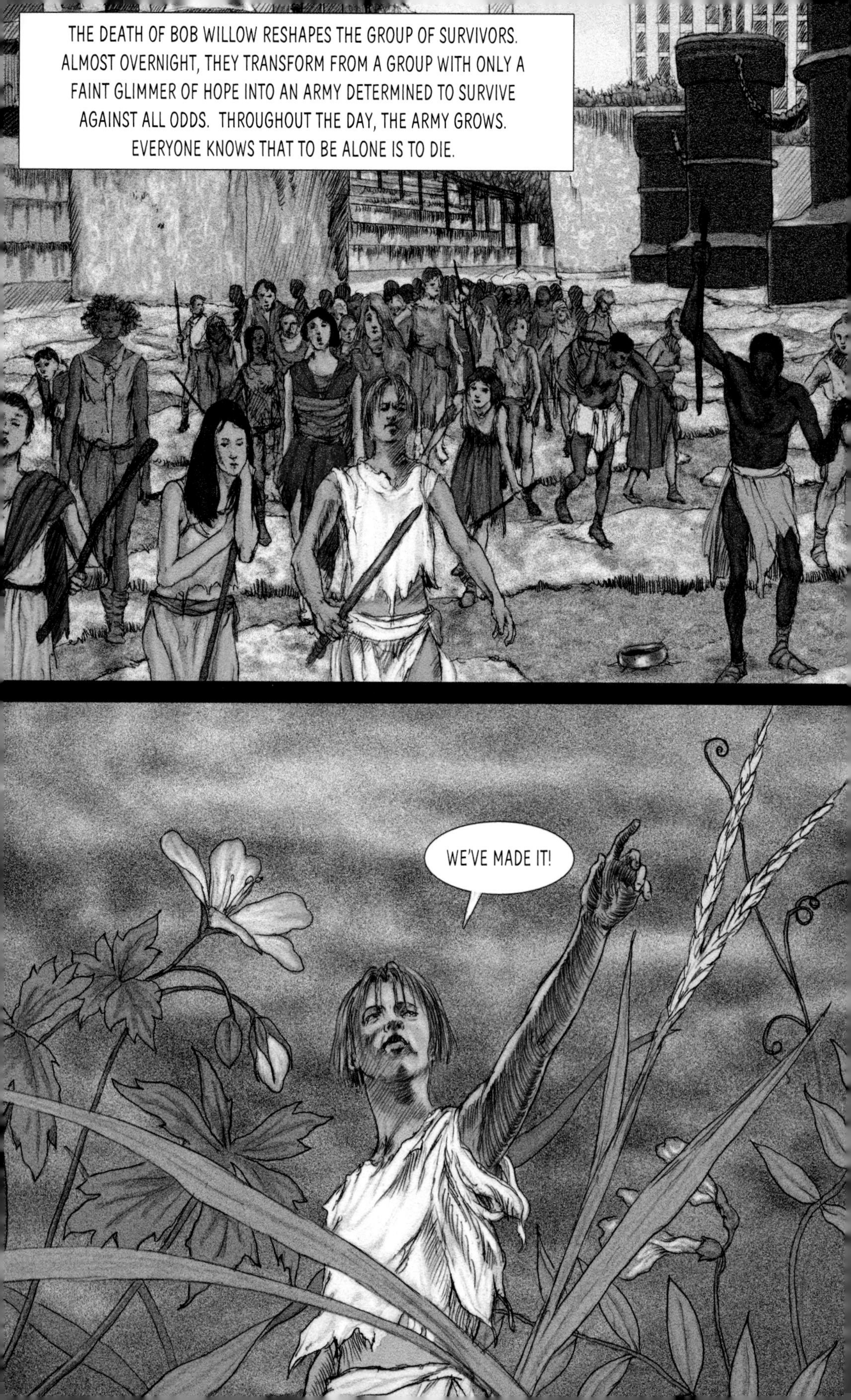
THE DEATH OF BOB WILLOW RESHAPES THE GROUP OF SURVIVORS. ALMOST OVERNIGHT, THEY TRANSFORM FROM A GROUP WITH ONLY A FAINT GLIMMER OF HOPE INTO AN ARMY DETERMINED TO SURVIVE AGAINST ALL ODDS. THROUGHOUT THE DAY, THE ARMY GROWS. EVERYONE KNOWS THAT TO BE ALONE IS TO DIE.
WE'VE MADE IT!

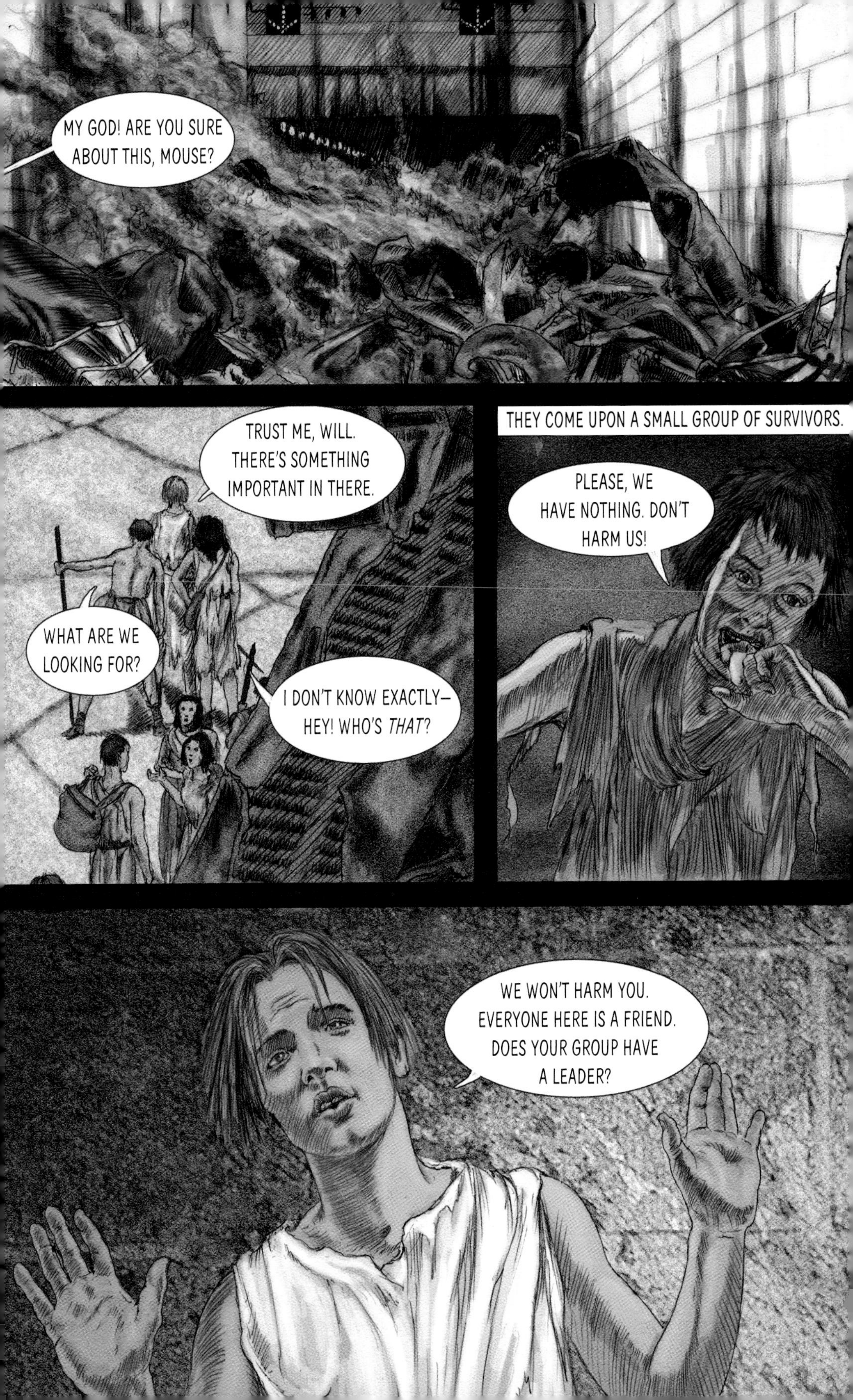
MY GOD! ARE YOU SURE ABOUT THIS, MOUSE?
TRUST ME, WILL. THERE'S SOMETHING IMPORTANT IN THERE.
WHAT ARE WE LOOKING FOR?
I DON'T KNOW EXACTLY— HEY! WHO'S *THAT*?
THEY COME UPON A SMALL GROUP OF SURVIVORS.
PLEASE, WE HAVE NOTHING. DON'T HARM US!
WE WON'T HARM YOU. EVERYONE HERE IS A FRIEND. DOES YOUR GROUP HAVE A LEADER?

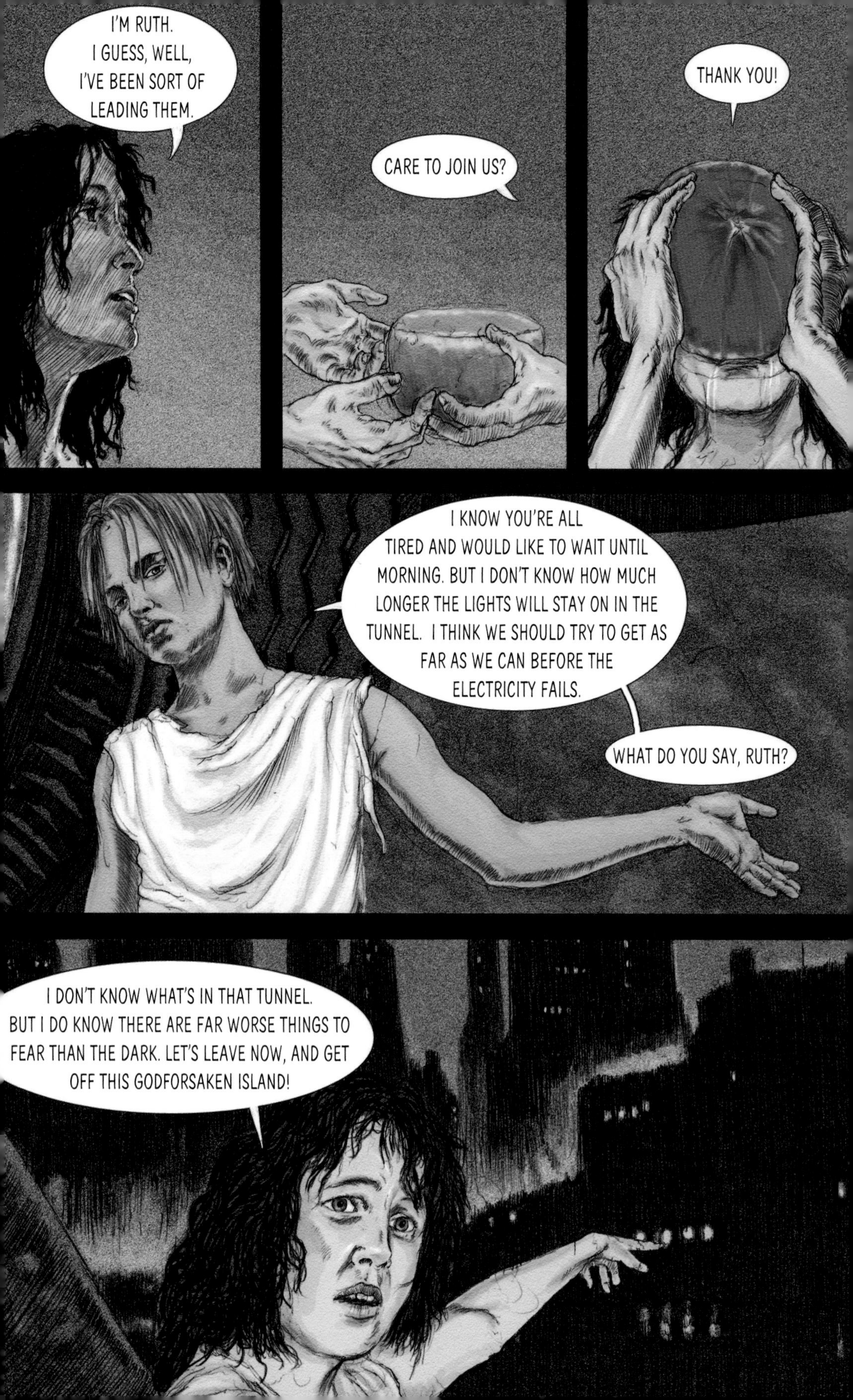
I'M RUTH. I GUESS, WELL, I'VE BEEN SORT OF LEADING THEM.
CARE TO JOIN US?
THANK YOU!
I KNOW YOU'RE ALL TIRED AND WOULD LIKE TO WAIT UNTIL MORNING. BUT I DON'T KNOW HOW MUCH LONGER THE LIGHTS WILL STAY ON IN THE TUNNEL. I THINK WE SHOULD TRY TO GET AS FAR AS WE CAN BEFORE THE ELECTRICITY FAILS.
WHAT DO YOU SAY, RUTH?
I DON'T KNOW WHAT'S IN THAT TUNNEL. BUT I DO KNOW THERE ARE FAR WORSE THINGS TO FEAR THAN THE DARK. LET'S LEAVE NOW, AND GET OFF THIS GODFORSAKEN ISLAND!

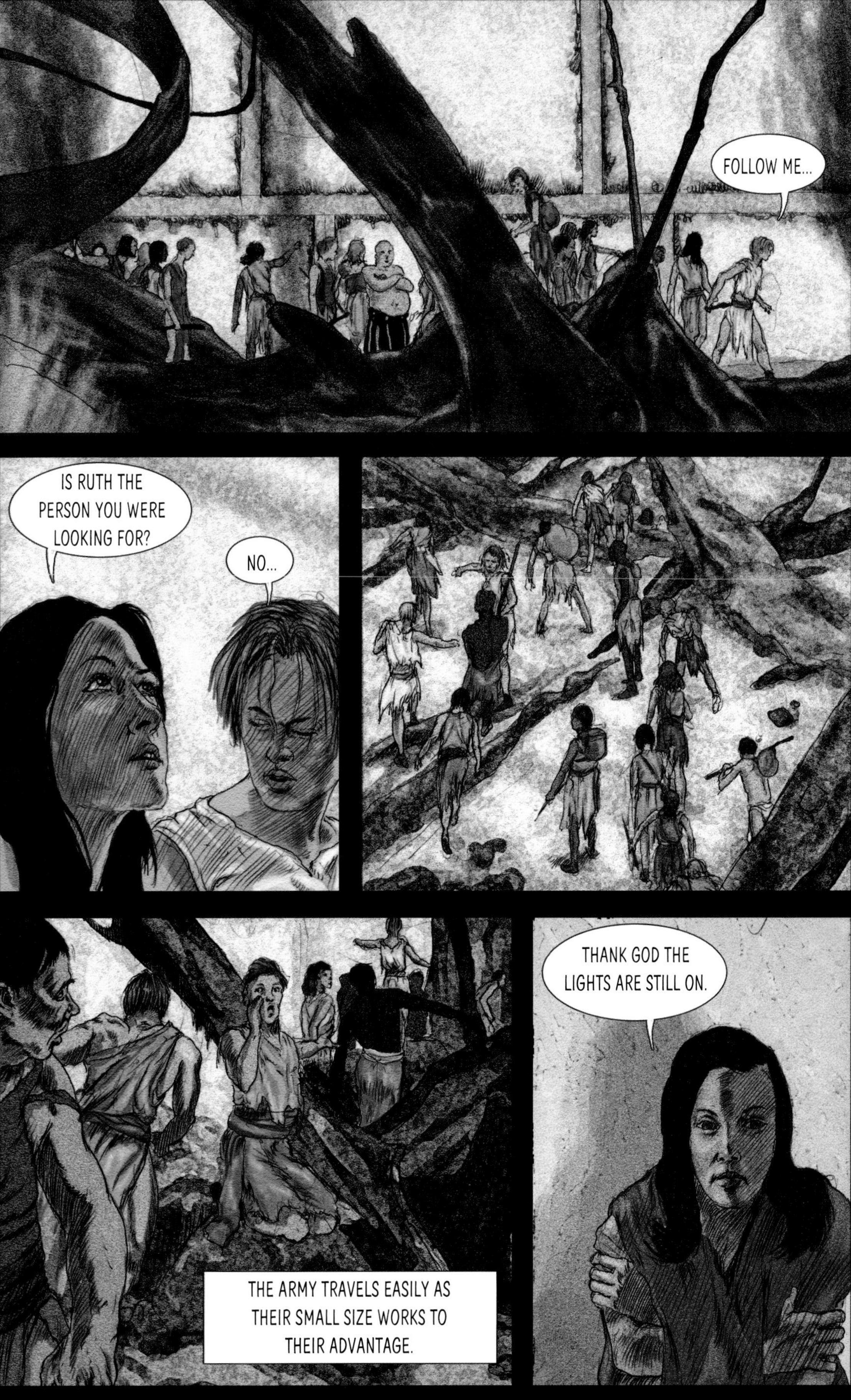
FOLLOW ME...
IS RUTH THE PERSON YOU WERE LOOKING FOR?
NO...
THE ARMY TRAVELS EASILY AS THEIR SMALL SIZE WORKS TO THEIR ADVANTAGE.
THANK GOD THE LIGHTS ARE STILL ON.

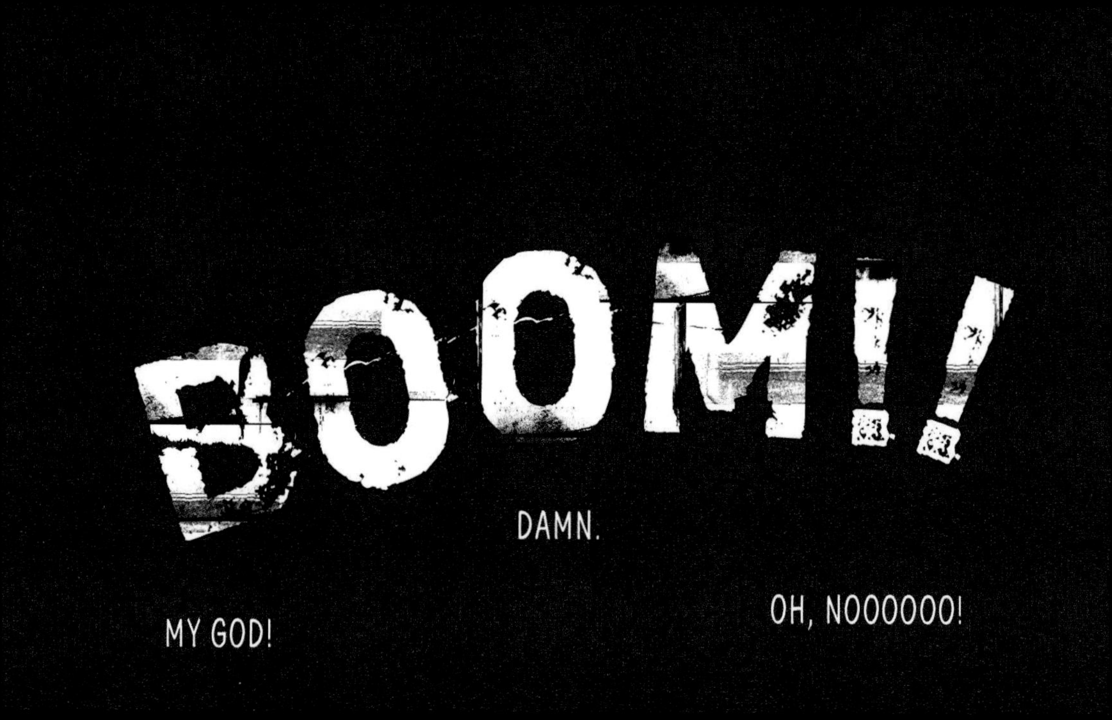
BOOM!!
DAMN.
MY GOD!
OH, NOOOOOO!

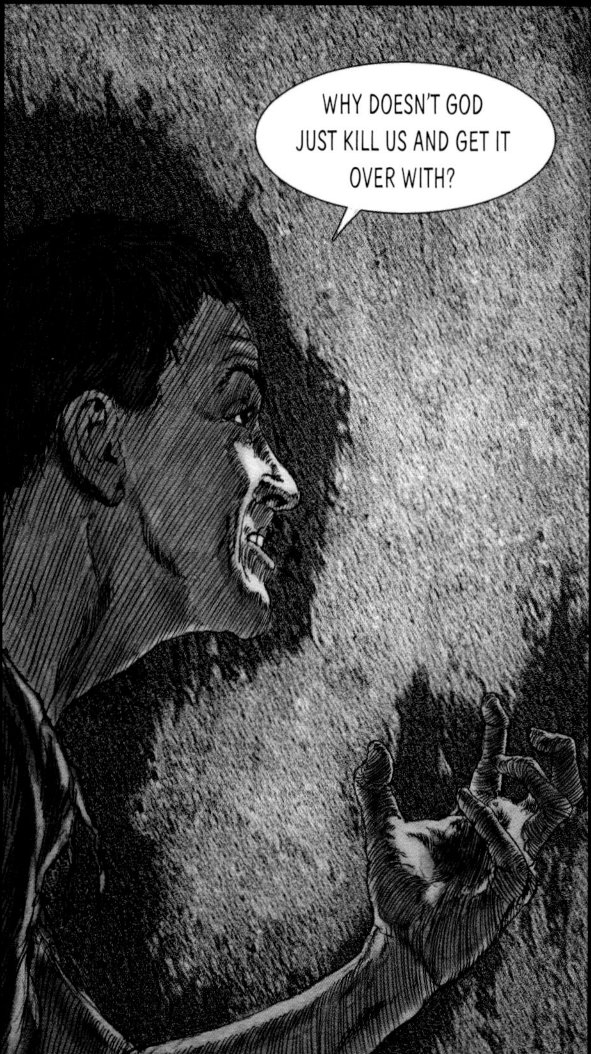
WHY DOESN'T GOD JUST KILL US AND GET IT OVER WITH?

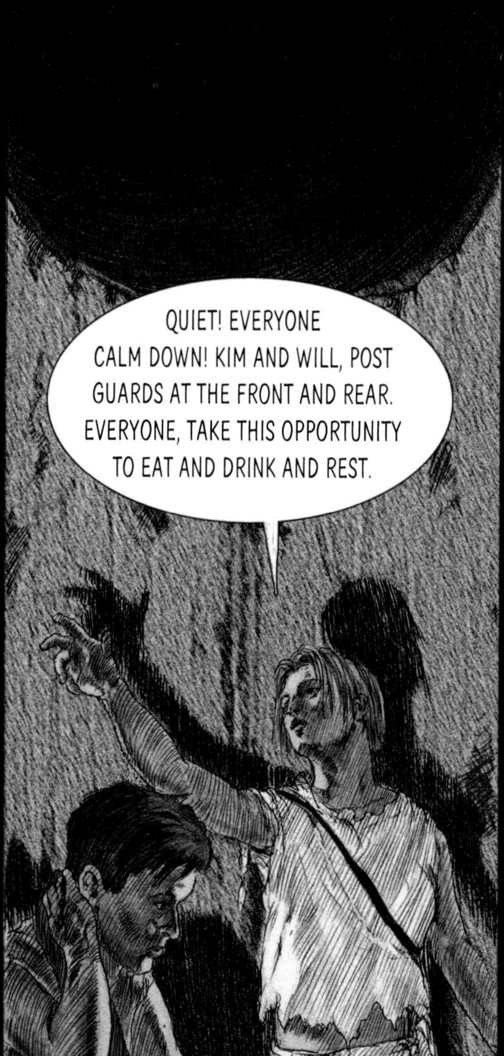
QUIET! EVERYONE CALM DOWN! KIM AND WILL, POST GUARDS AT THE FRONT AND REAR. EVERYONE, TAKE THIS OPPORTUNITY TO EAT AND DRINK AND REST.

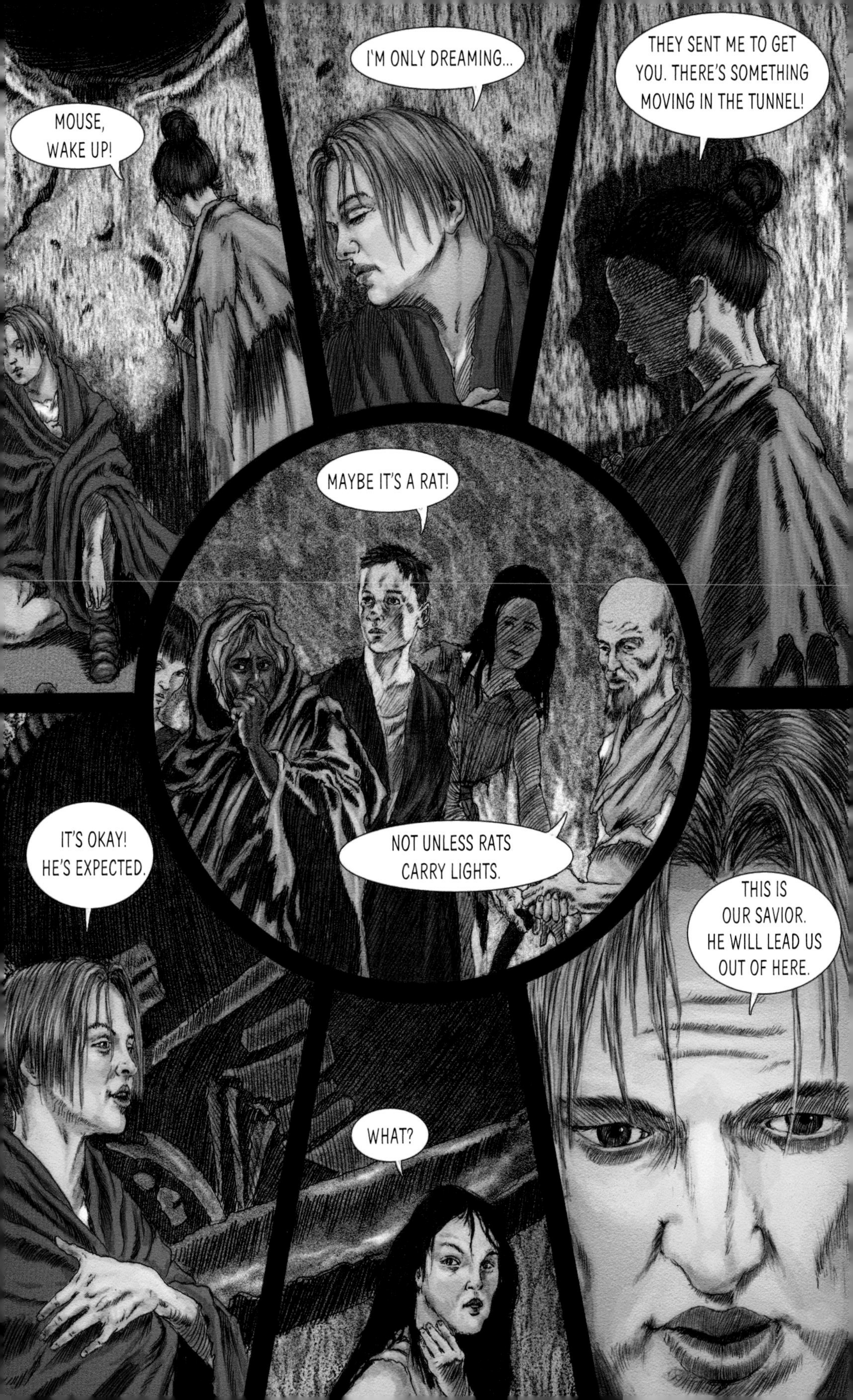
MOUSE,
WAKE UP!
I'M ONLY DREAMING...
THEY SENT ME TO GET YOU. THERE'S SOMETHING MOVING IN THE TUNNEL!
MAYBE IT'S A RAT!
NOT UNLESS RATS CARRY LIGHTS.
IT'S OKAY! HE'S EXPECTED.
WHAT?
THIS IS OUR SAVIOR. HE WILL LEAD US OUT OF HERE.

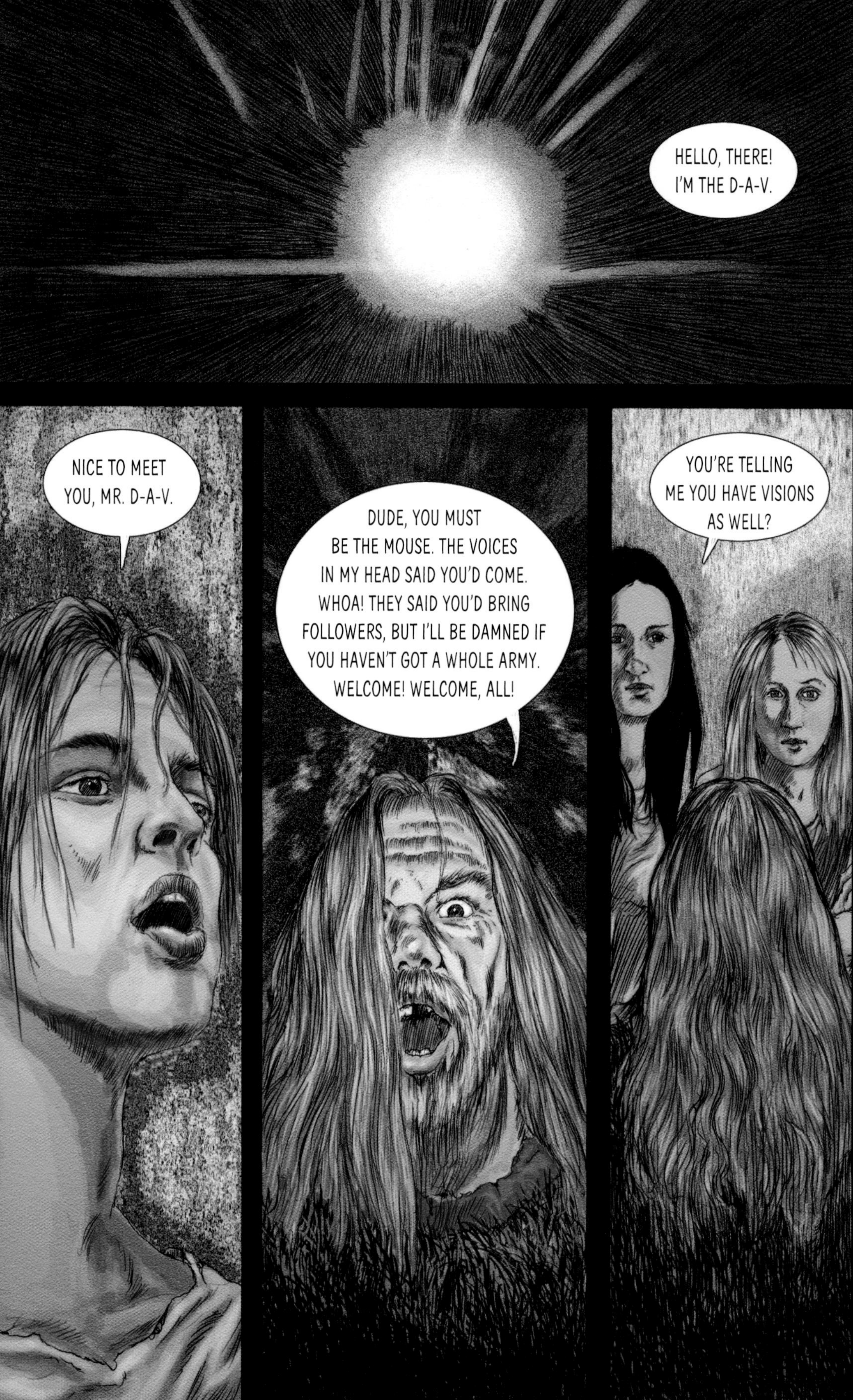
HELLO, THERE!
I'M THE D-A-V.
NICE TO MEET YOU, MR. D-A-V.
DUDE, YOU MUST BE THE MOUSE. THE VOICES IN MY HEAD SAID YOU'D COME. WHOA! THEY SAID YOU'D BRING FOLLOWERS, BUT I'LL BE DAMNED IF YOU HAVEN'T GOT A WHOLE ARMY. WELCOME! WELCOME, ALL!
YOU'RE TELLING ME YOU HAVE VISIONS AS WELL?

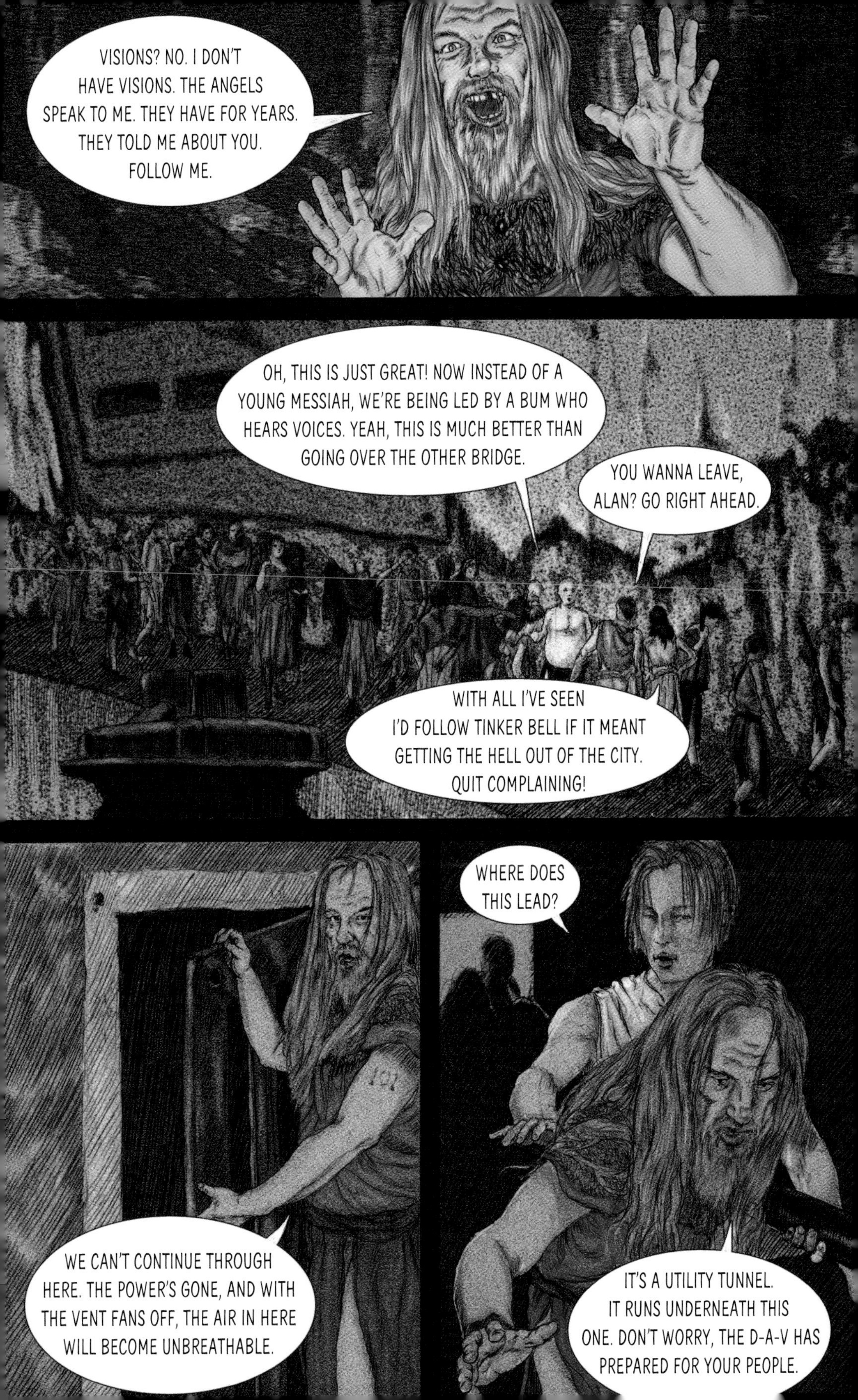
VISIONS? NO. I DON'T HAVE VISIONS. THE ANGELS SPEAK TO ME. THEY HAVE FOR YEARS. THEY TOLD ME ABOUT YOU. FOLLOW ME.
OH, THIS IS JUST GREAT! NOW INSTEAD OF A YOUNG MESSIAH, WE'RE BEING LED BY A BUM WHO HEARS VOICES. YEAH, THIS IS MUCH BETTER THAN GOING OVER THE OTHER BRIDGE.
YOU WANNA LEAVE, ALAN? GO RIGHT AHEAD.
WITH ALL I'VE SEEN I'D FOLLOW TINKER BELL IF IT MEANT GETTING THE HELL OUT OF THE CITY. QUIT COMPLAINING!
WE CAN'T CONTINUE THROUGH HERE. THE POWER'S GONE, AND WITH THE VENT FANS OFF, THE AIR IN HERE WILL BECOME UNBREATHABLE.
WHERE DOES THIS LEAD?
IT'S A UTILITY TUNNEL. IT RUNS UNDERNEATH THIS ONE. DON'T WORRY, THE D-A-V HAS PREPARED FOR YOUR PEOPLE.

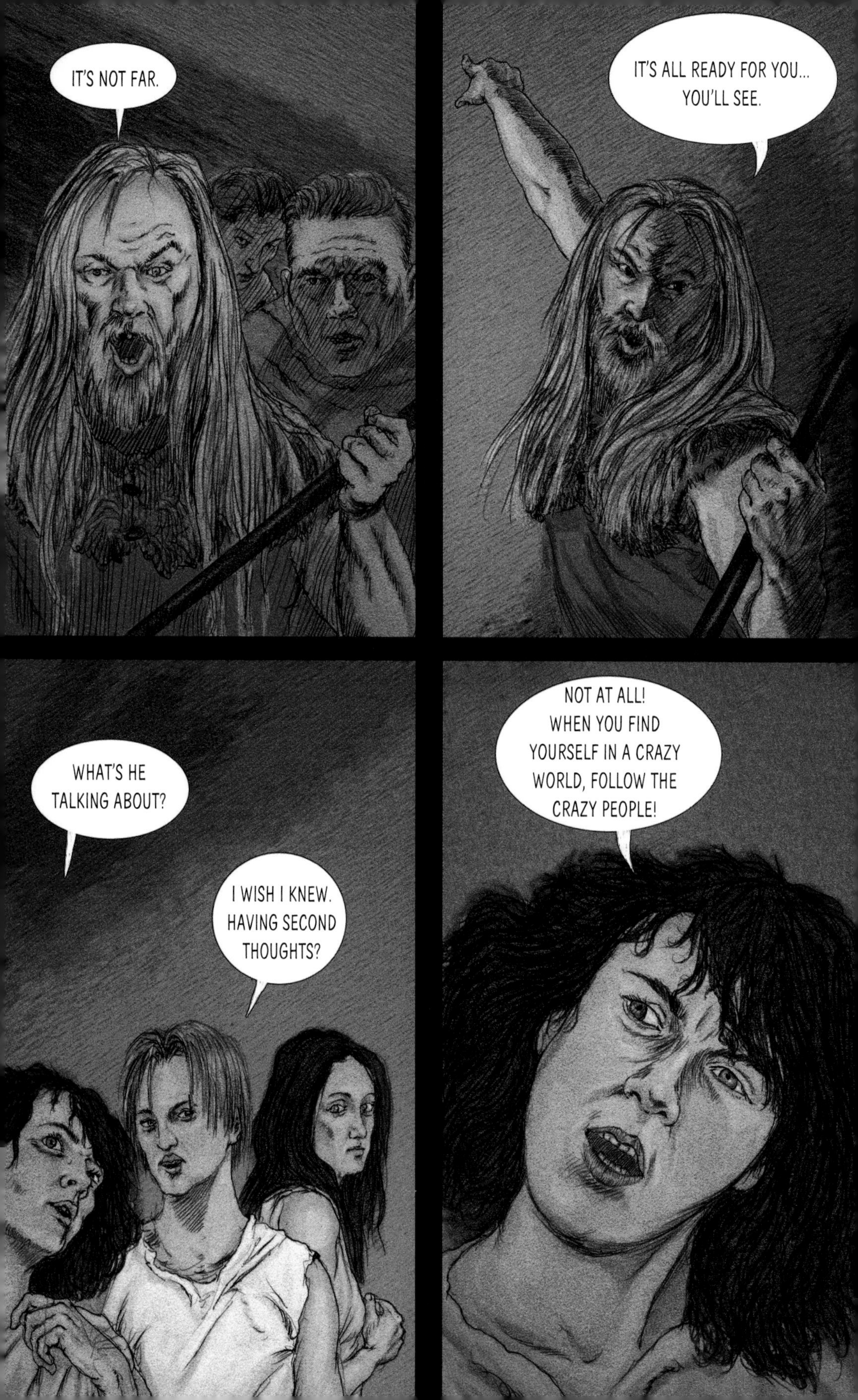
IT'S NOT FAR.
IT'S ALL READY FOR YOU... YOU'LL SEE.
WHAT'S HE TALKING ABOUT?
I WISH I KNEW. HAVING SECOND THOUGHTS?
NOT AT ALL! WHEN YOU FIND YOURSELF IN A CRAZY WORLD, FOLLOW THE CRAZY PEOPLE!

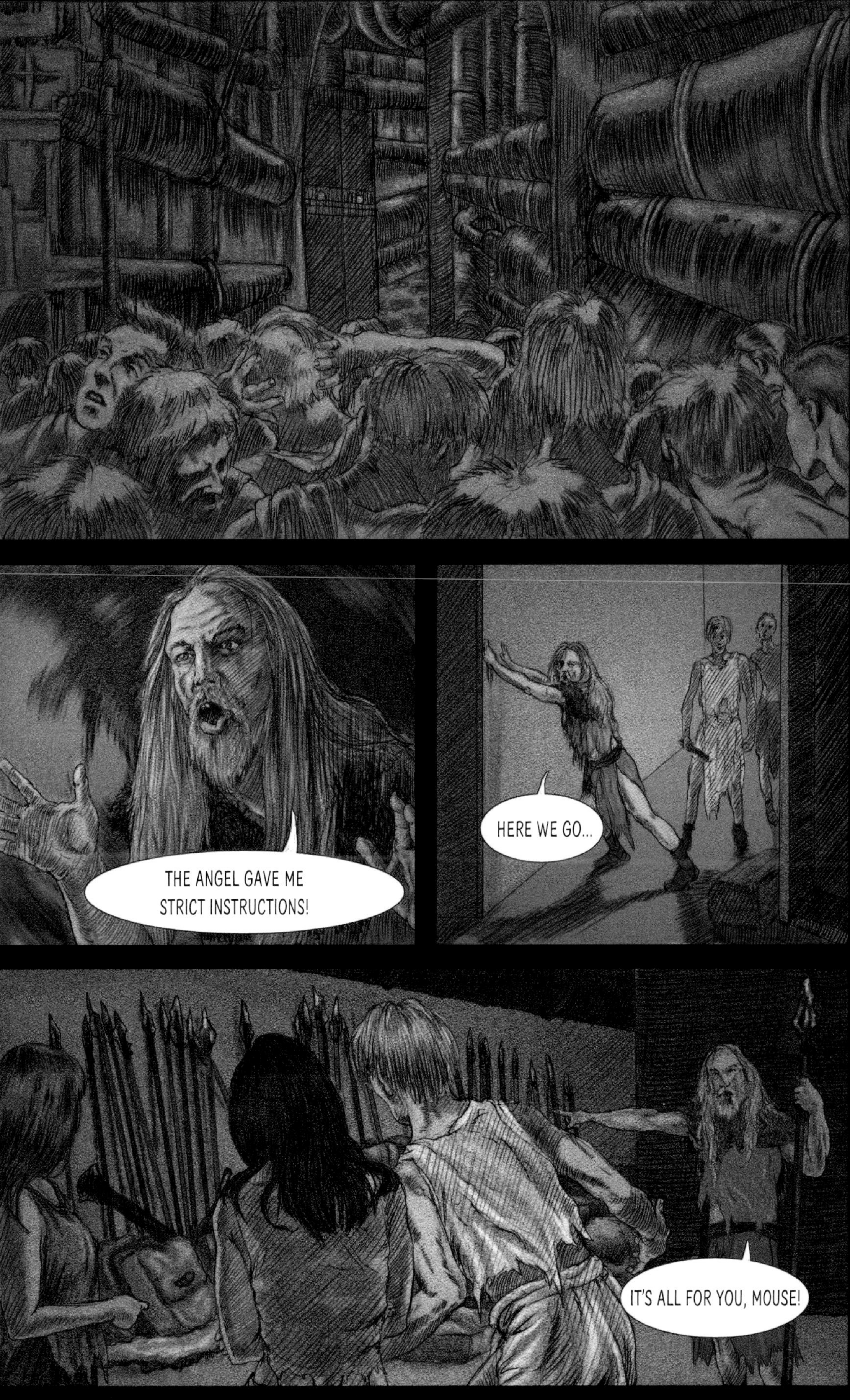
THE ANGEL GAVE ME STRICT INSTRUCTIONS!
HERE WE GO...
IT'S ALL FOR YOU, MOUSE!

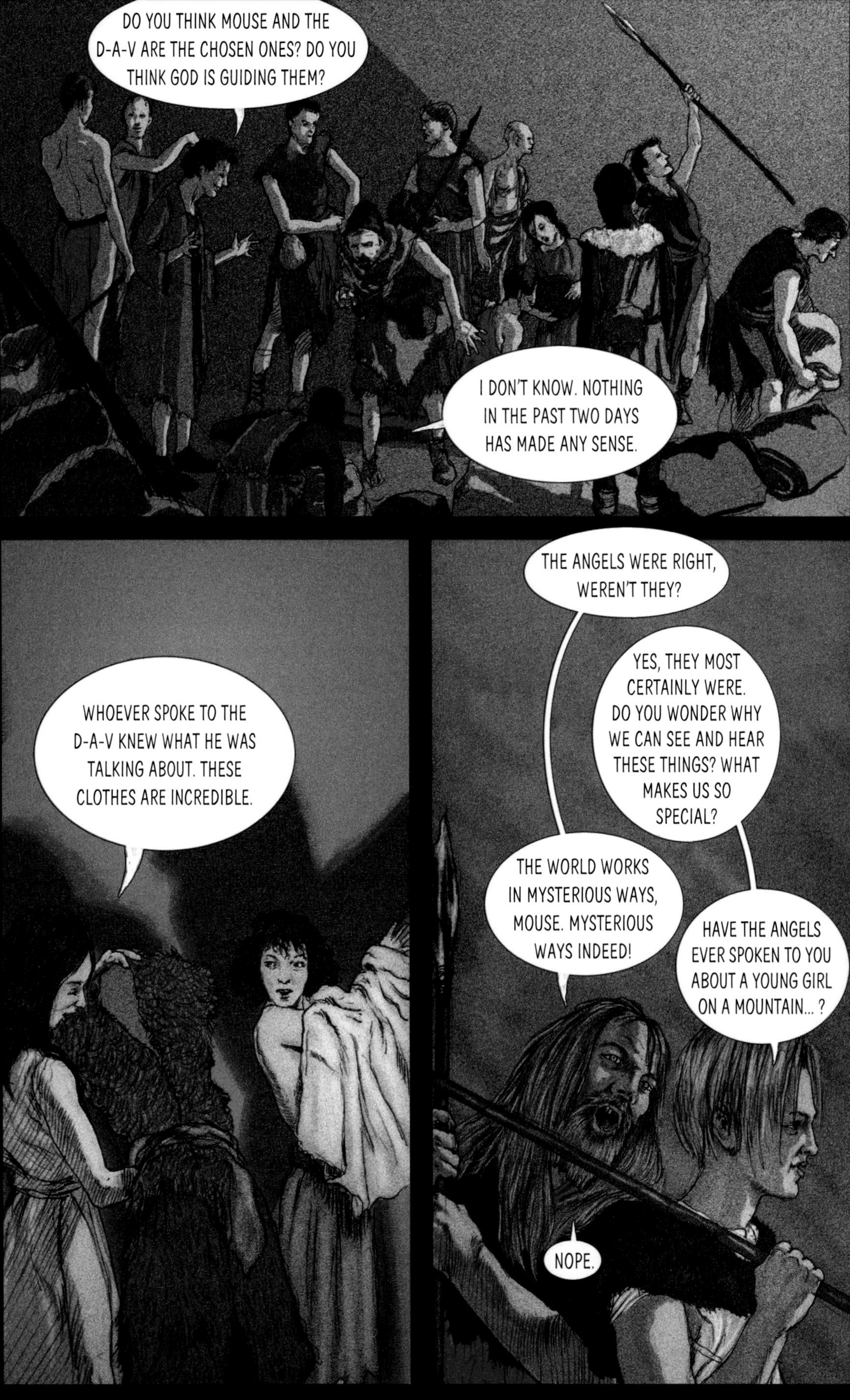
DO YOU THINK MOUSE AND THE D-A-V ARE THE CHOSEN ONES? DO YOU THINK GOD IS GUIDING THEM?
I DON'T KNOW. NOTHING IN THE PAST TWO DAYS HAS MADE ANY SENSE.
WHOEVER SPOKE TO THE D-A-V KNEW WHAT HE WAS TALKING ABOUT. THESE CLOTHES ARE INCREDIBLE.
THE ANGELS WERE RIGHT, WEREN'T THEY?
YES, THEY MOST CERTAINLY WERE. DO YOU WONDER WHY WE CAN SEE AND HEAR THESE THINGS? WHAT MAKES US SO SPECIAL?
THE WORLD WORKS IN MYSTERIOUS WAYS, MOUSE. MYSTERIOUS WAYS INDEED!
HAVE THE ANGELS EVER SPOKEN TO YOU ABOUT A YOUNG GIRL ON A MOUNTAIN... ?
NOPE.

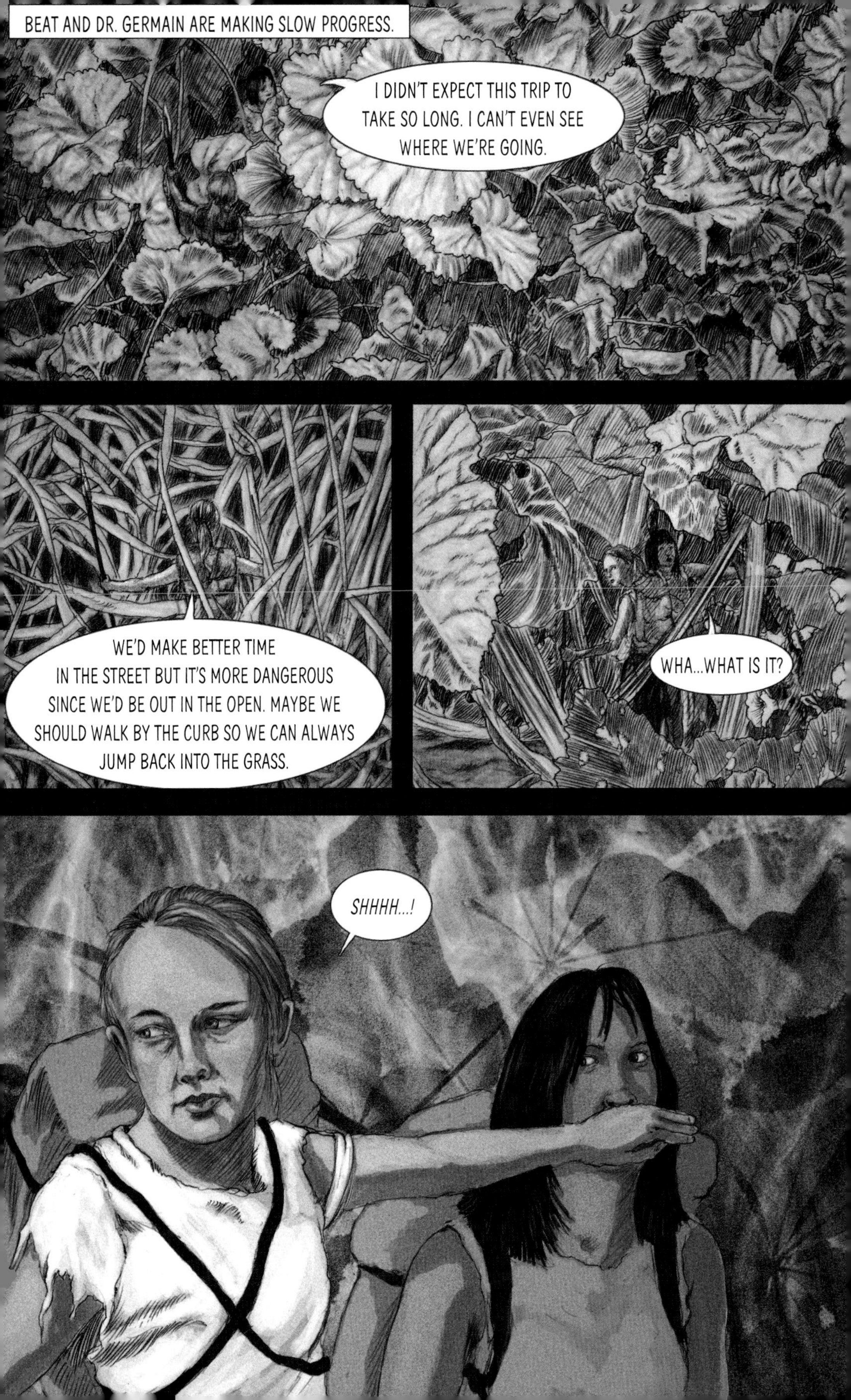
BEAT AND DR. GERMAIN ARE MAKING SLOW PROGRESS.
I DIDN'T EXPECT THIS TRIP TO TAKE SO LONG. I CAN'T EVEN SEE WHERE WE'RE GOING.
WE'D MAKE BETTER TIME IN THE STREET BUT IT'S MORE DANGEROUS SINCE WE'D BE OUT IN THE OPEN. MAYBE WE SHOULD WALK BY THE CURB SO WE CAN ALWAYS JUMP BACK INTO THE GRASS.
WHA...WHAT IS IT?
SHHHH...!

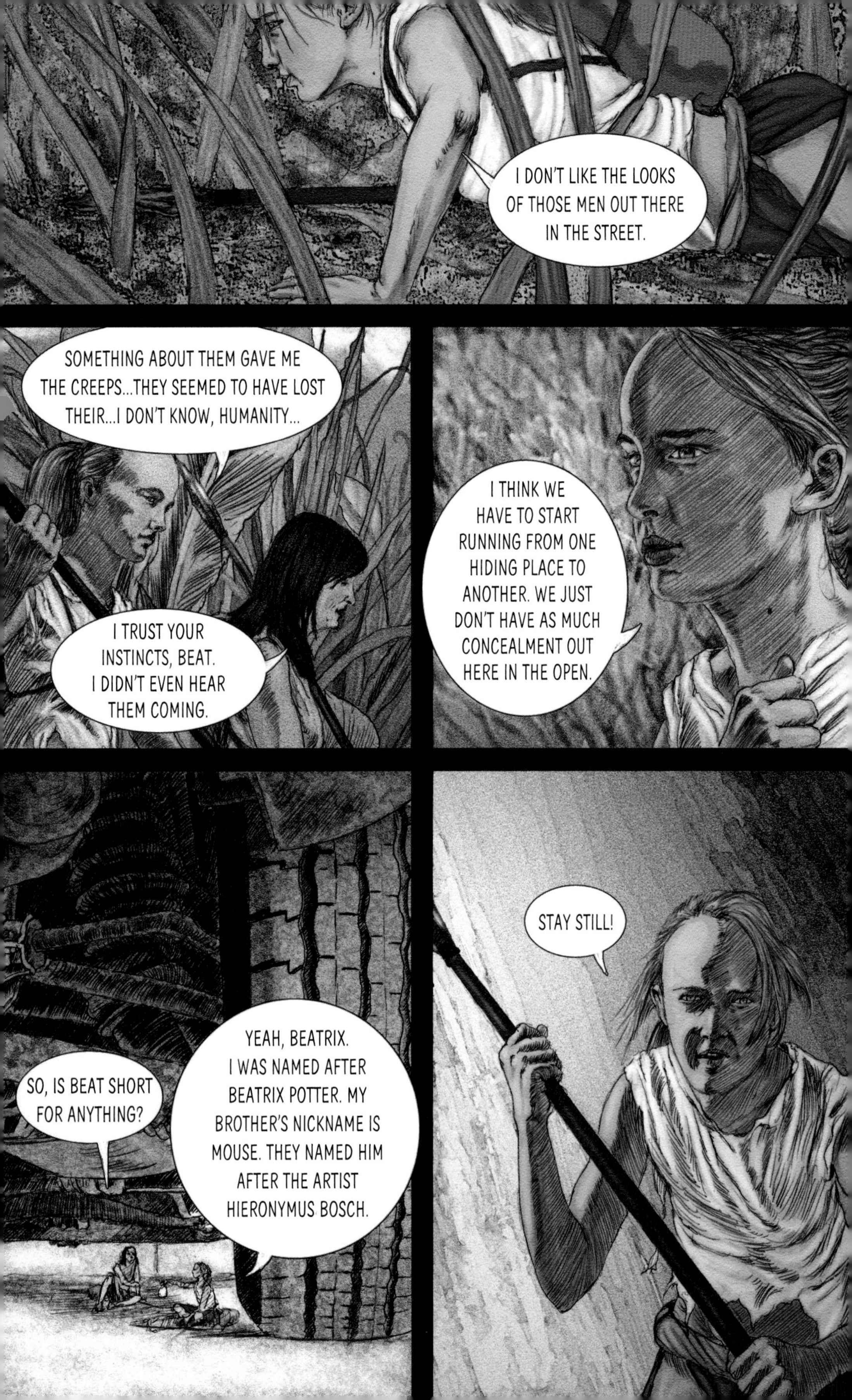
I DON'T LIKE THE LOOKS OF THOSE MEN OUT THERE IN THE STREET.
SOMETHING ABOUT THEM GAVE ME THE CREEPS...THEY SEEMED TO HAVE LOST THEIR...I DON'T KNOW, HUMANITY...
I TRUST YOUR INSTINCTS, BEAT. I DIDN'T EVEN HEAR THEM COMING.
I THINK WE HAVE TO START RUNNING FROM ONE HIDING PLACE TO ANOTHER. WE JUST DON'T HAVE AS MUCH CONCEALMENT OUT HERE IN THE OPEN.
SO, IS BEAT SHORT FOR ANYTHING?
YEAH, BEATRIX. I WAS NAMED AFTER BEATRIX POTTER. MY BROTHER'S NICKNAME IS MOUSE. THEY NAMED HIM AFTER THE ARTIST HIERONYMUS BOSCH.
STAY STILL!

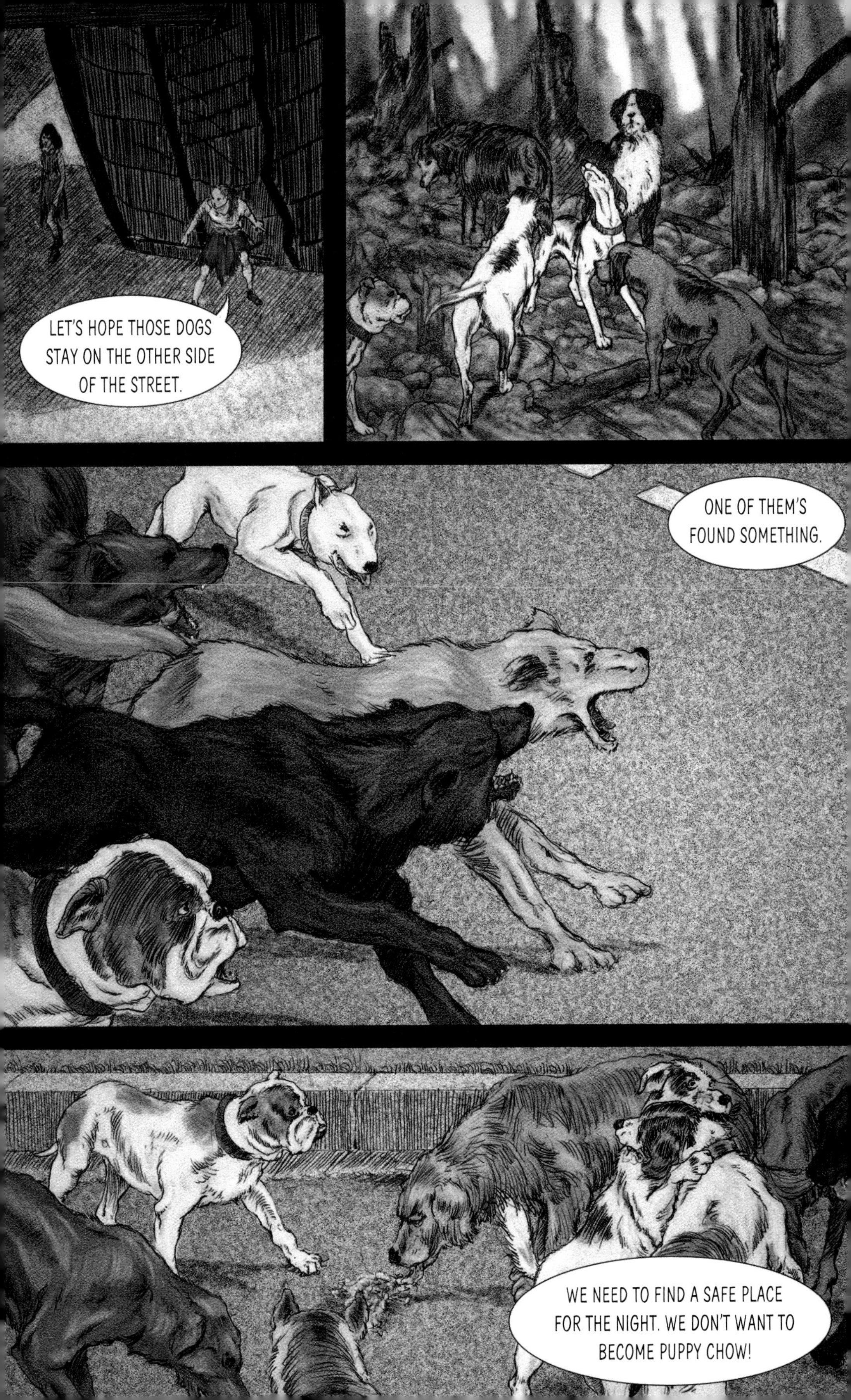
LET'S HOPE THOSE DOGS STAY ON THE OTHER SIDE OF THE STREET.
ONE OF THEM'S FOUND SOMETHING.
WE NEED TO FIND A SAFE PLACE FOR THE NIGHT. WE DON'T WANT TO BECOME PUPPY CHOW!

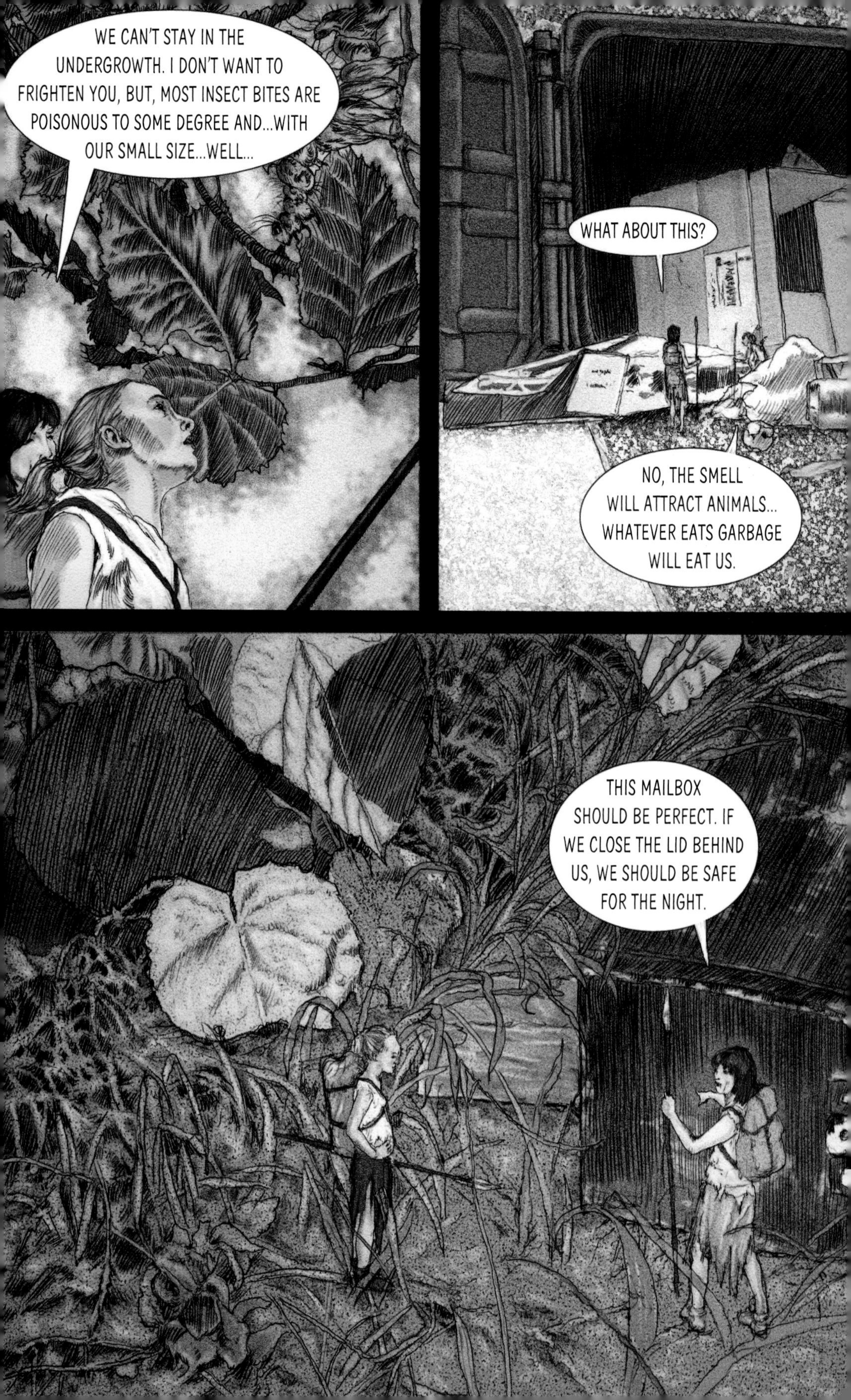
WE CAN'T STAY IN THE UNDERGROWTH. I DON'T WANT TO FRIGHTEN YOU, BUT, MOST INSECT BITES ARE POISONOUS TO SOME DEGREE AND...WITH OUR SMALL SIZE...WELL...
WHAT ABOUT THIS?
NO, THE SMELL WILL ATTRACT ANIMALS... WHATEVER EATS GARBAGE WILL EAT US.
THIS MAILBOX SHOULD BE PERFECT. IF WE CLOSE THE LID BEHIND US, WE SHOULD BE SAFE FOR THE NIGHT.

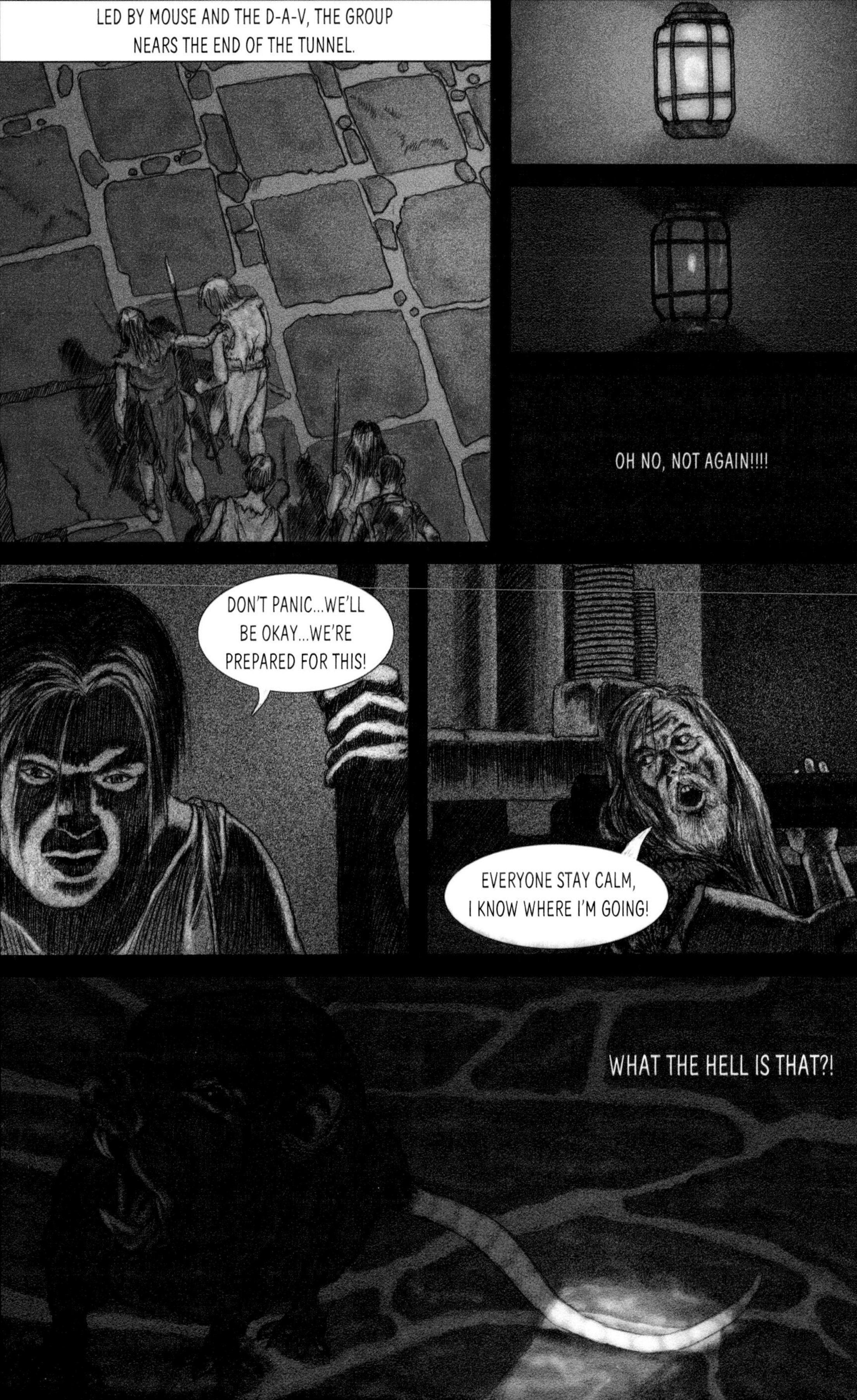
LED BY MOUSE AND THE D-A-V, THE GROUP NEARS THE END OF THE TUNNEL.
OH NO, NOT AGAIN!!!!
DON'T PANIC...WE'LL BE OKAY...WE'RE PREPARED FOR THIS!
EVERYONE STAY CALM, I KNOW WHERE I'M GOING!
WHAT THE HELL IS THAT?!

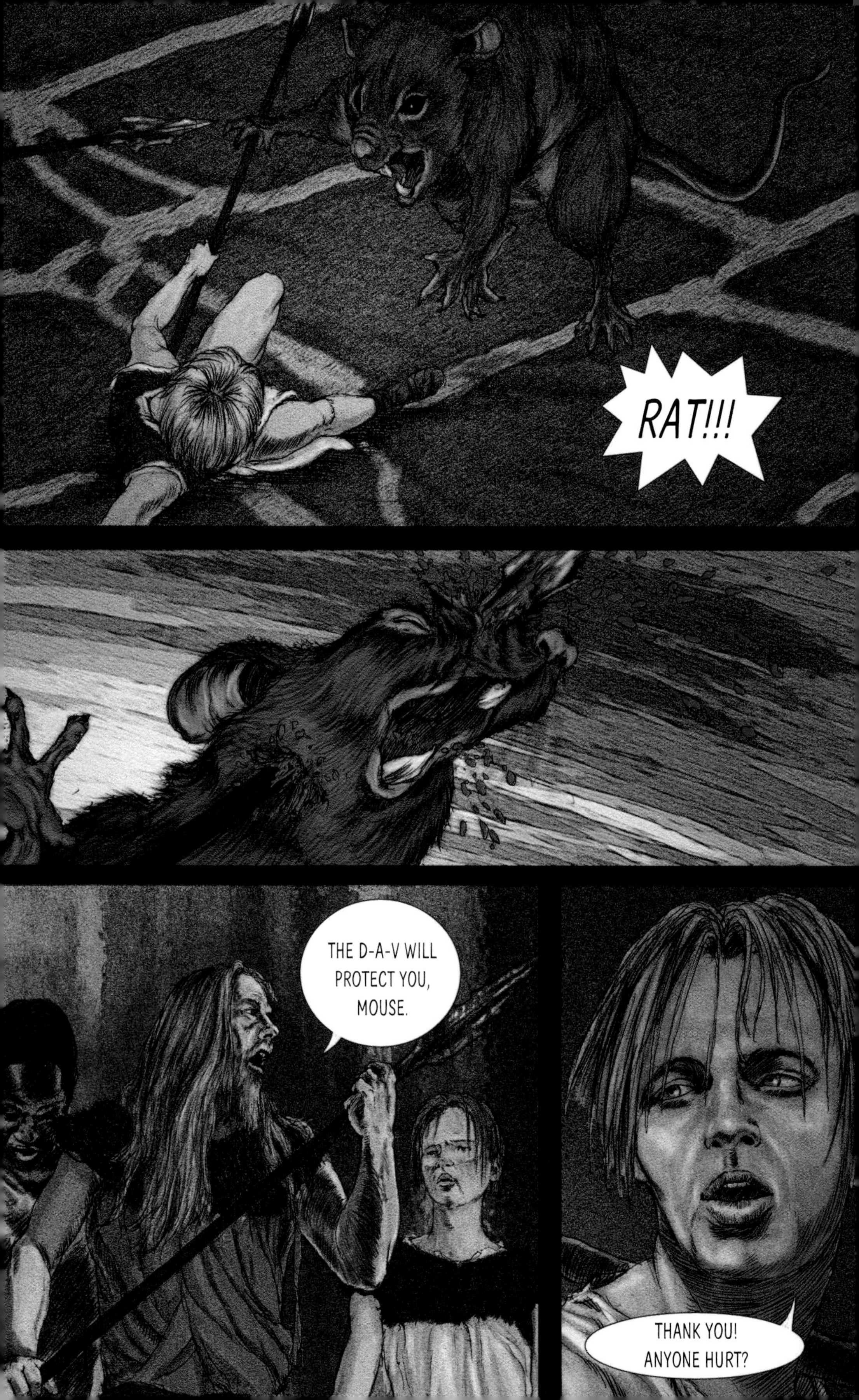
RAT!!!
THE D-A-V WILL PROTECT YOU, MOUSE.
THANK YOU! ANYONE HURT?

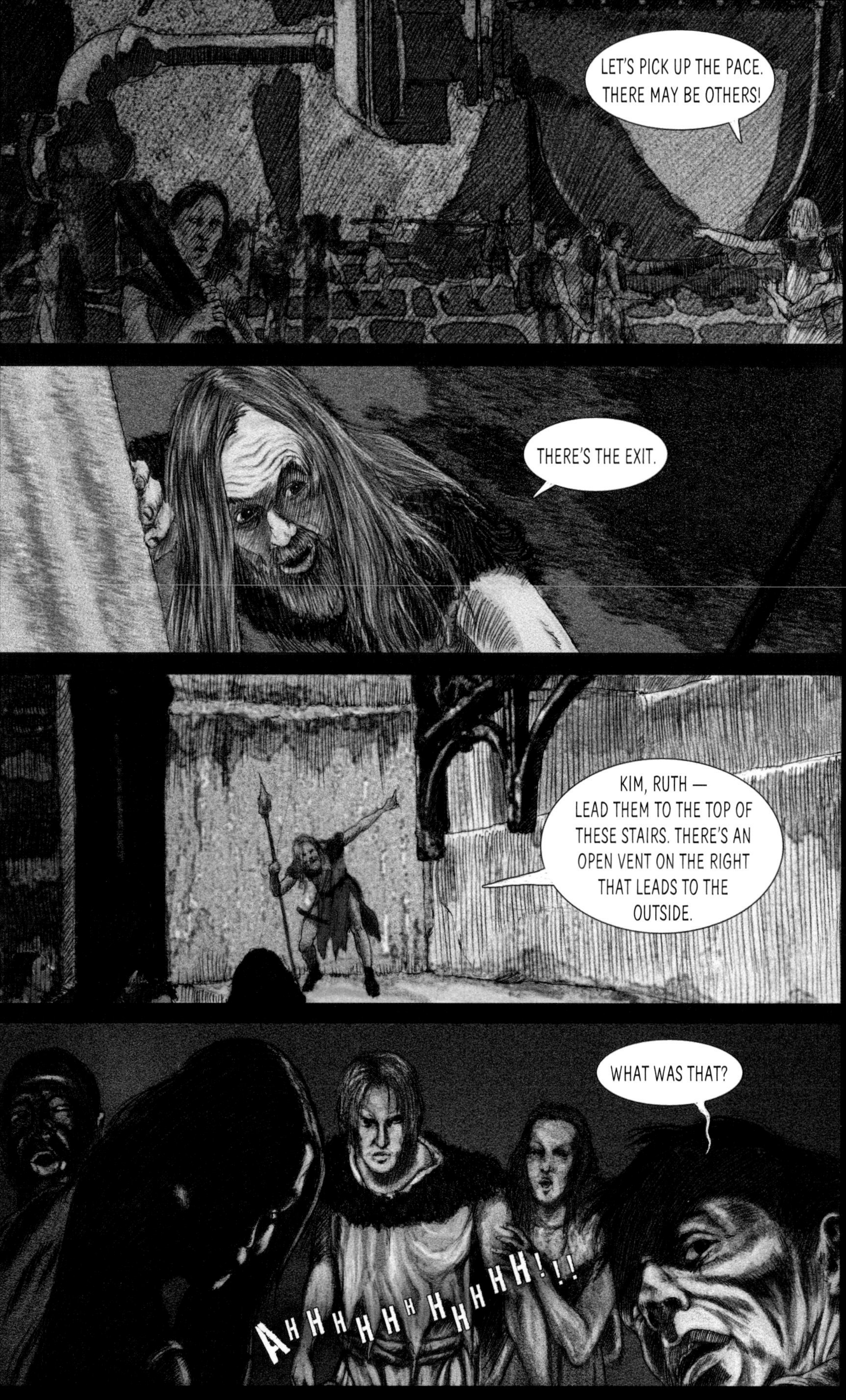
LET'S PICK UP THE PACE. THERE MAY BE OTHERS!
THERE'S THE EXIT.
KIM, RUTH — LEAD THEM TO THE TOP OF THESE STAIRS. THERE'S AN OPEN VENT ON THE RIGHT THAT LEADS TO THE OUTSIDE.
WHAT WAS THAT?
AHHHHHHHHHHHH!!!

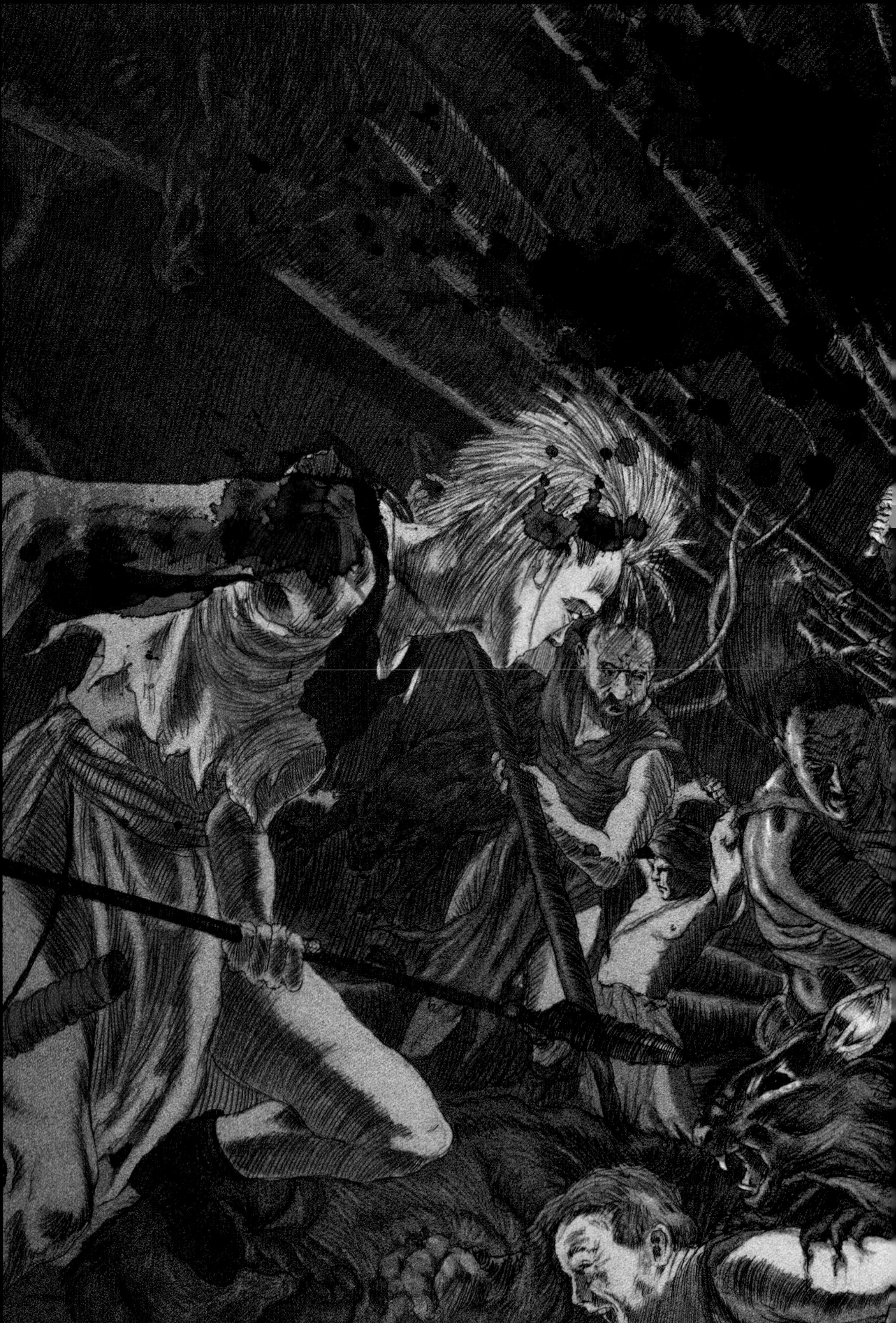

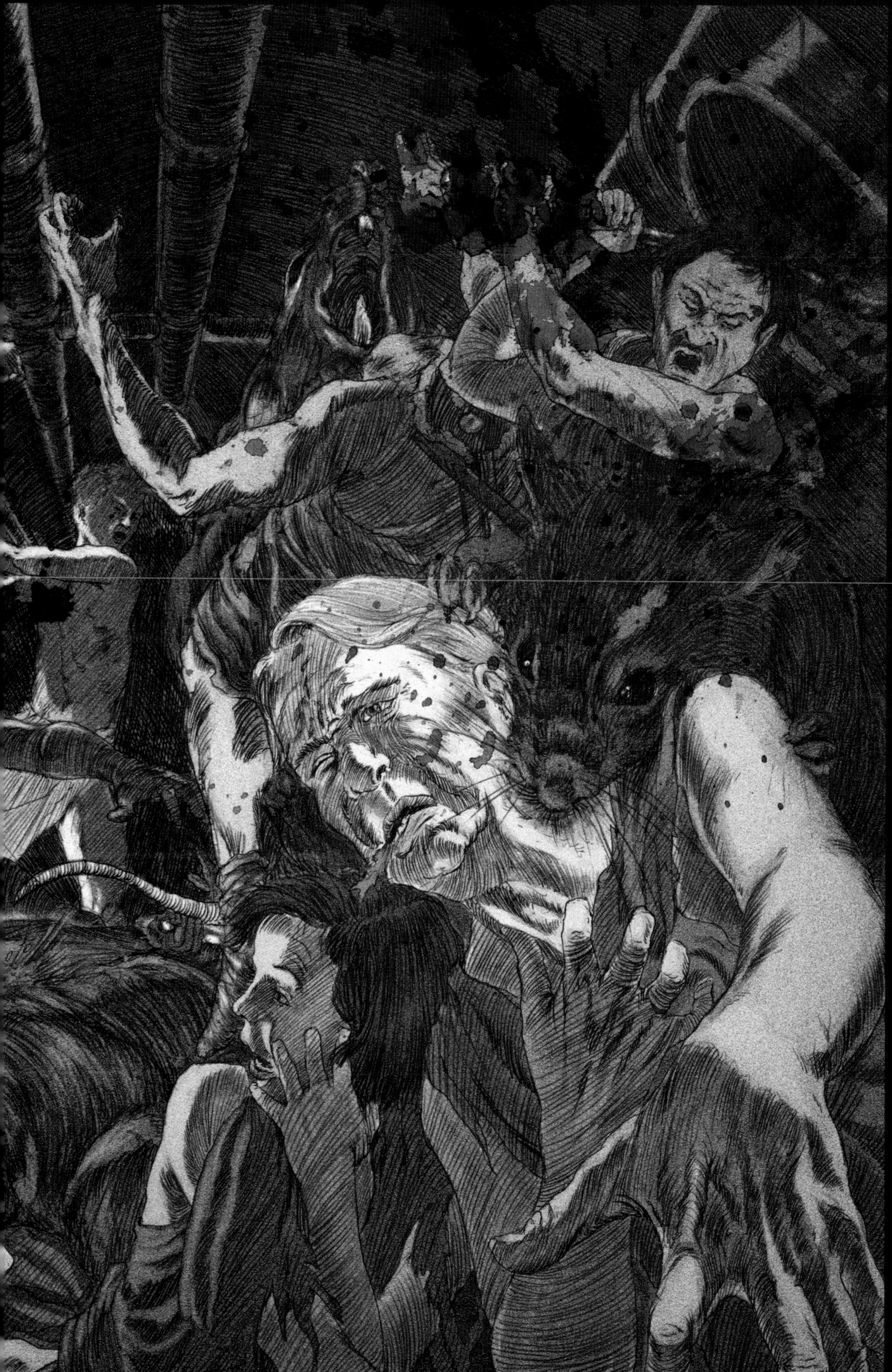

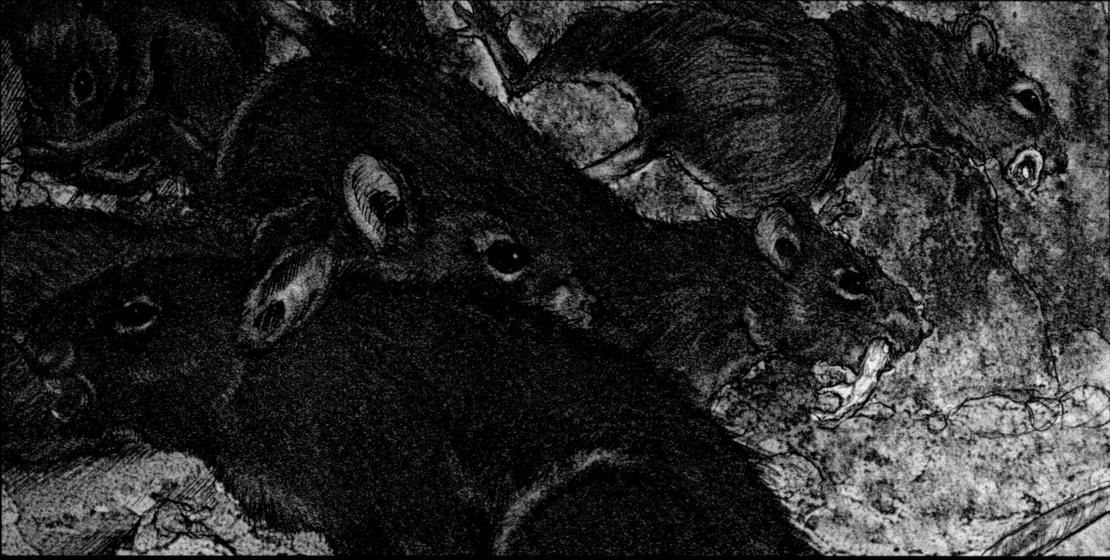

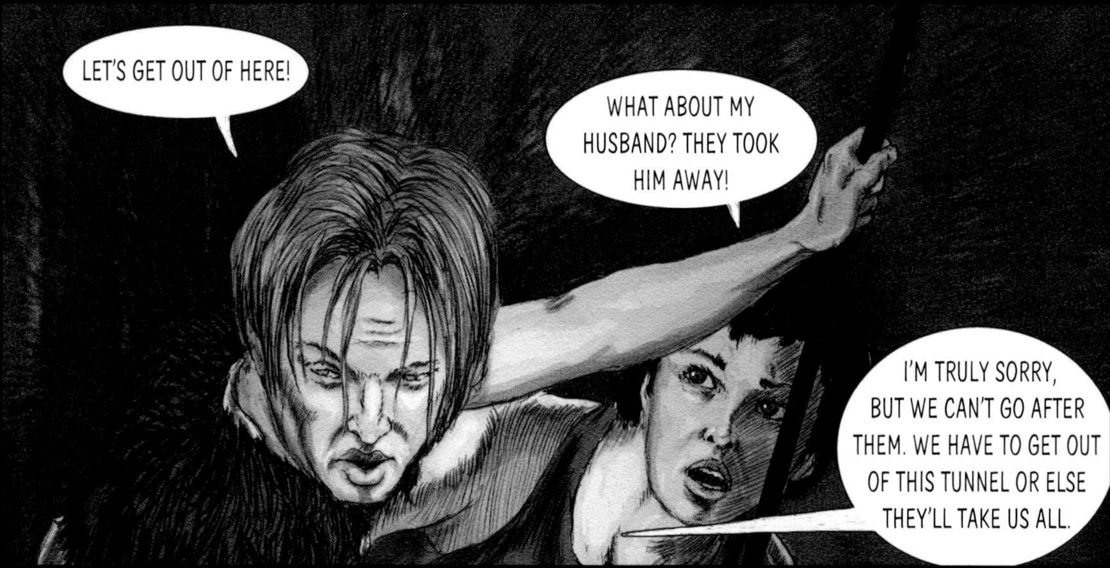
LET'S GET OUT OF HERE!
WHAT ABOUT MY HUSBAND? THEY TOOK HIM AWAY!
I'M TRULY SORRY, BUT WE CAN'T GO AFTER THEM. WE HAVE TO GET OUT OF THIS TUNNEL OR ELSE THEY'LL TAKE US ALL.

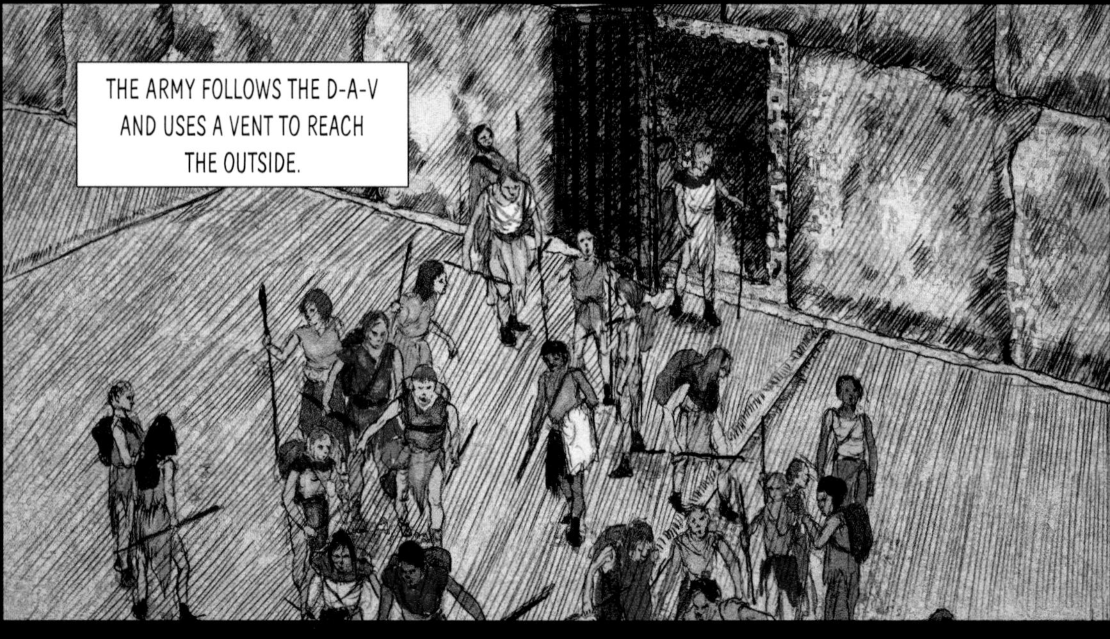
THE ARMY FOLLOWS THE D-A-V AND USES A VENT TO REACH THE OUTSIDE.

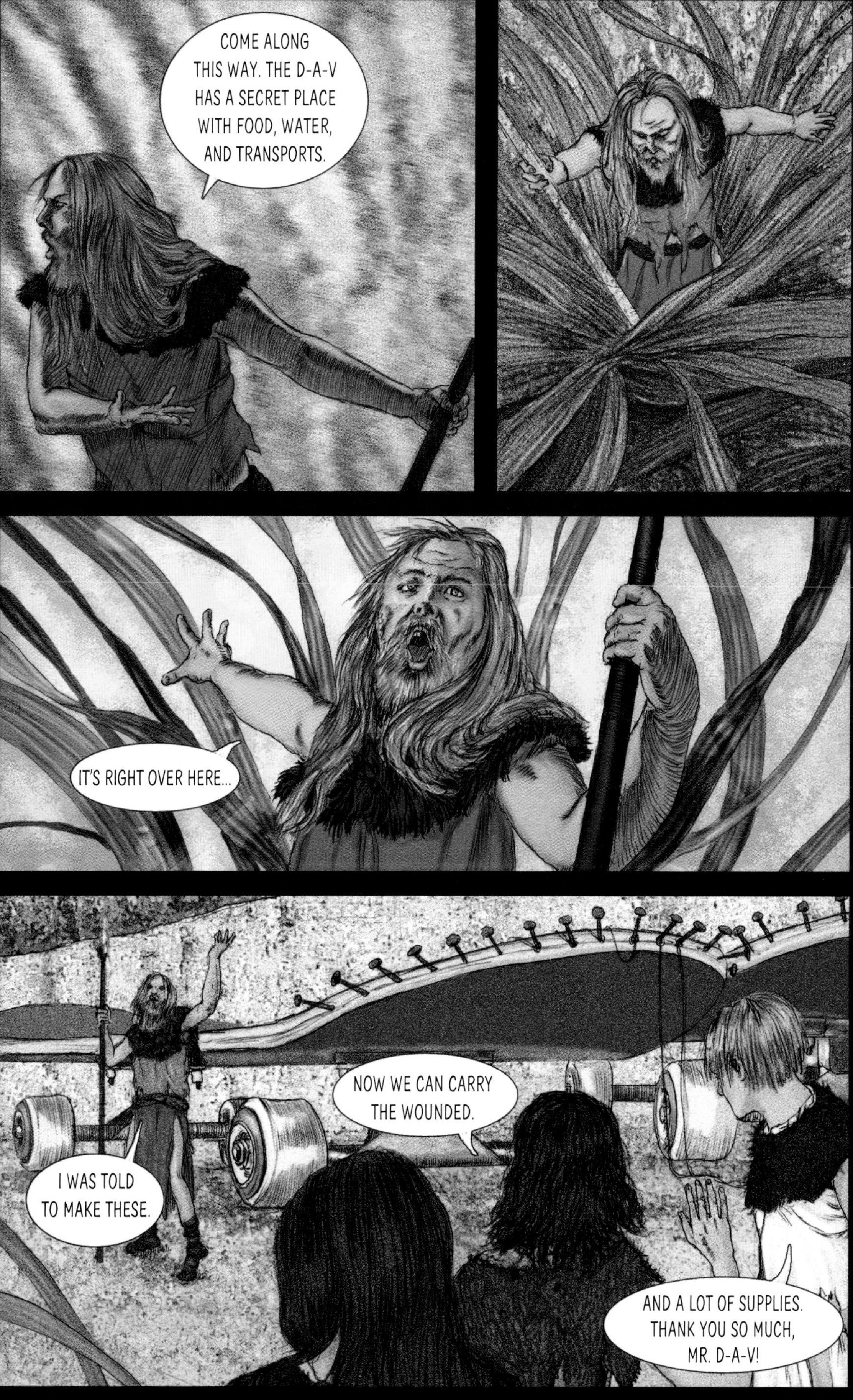
COME ALONG THIS WAY. THE D-A-V HAS A SECRET PLACE WITH FOOD, WATER, AND TRANSPORTS.
IT'S RIGHT OVER HERE...
I WAS TOLD TO MAKE THESE.
NOW WE CAN CARRY THE WOUNDED.
AND A LOT OF SUPPLIES. THANK YOU SO MUCH, MR. D-A-V!

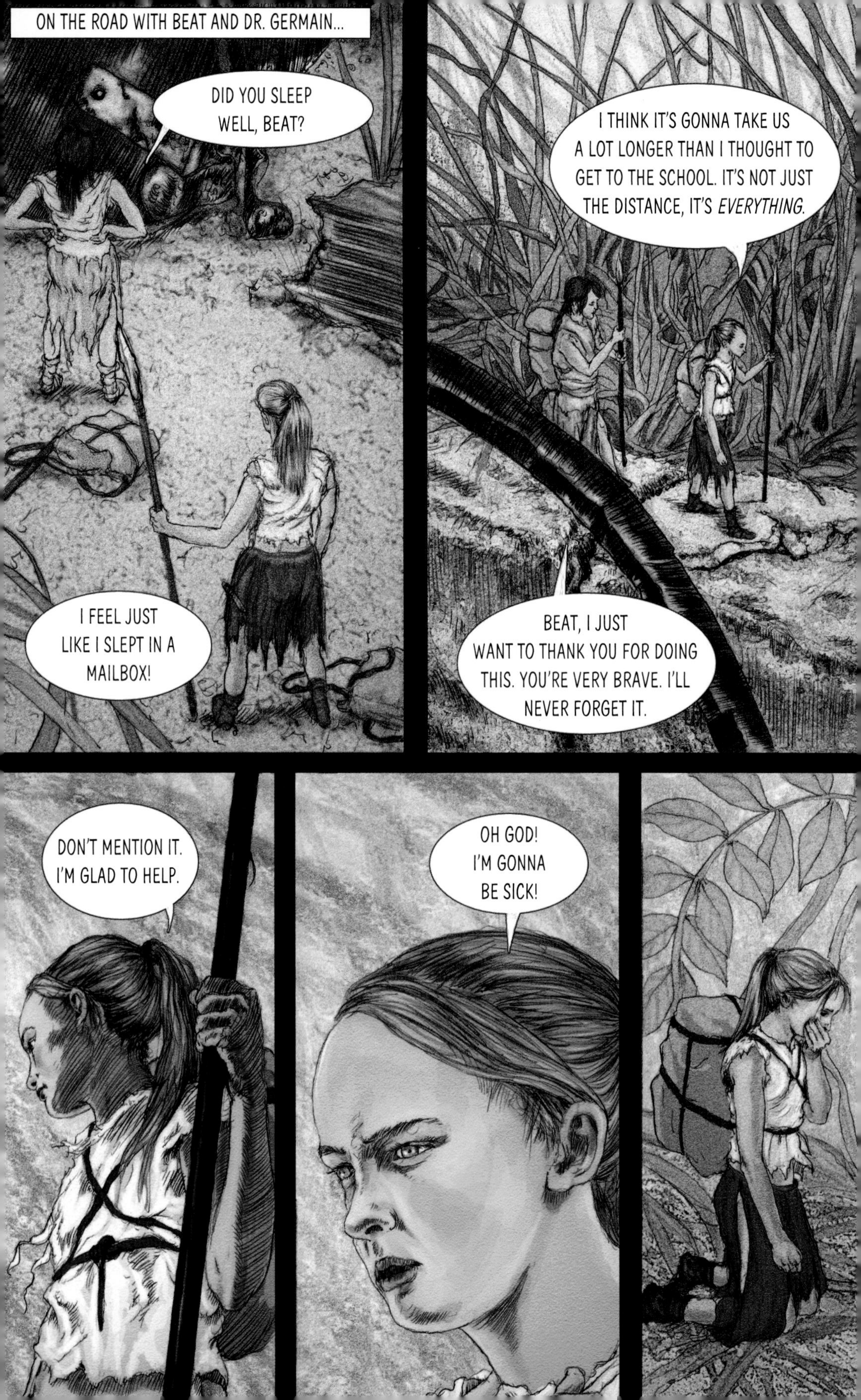
ON THE ROAD WITH BEAT AND DR. GERMAIN...
DID YOU SLEEP WELL, BEAT?
I FEEL JUST LIKE I SLEPT IN A MAILBOX!
I THINK IT'S GONNA TAKE US A LOT LONGER THAN I THOUGHT TO GET TO THE SCHOOL. IT'S NOT JUST THE DISTANCE, IT'S *EVERYTHING*.
BEAT, I JUST WANT TO THANK YOU FOR DOING THIS. YOU'RE VERY BRAVE. I'LL NEVER FORGET IT.
DON'T MENTION IT. I'M GLAD TO HELP.
OH GOD! I'M GONNA BE SICK!

I'M SO SORRY, HELEN. I NEED TO BE STRONGER. I NEED TO GET USED TO THINGS LIKE THIS.

BEAT, YOU HAVE NOTHING TO APOLOGIZE FOR. WE'RE ALL GOING TO HAVE TO LEARN TO DEAL WITH SEEING HORRORS LIKE THAT. BUT I DON'T THINK WE'LL EVER LEARN TO IGNORE IT.

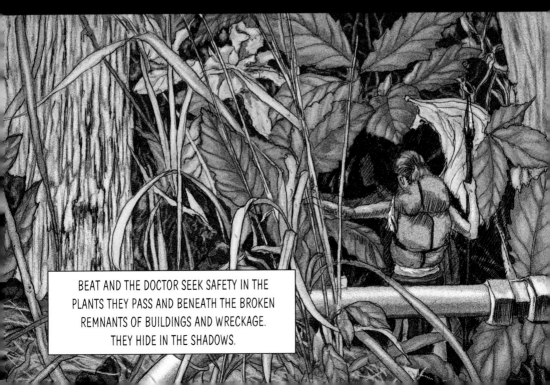

BEAT AND THE DOCTOR SEEK SAFETY IN THE PLANTS THEY PASS AND BENEATH THE BROKEN REMNANTS OF BUILDINGS AND WRECKAGE. THEY HIDE IN THE SHADOWS.

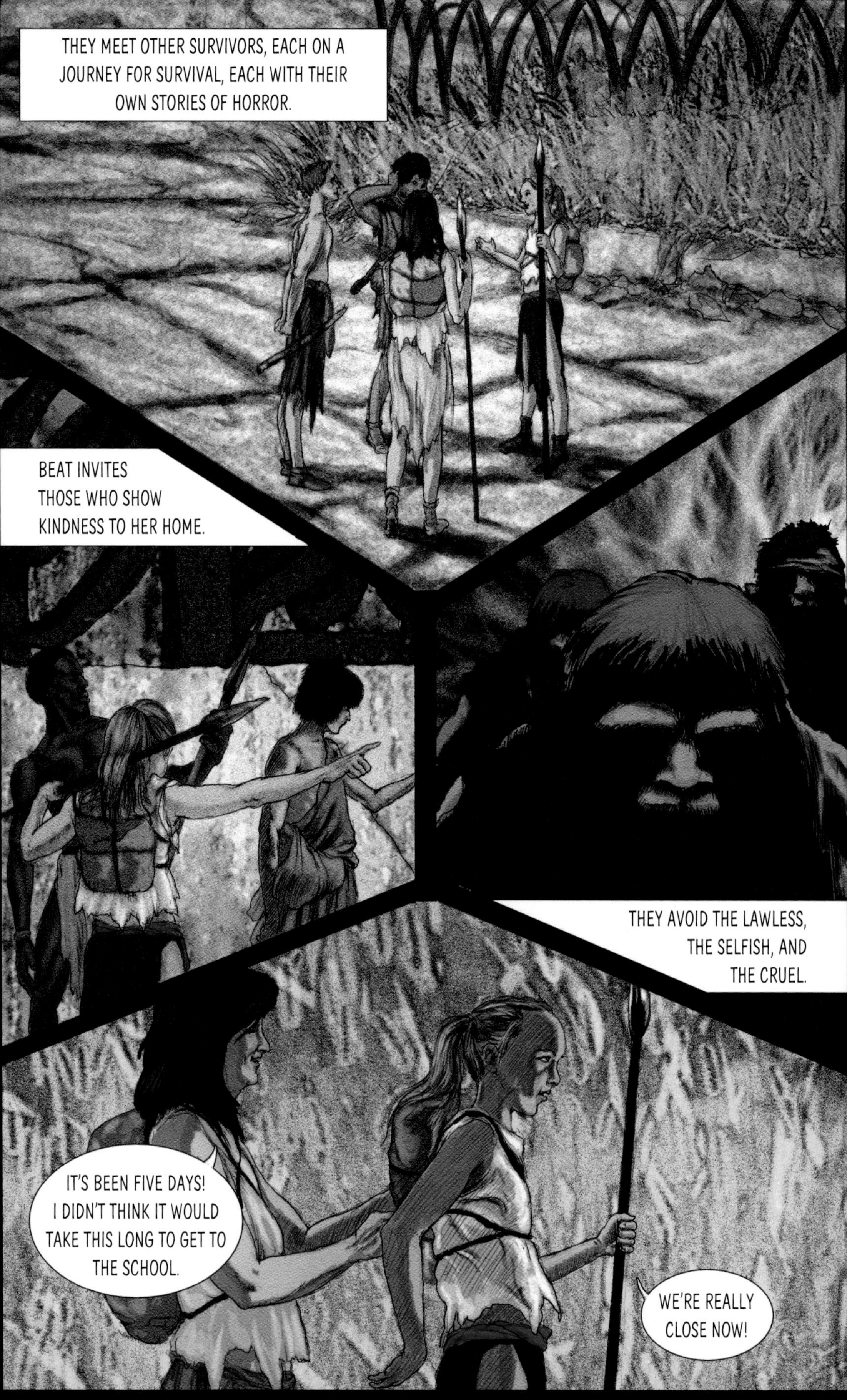
THEY MEET OTHER SURVIVORS, EACH ON A JOURNEY FOR SURVIVAL, EACH WITH THEIR OWN STORIES OF HORROR.
BEAT INVITES THOSE WHO SHOW KINDNESS TO HER HOME.
THEY AVOID THE LAWLESS, THE SELFISH, AND THE CRUEL.
IT'S BEEN FIVE DAYS! I DIDN'T THINK IT WOULD TAKE THIS LONG TO GET TO THE SCHOOL.
WE'RE REALLY CLOSE NOW!

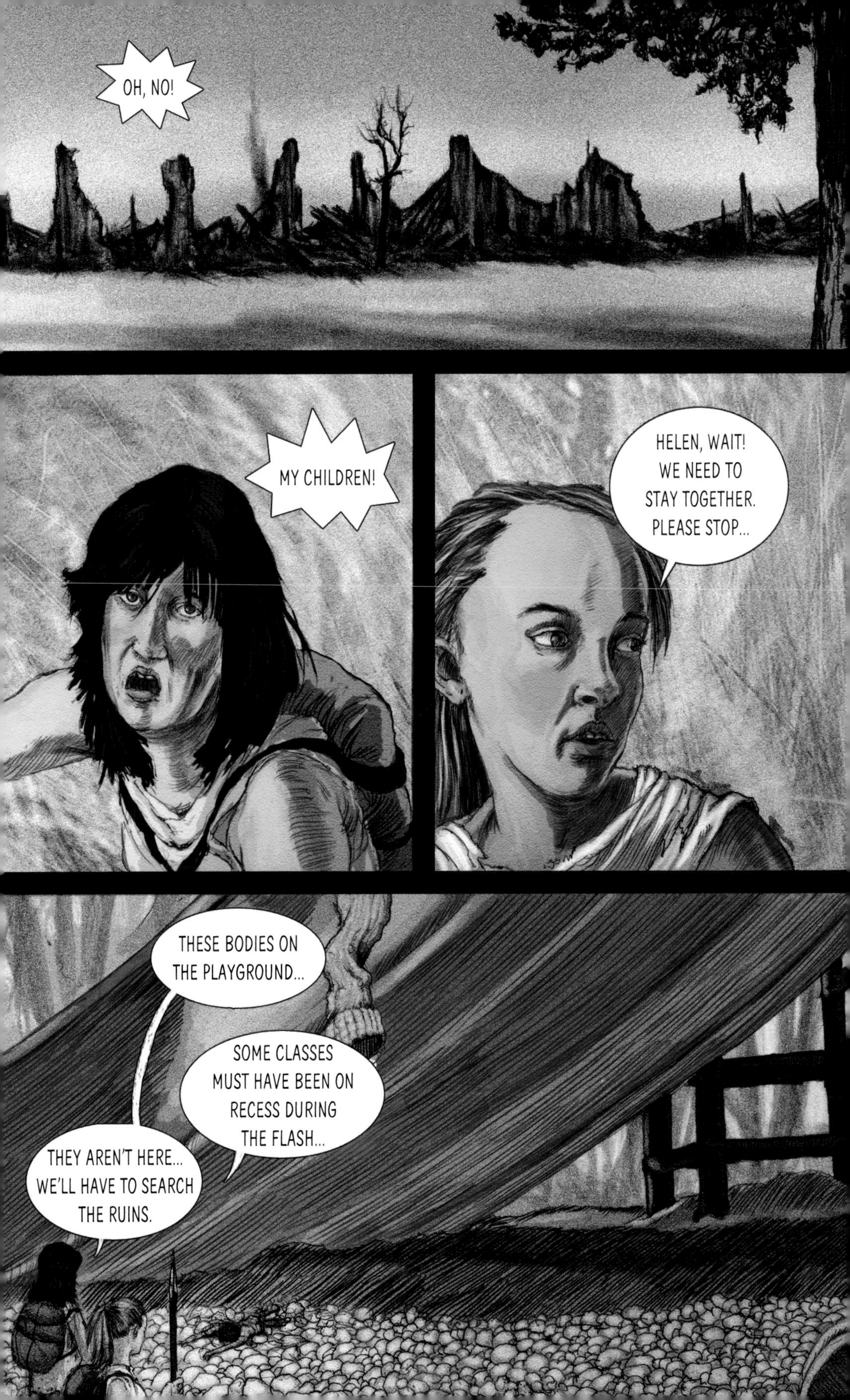
OH, NO!
MY CHILDREN!
HELEN, WAIT! WE NEED TO STAY TOGETHER. PLEASE STOP...
THESE BODIES ON THE PLAYGROUND...
SOME CLASSES MUST HAVE BEEN ON RECESS DURING THE FLASH...
THEY AREN'T HERE... WE'LL HAVE TO SEARCH THE RUINS.

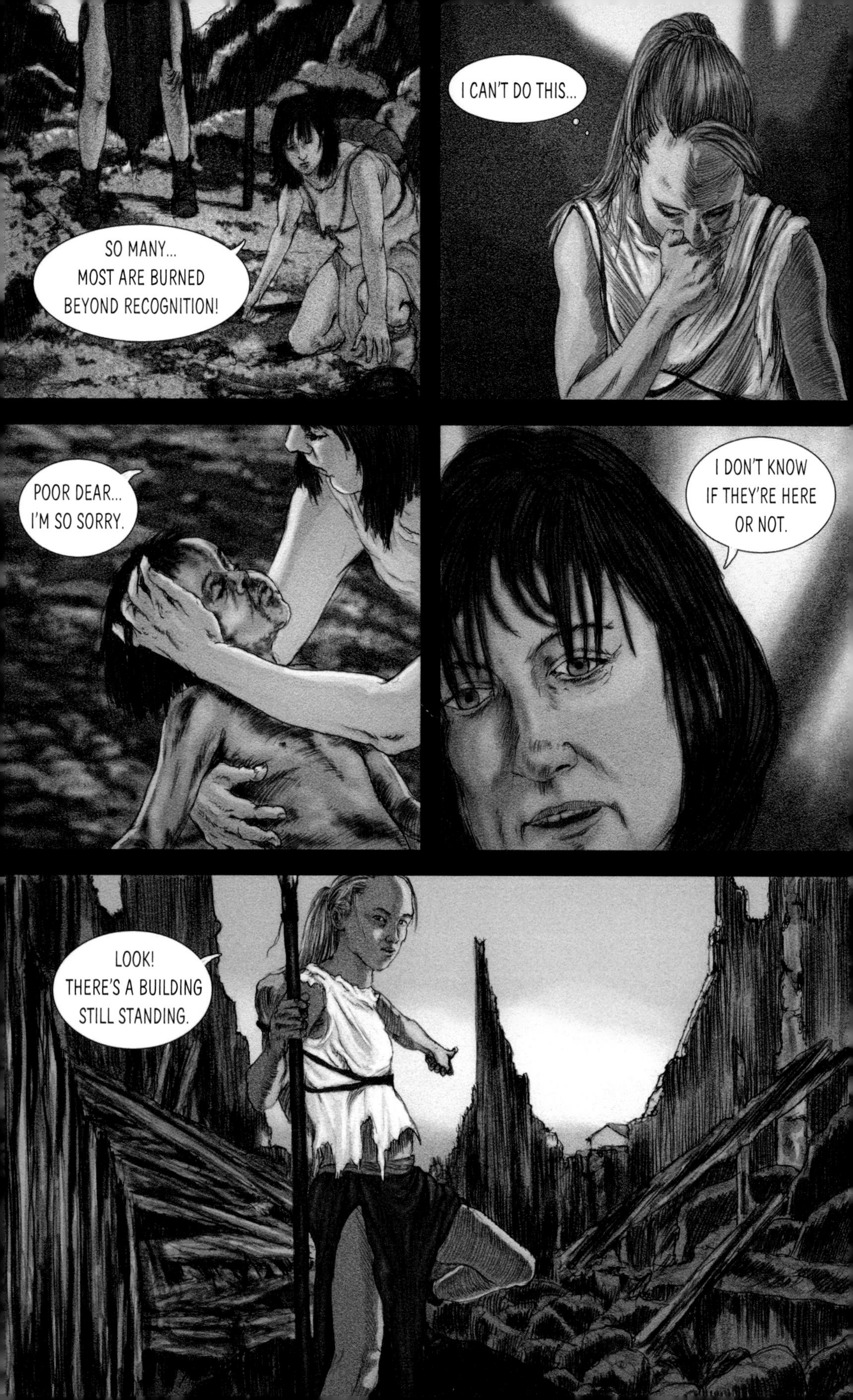
SO MANY...
MOST ARE BURNED
BEYOND RECOGNITION!
I CAN'T DO THIS...
POOR DEAR...
I'M SO SORRY.
I DON'T KNOW
IF THEY'RE HERE
OR NOT.
LOOK!
THERE'S A BUILDING
STILL STANDING.

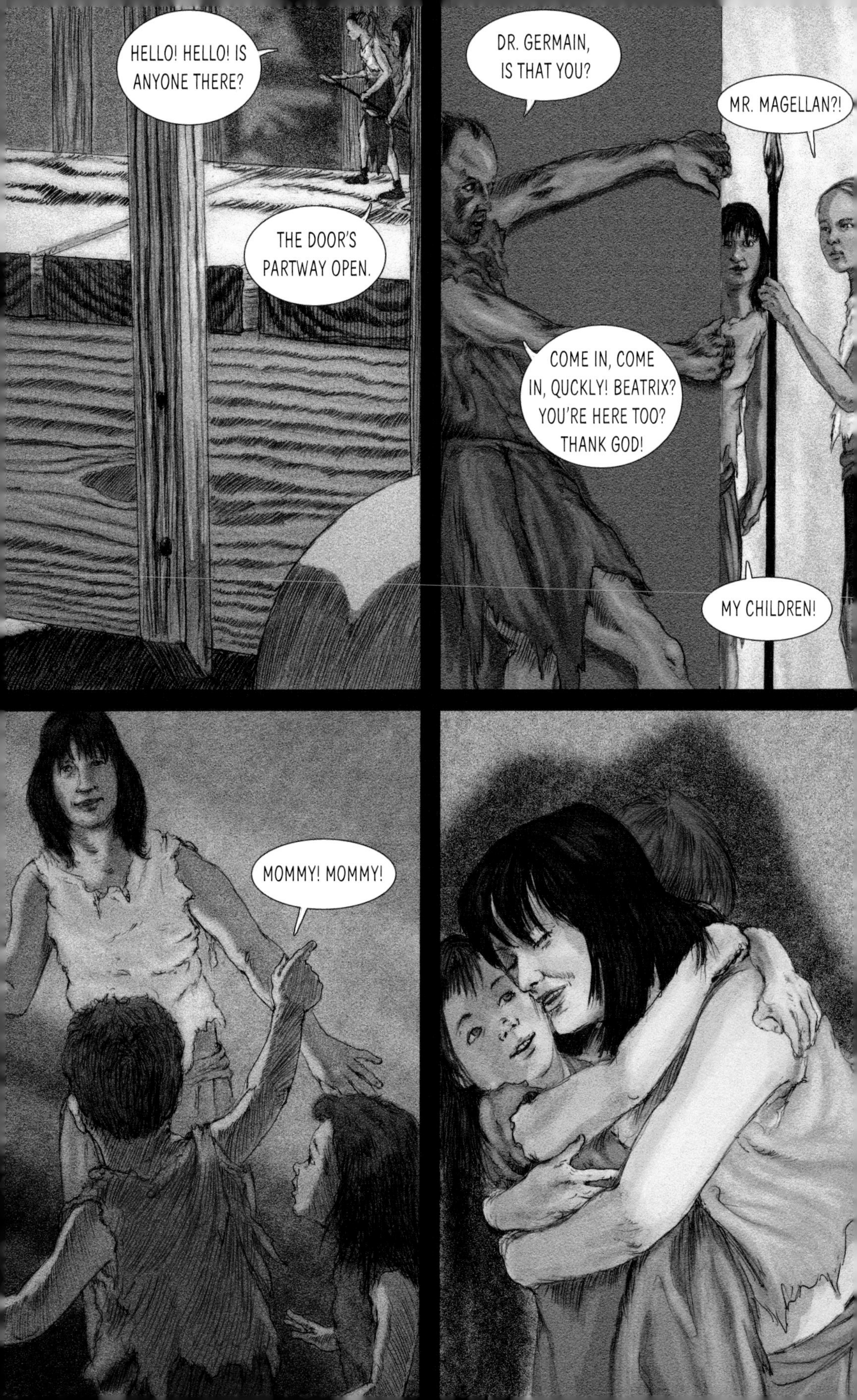
HELLO! HELLO! IS ANYONE THERE?
THE DOOR'S PARTWAY OPEN.
DR. GERMAIN, IS THAT YOU?
MR. MAGELLAN?!
COME IN, COME IN, QUCKLY! BEATRIX? YOU'RE HERE TOO? THANK GOD!
MY CHILDREN!
MOMMY! MOMMY!

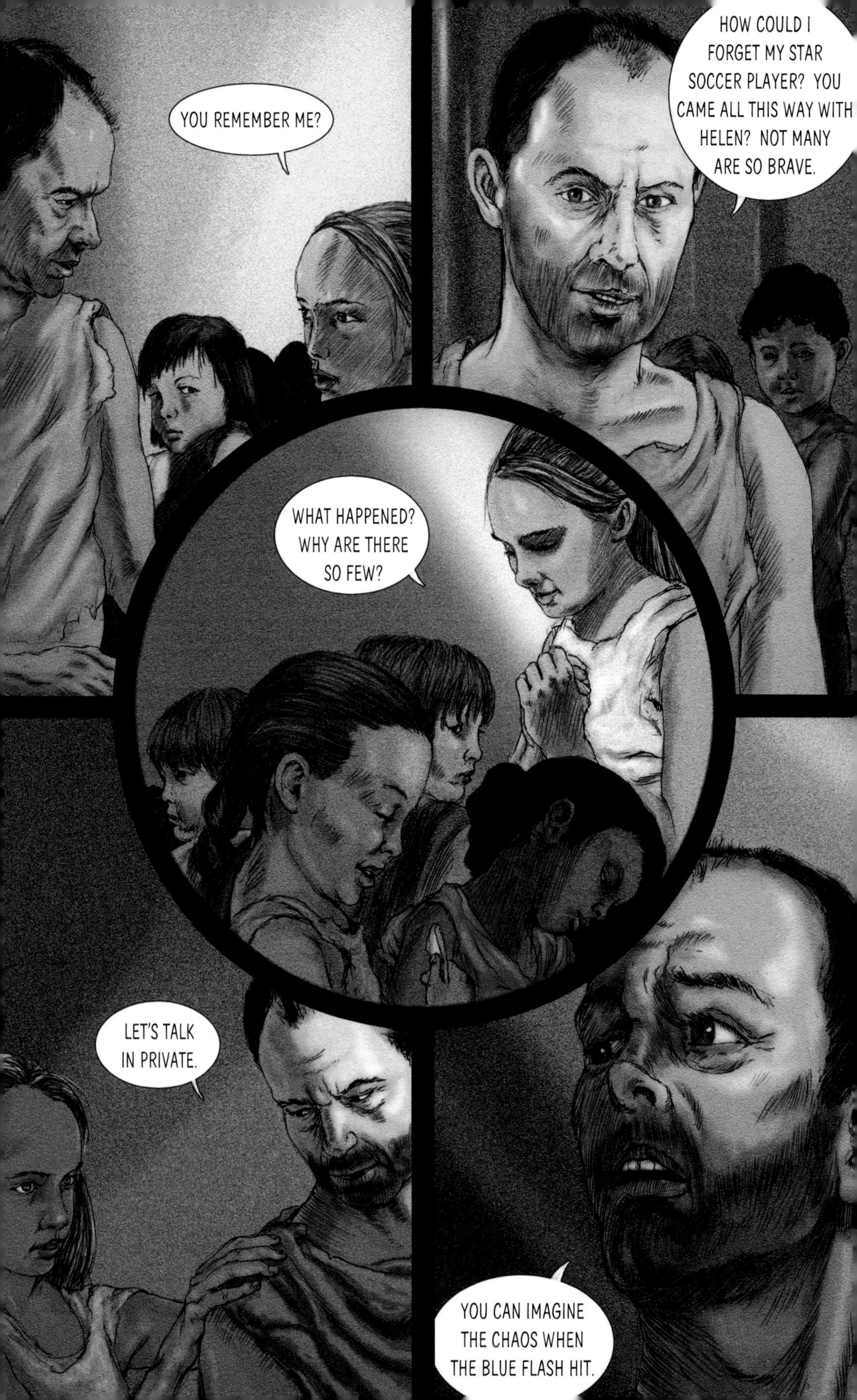
YOU REMEMBER ME?
HOW COULD I FORGET MY STAR SOCCER PLAYER? YOU CAME ALL THIS WAY WITH HELEN? NOT MANY ARE SO BRAVE.
WHAT HAPPENED? WHY ARE THERE SO FEW?
LET'S TALK IN PRIVATE.
YOU CAN IMAGINE THE CHAOS WHEN THE BLUE FLASH HIT.

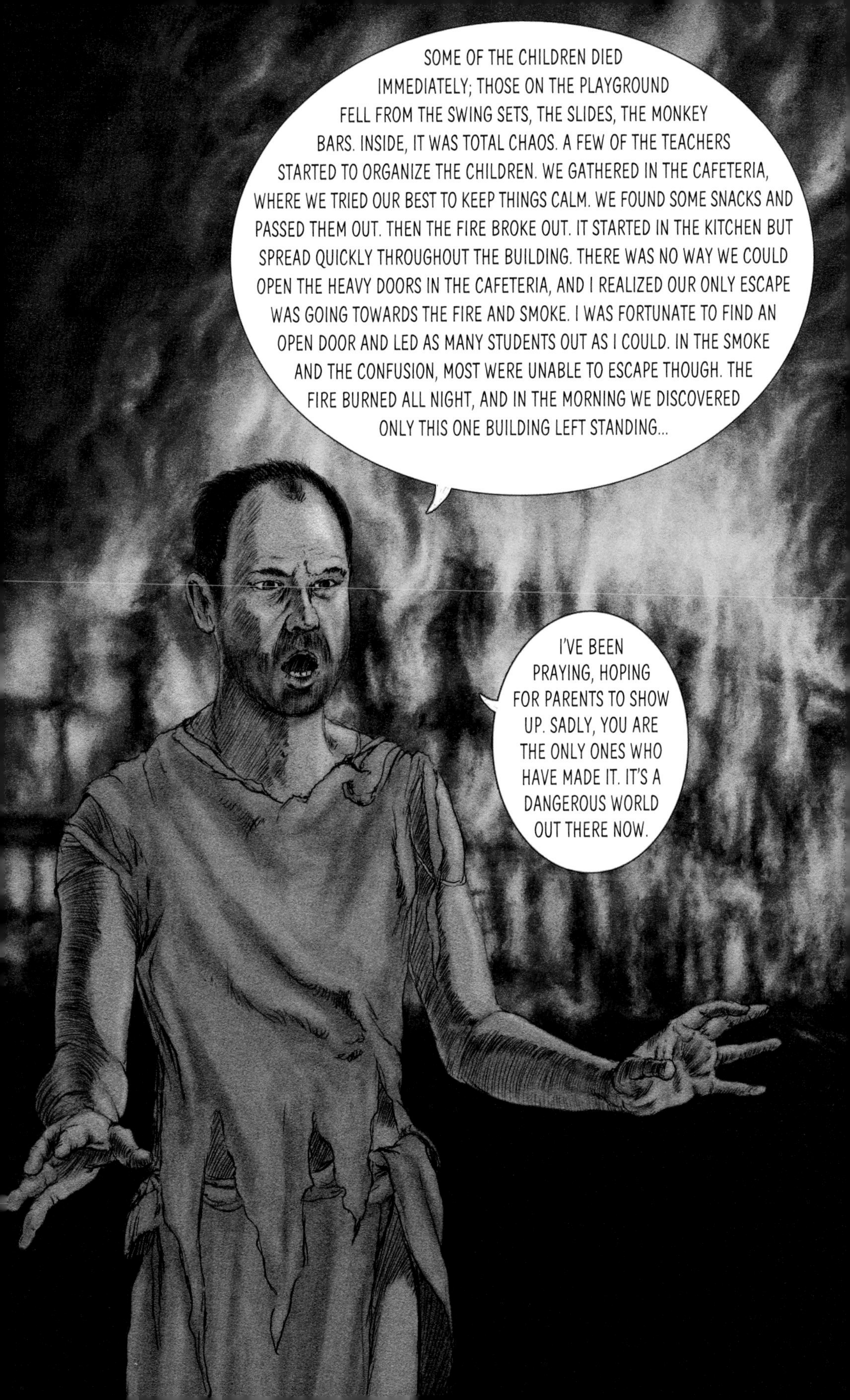
SOME OF THE CHILDREN DIED IMMEDIATELY; THOSE ON THE PLAYGROUND FELL FROM THE SWING SETS, THE SLIDES, THE MONKEY BARS. INSIDE, IT WAS TOTAL CHAOS. A FEW OF THE TEACHERS STARTED TO ORGANIZE THE CHILDREN. WE GATHERED IN THE CAFETERIA, WHERE WE TRIED OUR BEST TO KEEP THINGS CALM. WE FOUND SOME SNACKS AND PASSED THEM OUT. THEN THE FIRE BROKE OUT. IT STARTED IN THE KITCHEN BUT SPREAD QUICKLY THROUGHOUT THE BUILDING. THERE WAS NO WAY WE COULD OPEN THE HEAVY DOORS IN THE CAFETERIA, AND I REALIZED OUR ONLY ESCAPE WAS GOING TOWARDS THE FIRE AND SMOKE. I WAS FORTUNATE TO FIND AN OPEN DOOR AND LED AS MANY STUDENTS OUT AS I COULD. IN THE SMOKE AND THE CONFUSION, MOST WERE UNABLE TO ESCAPE THOUGH. THE FIRE BURNED ALL NIGHT, AND IN THE MORNING WE DISCOVERED ONLY THIS ONE BUILDING LEFT STANDING...
I'VE BEEN PRAYING, HOPING FOR PARENTS TO SHOW UP. SADLY, YOU ARE THE ONLY ONES WHO HAVE MADE IT. IT'S A DANGEROUS WORLD OUT THERE NOW.

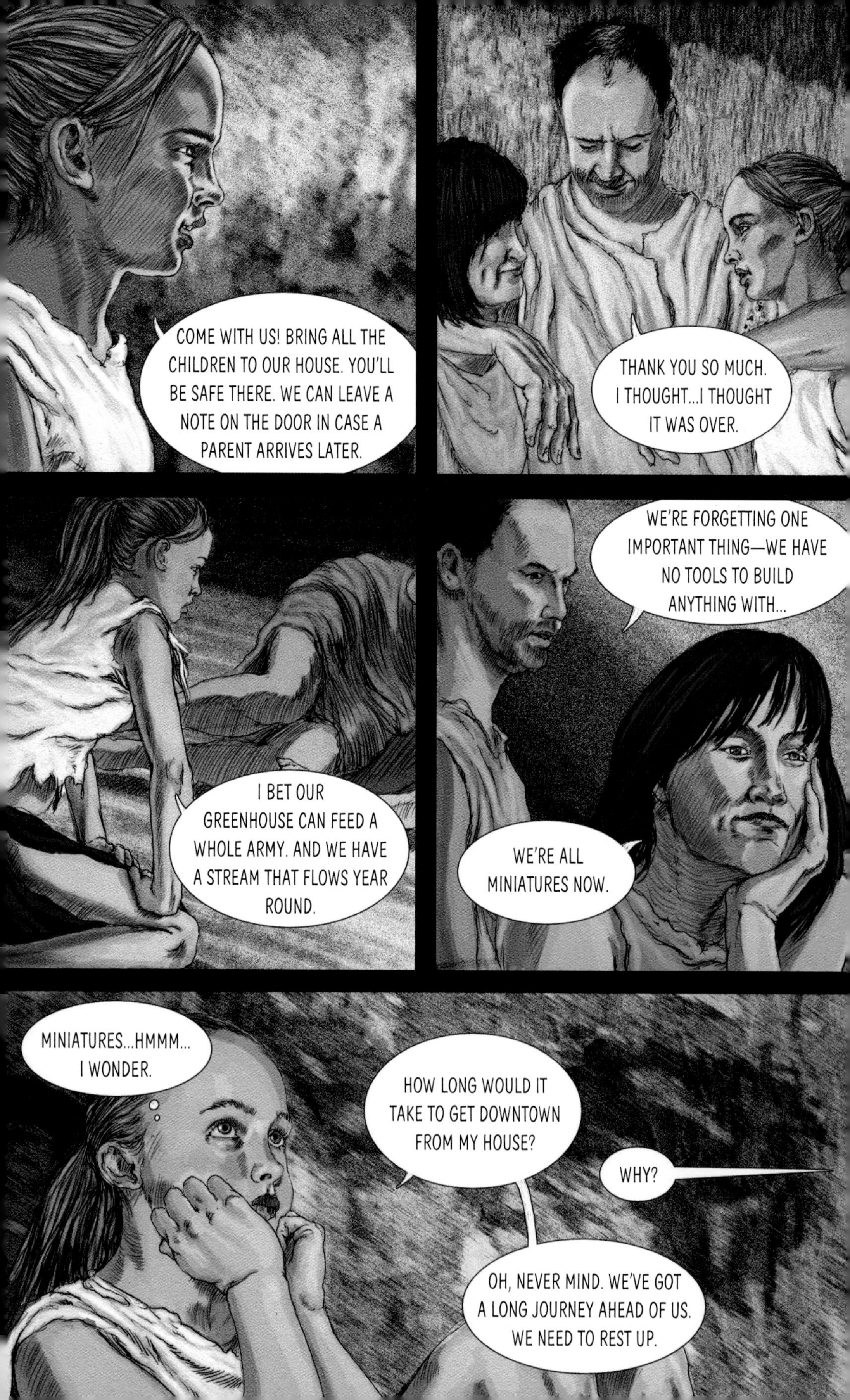

COME WITH US! BRING ALL THE CHILDREN TO OUR HOUSE. YOU'LL BE SAFE THERE. WE CAN LEAVE A NOTE ON THE DOOR IN CASE A PARENT ARRIVES LATER.
THANK YOU SO MUCH. I THOUGHT...I THOUGHT IT WAS OVER.
I BET OUR GREENHOUSE CAN FEED A WHOLE ARMY. AND WE HAVE A STREAM THAT FLOWS YEAR ROUND.
WE'RE FORGETTING ONE IMPORTANT THING—WE HAVE NO TOOLS TO BUILD ANYTHING WITH...
WE'RE ALL MINIATURES NOW.
MINIATURES...HMMM... I WONDER.
HOW LONG WOULD IT TAKE TO GET DOWNTOWN FROM MY HOUSE?
WHY?
OH, NEVER MIND. WE'VE GOT A LONG JOURNEY AHEAD OF US. WE NEED TO REST UP.

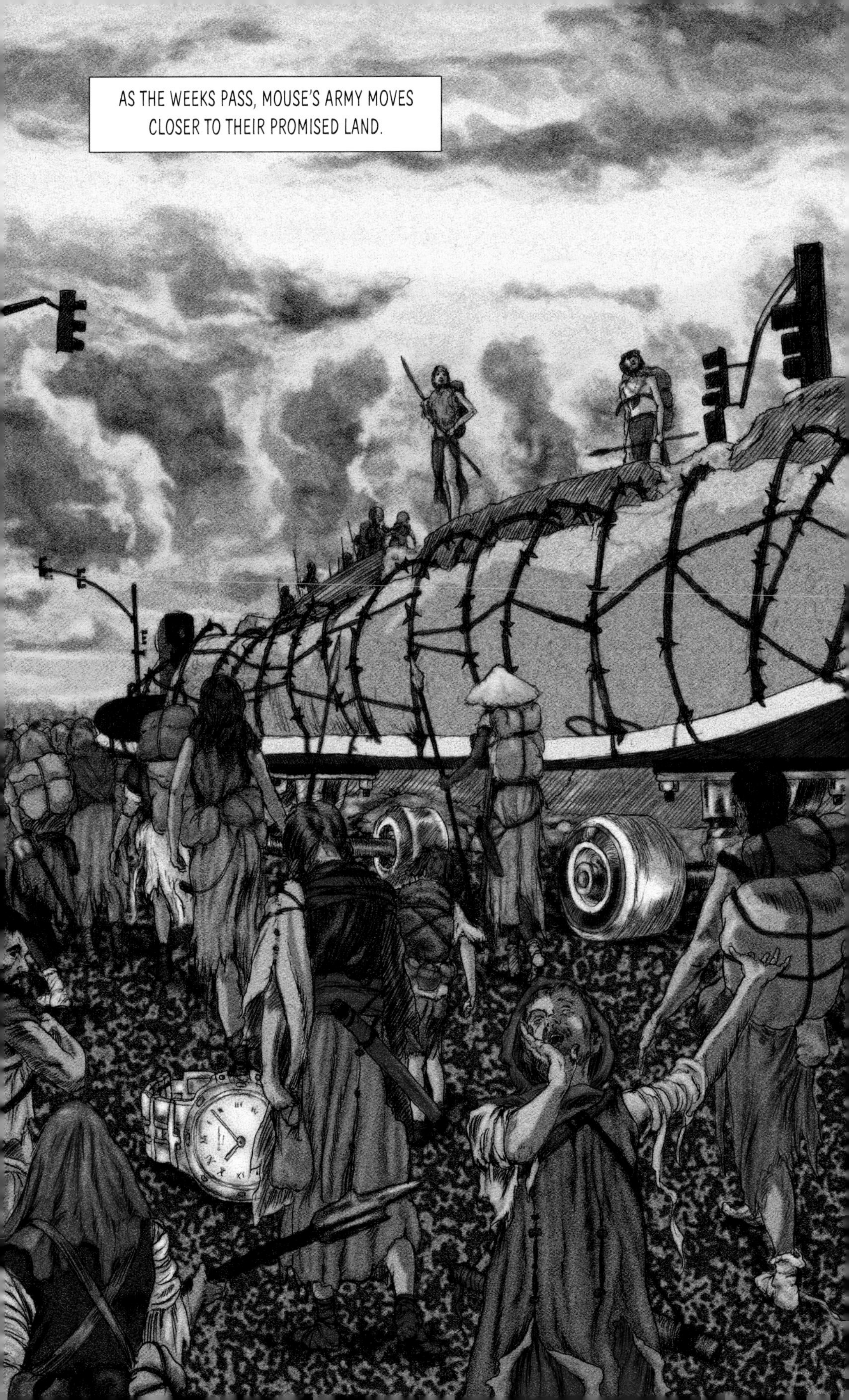
AS THE WEEKS PASS, MOUSE'S ARMY MOVES CLOSER TO THEIR PROMISED LAND.

THEY LIVE UNDER A STRICT SET OF RULES:
PROTECT THE WEAK...

AND PUNISH THE WICKED.

LIVING IN THE SMALL, THE ONCE FRIGHTENED
GROUP OF OFFICE WORKERS BLOSSOM INTO
SEASONED WARRIORS.

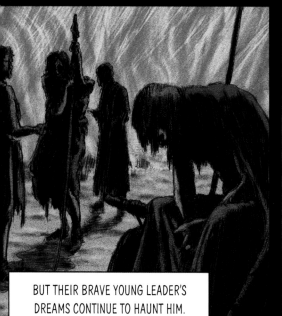

BUT THEIR BRAVE YOUNG LEADER'S
DREAMS CONTINUE TO HAUNT HIM.

AND HIS FATHER'S CRYPTIC MESSAGE PROVIDES
NO FURTHER CLUES TO THEIR FUTURE.

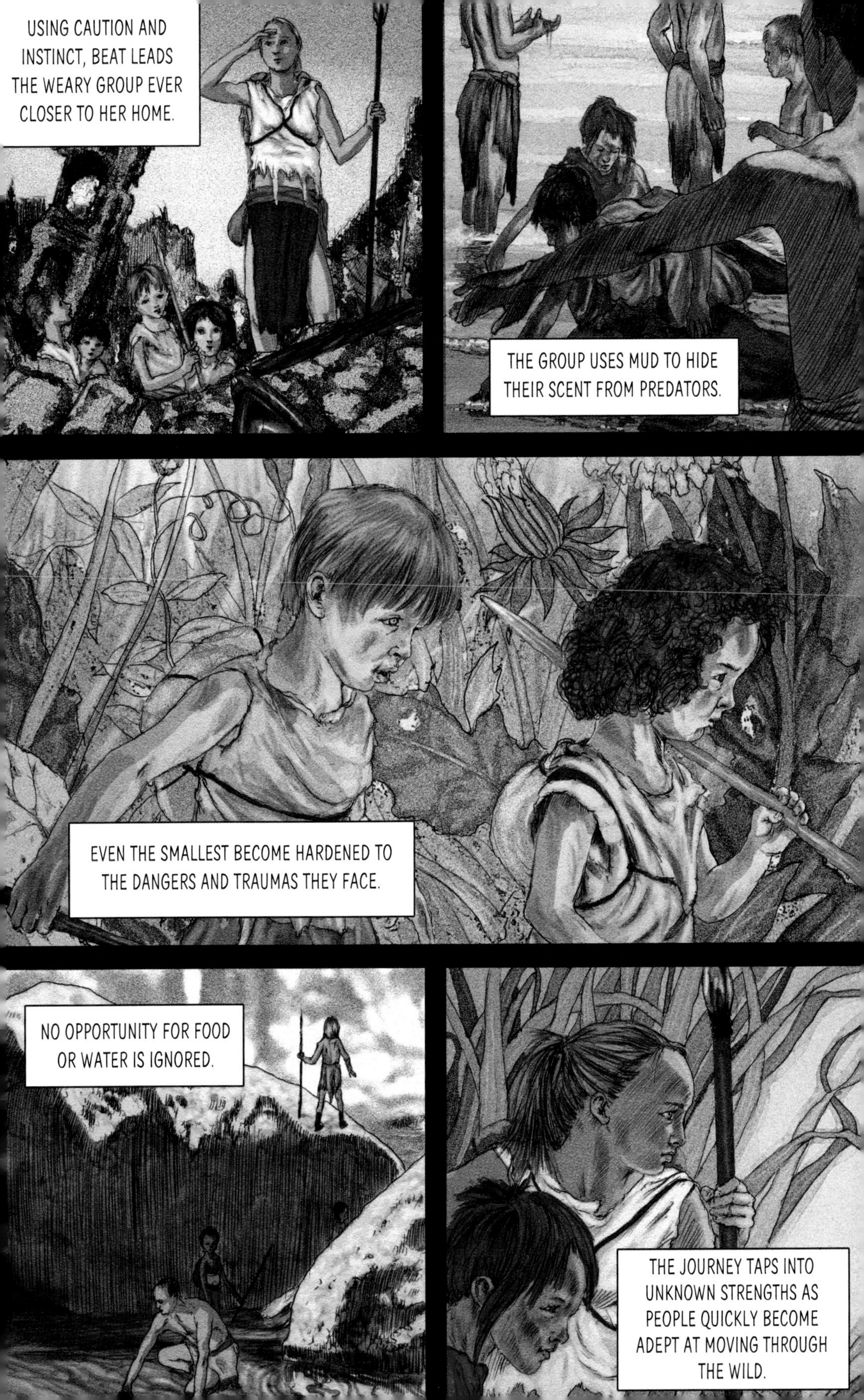
USING CAUTION AND INSTINCT, BEAT LEADS THE WEARY GROUP EVER CLOSER TO HER HOME.
THE GROUP USES MUD TO HIDE THEIR SCENT FROM PREDATORS.
EVEN THE SMALLEST BECOME HARDENED TO THE DANGERS AND TRAUMAS THEY FACE.
NO OPPORTUNITY FOR FOOD OR WATER IS IGNORED.
THE JOURNEY TAPS INTO UNKNOWN STRENGTHS AS PEOPLE QUICKLY BECOME ADEPT AT MOVING THROUGH THE WILD.

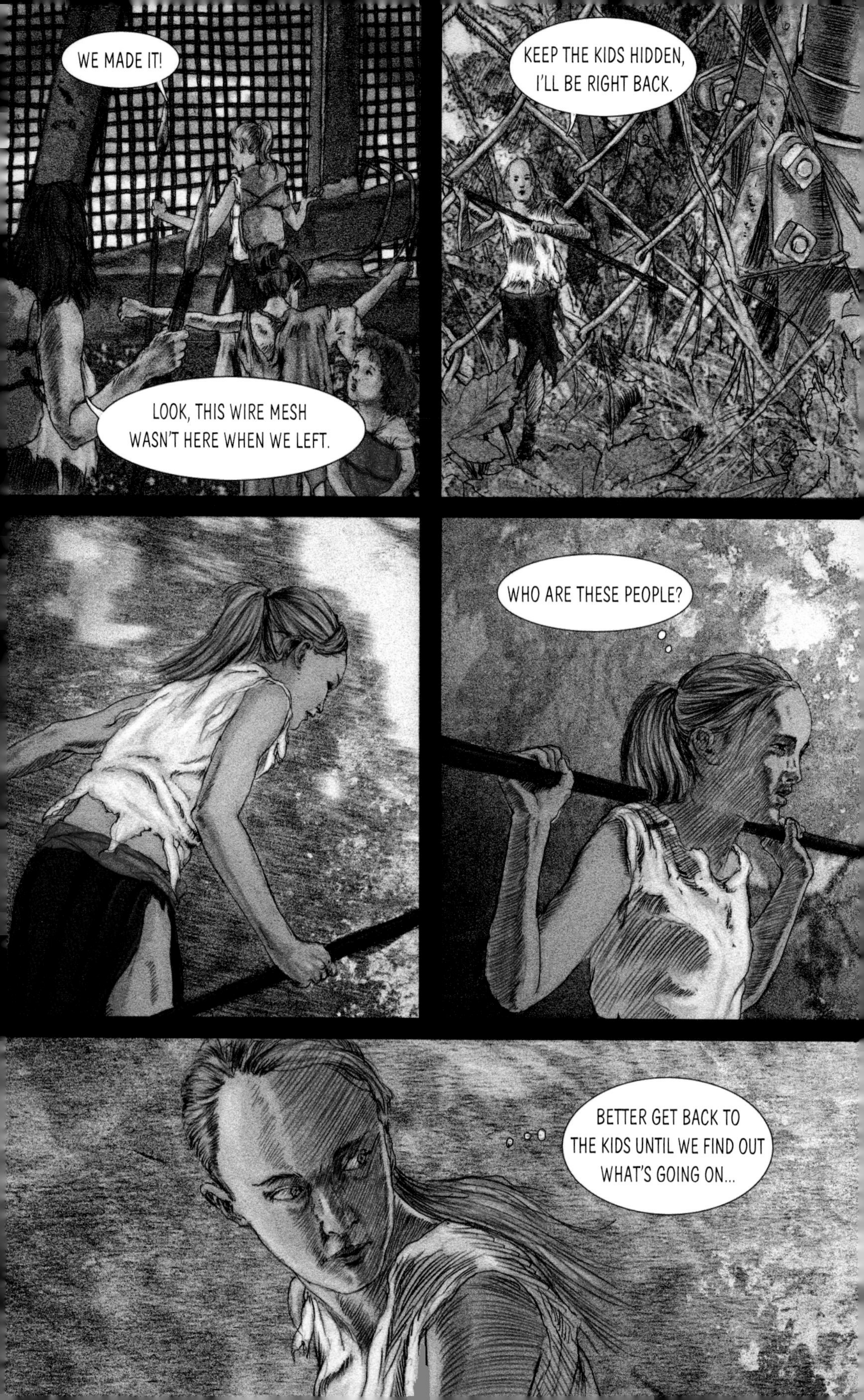
WE MADE IT!
LOOK, THIS WIRE MESH WASN'T HERE WHEN WE LEFT.
KEEP THE KIDS HIDDEN, I'LL BE RIGHT BACK.
WHO ARE THESE PEOPLE?
BETTER GET BACK TO THE KIDS UNTIL WE FIND OUT WHAT'S GOING ON...

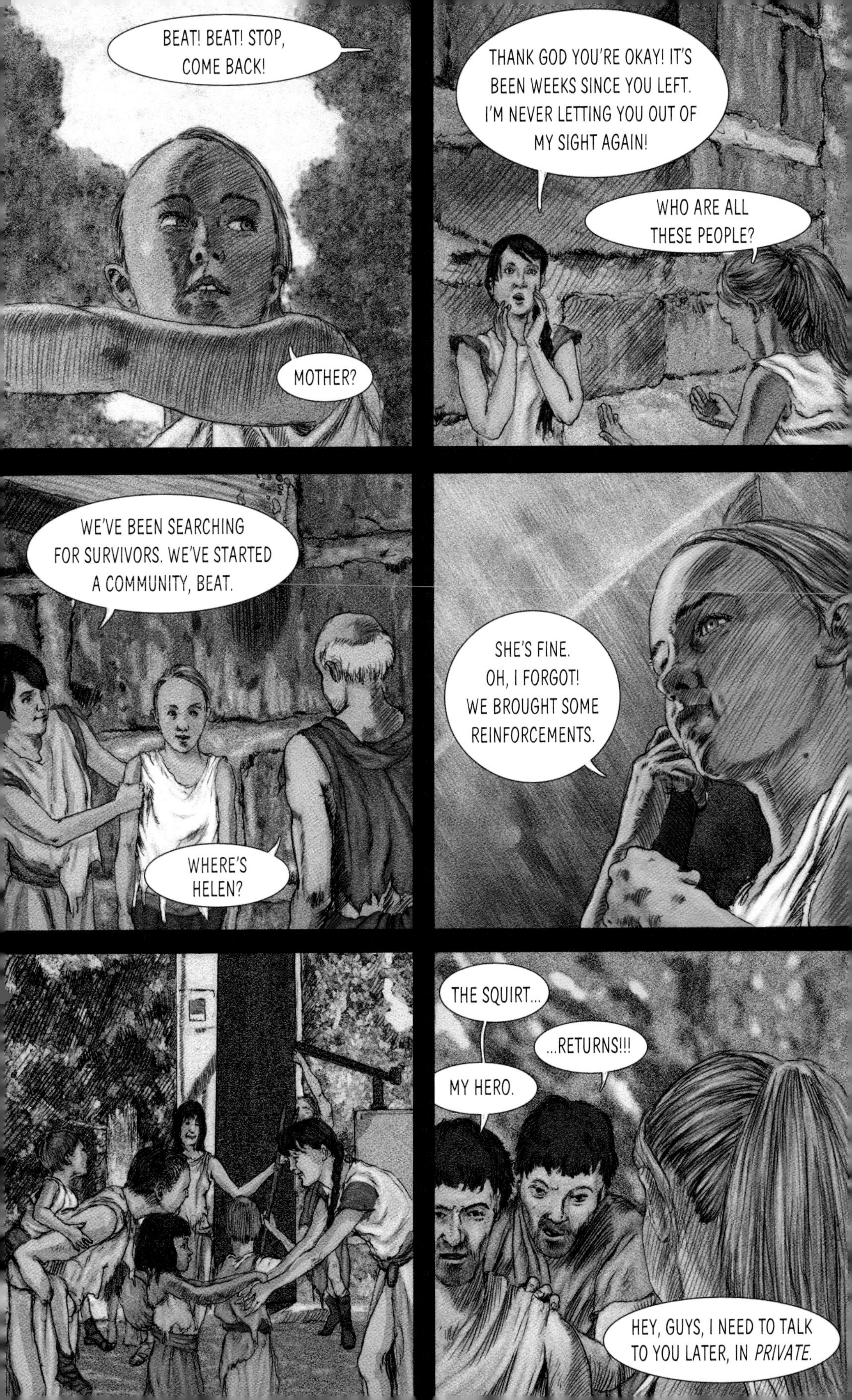
BEAT! BEAT! STOP, COME BACK!
MOTHER?
THANK GOD YOU'RE OKAY! IT'S BEEN WEEKS SINCE YOU LEFT. I'M NEVER LETTING YOU OUT OF MY SIGHT AGAIN!
WHO ARE ALL THESE PEOPLE?
WE'VE BEEN SEARCHING FOR SURVIVORS. WE'VE STARTED A COMMUNITY, BEAT.
WHERE'S HELEN?
SHE'S FINE. OH, I FORGOT! WE BROUGHT SOME REINFORCEMENTS.
THE SQUIRT...
...RETURNS!!!
MY HERO.
HEY, GUYS, I NEED TO TALK TO YOU LATER, IN *PRIVATE*.

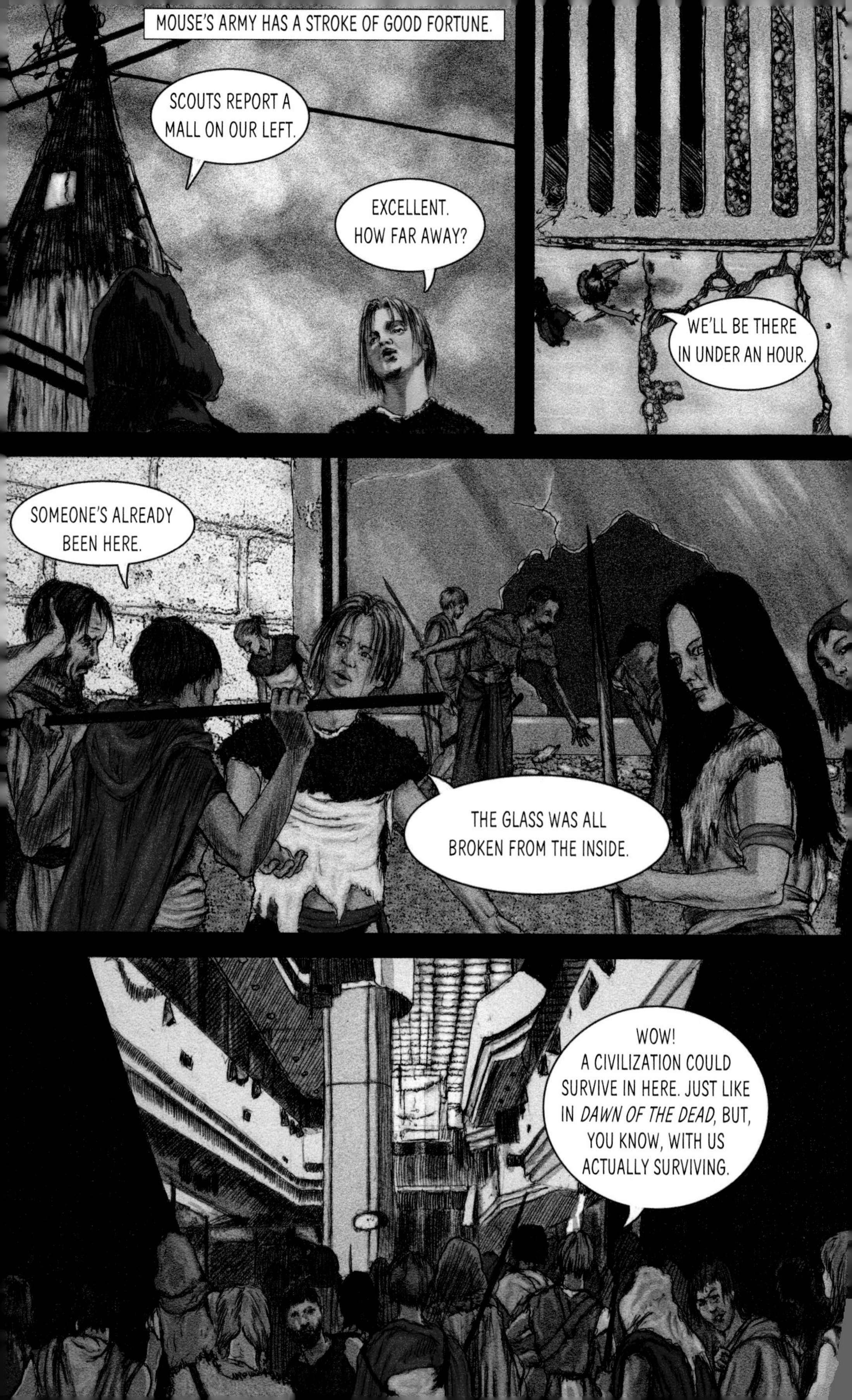
MOUSE'S ARMY HAS A STROKE OF GOOD FORTUNE.
SCOUTS REPORT A MALL ON OUR LEFT.
EXCELLENT. HOW FAR AWAY?
WE'LL BE THERE IN UNDER AN HOUR.
SOMEONE'S ALREADY BEEN HERE.
THE GLASS WAS ALL BROKEN FROM THE INSIDE.
WOW! A CIVILIZATION COULD SURVIVE IN HERE. JUST LIKE IN *DAWN OF THE DEAD*, BUT, YOU KNOW, WITH US ACTUALLY SURVIVING.

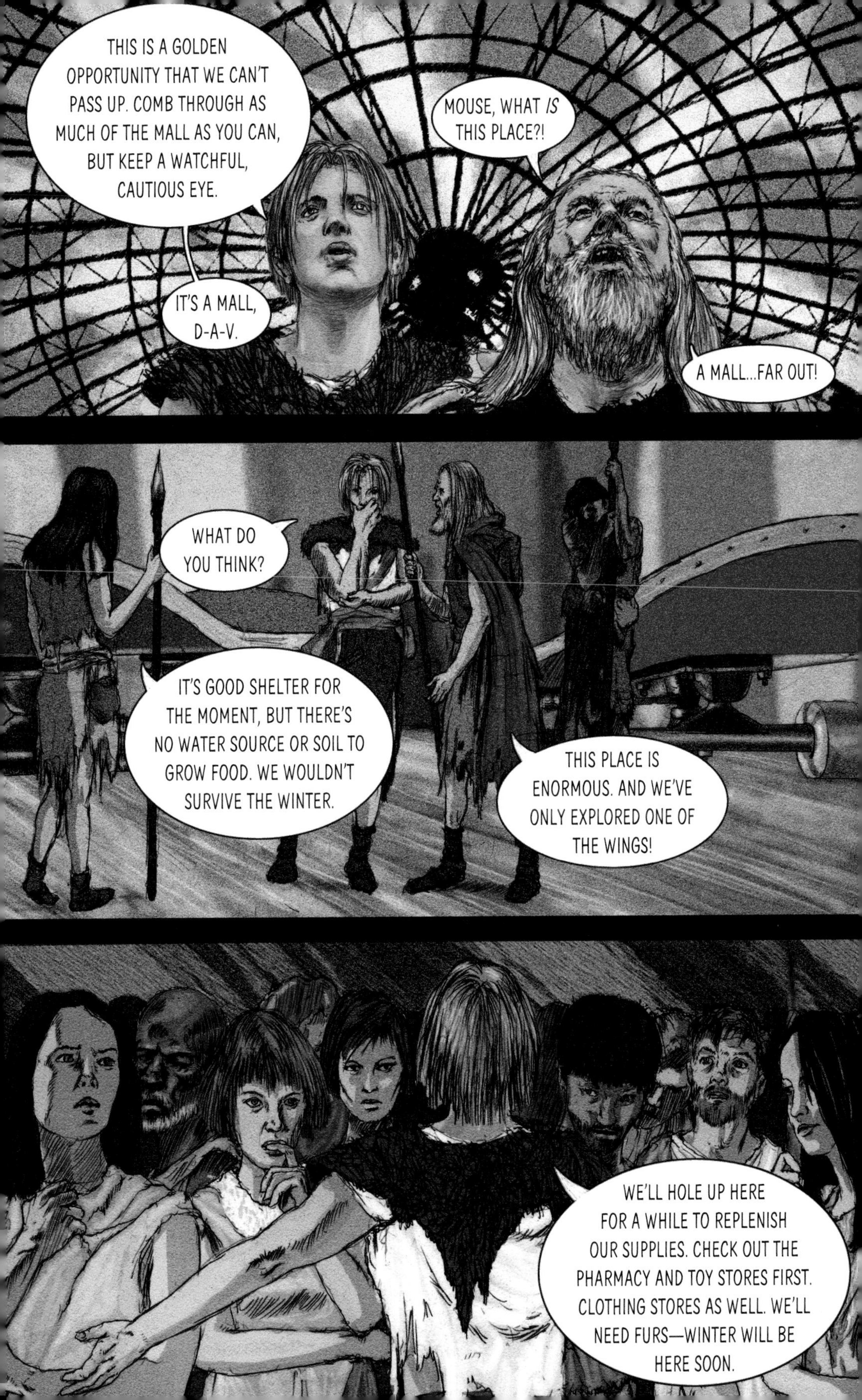
THIS IS A GOLDEN OPPORTUNITY THAT WE CAN'T PASS UP. COMB THROUGH AS MUCH OF THE MALL AS YOU CAN, BUT KEEP A WATCHFUL, CAUTIOUS EYE.
MOUSE, WHAT *IS* THIS PLACE?!
IT'S A MALL, D-A-V.
A MALL...FAR OUT!
WHAT DO YOU THINK?
IT'S GOOD SHELTER FOR THE MOMENT, BUT THERE'S NO WATER SOURCE OR SOIL TO GROW FOOD. WE WOULDN'T SURVIVE THE WINTER.
THIS PLACE IS ENORMOUS. AND WE'VE ONLY EXPLORED ONE OF THE WINGS!
WE'LL HOLE UP HERE FOR A WHILE TO REPLENISH OUR SUPPLIES. CHECK OUT THE PHARMACY AND TOY STORES FIRST. CLOTHING STORES AS WELL. WE'LL NEED FURS—WINTER WILL BE HERE SOON.

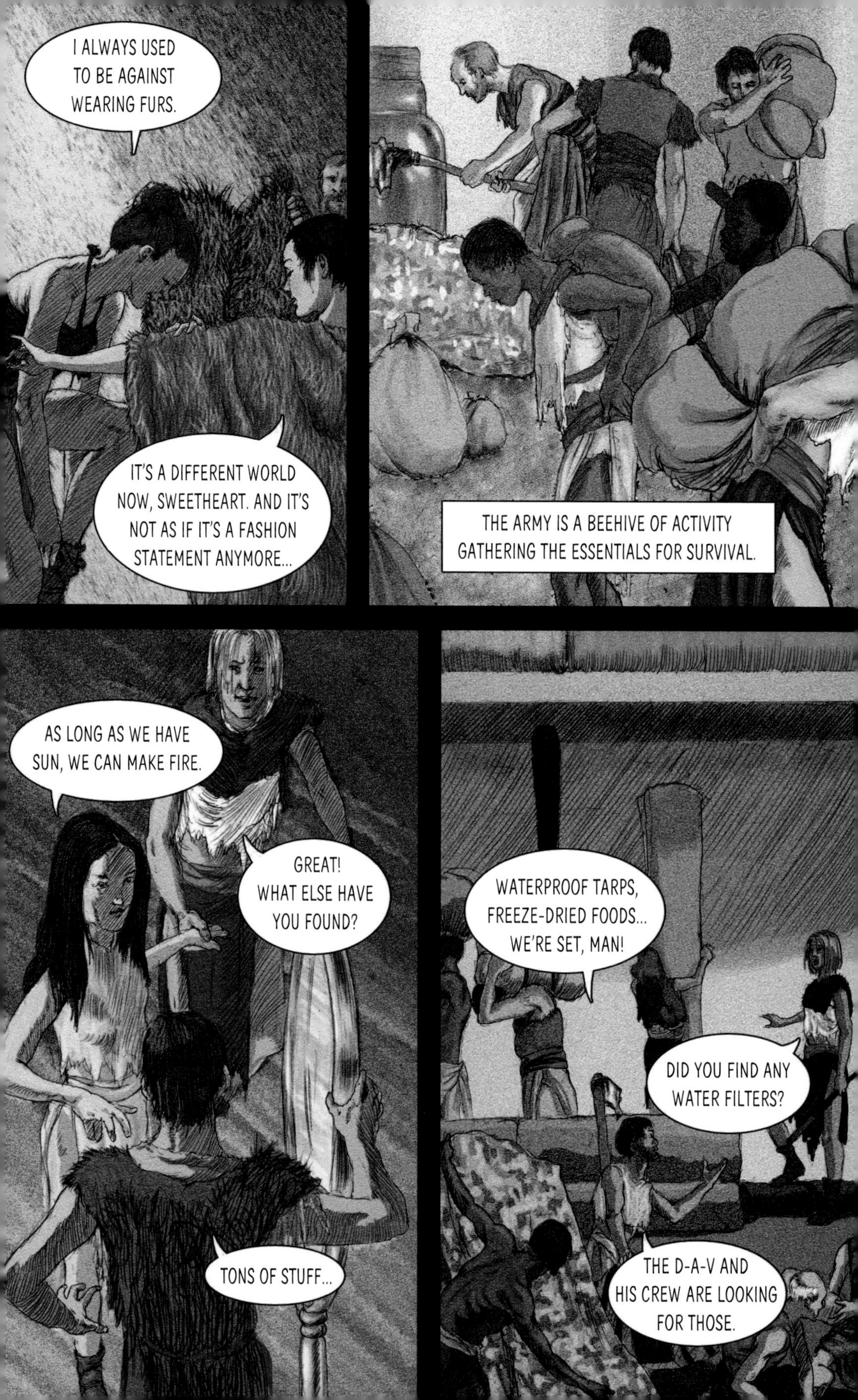
I ALWAYS USED TO BE AGAINST WEARING FURS.
IT'S A DIFFERENT WORLD NOW, SWEETHEART. AND IT'S NOT AS IF IT'S A FASHION STATEMENT ANYMORE...
THE ARMY IS A BEEHIVE OF ACTIVITY GATHERING THE ESSENTIALS FOR SURVIVAL.
AS LONG AS WE HAVE SUN, WE CAN MAKE FIRE.
GREAT! WHAT ELSE HAVE YOU FOUND?
TONS OF STUFF...
WATERPROOF TARPS, FREEZE-DRIED FOODS... WE'RE SET, MAN!
DID YOU FIND ANY WATER FILTERS?
THE D-A-V AND HIS CREW ARE LOOKING FOR THOSE.

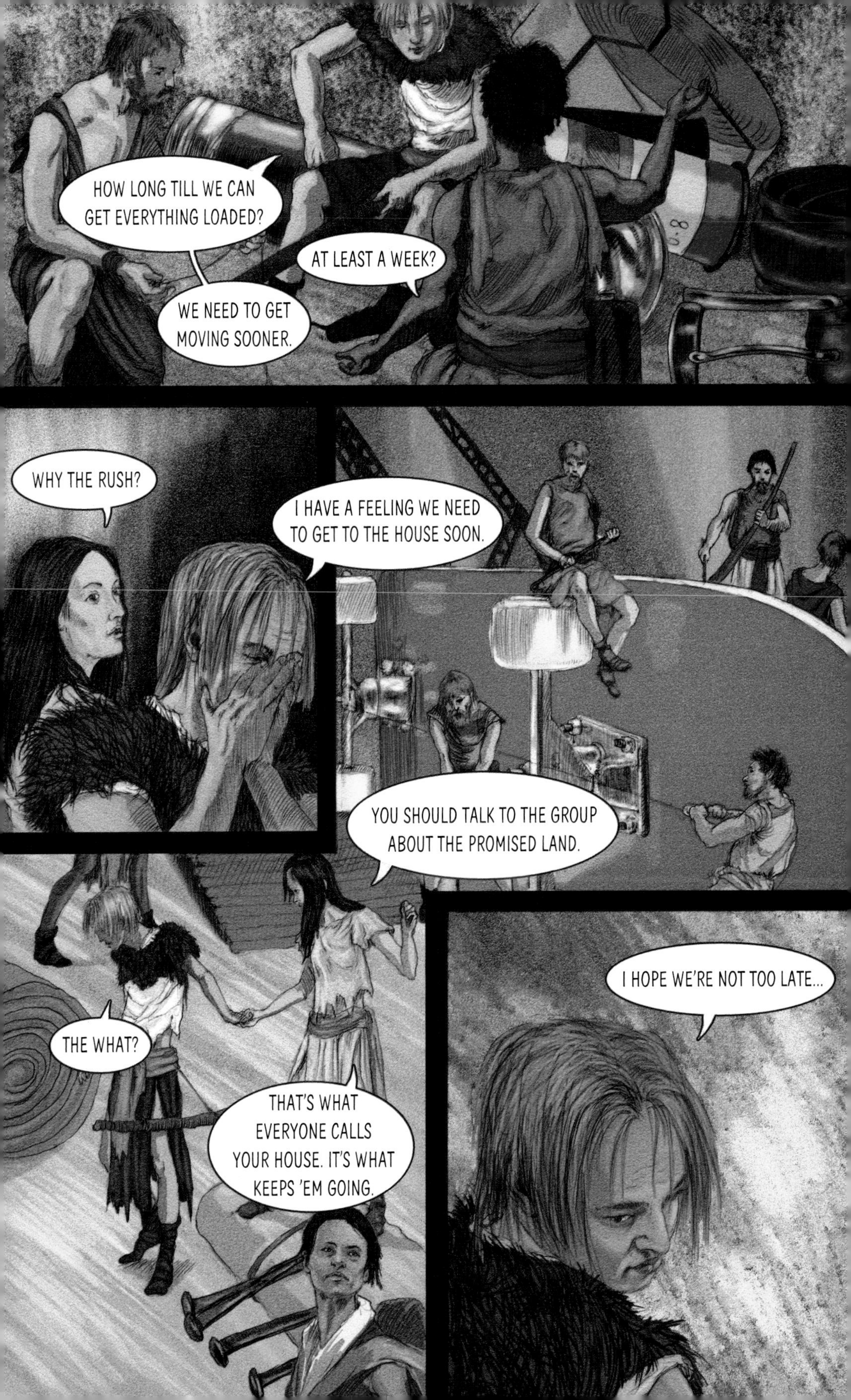
HOW LONG TILL WE CAN GET EVERYTHING LOADED?
AT LEAST A WEEK?
WE NEED TO GET MOVING SOONER.
WHY THE RUSH?
I HAVE A FEELING WE NEED TO GET TO THE HOUSE SOON.
YOU SHOULD TALK TO THE GROUP ABOUT THE PROMISED LAND.
THE WHAT?
THAT'S WHAT EVERYONE CALLS YOUR HOUSE. IT'S WHAT KEEPS 'EM GOING.
I HOPE WE'RE NOT TOO LATE...

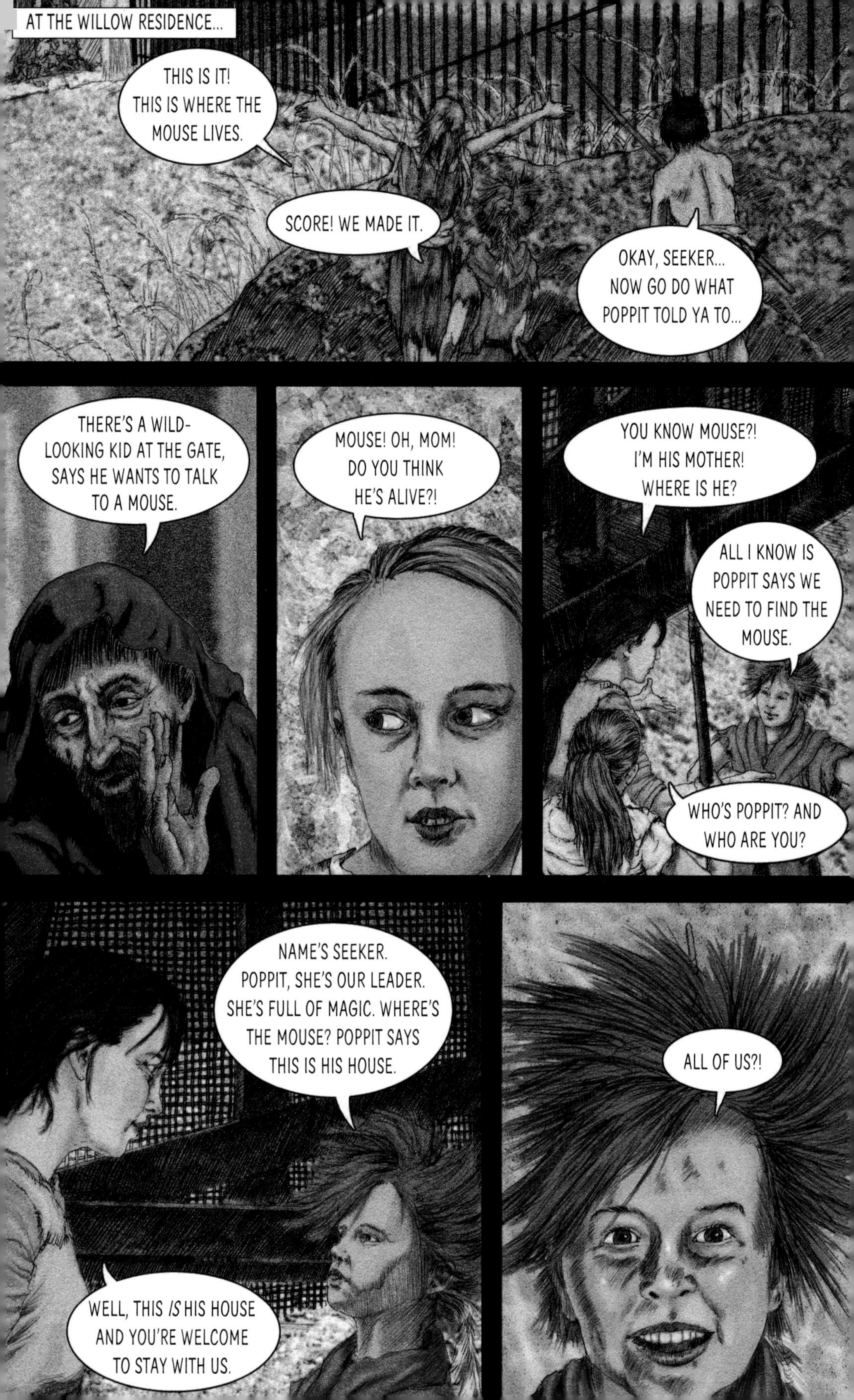
AT THE WILLOW RESIDENCE...
THIS IS IT! THIS IS WHERE THE MOUSE LIVES.
SCORE! WE MADE IT.
OKAY, SEEKER... NOW GO DO WHAT POPPIT TOLD YA TO...
THERE'S A WILD-LOOKING KID AT THE GATE, SAYS HE WANTS TO TALK TO A MOUSE.
MOUSE! OH, MOM! DO YOU THINK HE'S ALIVE?!
YOU KNOW MOUSE?! I'M HIS MOTHER! WHERE IS HE?
ALL I KNOW IS POPPIT SAYS WE NEED TO FIND THE MOUSE.
WHO'S POPPIT? AND WHO ARE YOU?
NAME'S SEEKER. POPPIT, SHE'S OUR LEADER. SHE'S FULL OF MAGIC. WHERE'S THE MOUSE? POPPIT SAYS THIS IS HIS HOUSE.
WELL, THIS *IS* HIS HOUSE AND YOU'RE WELCOME TO STAY WITH US.
ALL OF US?!

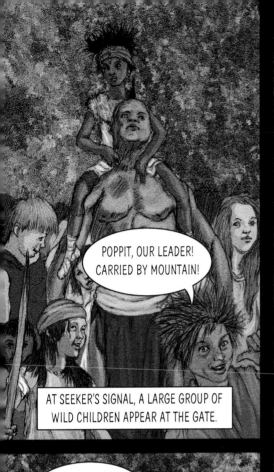

POPPIT, OUR LEADER! CARRIED BY MOUNTAIN!

AT SEEKER'S SIGNAL, A LARGE GROUP OF WILD CHILDREN APPEAR AT THE GATE.

IS IT TRUE? MOUSE ISN'T HERE? HOW DISTURBING...

HOW IS IT YOU KNOW MY SON?

POPPIT SEES EVERYTHING.

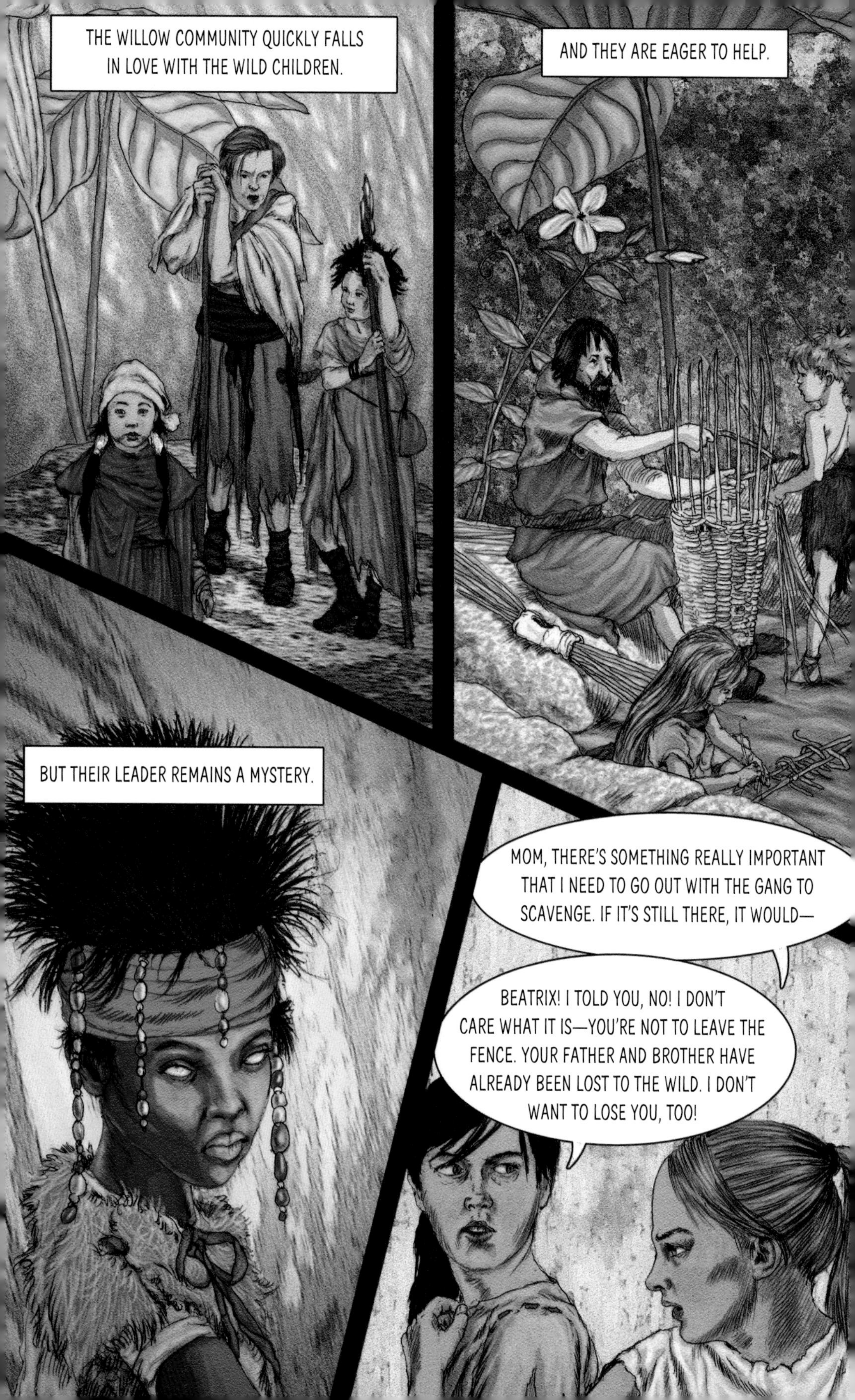
THE WILLOW COMMUNITY QUICKLY FALLS IN LOVE WITH THE WILD CHILDREN.
AND THEY ARE EAGER TO HELP.
BUT THEIR LEADER REMAINS A MYSTERY.
MOM, THERE'S SOMETHING REALLY IMPORTANT THAT I NEED TO GO OUT WITH THE GANG TO SCAVENGE. IF IT'S STILL THERE, IT WOULD—
BEATRIX! I TOLD YOU, NO! I DON'T CARE WHAT IT IS—YOU'RE NOT TO LEAVE THE FENCE. YOUR FATHER AND BROTHER HAVE ALREADY BEEN LOST TO THE WILD. I DON'T WANT TO LOSE YOU, TOO!

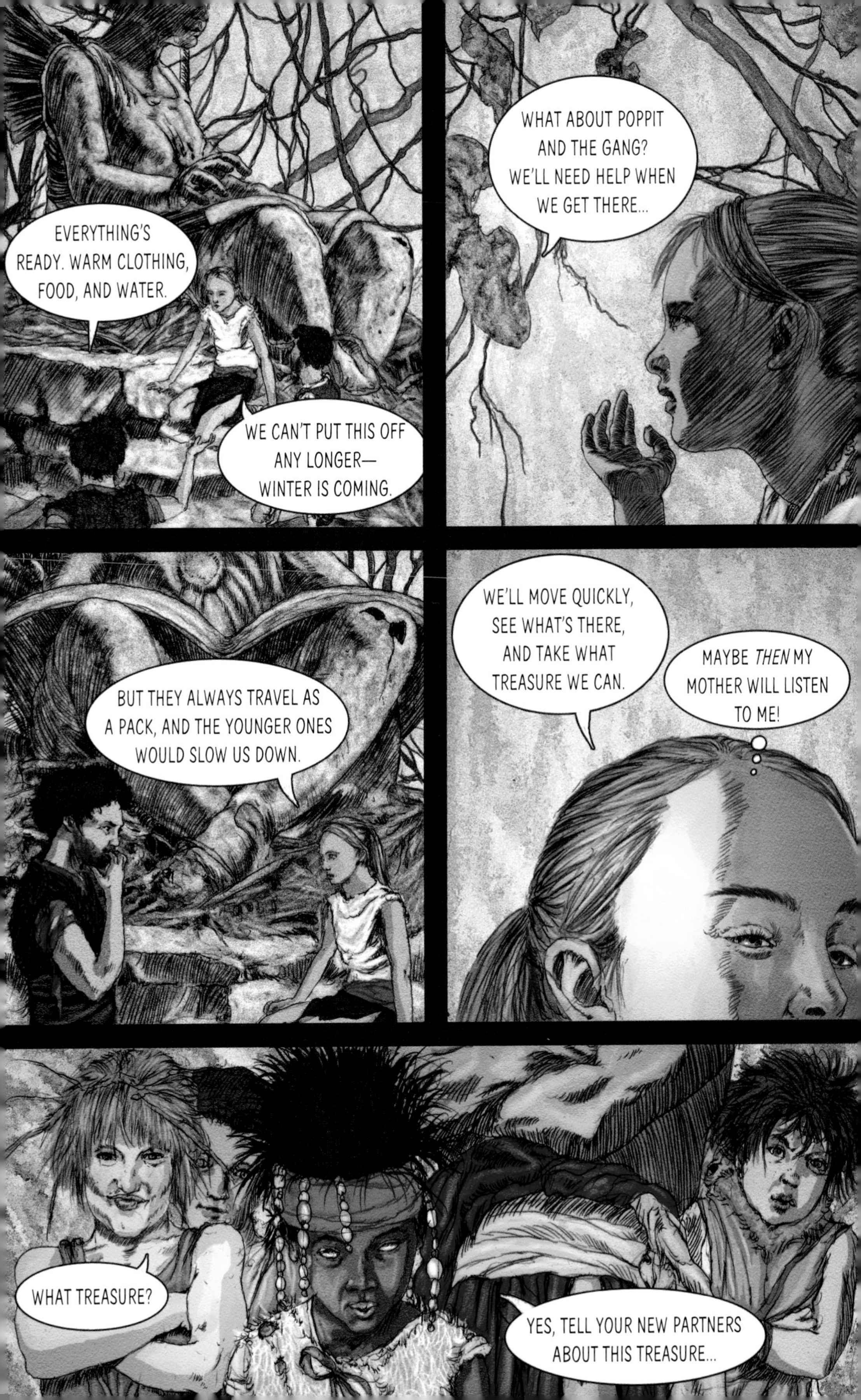
EVERYTHING'S READY. WARM CLOTHING, FOOD, AND WATER.
WE CAN'T PUT THIS OFF ANY LONGER— WINTER IS COMING.
WHAT ABOUT POPPIT AND THE GANG? WE'LL NEED HELP WHEN WE GET THERE...
BUT THEY ALWAYS TRAVEL AS A PACK, AND THE YOUNGER ONES WOULD SLOW US DOWN.
WE'LL MOVE QUICKLY, SEE WHAT'S THERE, AND TAKE WHAT TREASURE WE CAN.
MAYBE *THEN* MY MOTHER WILL LISTEN TO ME!
WHAT TREASURE?
YES, TELL YOUR NEW PARTNERS ABOUT THIS TREASURE...

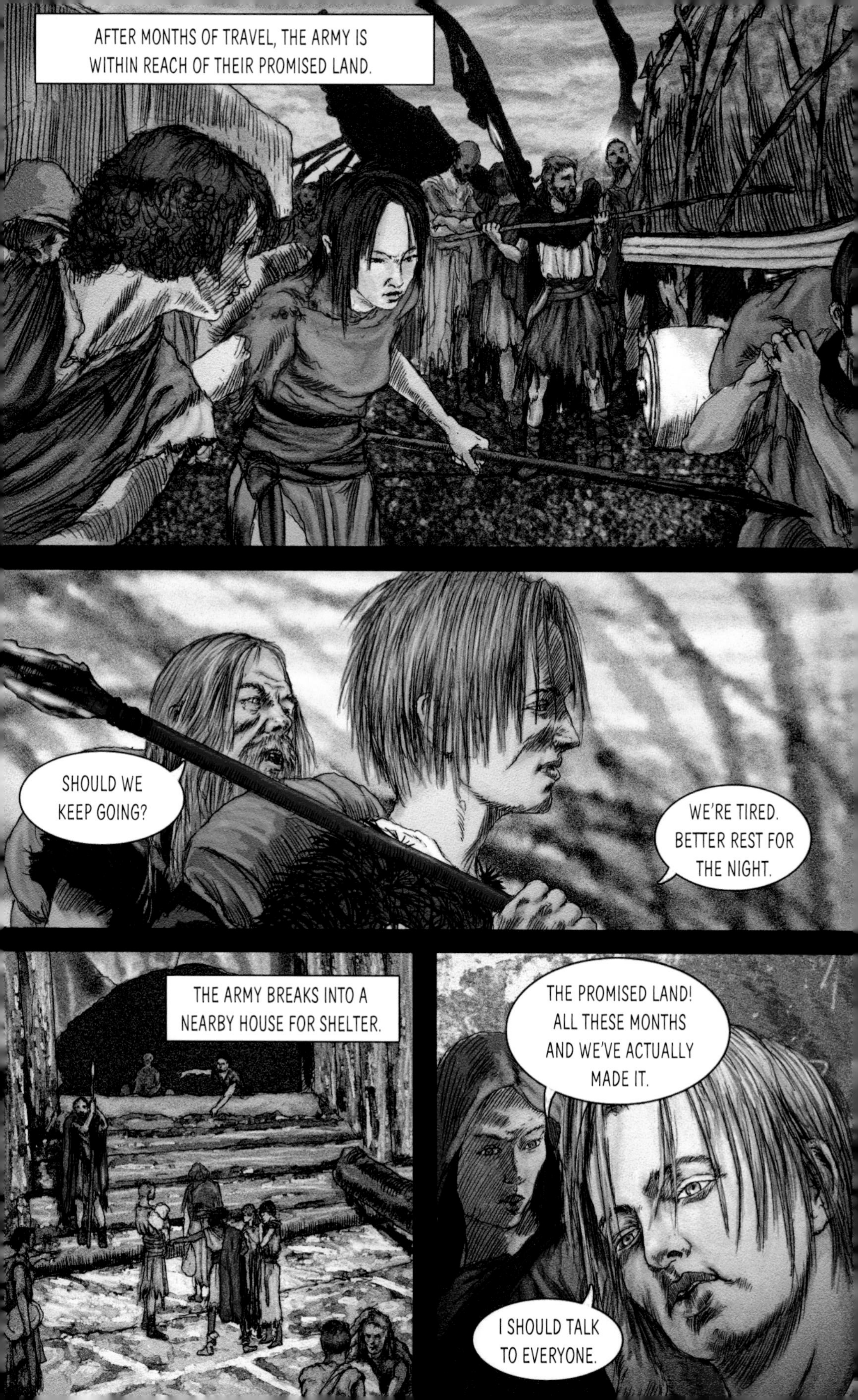
AFTER MONTHS OF TRAVEL, THE ARMY IS WITHIN REACH OF THEIR PROMISED LAND.
SHOULD WE KEEP GOING?
WE'RE TIRED. BETTER REST FOR THE NIGHT.
THE ARMY BREAKS INTO A NEARBY HOUSE FOR SHELTER.
THE PROMISED LAND! ALL THESE MONTHS AND WE'VE ACTUALLY MADE IT.
I SHOULD TALK TO EVERYONE.

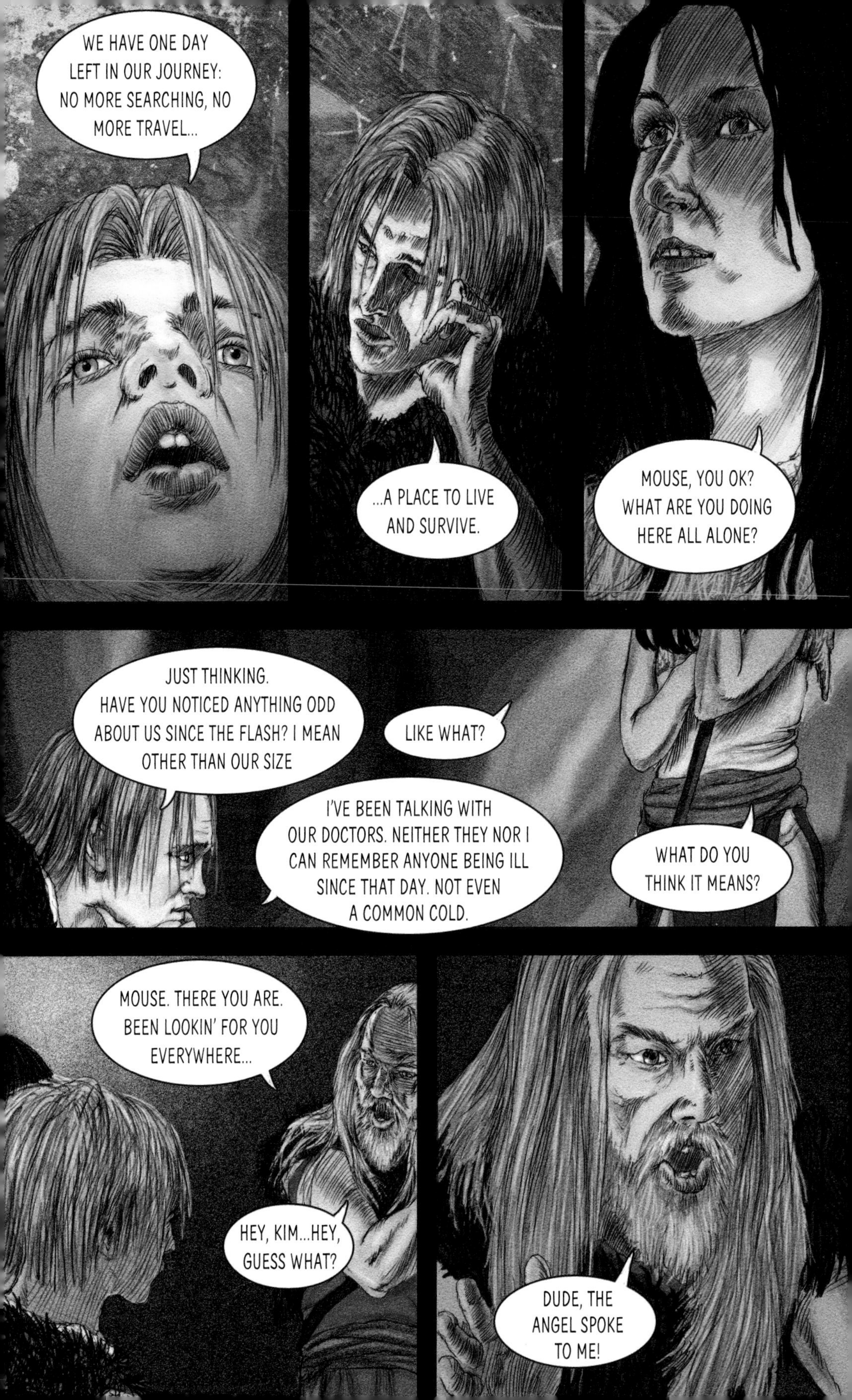
WE HAVE ONE DAY LEFT IN OUR JOURNEY: NO MORE SEARCHING, NO MORE TRAVEL...
...A PLACE TO LIVE AND SURVIVE.
MOUSE, YOU OK? WHAT ARE YOU DOING HERE ALL ALONE?
JUST THINKING. HAVE YOU NOTICED ANYTHING ODD ABOUT US SINCE THE FLASH? I MEAN OTHER THAN OUR SIZE
LIKE WHAT?
I'VE BEEN TALKING WITH OUR DOCTORS. NEITHER THEY NOR I CAN REMEMBER ANYONE BEING ILL SINCE THAT DAY. NOT EVEN A COMMON COLD.
WHAT DO YOU THINK IT MEANS?
MOUSE. THERE YOU ARE. BEEN LOOKIN' FOR YOU EVERYWHERE...
HEY, KIM...HEY, GUESS WHAT?
DUDE, THE ANGEL SPOKE TO ME!

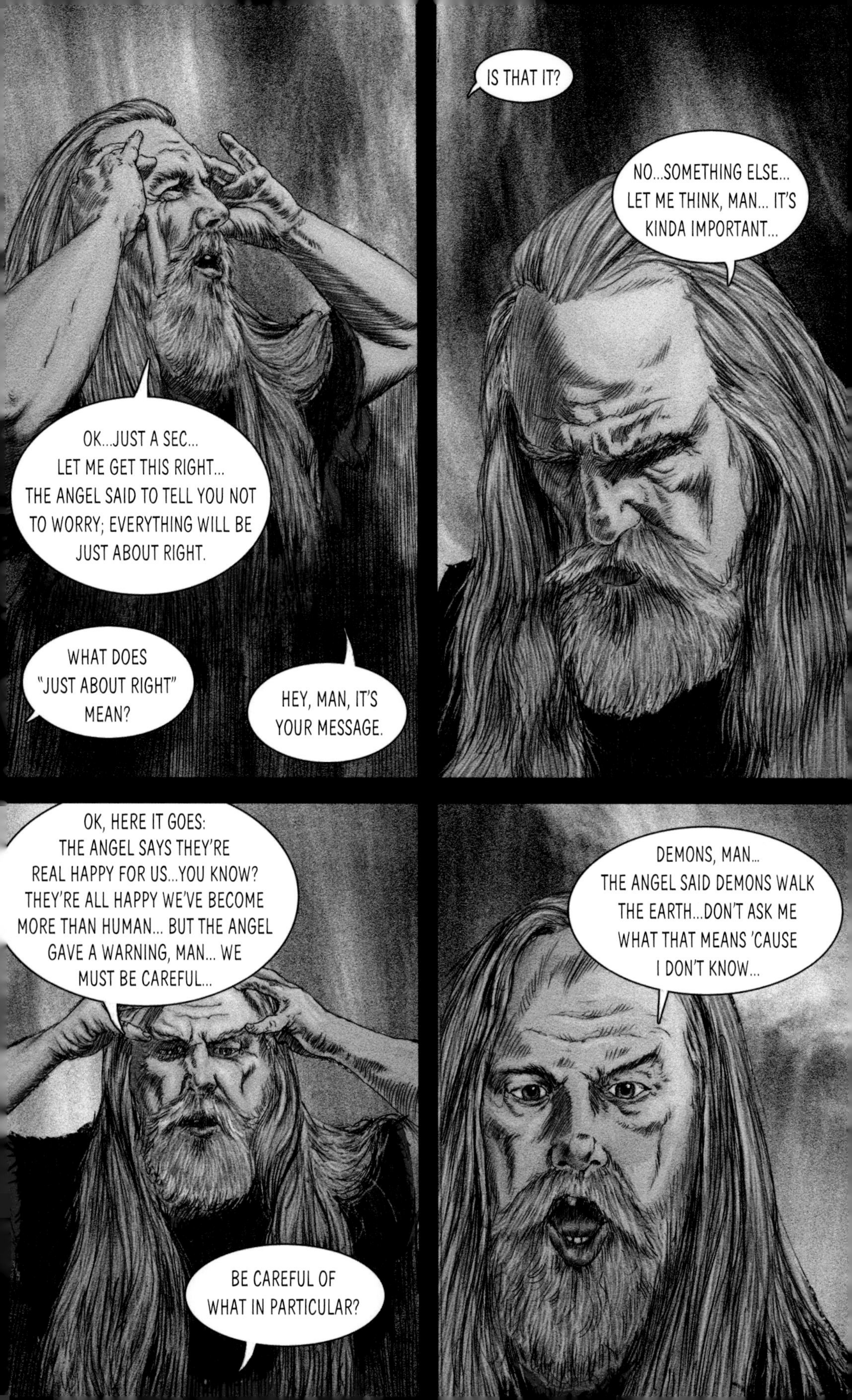
OK...JUST A SEC... LET ME GET THIS RIGHT... THE ANGEL SAID TO TELL YOU NOT TO WORRY; EVERYTHING WILL BE JUST ABOUT RIGHT.
WHAT DOES "JUST ABOUT RIGHT" MEAN?
HEY, MAN, IT'S YOUR MESSAGE.
IS THAT IT?
NO...SOMETHING ELSE... LET ME THINK, MAN... IT'S KINDA IMPORTANT...
OK, HERE IT GOES: THE ANGEL SAYS THEY'RE REAL HAPPY FOR US...YOU KNOW? THEY'RE ALL HAPPY WE'VE BECOME MORE THAN HUMAN... BUT THE ANGEL GAVE A WARNING, MAN... WE MUST BE CAREFUL...
BE CAREFUL OF WHAT IN PARTICULAR?
DEMONS, MAN... THE ANGEL SAID DEMONS WALK THE EARTH...DON'T ASK ME WHAT THAT MEANS 'CAUSE I DON'T KNOW...

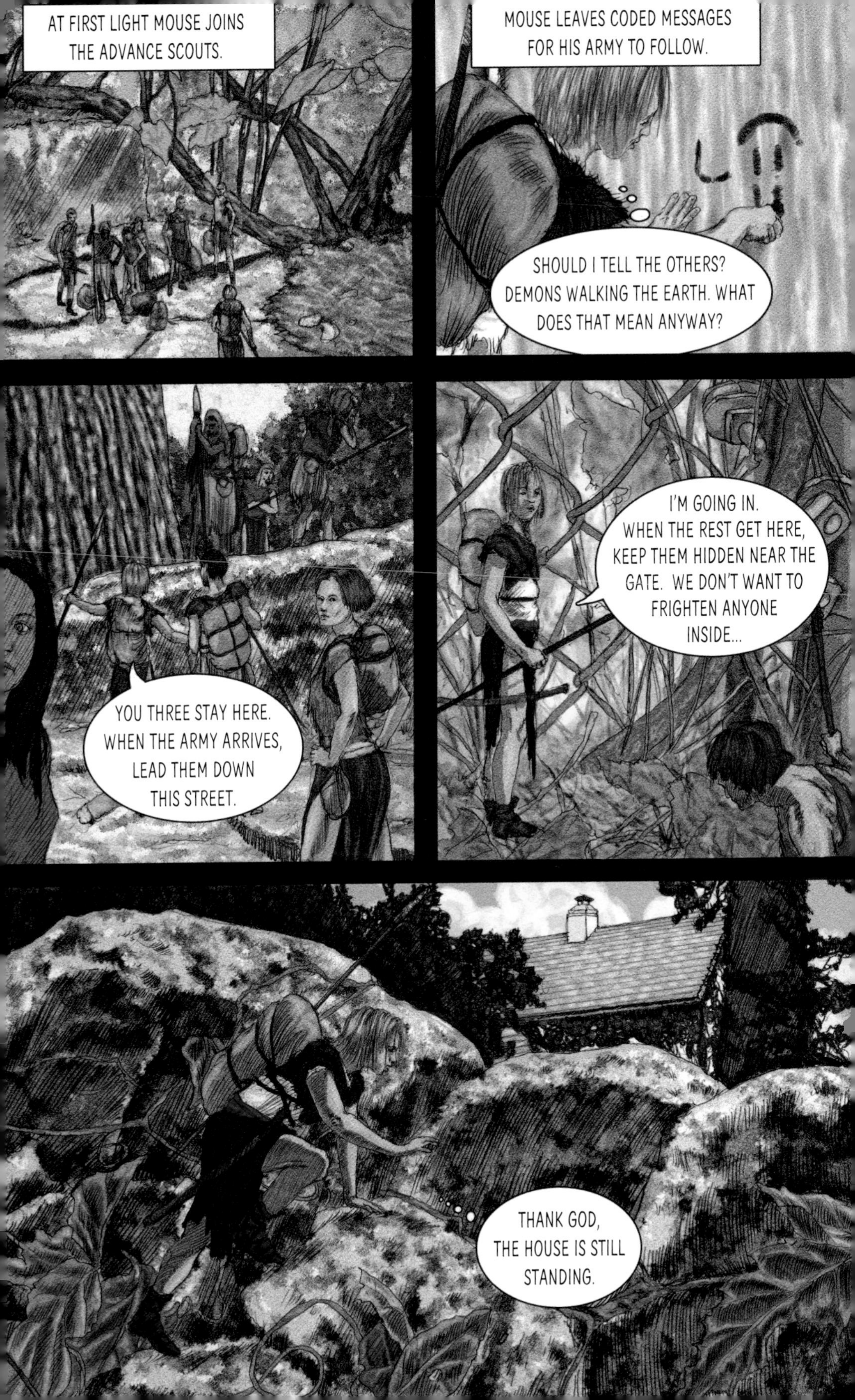
AT FIRST LIGHT MOUSE JOINS THE ADVANCE SCOUTS.
MOUSE LEAVES CODED MESSAGES FOR HIS ARMY TO FOLLOW.
SHOULD I TELL THE OTHERS? DEMONS WALKING THE EARTH. WHAT DOES THAT MEAN ANYWAY?
YOU THREE STAY HERE. WHEN THE ARMY ARRIVES, LEAD THEM DOWN THIS STREET.
I'M GOING IN. WHEN THE REST GET HERE, KEEP THEM HIDDEN NEAR THE GATE. WE DON'T WANT TO FRIGHTEN ANYONE INSIDE...
THANK GOD, THE HOUSE IS STILL STANDING.

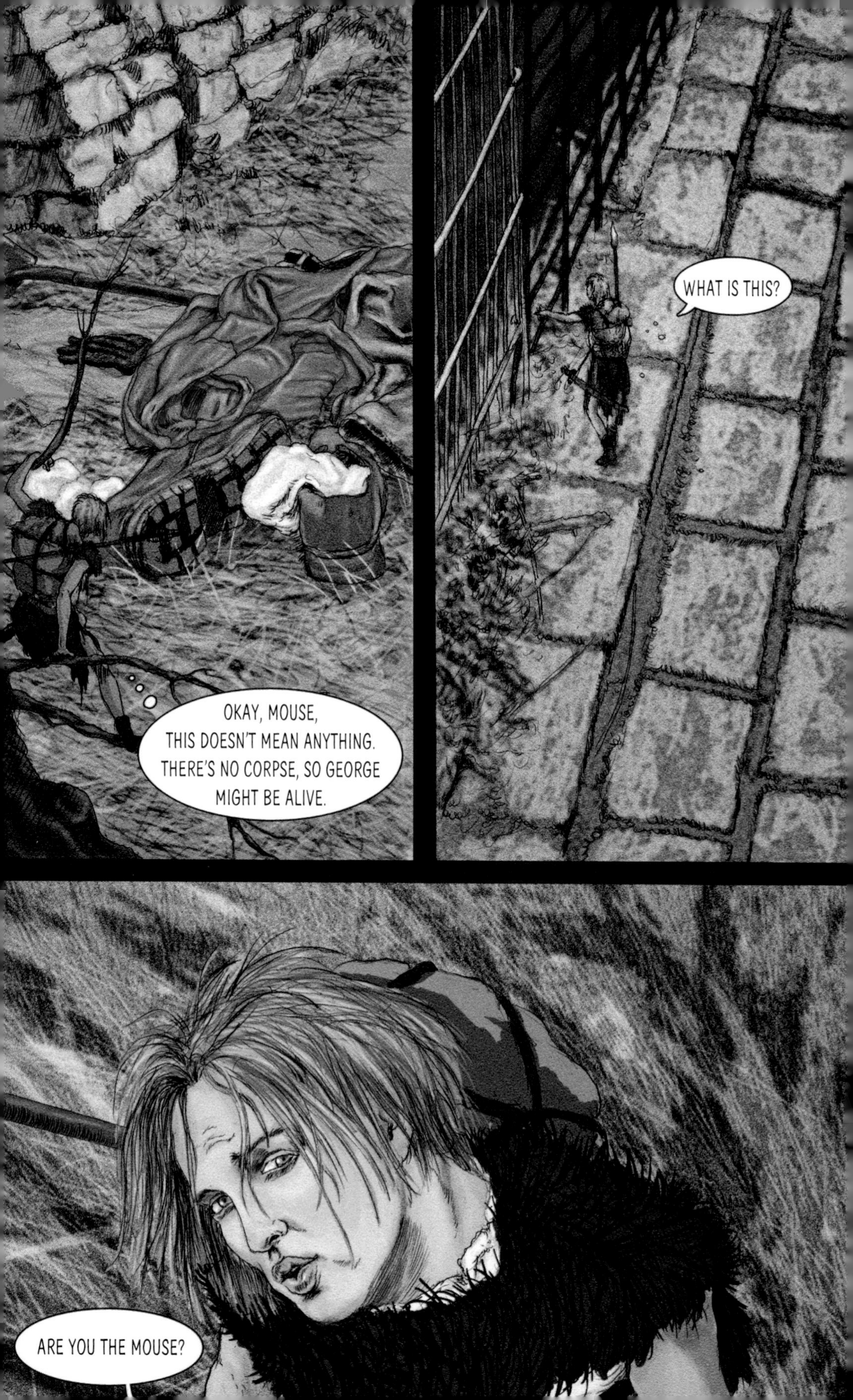
OKAY, MOUSE, THIS DOESN'T MEAN ANYTHING. THERE'S NO CORPSE, SO GEORGE MIGHT BE ALIVE.
WHAT IS THIS?
ARE YOU THE MOUSE?

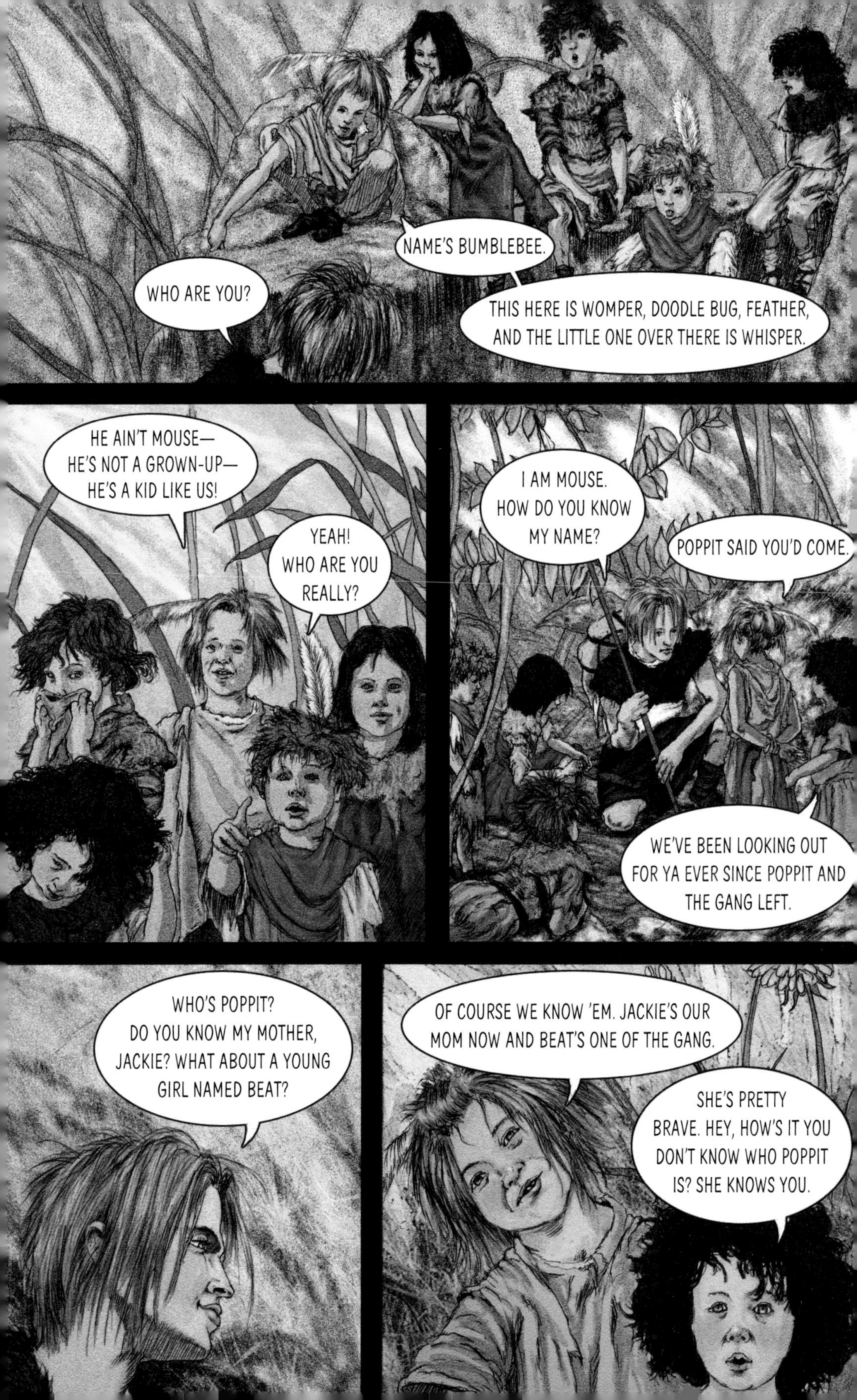
WHO ARE YOU?
NAME'S BUMBLEBEE.
THIS HERE IS WOMPER, DOODLE BUG, FEATHER, AND THE LITTLE ONE OVER THERE IS WHISPER.
HE AIN'T MOUSE— HE'S NOT A GROWN-UP— HE'S A KID LIKE US!
YEAH! WHO ARE YOU REALLY?
I AM MOUSE. HOW DO YOU KNOW MY NAME?
POPPIT SAID YOU'D COME.
WE'VE BEEN LOOKING OUT FOR YA EVER SINCE POPPIT AND THE GANG LEFT.
WHO'S POPPIT? DO YOU KNOW MY MOTHER, JACKIE? WHAT ABOUT A YOUNG GIRL NAMED BEAT?
OF COURSE WE KNOW 'EM. JACKIE'S OUR MOM NOW AND BEAT'S ONE OF THE GANG.
SHE'S PRETTY BRAVE. HEY, HOW'S IT YOU DON'T KNOW WHO POPPIT IS? SHE KNOWS YOU.

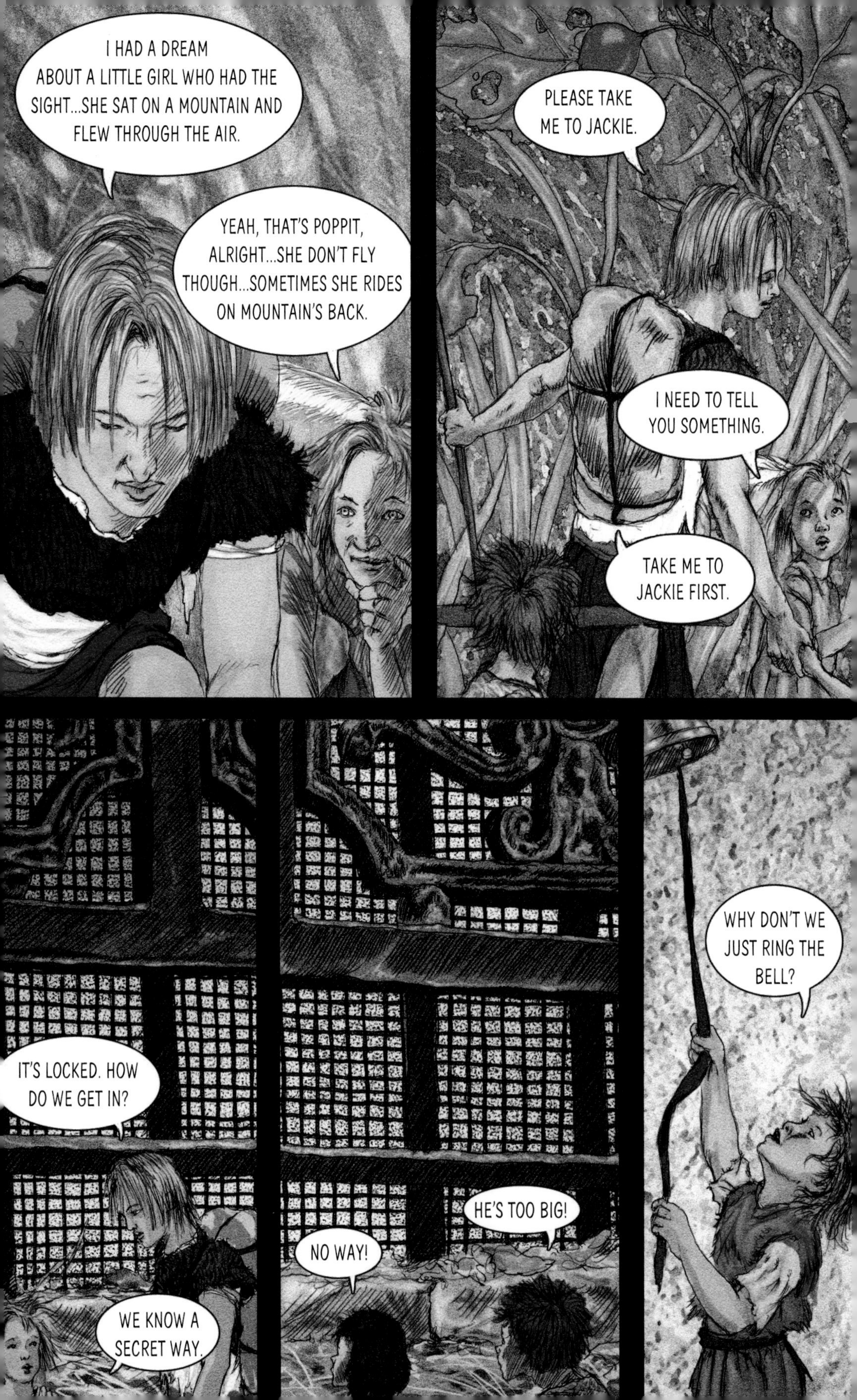
I HAD A DREAM ABOUT A LITTLE GIRL WHO HAD THE SIGHT...SHE SAT ON A MOUNTAIN AND FLEW THROUGH THE AIR.
YEAH, THAT'S POPPIT, ALRIGHT...SHE DON'T FLY THOUGH...SOMETIMES SHE RIDES ON MOUNTAIN'S BACK.
PLEASE TAKE ME TO JACKIE.
I NEED TO TELL YOU SOMETHING.
TAKE ME TO JACKIE FIRST.
IT'S LOCKED. HOW DO WE GET IN?
WE KNOW A SECRET WAY.
NO WAY!
HE'S TOO BIG!
WHY DON'T WE JUST RING THE BELL?

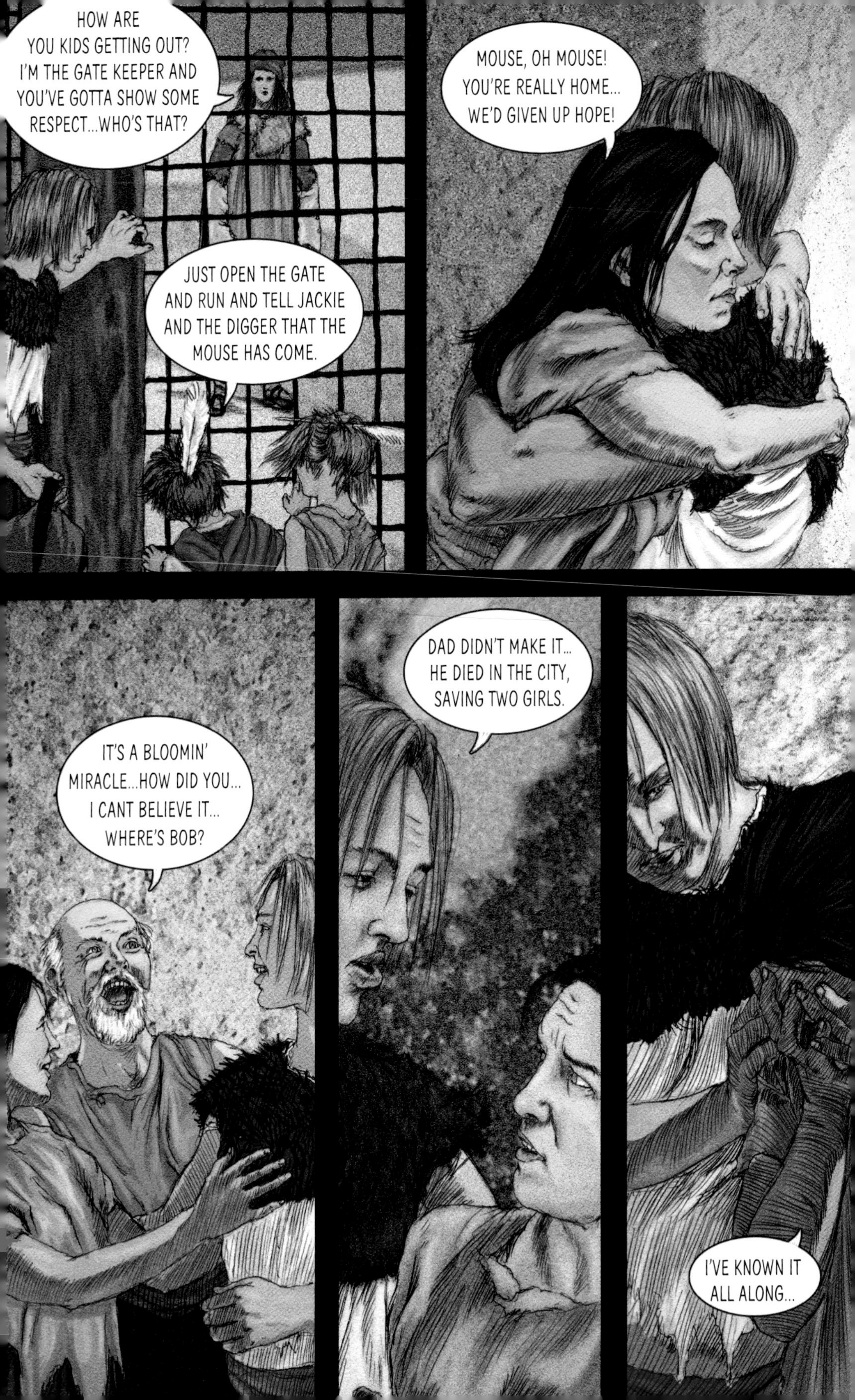
HOW ARE YOU KIDS GETTING OUT? I'M THE GATE KEEPER AND YOU'VE GOTTA SHOW SOME RESPECT...WHO'S THAT?
JUST OPEN THE GATE AND RUN AND TELL JACKIE AND THE DIGGER THAT THE MOUSE HAS COME.
MOUSE, OH MOUSE! YOU'RE REALLY HOME... WE'D GIVEN UP HOPE!
IT'S A BLOOMIN' MIRACLE...HOW DID YOU... I CANT BELIEVE IT... WHERE'S BOB?
DAD DIDN'T MAKE IT... HE DIED IN THE CITY, SAVING TWO GIRLS.
I'VE KNOWN IT ALL ALONG...

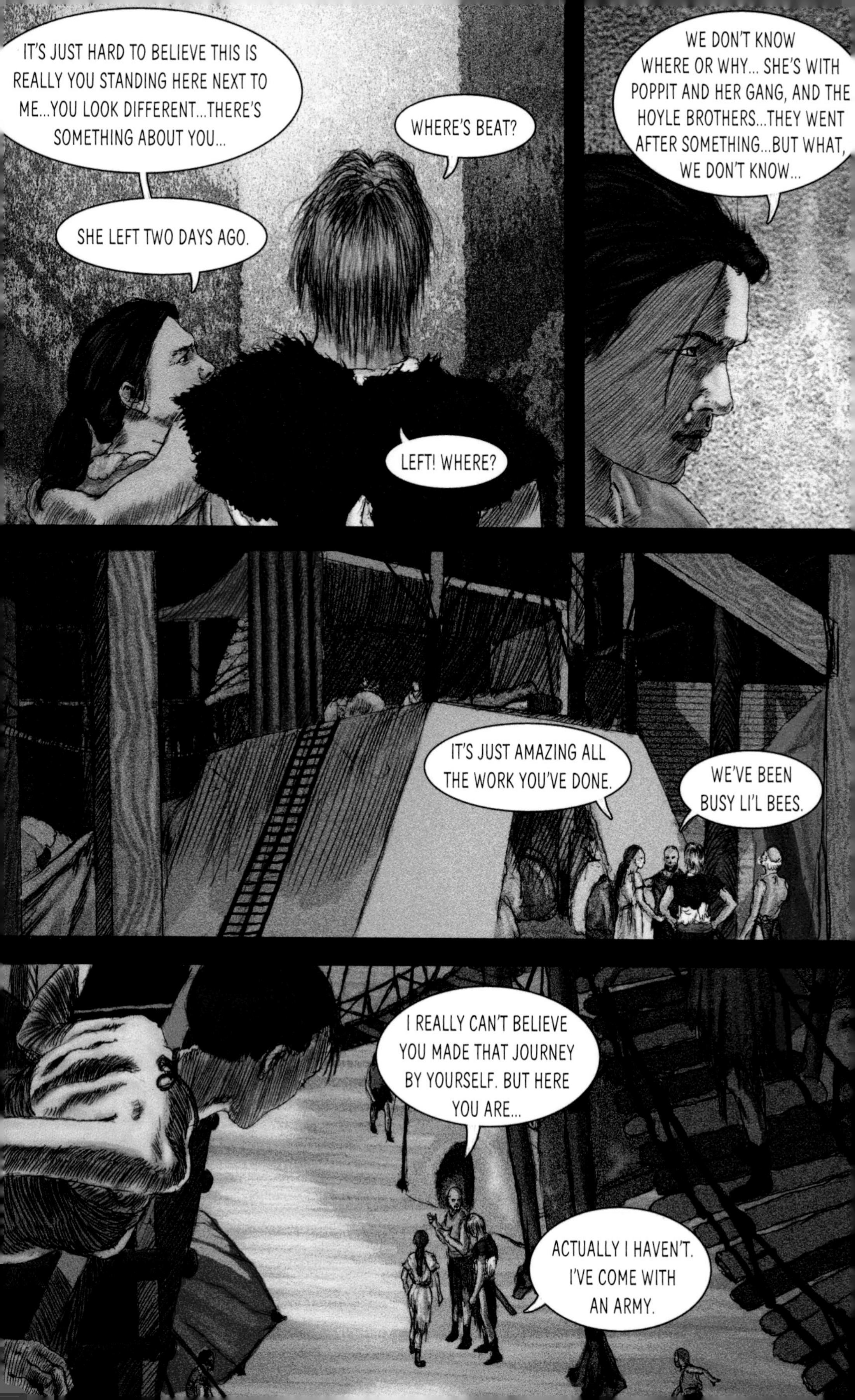
IT'S JUST HARD TO BELIEVE THIS IS REALLY YOU STANDING HERE NEXT TO ME...YOU LOOK DIFFERENT...THERE'S SOMETHING ABOUT YOU...
WHERE'S BEAT?
SHE LEFT TWO DAYS AGO.
LEFT! WHERE?
WE DON'T KNOW WHERE OR WHY... SHE'S WITH POPPIT AND HER GANG, AND THE HOYLE BROTHERS...THEY WENT AFTER SOMETHING...BUT WHAT, WE DON'T KNOW...
IT'S JUST AMAZING ALL THE WORK YOU'VE DONE.
WE'VE BEEN BUSY LI'L BEES.
I REALLY CAN'T BELIEVE YOU MADE THAT JOURNEY BY YOURSELF. BUT HERE YOU ARE...
ACTUALLY I HAVEN'T. I'VE COME WITH AN ARMY.

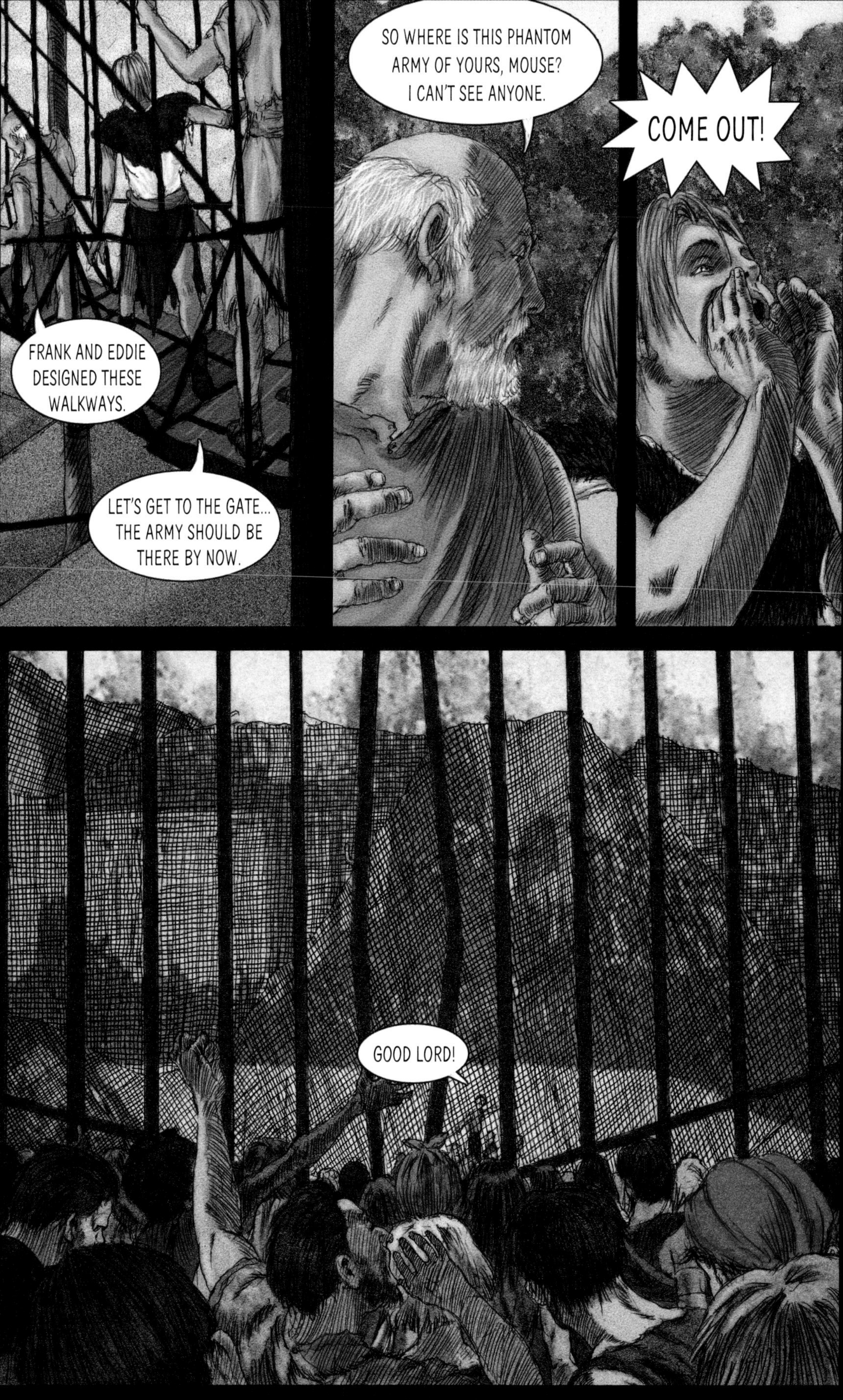
FRANK AND EDDIE DESIGNED THESE WALKWAYS.
LET'S GET TO THE GATE... THE ARMY SHOULD BE THERE BY NOW.
SO WHERE IS THIS PHANTOM ARMY OF YOURS, MOUSE? I CAN'T SEE ANYONE.
COME OUT!
GOOD LORD!

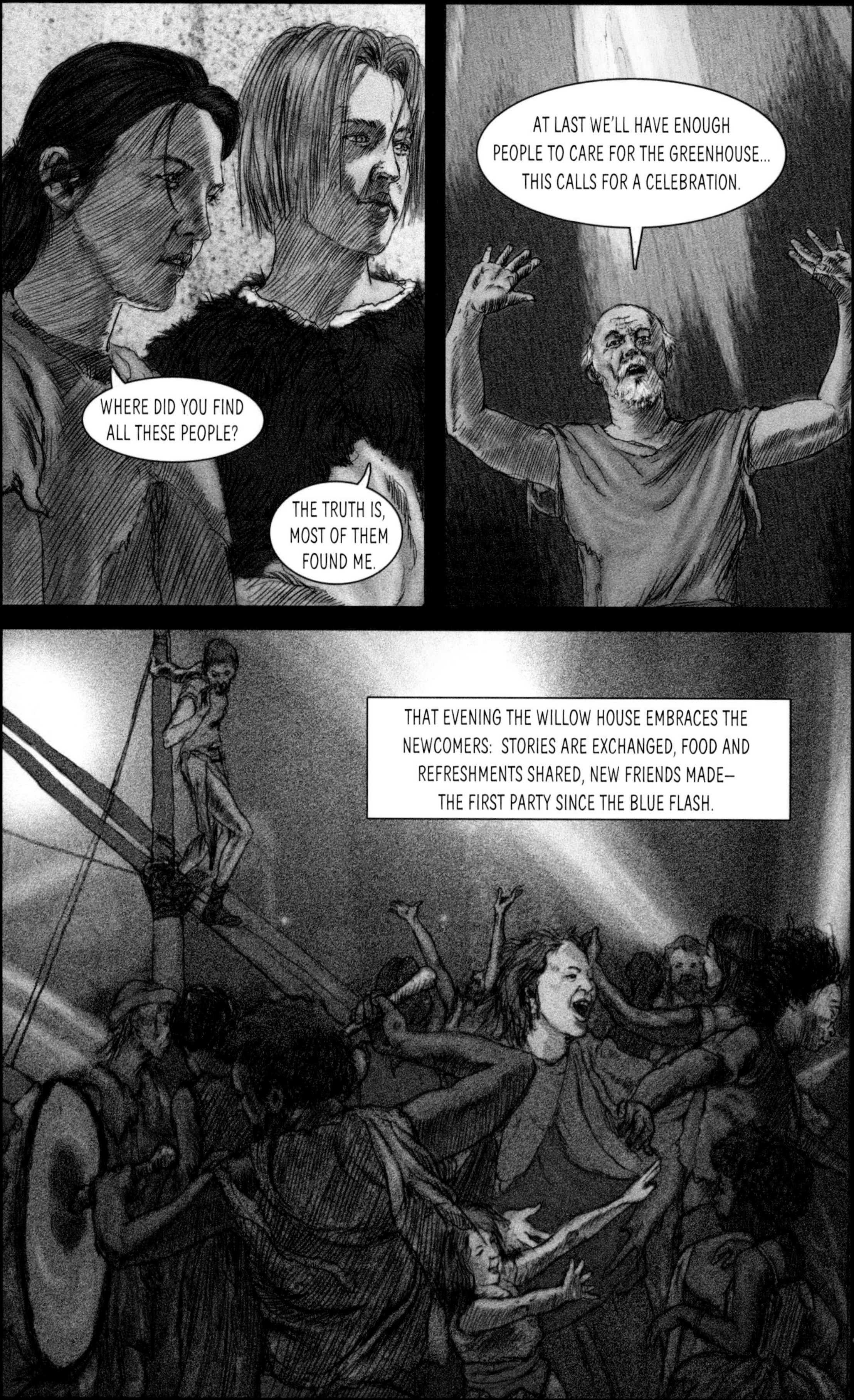
WHERE DID YOU FIND ALL THESE PEOPLE?
THE TRUTH IS, MOST OF THEM FOUND ME.
AT LAST WE'LL HAVE ENOUGH PEOPLE TO CARE FOR THE GREENHOUSE... THIS CALLS FOR A CELEBRATION.
THAT EVENING THE WILLOW HOUSE EMBRACES THE NEWCOMERS: STORIES ARE EXCHANGED, FOOD AND REFRESHMENTS SHARED, NEW FRIENDS MADE— THE FIRST PARTY SINCE THE BLUE FLASH.

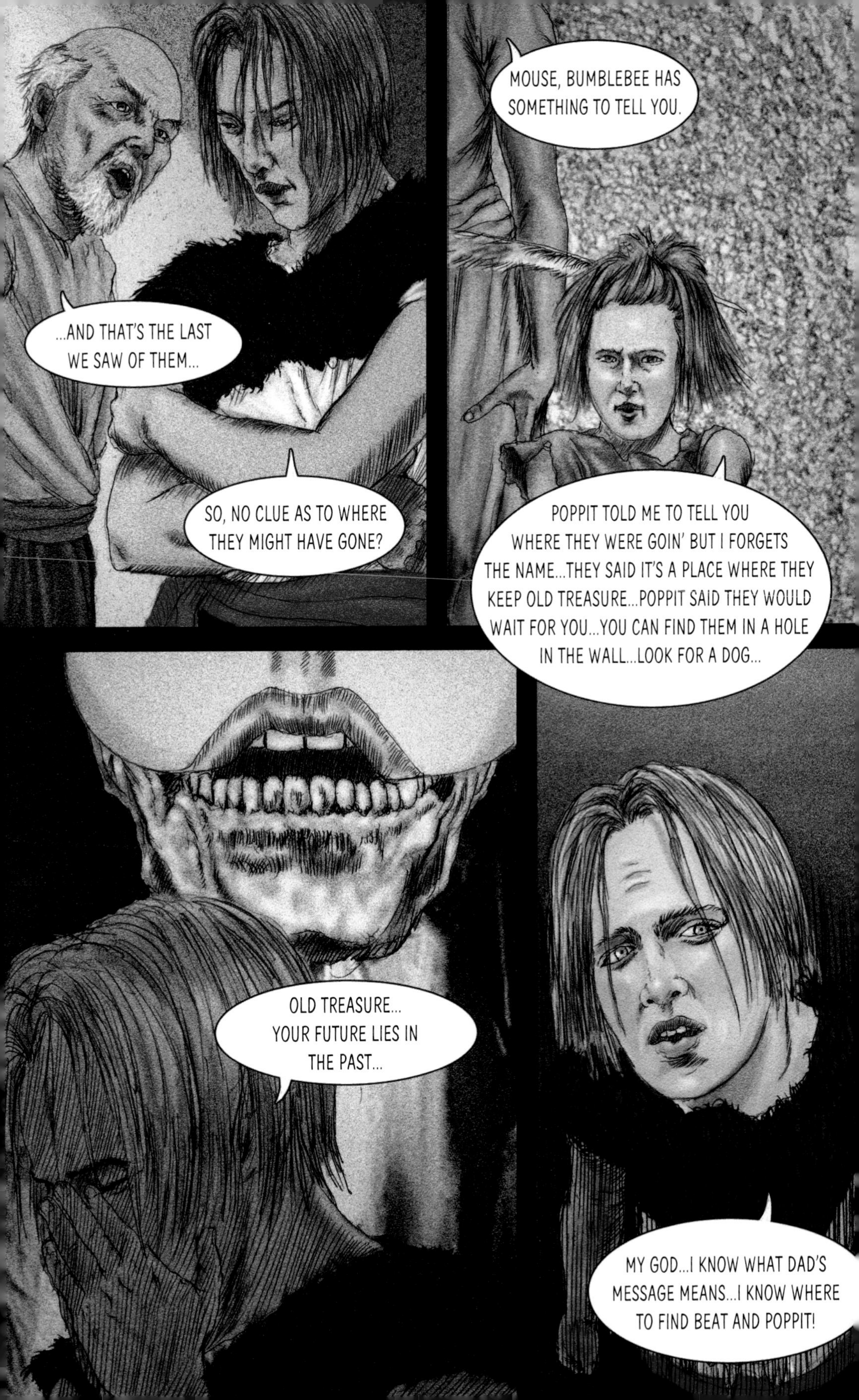
...AND THAT'S THE LAST WE SAW OF THEM...
SO, NO CLUE AS TO WHERE THEY MIGHT HAVE GONE?
MOUSE, BUMBLEBEE HAS SOMETHING TO TELL YOU.
POPPIT TOLD ME TO TELL YOU WHERE THEY WERE GOIN' BUT I FORGETS THE NAME...THEY SAID IT'S A PLACE WHERE THEY KEEP OLD TREASURE...POPPIT SAID THEY WOULD WAIT FOR YOU...YOU CAN FIND THEM IN A HOLE IN THE WALL...LOOK FOR A DOG...
OLD TREASURE... YOUR FUTURE LIES IN THE PAST...
MY GOD...I KNOW WHAT DAD'S MESSAGE MEANS...I KNOW WHERE TO FIND BEAT AND POPPIT!

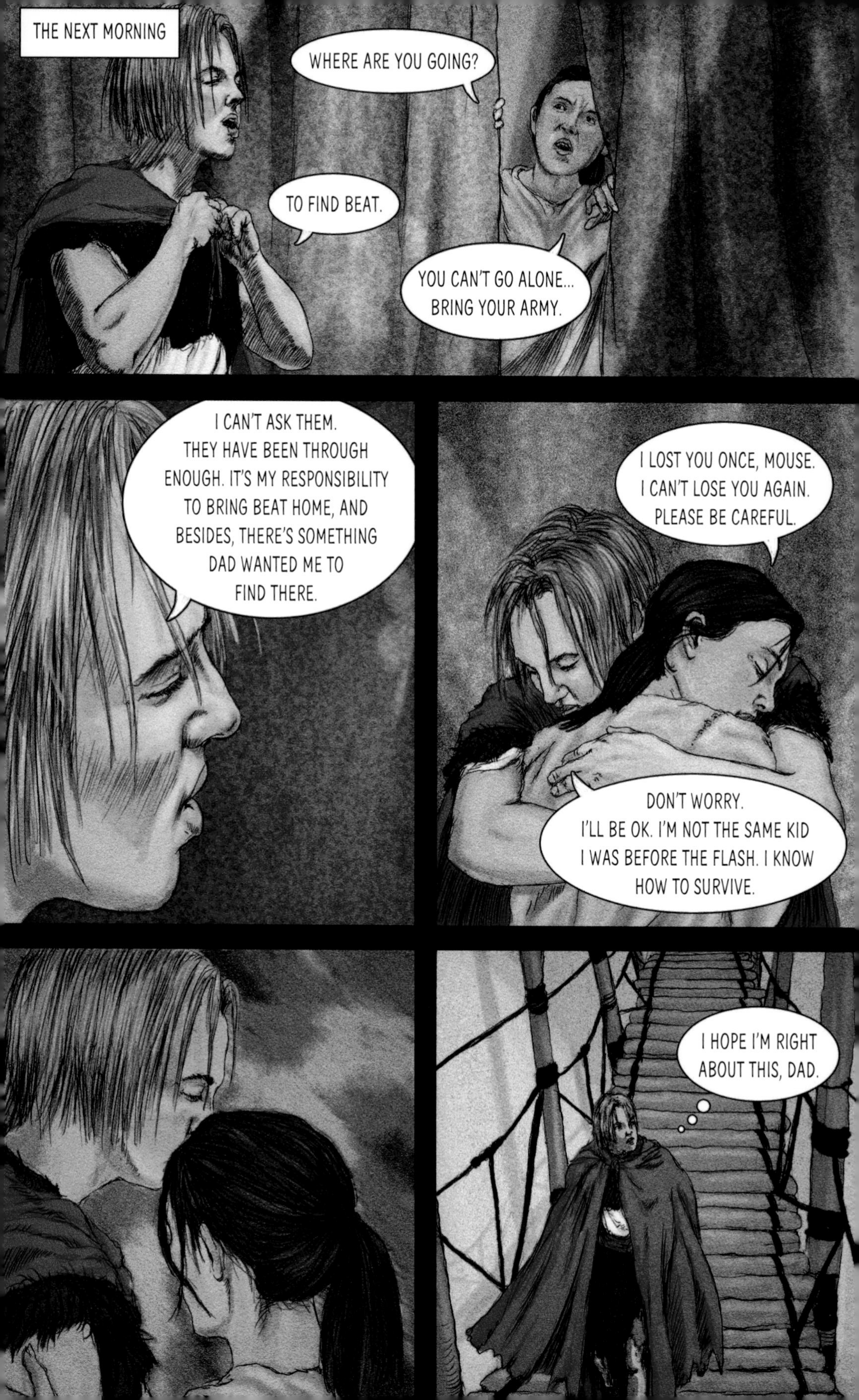
THE NEXT MORNING
WHERE ARE YOU GOING?
TO FIND BEAT.
YOU CAN'T GO ALONE... BRING YOUR ARMY.
I CAN'T ASK THEM. THEY HAVE BEEN THROUGH ENOUGH. IT'S MY RESPONSIBILITY TO BRING BEAT HOME, AND BESIDES, THERE'S SOMETHING DAD WANTED ME TO FIND THERE.
I LOST YOU ONCE, MOUSE. I CAN'T LOSE YOU AGAIN. PLEASE BE CAREFUL.
DON'T WORRY. I'LL BE OK. I'M NOT THE SAME KID I WAS BEFORE THE FLASH. I KNOW HOW TO SURVIVE.
I HOPE I'M RIGHT ABOUT THIS, DAD.

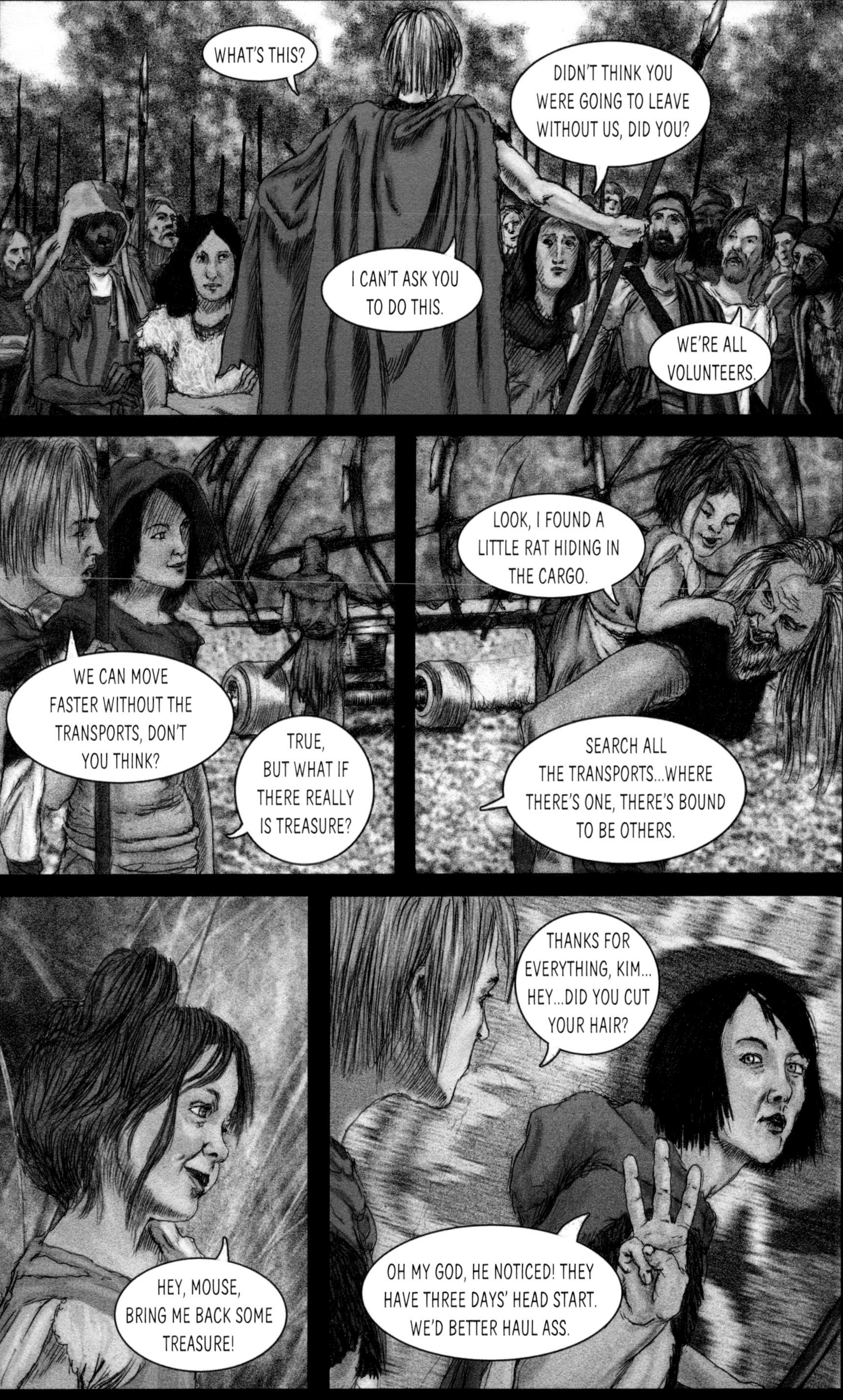
WHAT'S THIS?
DIDN'T THINK YOU WERE GOING TO LEAVE WITHOUT US, DID YOU?
I CAN'T ASK YOU TO DO THIS.
WE'RE ALL VOLUNTEERS.
WE CAN MOVE FASTER WITHOUT THE TRANSPORTS, DON'T YOU THINK?
TRUE, BUT WHAT IF THERE REALLY IS TREASURE?
LOOK, I FOUND A LITTLE RAT HIDING IN THE CARGO.
SEARCH ALL THE TRANSPORTS...WHERE THERE'S ONE, THERE'S BOUND TO BE OTHERS.
HEY, MOUSE, BRING ME BACK SOME TREASURE!
THANKS FOR EVERYTHING, KIM... HEY...DID YOU CUT YOUR HAIR?
OH MY GOD, HE NOTICED! THEY HAVE THREE DAYS' HEAD START. WE'D BETTER HAUL ASS.

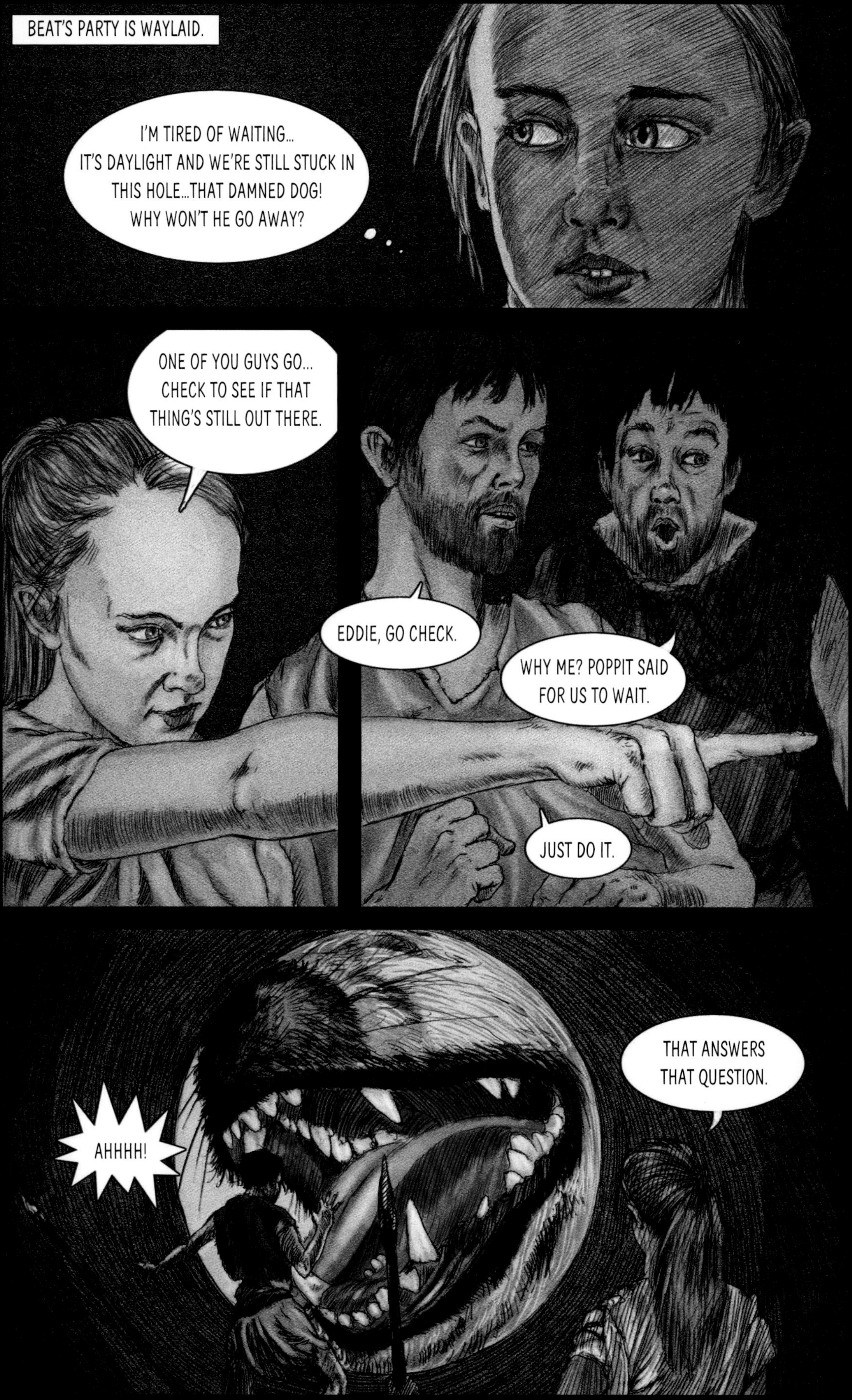
BEAT'S PARTY IS WAYLAID.
I'M TIRED OF WAITING... IT'S DAYLIGHT AND WE'RE STILL STUCK IN THIS HOLE...THAT DAMNED DOG! WHY WON'T HE GO AWAY?
ONE OF YOU GUYS GO... CHECK TO SEE IF THAT THING'S STILL OUT THERE.
EDDIE, GO CHECK.
WHY ME? POPPIT SAID FOR US TO WAIT.
JUST DO IT.
AHHHH!
THAT ANSWERS THAT QUESTION.

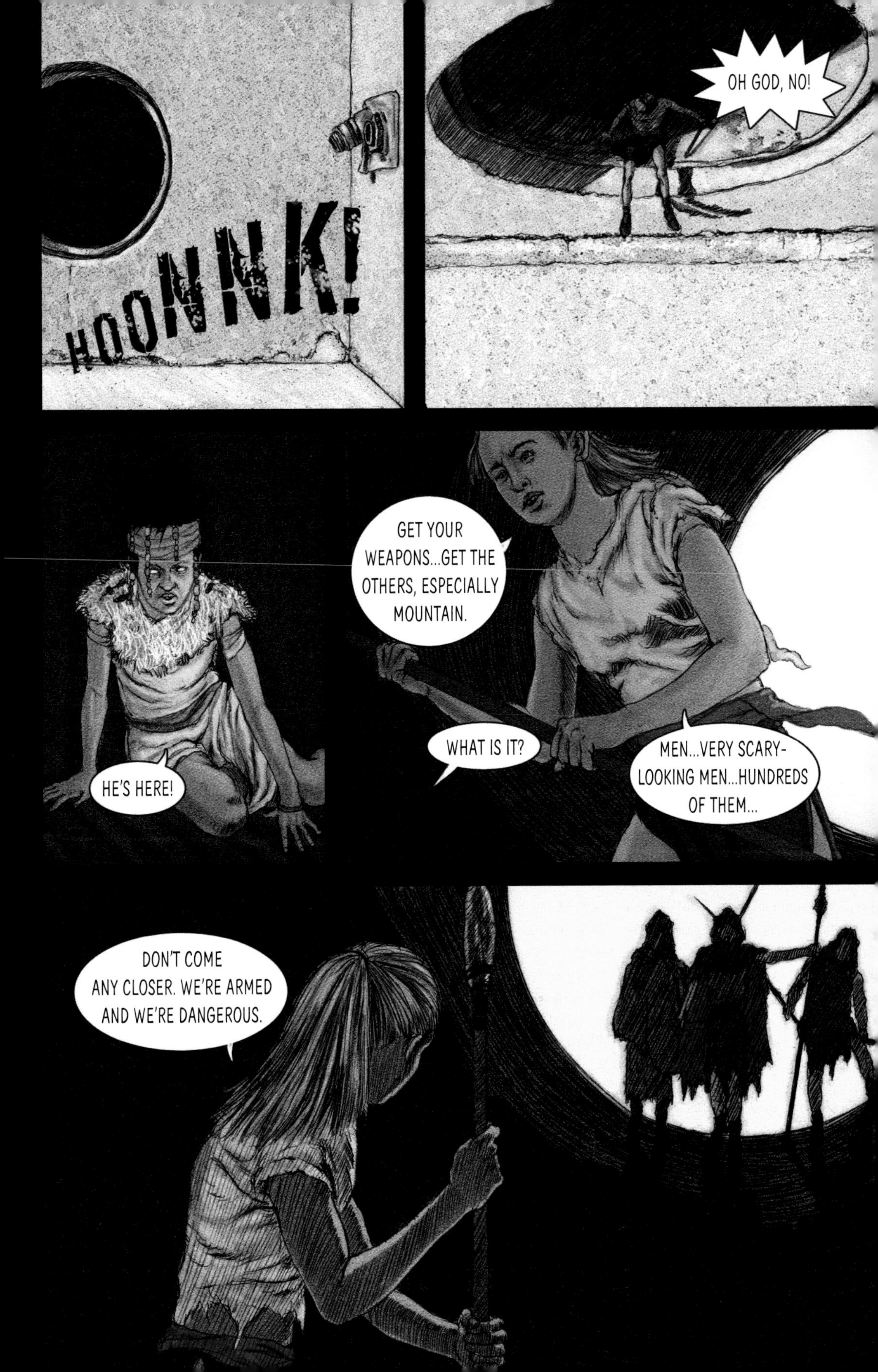
HOONNK!
OH GOD, NO!
GET YOUR WEAPONS...GET THE OTHERS, ESPECIALLY MOUNTAIN.
HE'S HERE!
WHAT IS IT?
MEN...VERY SCARY-LOOKING MEN...HUNDREDS OF THEM...
DON'T COME ANY CLOSER. WE'RE ARMED AND WE'RE DANGEROUS.

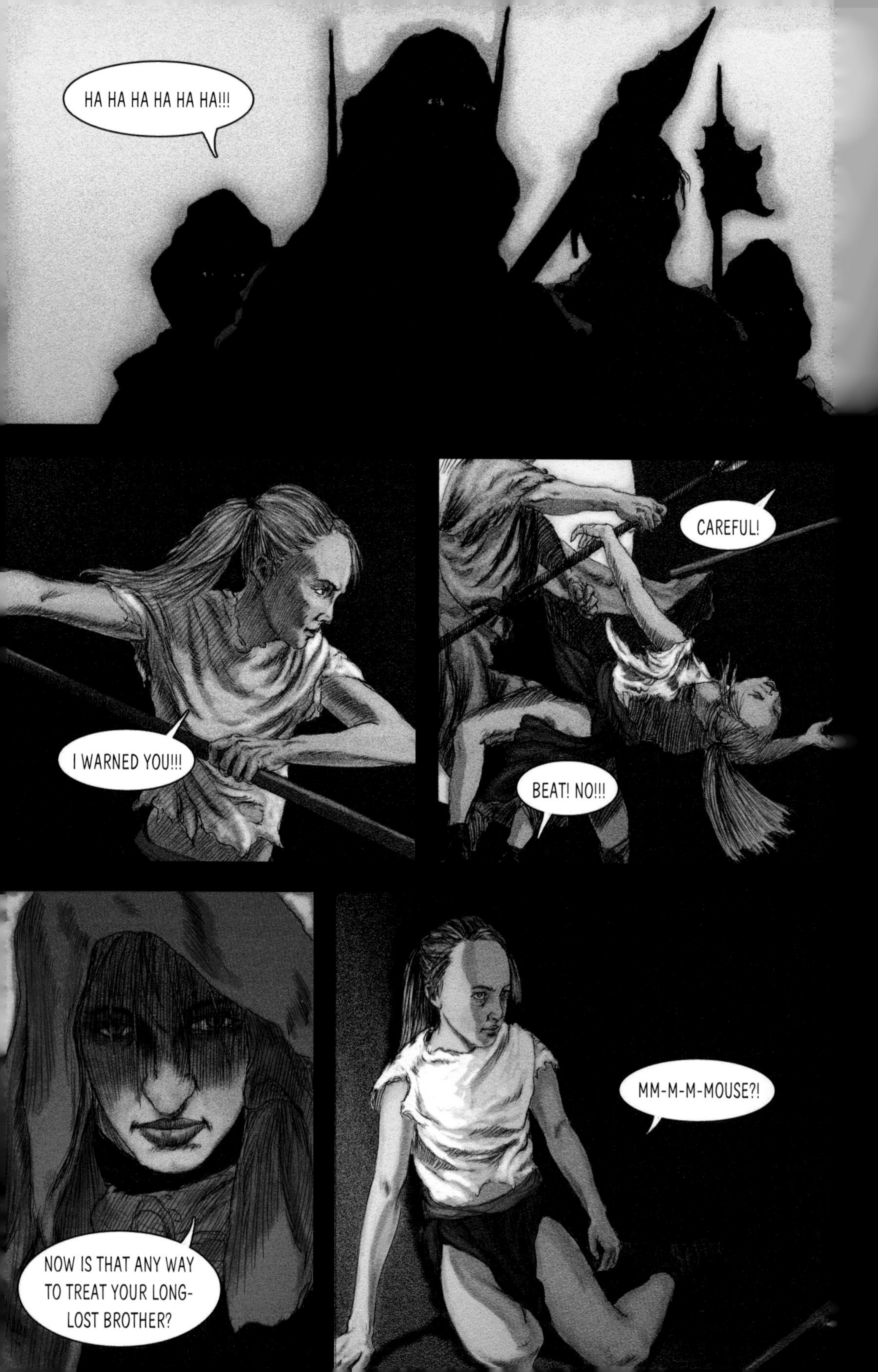
HA HA HA HA HA HA!!!
I WARNED YOU!!!
CAREFUL!
BEAT! NO!!!
NOW IS THAT ANY WAY TO TREAT YOUR LONG-LOST BROTHER?
MM-M-M-MOUSE?!

YOU'RE ALIVE! HOW DID YOU...WHO ARE ALL THESE PEOPLE...WHERE'S DAD?

DAD'S GONE... I'LL EXPLAIN LATER.

I KIND OF HAD A FEELING ALL ALONG. I ONLY WISH I COULD HAVE SEEN HIM ONE MORE TIME. I'M SO SORRY I ATTACKED YOU...IN THE SHADOWS YOU LOOKED LIKE SOME KIND OF DEMON...

DON'T EVER SAY THAT, BEAT! NEVER SAY THAT AGAIN!

WHAT?

YOU MUST BE POPPIT.

MOUSE, AT LAST. WE HAVE BEEN WAITING FOR YOU.

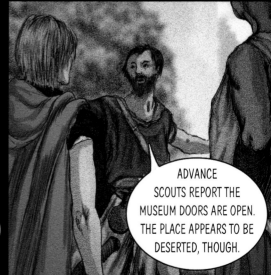

ADVANCE SCOUTS REPORT THE MUSEUM DOORS ARE OPEN. THE PLACE APPEARS TO BE DESERTED, THOUGH.

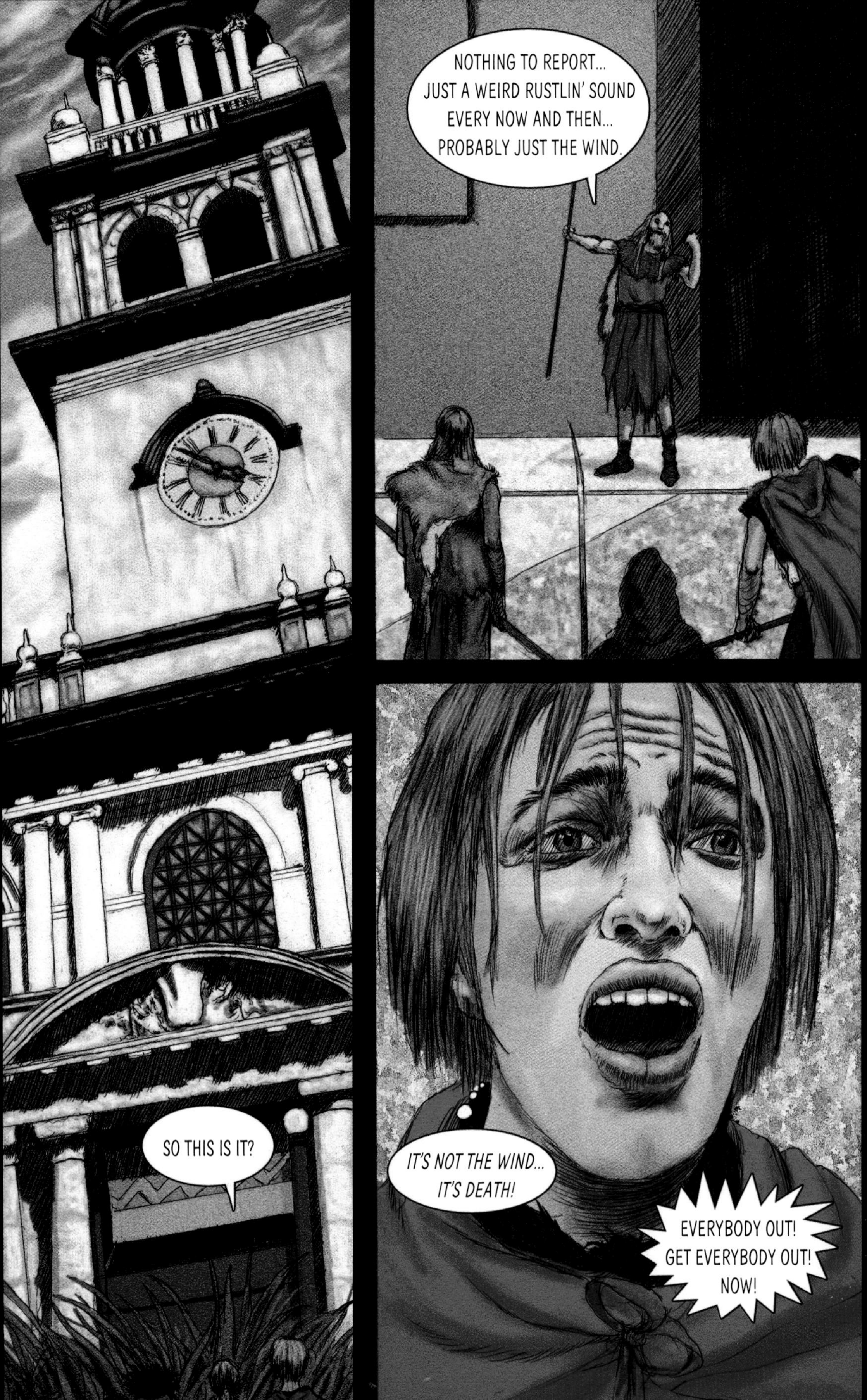
NOTHING TO REPORT... JUST A WEIRD RUSTLIN' SOUND EVERY NOW AND THEN... PROBABLY JUST THE WIND.
SO THIS IS IT?
IT'S NOT THE WIND... IT'S DEATH!
EVERYBODY OUT! GET EVERYBODY OUT! NOW!

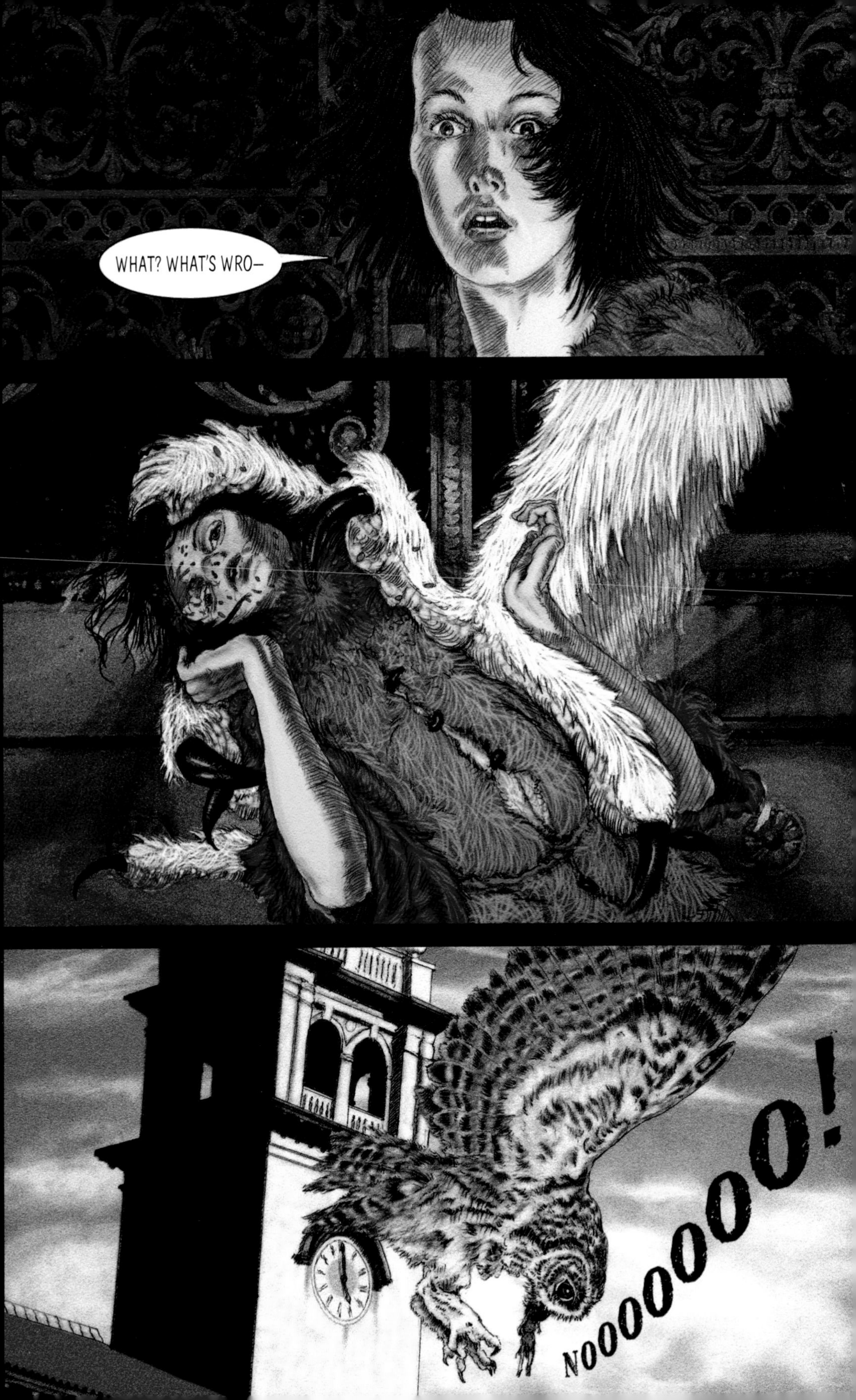
WHAT? WHAT'S WRO–
NOOOOOOOO!

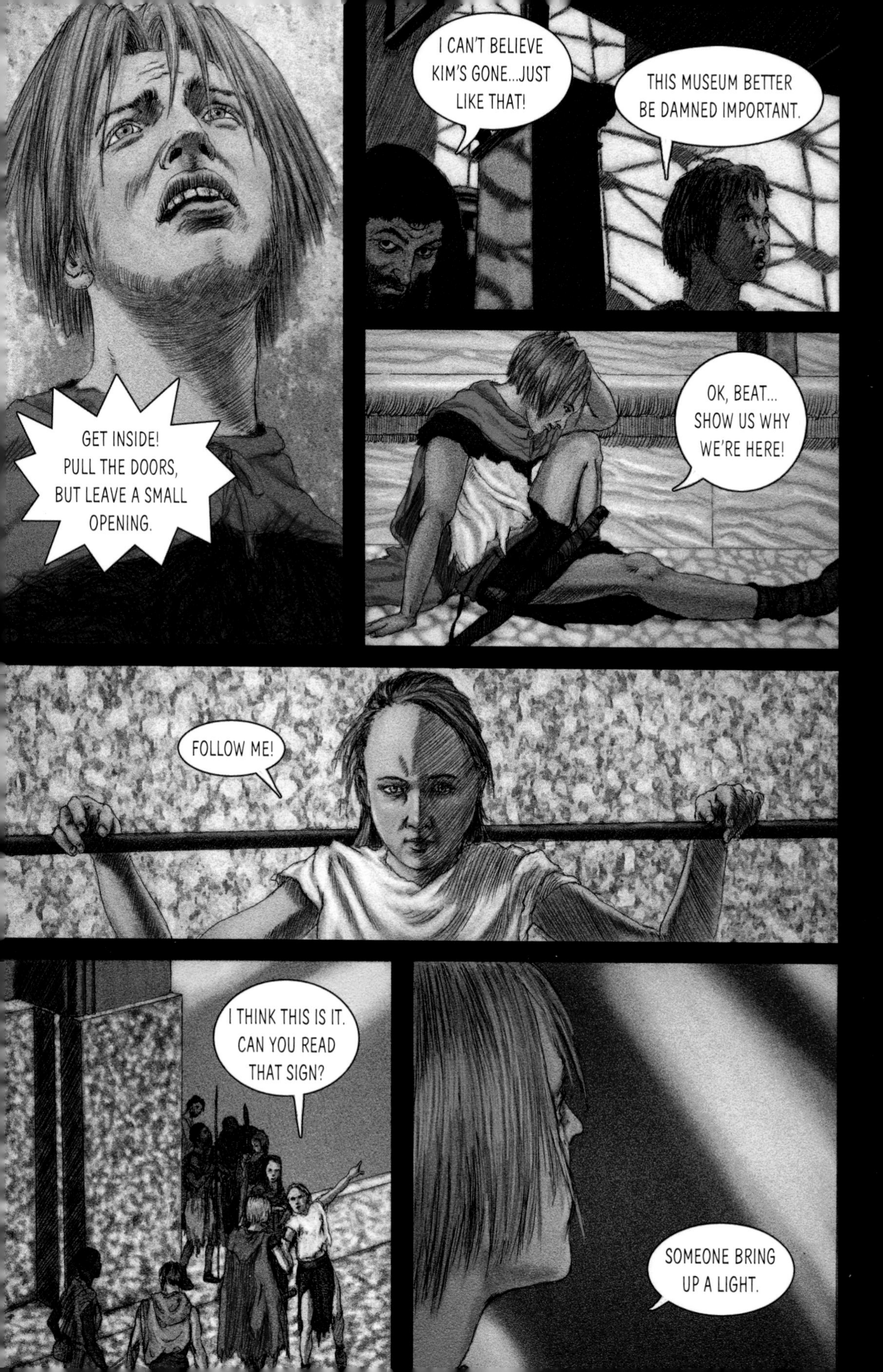
GET INSIDE! PULL THE DOORS, BUT LEAVE A SMALL OPENING.
I CAN'T BELIEVE KIM'S GONE...JUST LIKE THAT!
THIS MUSEUM BETTER BE DAMNED IMPORTANT.
OK, BEAT... SHOW US WHY WE'RE HERE!
FOLLOW ME!
I THINK THIS IS IT. CAN YOU READ THAT SIGN?
SOMEONE BRING UP A LIGHT.

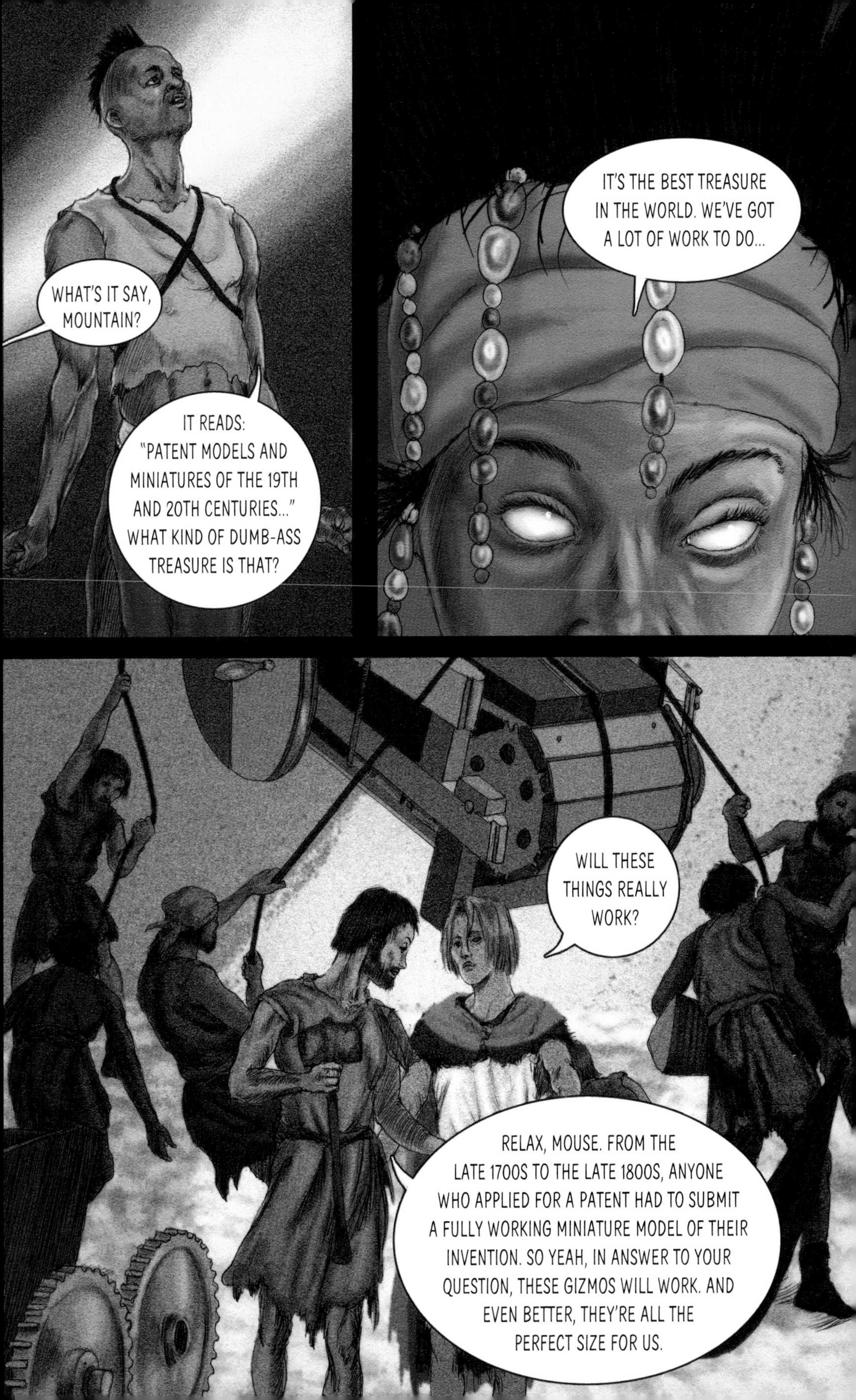
WHAT'S IT SAY, MOUNTAIN?
IT READS: "PATENT MODELS AND MINIATURES OF THE 19TH AND 20TH CENTURIES..." WHAT KIND OF DUMB-ASS TREASURE IS THAT?
IT'S THE BEST TREASURE IN THE WORLD. WE'VE GOT A LOT OF WORK TO DO...
WILL THESE THINGS REALLY WORK?
RELAX, MOUSE. FROM THE LATE 1700S TO THE LATE 1800S, ANYONE WHO APPLIED FOR A PATENT HAD TO SUBMIT A FULLY WORKING MINIATURE MODEL OF THEIR INVENTION. SO YEAH, IN ANSWER TO YOUR QUESTION, THESE GIZMOS WILL WORK. AND EVEN BETTER, THEY'RE ALL THE PERFECT SIZE FOR US.

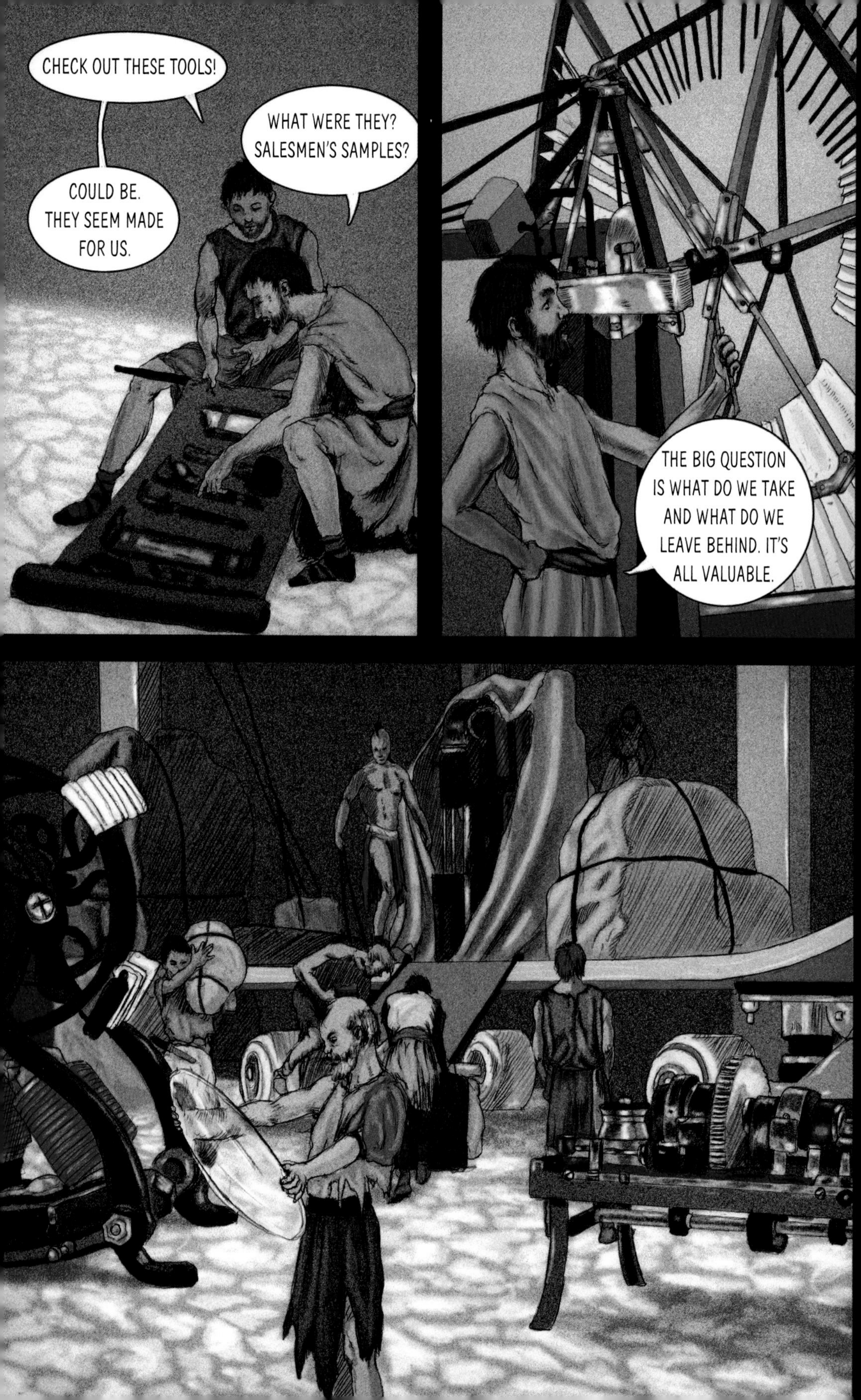
CHECK OUT THESE TOOLS!
WHAT WERE THEY? SALESMEN'S SAMPLES?
COULD BE. THEY SEEM MADE FOR US.
THE BIG QUESTION IS WHAT DO WE TAKE AND WHAT DO WE LEAVE BEHIND. IT'S ALL VALUABLE.

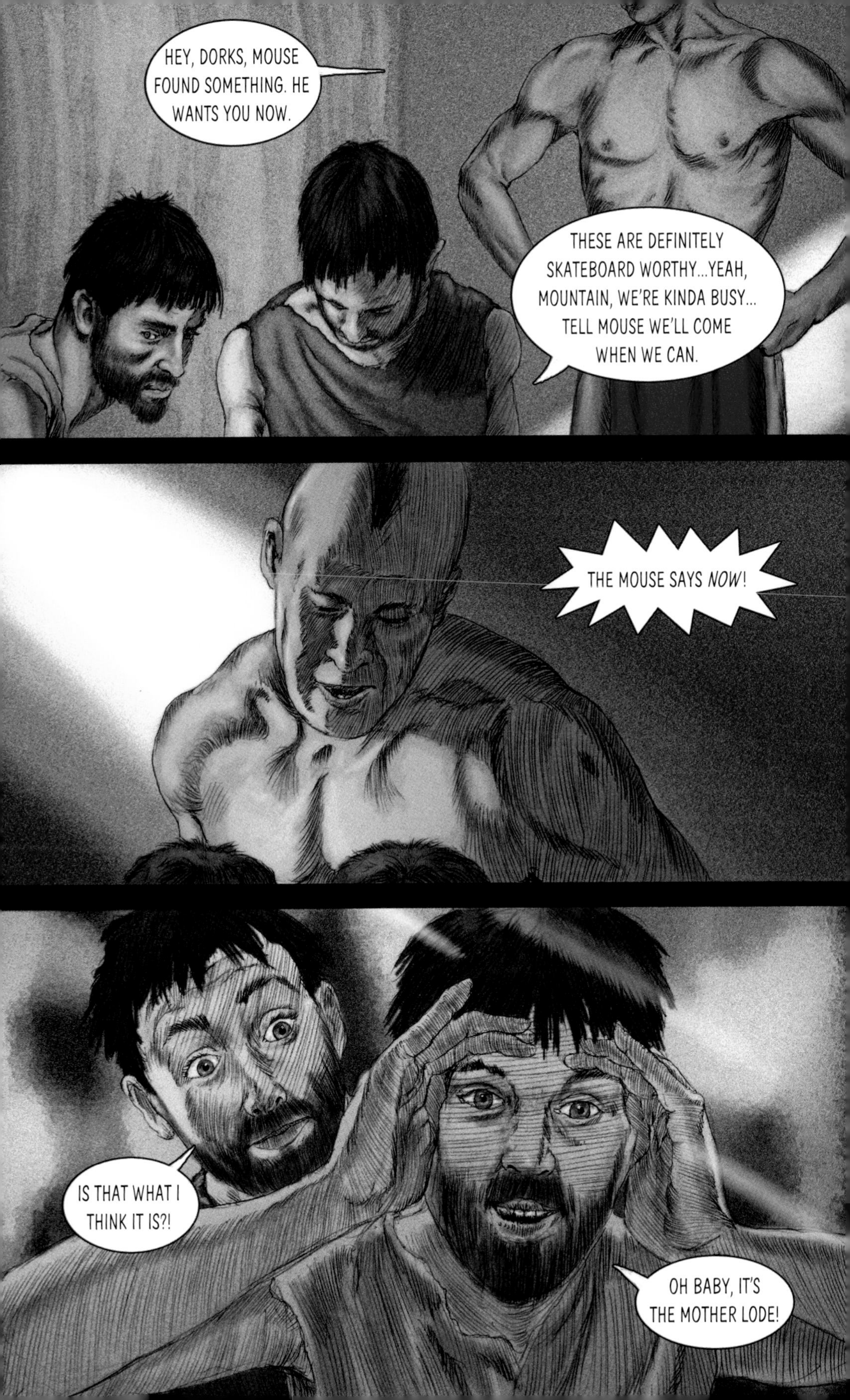
HEY, DORKS, MOUSE FOUND SOMETHING. HE WANTS YOU NOW.
THESE ARE DEFINITELY SKATEBOARD WORTHY...YEAH, MOUNTAIN, WE'RE KINDA BUSY... TELL MOUSE WE'LL COME WHEN WE CAN.
THE MOUSE SAYS *NOW*!
IS THAT WHAT I THINK IT IS?!
OH BABY, IT'S THE MOTHER LODE!

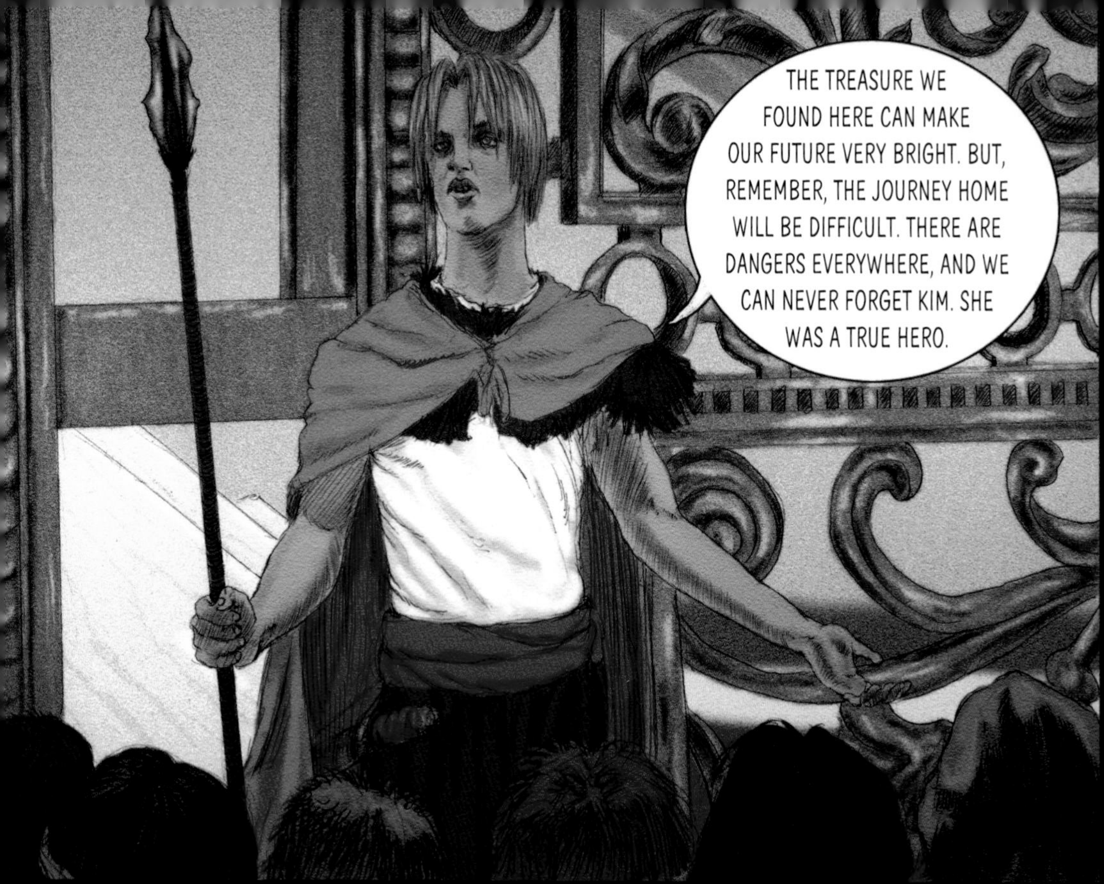
THE TREASURE WE FOUND HERE CAN MAKE OUR FUTURE VERY BRIGHT. BUT, REMEMBER, THE JOURNEY HOME WILL BE DIFFICULT. THERE ARE DANGERS EVERYWHERE, AND WE CAN NEVER FORGET KIM. SHE WAS A TRUE HERO.

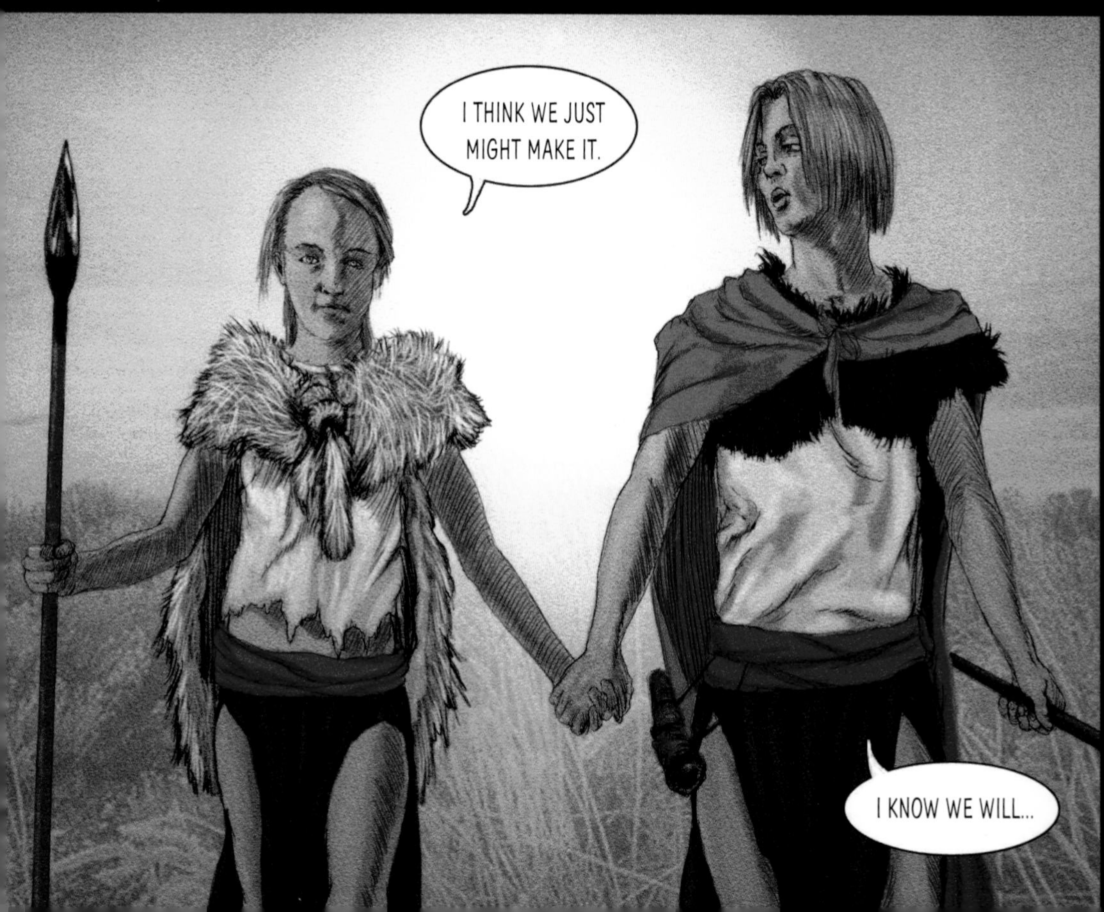
I THINK WE JUST MIGHT MAKE IT.
I KNOW WE WILL...

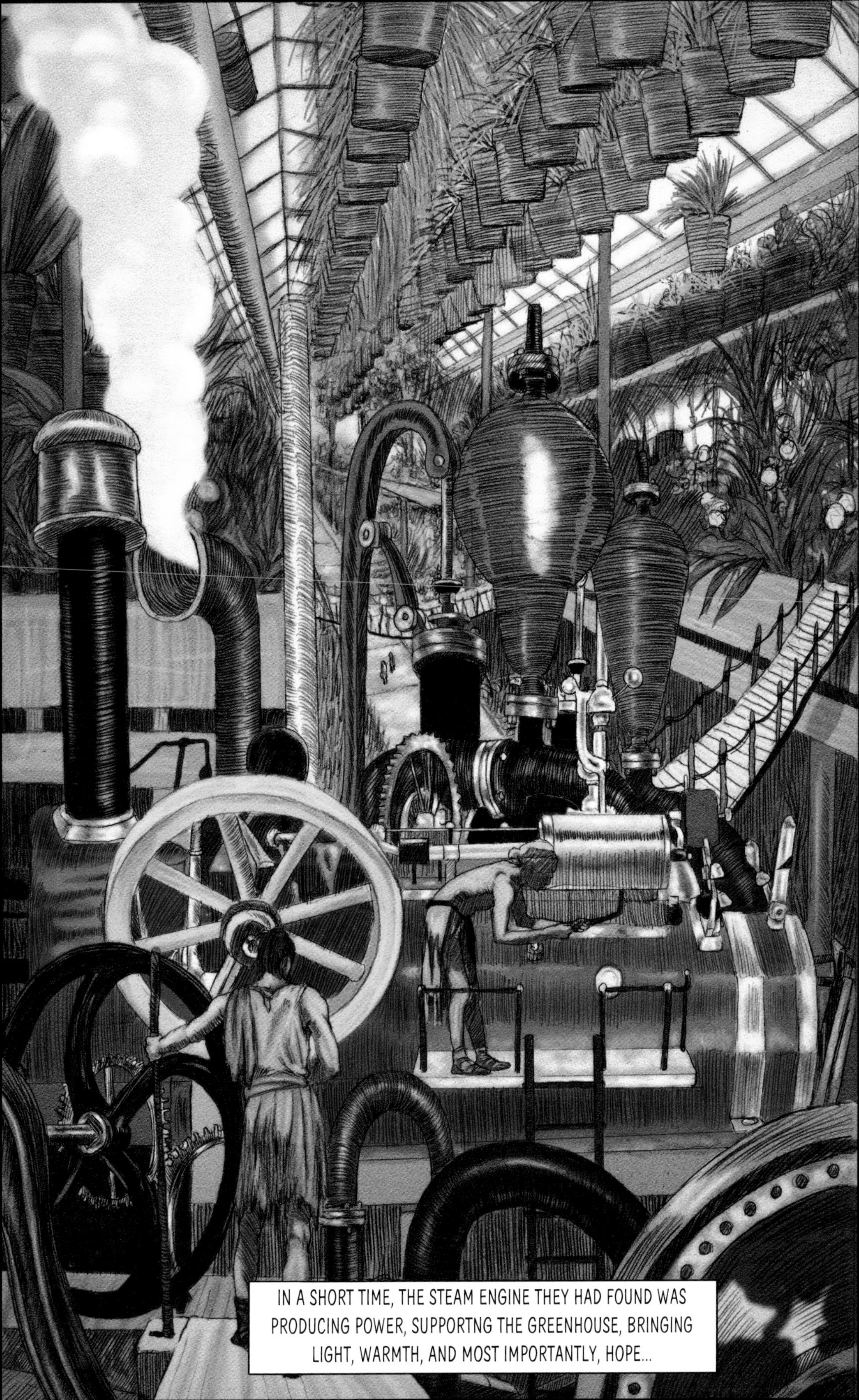
IN A SHORT TIME, THE STEAM ENGINE THEY HAD FOUND WAS PRODUCING POWER, SUPPORTNG THE GREENHOUSE, BRINGING LIGHT, WARMTH, AND MOST IMPORTANTLY, HOPE...

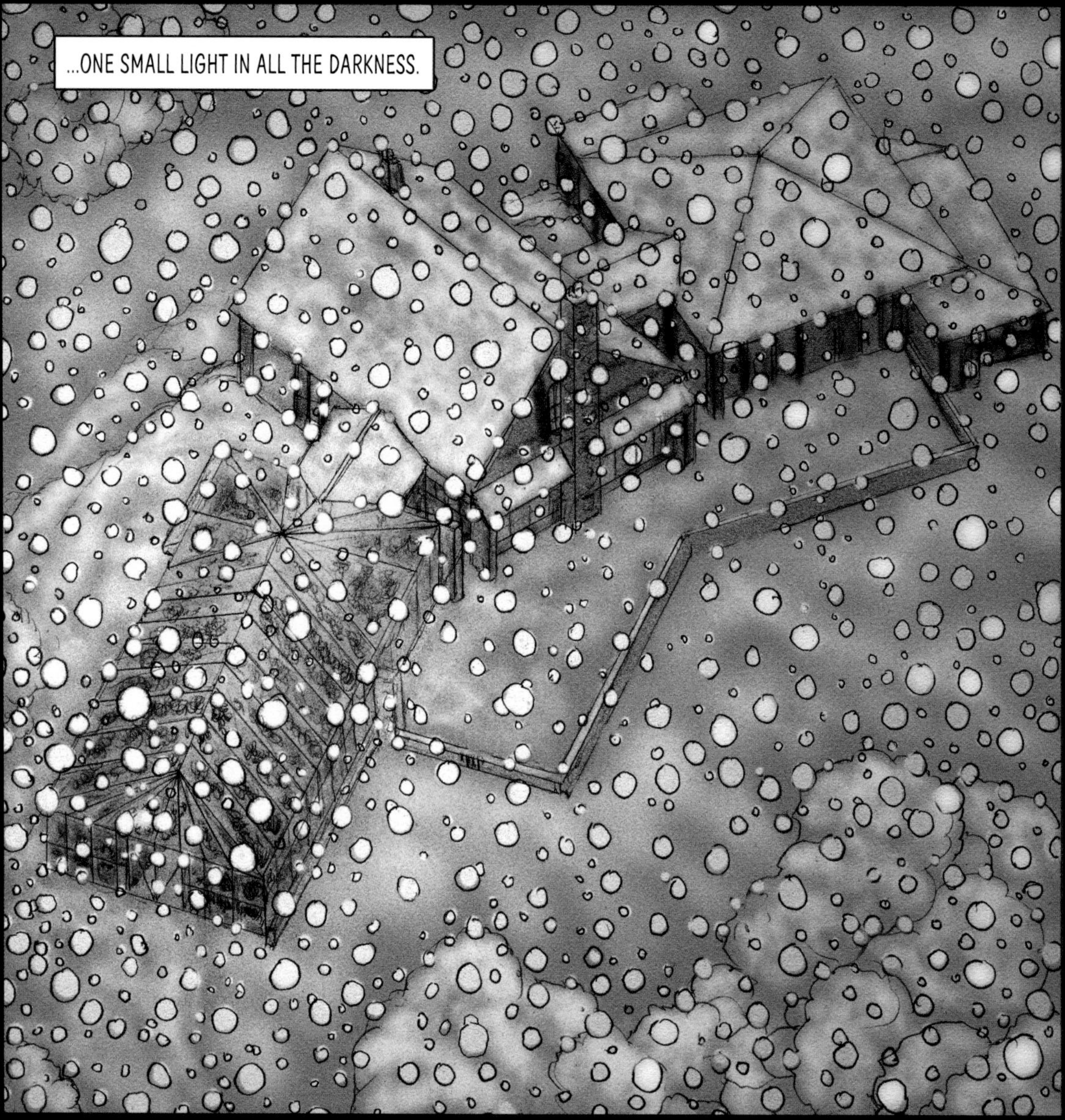
...ONE SMALL LIGHT IN ALL THE DARKNESS.

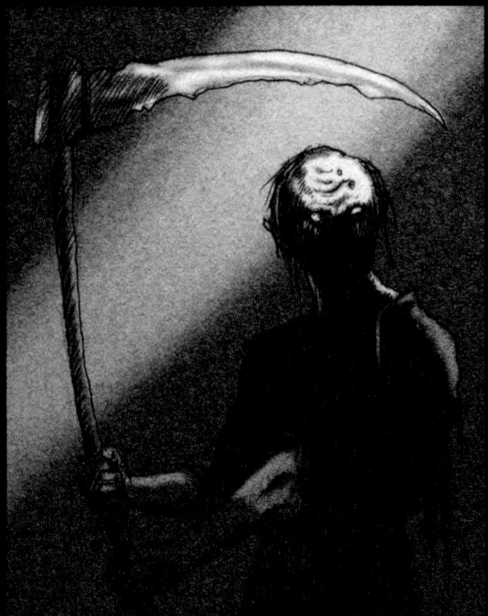
MEANWHILE, FAR FROM HOME...

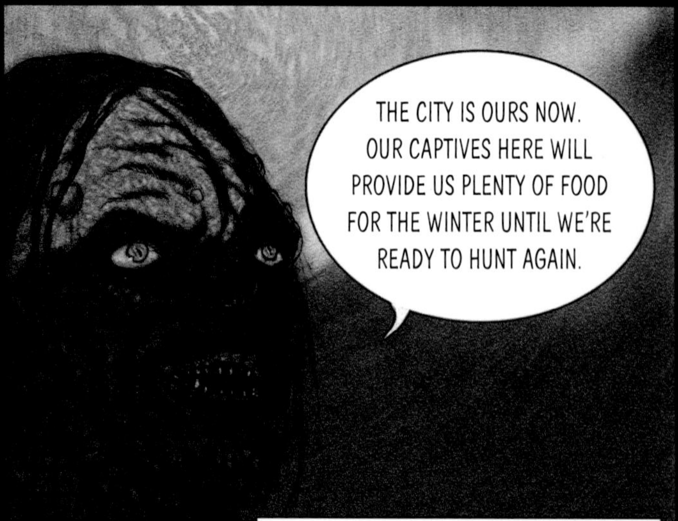
THE CITY IS OURS NOW. OUR CAPTIVES HERE WILL PROVIDE US PLENTY OF FOOD FOR THE WINTER UNTIL WE'RE READY TO HUNT AGAIN.
BY THE SPRING, THE TRANSFORMATION OF HUMAN TO DEMON WOULD BE COMPLETE.